Cana

The Globe an

"Canadians rejoice! Our Vonnegut has finally arrived!
Morgan Murray's debut is a great, brawling, sprawling,
muscular glory of a story. Funny, dark, and wholly original."
—WILL FERGUSON, winner of the Scotiabank Giller Prize

"Murray's *Dirty Birds* is a brilliant, antic, absurd and cut-to-
the-quick satire of millennial life. There's a laugh and
beautifully conjured insight on every page of this joyful
extravaganza. A very, very funny and boldly imagined novel."
—LISA MOORE, winner of Canada Reads

"There's work and care in the writing; the experiences,
however foolish, feel earned. At the same time it's kinetic:
the words, like birds, take flight."
—JOAN SULLIVAN, *The Telegram*

"This gigantic novel won't shut up."
—NATHANIEL G. MOORE, *Atlantic Books Today*

"*Dirty Birds* is an ambitious debut that humorously chronicles
an alternate version of recent Montreal history."
—JEFF MILLER, *Montreal Review of Books*

"The most compelling aspect of Murray's humour
is his sneering take on the artist novel, which often
features a sad young man who takes himself too seriously
as he pines for an elusive, free-spirited young woman.
Murray takes these tropes and sets them on fire."
—TOM HALFORD, *Canadian Notes & Queries*

"A weird and wonderful novel with two pages of
wisdom that makes the whole story so poignantly beautiful
that it will live on in my heart for many, many years."
—SARAH BUTLAND, *The Miramichi Reader*

"I LOVED this book, and I kind of want a sequel,
and the idea of a sequel about a guy who's arguably
learned nothing is maybe a TERRIBLE idea and that
makes me love this book even more."
—JENNY MITCHELL, Bird City and CFRU Radio, Guelph

DIRTY BIRDS

MORGAN MURRAY

COVER ART: KATE BEATON
INTERIOR ART: MORGAN MURRAY

BREAKWATER
P.O. BOX 2188, ST. JOHN'S, NL, CANADA, A1C 6E6
WWW.BREAKWATERBOOKS.COM

ISBN 978-1-55081-807-9
A CIP catalogue record for this book is available from Library and Archives Canada
COPYRIGHT © 2020 Morgan Murray
Cover Art: Kate Beaton
Interior Art: Morgan Murray

All of the characters and events portrayed in this book are fictitious. Any resemblance to actual persons, living or deceased, is purely coincidental.

The main typeface used throughout this book is Averia Serif. Designed by Dan Sayers, Averia Serif was created by finding the geometric average letter shapes of 725 other fonts. Of all the fonts, it is by far the most incredibly, spectacularly, remarkably average.

Second Printing

We acknowledge the support of the Canada Council for the Arts. We acknowledge the financial support of the Government of Canada and the Government of Newfoundland and Labrador through the Department of Tourism, Culture, Arts and Recreation for our publishing activities.

PRINTED AND BOUND IN CANADA.

Canada Council   Conseil des arts
for the Arts   du Canada

Canada

Newfoundland
Labrador

Breakwater Books is committed to choosing papers and materials for our books that help to protect our environment. To this end, this book is printed on a recycled paper and other sources that are certified by the Forest Stewardship Council®.

For Tamara & Logan

• • •

CONTENTS

FIGURES

Such is the first poet, he is young, he is cynical.
–Victor Hugo, "Preface" to *Cromwell*

[Disneyland is] meant to be an infantile world, in order to make us believe that the adults are elsewhere, in the "real" world, and to conceal the fact that real childishness is everywhere, particularly among those adults who go there to act the child in order to foster illusions of their real childishness.
- Jean Baudrillard, *Simulacra and Simulations*

Like a bird on the wire
Like a drunk in a midnight choir
I have tried in my way to be free
- Leonard Cohen, "Bird on a Wire"

I've lived history. I've made history, and I know I'll have my place in history. That's not egoism.
– Hon. John Diefenbaker, *MacLean's*, 1973

If the children don't grow up
Our bodies get bigger but our hearts get torn up
We're just a million little gods causing rain storms
Turning every good thing to rust
– Arcade Fire, "Wake Up"

All those people drinking lover's spit
They sit around and clean their face with it
You know it's time that we grow old and do some shit
– Broken Social Scene, "Lover's Spit"

PART ONE

SASKATCHEWAN

ONE
MILTON OF NOWHERE

Milton Ontario

Milton Ontario—not to be confused with Milton, Ontario[1]—sits on a bus as it grumbles across the frozen Prairie.

It's cold like winter, but technically still fall, late 2007. In just over a year, the world's economy will collapse, a Junior Senator from Illinois will be elected America's first Black president, *Beverly Hills Chihuahua* will be the highest grossing film in theatres, and Milton will be back on this same bus going in the opposite direction.

But for now, Milton has left his parent's basement in the middle of nowhere with all his earthly possessions, hopes, and dreams packed into an old hockey bag with a bum zipper, wrapped in half a roll of duct tape, headed for the most romantic city in North America: Montreal.

He's left his nowhere behind for somewhere. For something. To become someone. To become, at long last, what he's going to be when he grows up.

Or that's his half-assed plan.

---

[1] The Upper Canadian gristmill town turned square-head screw capital turned Toronto suburb, named after poet John Milton, best known for his epic poem about the Greater Toronto Area, *Paradise Lost*. (1667)

The trouble is, Milton has decided the thing he'll be is a poet.

A poet.

Not a doctor or lawyer like his mother encouraged. Not a welder or pipefitter like his father insisted. A poet.

A poet and a ladies' man. Like his hero, Leonard Cohen.

Never mind that he doesn't know anyone in Montreal, has no money, no job, no prospects, and—as he sets off from the Montreal bus station on foot, dragging his 80-pound duct-tape bag, towards the Mile End apartment he's renting sight-unseen from Craigslist with three strangers—he isn't even sure if Leonard Cohen is still alive.

Never mind that he is not particularly talented, nor motivated, nor clever.

Never mind that Milton has never kissed a girl.

And never mind that Milton Ontario is incredibly, spectacularly, remarkably average. Plain. Boring. Humdrum. Bland. Dull. Beige down to his very soul.

Never mind that if all of humanity was charted on a single chart for averageness, Milton would be a pimple on the nipple of the distribution curve of averageness.

No, never mind that every force in the universe is pulling Milton, with all of its might, towards the mean. Towards an absolutely average life, with an exceedingly average wife, and 1.8 devastatingly average kids. Towards an over-crowded half-furnished split-level bungalow with an attached one-and-one-half car garage and seven socks lost forever under the second-hand couch. Towards fifteen years of showing up fifteen minutes late to teacher-parent meetings. Towards soccer practice and hockey practice and piano practice. Towards cable subscriptions and cell contracts and car payments and crippling credit-card debt. Towards a surprise 25th wedding anniversary at the Legion Hall with a catered ham lunch served on paper plates. Towards accepting an early

Fig. 1. All his earthly possessions

retirement package from the Wheat Pool when the grain elevator he's spent 30 years at is sold to the Chinese and closed down then blown up. Towards chronic pain. Towards chronic numbness. Towards chronic disappointment. Towards his heart giving up several years after he had.

Never mind all of that, because Milton Ontario, some-how, against all sense, doesn't.

Never mind every force in the universe. Milton has decided to become a poet when he grows up. Whenever that might be.

• • •

Janne Alatalo

How such an outrageous idea—becoming a poet when he grows up—comes to nest in the mind of an altogether incredibly average man-child living in the middle of absolute nowhere was entirely an accident. Just like Milton.

He was just the latest accidental kid in a long line of accidental Saskatchewan dirt-farming Ontarios made in pick-up trucks and tractors and farm houses and grain bins and sod huts and wood sheds and, at least twice, in the only bathroom in the old Legion Hall during the Chaff Days Cabaret.

A long chain of extraordinarily average dirt farmers who, one after another, worked and drank themselves to unremarkable deaths, but not always in that order, beginning with Janne Alatalo.

Janne was the illiterate seventh son of a Finnish cobbler from the tiny village of Meskusvaara near the tiny town of Kuusammo not far from the Russian border.

In the 18-somethings he fled a Finnish famine to take Canada up on 160 acres of free land in the middle of the bald-headed Prairie.

Bald-headed Prairie that for some 12,000 years or so had fed the Očhéthi Šakówiŋ (Sioux), Niitsítapi (Blackfoot),

Néhinaw (Cree), and later the Métis just fine, until the king of England stole it and gave it to his cousin's start-up—a company that traded trinkets for beaver pelts to keep the old country plutocracy in fancy hats.[2]

Hats!

The history of Canada—the fancy hats, the department store running half a continent, the free land—would be a hilarious Monty Python sketch were it not underwritten by 400-and-some years' (and counting) of passive-aggressive genocide.

But, when it comes down to it, Canada isn't really a country. Not in the communally-governed-chunk-of-earth inhabited-by-people-belonging-to-the-same-tribe sense. It is just a really big company town built around stockpiles of foreign-owned riches.

Riches, it was decided through centuries of squabbles amongst various versions of rich white Christian Europeans, that were most effectively exploited by poor white Christian refugees fleeing the endless squabbles and turnip famines in Europe rather than the millions of locals who had the galling tendency to not be white, Christian, European, nor easily bought.

---

[2]   In 1670, King Charles II gave the Hudson's Bay Company, founded by his cousin Rupert and a pair of disgruntled French fur traders, control over one-third of what eventually became Canada—one-and-a-half million square miles of land that wasn't his to give (everything that drained into Hudson's Bay). The company made a killing collecting beaver pelts from fur traders in the New World and shipping them back to Britain to be made into fancy hats, which were all the rage. This went on for nearly 200 years before fancy silk hats replaced fancy beaver hats as the hottest head ornament for the fabulously wealthy, at which point the company sold Rupert's Land to a brand-new Canada. The company still exists, almost 350 years later. Now headquartered in the Toronto suburb of Brampton, they own a number of department-store chains worldwide, including The Bay, in Canada, which is best known for its Canadian Olympic mittens—the ones with the maple leafs on the palms.

The Crown, the Hudson's Bay Company, the Church, the Royal Navy, the Queen's Own Rifles, and the North-West Mounted Police built the world's biggest company town and gave vast chunks of it freely to illiterate cobbler's sons with no farming/fishing/mining/logging experience because they were more than happy to break their backs digging up, chopping down, and scooping up the riches of the land and sea for Big Hats, Big Coal, Big Oil, Big Ag, Big Timber, and Big Fish.

This particular cobbler's son didn't speak a word of the Queen's English, which didn't much matter on the Prairie where it was just a stew of Slavic-Nordic Germanic dialects and whatever Finnish is, but it mattered when he landed in Montreal and the customs officer asked him his name.

After an elaborate game of yelly charades: "Janne!" "Johnny?" "Janne!" "Johnny?" "Janne!" "Johnny?" "Janne!" Janne Alatalo became Johnny Ontario and was sent by train to collect his 160 acres near what would become Belly-button, Saskatchewan.

• • •

Bellybutton[3]

Saskatchewan is the distillation of geography into the purest mathematical form of utilitarian colonial averageness.

It's what happens when history and landscape are erased, and a kind of bland Victorian modernist utopia is designed from scratch by bureaucrats who had never seen a prairie sky in its full spring fury, who had never had a whiff of native prairie grasses in late summer, who had never had their nostrils freeze shut in a cold prairie winter.

---

[3] According to the authoritative local history book, *Puddles of the Past*, written by the Royal Prairie Dog Women's Auxiliary Society on the occasion of Saskatchewan's 75th anniversary in 1980, Bellybutton was named by Mrs. Eddie Stankowski, who ran the post-office that grew into the village, for its proximity to the neighbouring towns of Elbow, Eyebrow, and Central Butte.

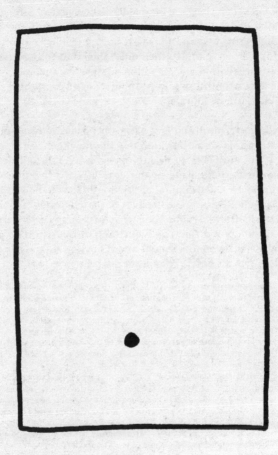

Fig. 2. Bellybutton, Saskatchewan

DIRTY BIRDS

The Queen's Own Rulers and Her Majesty's Protractors drew a perfect rectangle in the middle of an imperfect continent. Nothing to define it but four lines drawn arbitrarily through the southern dust and northern bogs and then cut into a million perfect six-mile, then mile, then half-mile squares. Just squares within squares within one massive square. Everything in two dimensions. Everything straight, everything flat. Infinite flatness. Infinite.

Bellybutton is mostly nothing to mostly no one in the absolute middle of this absolutely infinitely flat nowhere.

It sits, most notably, near the banks of Lake Diefenbaker—a man-made lake made in the year of Canada's glorious centenary by the damming of the South Saskatchewan and Qu'Appelle Rivers[4] and named for Saskatchewan's favourite son: the ineffectual Prime Minister John George Diefenbaker.[5]

Once upon a time, Bellybutton had a post office and a grain elevator and a school and a hockey rink and a gas station with a Chinese restaurant.

[4] The damming of the South Saskatchewan and Qu'Appelle Rivers brought much needed irrigation, electricity, and water skiing to this dark, dusty, and dull corner of Saskatchewan, but it also flooded Mistaseni. Cree for "Big Rock," after a giant rock dumped in the middle of the prairie by glaciers 12,000 years ago, Mistaseni was a sacred Cree site for thousands of years until it got in the way of progress. Instead of moving the rock, as requested, the government packed it full of dynamite and blew it up.

[5] John George Diefenbaker (b.1895-d.1979) was Canada's 13th Prime Minister (1957-1963). Born in Ontario, his family moved to Saskatchewan when he was a boy. Before becoming prime minister, he was a lawyer and a loser—losing five straight elections, including a race for mayor of Prince Albert. He finally won a seat in parliament in 1940, then lost four straight bids for Tory leadership, before winning in 1956. Then, somehow, he became one of the first modern populist rock star politicians, leading a stunning upset of the long-reigning Liberals in 1957, which he parlayed into a record-setting landslide win in a snap election the next year. Then, things fell apart. As good as he was at campaigning, 'Dief' was even worse at governing. He bumbled, stumbled, fumbled his way through a rough five years and promptly gave power back to the Liberals for another 20+ years.

Fig. 3. John G. Diefenbaker, Patron saint of Saskatchewan

It used to be a proper Prairie town.

But all of that has gone away. All the young people have left. Convinced there was nothing for them at home. That something was somewhere else. In a city. In a college. In an office. In anywhere other than the cab of a tractor or at the end of a shovel.

So, they've gone and taken most everything with them. The post offices, the grain elevators and the schools and the hockey rinks and the gas stations with Chinese restaurants. Not much is left. Just like all the other Prairie towns.

By the time Milton was on a bus retracing the footsteps of his great-great-great-great grand Janne/Johnny back to Montreal, less than 100 people lived in Bellybutton.

It's just a dusty two-combine-wide main street, a mostly empty grocery store with always-wilted lettuce, a motel with a tavern but no rooms, and a café with 42 items on the menu but only ever enough ingredients to make about seven.

• • •

Birth of a Ladies' Man

Like Milton's coming to be in Bellybutton being an accident of the most average kind, so was his coming to wanting to be a poet.

His childhood was average. He spent it fruitlessly trying to kiss girls, and endlessly horsing around with his friends—playing hockey, riding bikes, making fart noises with their armpits, calling each other gay, shooting each other in the ass with Joey Flipchuk's BB gun, stealing beer from their dads' fridges and puking in the woods after shot-gunning a single can of Old Style Pilsner, stealing cigarettes from their moms' purses and puking in the woods after chain-smoking half a pack of Player's Light Menthols, stealing porn magazines from underneath older brothers' beds and awkwardly hiding erections in the woods while making lewd comments about the "jugs" and "cans" on Ms. September, lying at sleepovers about

Fig. 4. Misspent youth

making out with one of the seven Ashleys from their class in those same woods.

He was a little shit, just like all the other little shits. And well on his way to being an average, everyday, normal shit.

Milton was well on his way to the same sameness as everyone else. Or he would have been, were it not for a conspiracy of ninth-grade hormones, the Saskatchewan Board of Education pension policy, the inventory turnover of the seven rental videos at Roy's Gas & Grocery, his father's refusal to throw anything away, his inability to skate backwards, and the incessant questions about what he was going to be when he grew up he'd been getting since before he could even talk, that gave him the foolish notion he had a say in the matter.

Had any of those things been different, even slightly, everything would have been different.

Had he started puberty a few months earlier like most of his friends; had Mrs. Jankowski not been eligible for her full pension for one more year; had something with more explosions than Baz Luhrman's *Romeo + Juliet* been available at Roy's for Ashley B.'s 14th birthday party; had he made the Central Butte Bantam "A" Rep team and been at a tournament in Biggar the night of the party...

Had anything been even a little different, everything would have been a lot different.

But it wasn't.

Milton sat next to Ashley D. at Ashley B.'s 14th birthday party as Claire Danes drank the poison.

As Juliet took her last breath, Milton drank in the smell of Ashley D.'s intoxicating cherry lip gloss, falling hopelessly in love with her.

The next morning, Todd Strubey, a 22-year-old from Vancouver who went to university in Montreal, was hired to replace Mrs. Jankowski as the English, Social Studies, and Shop teacher at Bellybutton Regional.

Mr. Strubey, who insisted his students called him Todd, was the first man Milton had ever seen wear a full beard; he owned the only Volvo in all of Saskatchewan, which he'd smoke weed in after school every day in the parking lot; and in the poetry unit of grade nine English, instead of the government-mandated curriculum of boring dead old white guys, he surreptitiously taught the poems and semi-lewd love songs of Leonard Cohen.

"The man is a god," he'd say as he drilled the lascivious themes of "Death of a Ladies Man" into impressionable, hormone-addled minds.

Milton didn't really understand any of it, but between the coolness of Todd and that Leonard Cohen seemed to be speaking only to Milton, coaching him through the heartache of his unrequited, burning love for Ashley D., Milton was hooked.

Todd, being cool like that, lent Milton a bunch of old Leonard Cohen records.

Milton ran home and dug through the shed for his dad's old record player. He found it buried under rat-eaten boxes of his ancient baby clothes and his grandmother's 44-pound, 98-year-old Underwood No. 3 typewriter.

He hauled both giant machines under his bed and began clackity-clacking his innermost feelings just like Leonard Cohen, while listening to *I'm Your Man* for hours, trying to decipher what "I'd howl at your beauty like a dog in heat," meant, until his dad would smash on the wall and tell him, in not so many words, to "stop feeling things."

• • •

Fig. 5. Leonard Cohen, Our Lord and Saviour/Ladies Man

Death of a Ladies' Man

Milton played out his pubescence through awful,terrible, sappy lovesick poems with barely visible ks, and fs, and •s that hit too hard and left tiny holes in the paper.

He would nurture one look from Ashley D. at lunch into pages and pages of lovesick agony. Horrid poems about how impossible love was. Things that started with lines like:

```
love is imp•ssible!
```

And ran several pages long full of poorly rhyming similes emphasizing this point:

```
like a fun time at the h•spital
like a d•uble backflip •ff a c•mbine
like g•ing back in time
like a sax•phone impr•ving a r•ck s•ng
like mr calvin n•t dr•ning •n
```

And ending, pages later, with lines like:

```
alas send my heart t• the h•spital
l•ve is imp•ssible
```

These first poems Milton wrote, despite his later insistence that he might become a professional poet—so much as there are "professional" poets—were probably his best, or at least his most honest.

He never did work up the courage to ask Ashley D. out. The closest he came was writing her a letter. A love letter. The greatest love letter ever written. The love letter to end all love letters:

DIRTY BIRDS

my dearest ashley

your cheeks are like a fawns on a spring
morn sparkling like mildew youre heart
my love is delicate like a flower but
thunders like a thousand galloping lionesses
returning from the hunt filled with the
blood of your pray and its my heart my love
that is your prey for i am at your mercy i
prey daily for your look your laugh my
heavens your touch i pray to be your prey
forevermore would you allow it pray tell to
be so twould you i twould be yours and yours
alone you feasting on my heart me in revelry
alas pray tell shallt be so so shallt be
that i be yours and you i prey come to me

will you go out with me

circle yes or no

yes

your pray
milton ontario

He carried the letter around in his backpack for a year and a half before Ashley D. showed up for homeroom wearing Joey Flipchuk's Sk8 or Di[6] sweatshirt.

Milton vowed revenge.

• • •

Revenge of a Ladies' Man

Each year, the twelfth-grade class would take an overnight trip to the John G. Diefenbaker Museum and Gas Station in Prince Albert (a good four hours into the northern Saskatchewan wilderness).

The timing of Milton's twelfth-grade trip coincided with a particularly vicious bedbug outbreak in his older brother's room. So, as any truly great revenge plot begins, Milton, with tweezers and a magnifying glass, snuck into his brother's room and collected dozens of barely seeable, particularly vicious bedbugs.

He carried them in a jar with him all the way to Prince Albert where, in the middle of the night, he emptied the jar into Joey's bunk.

These particularly vicious bedbugs, though, weren't actually bedbugs at all.

Between Milton's brother's general sloth, filth, and promiscuity, and their dog being the same, these were some kind of super bugs created by the extensive cross- and inter-breeding of bedbugs, fleas, crabs, and fruit flies, all infected with a particularly vicious strain of the herpes simplex virus.

However, rather than causing immediate death like one would suspect, or even minor irritation as Milton had hoped, this super insect caused sudden-onset penile hypertrophy, or gigantism of the penis—a condition that enlarged Joey's penis to 10 times the average size.

---

[6] A short-lived Vancouver-based skateboard apparel company that used the likeness of Diana, Princess of Wales, to sell t-shirts until they received a very convincing cease and desist letter from Her Majesty's Solicitor.

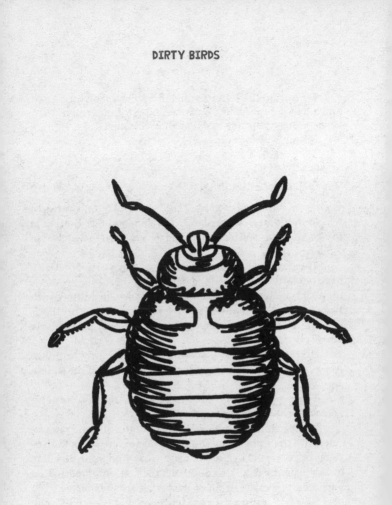

Fig. 6. Super bug

It was a big deal at the time, the sudden-onset penile hypertrophy. Joey was hospitalized and no one knew why. Milton was worried his revenge plot had worked a little too well and he'd killed Joey. But word soon spread around school that Joey got "bitten by a radioactive spider on the dick" and that the swelling was immense, "like a third leg."

The front page of *The Herald* ran a picture of Joey from his hospital bed, giving the thumbs up, the shape of his new third leg clearly visible under the blankets, Ashley D. in his Sk8 or Di sweatshirt, out of focus at his bedside. The headline read: "Local Boy's Bits Bitten by Radioactive Arachnid."

Joey got a hero's welcome when he returned to school. Everyone assembled in the gym, with their "Welcome Back Joey" banners, and cheered wildly when he came in wearing his team jacket and a special giant penis brace, making a humping motion as he walked.

Principal Flipchuk, Joey's uncle, gave a teary speech about bad things happening to good people and finding a silver lining in even the darkest clouds.

"Bad things sometimes happen to good people. It's important, though, to always look for silver linings in even the darkest clouds. Take young Joey here. He's been stricken by a tragic insect bite on his...ahem...tallywhacker, and he could have chosen to shrivel and die, but no. He is here. He is back. Bigger and better than ever!"

Mrs. Marichinko's third-grade class sang "How Great Thou Art" at the tops of their lungs. Everyone but Milton was moved to tears.

"He's been through so much!" they said.

"That poor boy!" they said.

"Look at the size of that thing," they said.

"Like one of Berta Federko's overgrown zucchinis," they said.

Nine beers deep into an unsanctioned bush party that Friday, Joey debuted his new party trick: "The Big Reveal." Someone would dare him to "whip that thing out" and he'd unspool "that thing" from his pants like a garden hose and chase people around with it, cracking it like Indiana Jones's whip.

• • •

Who by Fire

Milton was humiliated and heartbroken. As an attempt to heal he decided to burn the love letter and all the poems, the endless pages of poems.

He made a thing of it.

About to leave for college in Moose Jaw, he went to the edge of a cliff overlooking the lake and set a small fire, feeding it pages of:

```
my heart is a dessert
you walk through like a lizard
but you dont drink
and that stinks
```

But the trouble with rituals in the time of *Friends*, Furbies, and Y2K was that everything felt phony.

Hoping to be cleansed, or to be shown the great secrets of the universe—or to feel whatever Abraham must have felt as he tried lighting the match under his only son—Milton, a late-onset pubescent 17-year-old feeding unsent love letters and poorly-written poems into a fire that took him and his mis-remembered Boy Scout training far too long to start, felt nothing. Then he felt angry because he felt nothing. Then he felt silly for feeling anything at all. Then he felt panicked as the fire spread to the nearby prairie grasses, dry with drought. Then he felt embarrassed when his courtroom picture was later splashed across the front page of *The Herald* with the headline "Local Boy's Broken Heart Starts Bellybutton Blaze."

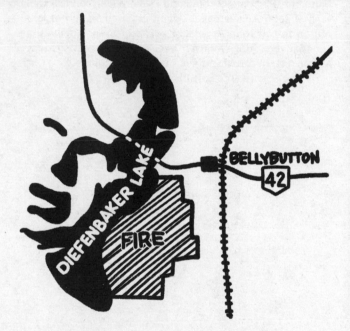

Fig. 7. The Great Bellybutton Heartbreak Fire of 2002

He was still a minor, so he avoided getting a criminal record. But, for starting and stoking with heartbreak a fire that burned 12,000 acres of John Angelstad's nearly ready soy beans and snap peas, Judge Marshall Johnson sentenced Milton to 100 hours of community service (i.e., hand cleaning each of John Angelstad's 37 giant grain bins), and ordered Milton to pay John Angelstad's crop-insurance deductible and legal fees. Judge Johnson, a renowned hard-ass, also gave Milton a stern dressing down in the courtroom.

"You're soft, son. Soft like baby shit."

TWO
COLLEGE

PUS

The heartbreak, the sudden-onset penile hypertrophy, the fire, the trial, the community service—this was, for the moment at least, the last straw.

Milton gave up all hope of becoming a poet, of getting laid, of becoming someone who was somebody who did something. He quit listening to Leonard Cohen. He quit clackity-clacking under his bed. He resigned himself to his fate: a faceless, nameless nobody somewhere out in the Alberta Oil Patch. Like everybody else.

So, as every person younger than his parents who lived in a town smaller than Moose Jaw has had to do since even the worst job started requiring a degree or a diploma, Milton packed his everything and moved to the city to enrol in the Instrumentation Diploma program at the Polytechnic University of Saskatchewan's Moose Jaw campus.

He had no real interest in instrumentation. He didn't even know what it was. Just that his Uncle Ronnie was "making good money" in the oil patch as an instrumentation technician "fucking the dog all day for journeyman wages," according to his father.[7]

---

[7] "Fucking the dog" is a technical term in the oil and gas industry meaning "not working very hard."

Instrumentation—the installation and maintenance of the precision instruments used in the oil and gas industry to measure production and control various processes—he discovered, was dreadfully dull.

It was the refuge of broken-down has-been junior hockey players with their lips full of chewing tobacco, forever spitting brown globs of 'snus' or 'chaw' into empty Gatorade bottles, and one never-was poet who'd given up on his dreams and resigned himself to his Oil Patch fate.

Milton's classes were all taught by retired instrument men—they were all men—with moustaches, ball caps, and steel-toed boots, whose teaching styles fell somewhere on the spectrum between comatose and root canal.

Every day, from 9:00 to 5:00 with two 15-minute "smoke breaks," and 45 minutes for lunch, Milton would sit in a white cinderblock and linoleum classroom and try to stay awake through the drone of Larry the Has-Been Flin Flon Bomber turned Has-Been Instrument Man reading word-for-word out of the text book.

Milton's college life became very monastic: studious, silent, celibate, dreadfully tedious, obsessed with an unrequited high-school love, and religiously jerking off into an old sock several times per day.

Each day after class, Milton would go to the PUS library to do his homework, then go home to his "apartment"—a windowless bedroom in a basement with a microwave and mini-fridge—and eat a frozen dinner in front of whatever was on the two channels he sort of got through the tinfoil bunny ears he'd jammed into the back of an antique 12-inch TV until it was time to go to work.

He had landed a part-time nighttime shelf-stocking gig at Farmtime, the Walmart of Saskatchewan farm stores. He'd work four nights per week from when the store closed at 9:00 p.m. until 1:00 a.m., stocking shelves with a deaf-mute ex-con named Charlie. Then back to his basement studio apartment to watch infomercials until he fell asleep.

• • •

The Boys

Milton did his best to stick to his involuntary vow of friend-less, celibate silence. But after the mid-term exam the entire class—"No exceptions, you assholes"—went to the campus bar, Gassy's, for beers; Milton didn't have a choice.

He ended up as one of eight wedged around a corner booth meant for five—six, tops—silently sipping cheap beer and staring over one another's ball caps at different TVs playing the LPGA Idaho Potato Insurance Invitational from Spokane, Washington, on GolfTV with the sound off and the black closed-caption boxes covering the lower third of the screen.

After about an hour, with only nods, "welps," and one-way trips to the pisser, the group had dwindled to a threesome. The three of them—Milton, who desperately wanted to go home but was stuck in the corner, and two dudes in ball caps—sat in silence for a long while, half-watching golf over one another's heads.

"You boys from here?"

"I'm from Bellybutton."

"Where in the feck is that?"

"By Diefenbaker Lake."

"Ah. Right on, man."

They all returned to watching golf, until a commercial.

"I'm from Mantario."

"Where's that?"

"It's a fecking hole, man, just south of Alsask."

"Right on. Man."

Milton and Ball Cap 1 both waited for Ball Cap 2 to say something, anything. He didn't. He just silently sipped his beer, eyes glued on the TV over Milton's head.

"Who you boys like for the cup this year?"

"I dunno, the Habs look good."

Fig. 8. Regrets

"..."

"Yeah. If they get Koivu back."

"..."

"You guys play?"

"Uh... I did... A bit. You?"

"Yeah, five years in the ess-jay[8] for seven teams: La Ronge, Melfort—that place blows, feck me!—Kindersley, Estevan, Weyburn, Melville—not much better than Melfort! Feck that place too!—and then Yorkton, but luckily not Flin Flon, that place is the fecking moon, man!"

"Cool. That's pretty good."

"Not really. I shoulda got a scholly,[9] but I got fecked."

"Like hurt?"

"Nah, like a bunch of things. Coaches and shit."

"That sucks."

"Yeah, man. Like, I fecked the coach's daughter in Melville, eh. And he gets all pissy about it. Like, what did he expect to happen? She was a smoke show. And it's not like I knocked 'er up or anything! Jesus! But the asshole trades me to feckin' Yorkton in my overage year for a feckin' space heater for the dressing room. We won three games all year, man. I led the team in PIMs,[10] and was third on the team in apples,[11] but I got fecked... Where'd you play?"

"Uh... Nowhere, really. Just Midget last year."

"Midget trips?"[12]

---

8   The ess-jay is the Saskatchewan Junior Hockey League (SJHL), one of several junior "A" leagues in Canada. Junior A is the second-highest tier of hockey for players between 16 and 20 years old. The highest is major junior in the Canadian Hockey League, which is made up of three smaller leagues: the Western Hockey League (WHL, or the Dub), the Ontario Hockey League (OHL, or the Oh), and the Quebec Major Junior Hockey League (QMJHL, or the Q).

9   Because Major Junior players are paid a very small stipend, they are considered "professional" by the NCAA, and thus ineligible for US college scholarships. Many Canadians hoping to get scholarships to American schools play junior A hockey through high school.

10 Penalty minutes.

11 Assists.

12 Midget is the oldest age category in Canadian minor hockey, for players 15 to 17. Minor hockey is divided into lettered tiers, triple-A (AAA or "trips") being the highest calibre.

"Uh... I guess. I went to camp in Battleford, but... uh... hurt my... um... shoulder."[13]

"Shitty... What about you, boss? You play?"

"..."

"Chatty one, aren't yah?"

"..."

Milton shrugged.

They sat sipping their beers and watching golf for a long while. Finally, Ball Cap 2 spoke, without taking his eyes off the TV.

"I did a few years in PA in the dub and then got dumped in the ay-jay after I got suspended for pitching my lid at some donkey in Swift. Got a few games in Boise in the Coast in '93. Bitzy Federko was my D-partner, Bernie's nephew. I was a plug though, better at drinkin' and screwin'. So, I've done that and a lot of blow for the last 15 years loadin' shit at a feedlot in Meddy Hat. But now I'm 37, got three kids with three broads, time to grow up, I guess, quit drinkin', make some real money."[14]

---

[13] This was a lie. Milton did play hockey, but not "Midget trips." He played for the Bellybutton Midget "D" Combine Pilots. He did go to a camp in North Battleford, but not the camp where the Battlefords North Stars SJHL team is chosen each fall. He went to a summer recruiting camp/cash grab to which any boy (no girls allowed) between the ages 15 and 20 can pay $100 to play in three scrimmages. And Milton didn't hurt his shoulder. He just wasn't good enough. He cared more about his poetry and Ashley D. than hockey. He only went because his friend Cory needed a ride. Cory didn't make the cut either.

[14] In English: "I played for a short while with the Prince Albert (Saskatchewan) Raiders of the Western Hockey League (major junior). However, I was demoted to the Alberta Junior Hockey League (junior "A") after throwing my helmet at a fan during a game against the Swift Current (Saskatchewan) Broncos. Following my junior career, I spent some time during the 1993 season with the Boise (Idaho) Noise in the Pacific Coast Hockey League (now defunct), where my defence partner was the nephew of Hall of Famer and Saskatchewan-born Bernie Federko. I was not a very proficient player, due to alcoholism and womanizing. Following my retirement from hockey I have spent the past 15 years working at a beef feedlot in Medicine Hat, Alberta. After years of sex, drugs, and alcohol, and fathering three children with three different women, I've decided, at long last, to change my ways. I am sober now and working to find a more stable career."

Fig. 9. Bitzy Federko, Defence, Boise Noise, PCHL, 1992-93

With that he downed the last half of his beer, belched, slammed his hand on the table, nodded at Milton and Ball Cap 1, and left.

Ball Cap 1 and Milton stared into the bottom of their empty beer glasses for a long time before leaving. Milton walked to the library, in the cold, and looked up the 1993 Boise Noise on hockeystats.com.

• • •

A Poet's Heart

The night out with the boys was never repeated. Milton stuck to the school-work-school-work-repeat for as long as he could stand it, but couldn't bear it much past the end of January.

He had cultivated a poet's heart. And a poet's heart, he decided, could not be satiated by the drudgery of thermal expansion coefficients or PID action pneumatic controller functions.

He stopped going to class, started reading books by Bukowski and Kerouac and Hemingway, skipped the Instrumentation final exam, and didn't take a summer apprenticeship placement in the Oil Patch like he was supposed to.

He started writing poetry again. He read more of the classics. He convinced himself that he wasn't meant to be an Instrument Man. He was meant to be a poet. An artist. He was meant to carry the mantle for Bukowski and Ginsberg. For Leonard Freaking Cohen.

The more he read, the more he began to think he might be one of these men. These great men. These men who've swallowed all the unfairness of the world—the unfairness of being unloved and unappreciated and miscast—and turned all that pain into righteous indignation and rage. Into beautiful fever-dream novels that made Milton feel at home in the world for the first time. These men. These beautiful, great men. These heroes. These martyrs. These brightest minds of their generations. Died so that Milton might live. Lived so that

Milton might too. That Milton might live forever, like them.

He was ready to fulfill this destiny. But first, he had to convince his parents of his impending immortality.

They would absolutely shit if they found out Milton wanted to drop out and be a poet.

He headed home for the summer to work at Uncle Randy's Farm Supply and try and talk his parents into lending him enough money to move somewhere better and help him get started on a career in poetry.

"Poetry? Poetry! There ain't no money in poetry! That's the dumbest thing I've ever heard. Poetry! Finish school and get a job. Poetry? Instrumentation is a good job. Your Uncle Ronnie makes good money at it. He fucks the dog all day and drives a new truck every year."

"Ronnie drives a new truck every year, hon, because he writes them off drunk driving all the time."

"Well, at least he can afford it."

No amount of begging, pleading, research into earning potential of poets—which, at the highest end of the spectrum on pickyourjob.com, was quite a bit less than first year instrumentation apprentice—no amount of anything could help his parents see the light. But they didn't protest too loudly when Milton mentioned changing his program as he got out of the car the next September when they dropped him back off at PUS.

"We're worried about you, hon. We don't want you turning into a deadbeat like your Uncle Jeff."

"Just get out."

Each summer played out the same as the first. Milton would start a new program in the Fall, hate it, come home in the Spring wanting to drop out entirely and go be a poet somewhere, anywhere. His parents would insist he continue, he'd enrol in a new program, and on and on.

Fig. 10. The classics

He tried instrumentation, welding, pipefitting, carpentry, and a brief flirtation with electrical before finding a program he could stomach in his fifth year: Artistic Sciences.

• • •

Artistic Sciences

The Artistic Sciences was an altogether made-up discipline that PUS administration concocted to "tap a lucrative market for students who eschew stable careers in favour of mislaid conceptions of illusory personal 'fulfillment'," according to a secret internal memo turned over to the *Moose Jaw Times Herald* through a Freedom of Information request as part of a sweeping investigation into the bankruptcy of PUS years later.

Thanks to Milton's four year tour through the trades, he only needed to complete the final course: ARTSCI1000: Applied Arts Sciences.

Semi-retired millwright Instructor Mr. Moustache Ball Cap Steel-Toed Boots led a class of misfit toys through such topics as theatre-set framing and wiring, sculpting with pipe, live figure AutoCAD drafting, and a final self-directed project.

Milton's final project was a book of semi-lewd poems entitled *O, AD*. A clever secret reference to the hollowness of his heart without Ashley D. in it.

O, AD was 536 pages long. Milton sent it away to be leather-bound at a specialty book bindery in Iceland. Sorglegt Poka LLC from Reykjavík had pioneered a method of compressing many types of organic fibers into a kind of synthetic suede that could be used for things like book covers. Milton paid $1,200—every last cent he had—to have them turn thin slices of dehydrated reindeer heart into a lavishly plush book cover with the title and his name, albeit misspelled and a minimalist sketch of the Mona Lisa embossed in gold on the cover.

Fig. 11. 0, AD, by Martin Ortanio

His masterpiece contained poems such as the eponymous "O, AD," which contained lines like:

```
w●e w●e is the heart
that d●es n●t start
t● break s● fast
because it was c●nsumed as breakfast

w●e w●e is the heart
that d●es n●t mark
the passing ●f time
because it d●es n●t have a dime

w●e w●e is the heart
that cann●t part
because it has n● past
●nly eyes for that ass¹⁵
```

Milton poured his heart into the project. He was sure it was going to get an A+, and Mr. Moustache Ball Cap Steel-Toed Boots would send a copy immediately to his cousin at Random House in New York, and *O, AD* would become an instant smash hit bestseller, and he would return to Bellybutton richer than a first-year instrumentation apprentice, and his parents would apologize and tell him how wrong they were to doubt him, and he'd be made the Marshall of the Chaff Days Parade, and as the parade pulled back into the Legion parking lot after its three-block lap around town, he would see Ashley D. in a sundress squinting into the light reflected off the pristine green paint of the John Deere S700 combine they let the Marshall drive in the parade each year, and he would hop down from the climate-controlled, surround-sound-with-satellite-radio cab and take her by the hand and run off to the shore of Diefenbaker Lake and he would give her the reindeer heart bound original *O, AD*, and she would swoon and they'd make love right there on shore.

---

¹⁵ It was supposed to read "for that lass," but Milton didn't have time to proofread his masterpiece before sending it to Sorglegt Poka.

He was sure of all of this. Well most of it. He wasn't sure if there was a new S-series combine out this year or not, but if there was, Central Butte Machine would provide the newest model to the Parade Marshall. Other than that, he was sure of every last detail.

But, Mr. Moustache Ball Cap Steel-Toed Boots wasn't a connoisseur of poetry and didn't even have a cousin at Random House. His criteria for grading final projects was "potential financial value" and "employable skills exhibited." So, when Milton got his priceless final project back, there was a giant "D-" scratched in red Sharpie on the inside cover with the comment:

> Poetry is a dead medium that has long been surpassed by newer stuff like TV and videos. A quick search of the Google shows that the few poetry books that still get made don't make any money at all, and that poets usually die poor and by suicide. These poems, or at least the first 30 I got through, are all so sad, and not very good, and you seem to be obsessed with some guy named Andy. Overall, this is worthless art, you've shown little employable skills. This would have been a fail, but for the fine leather work on the cover, might I suggest changing to our leather work program, here is a brochure.

• • •

The Graduate

Milton's parent's drove down for Milton's graduation ceremony and, mostly, to take him back to Bellybutton. The celebration only lasted until they were out of the parking lot.

"Do you have a job lined up yet?"

"Not yet. Maybe Randy's for now."

"I ran into Karen the other day at the post-office."

"Randy's? You went to school for five years to stock shelves at Randy's?"

"She said Roger has the gout pretty bad."

"Should've stayed with instrumentation."

"I told Karen that Roger needs to get off the sweets. They're just so bad for you."

"Good money in it."

"It's so bad Karen wasn't sure he'd be able to go up to Edmonton this weekend."

"Remember Tiny Schmautz's boy, Teeny from hockey? Could barely lick his lips?"

"Ashley is graduating from medical school."

"He finished his instrumentation three friggin' years ago, he's working in Fort Mac, fucks the dog all day for $65 an hour."

"Hon, I wish you wouldn't curse so much in front of him."

"What'd I say?"

"The... the thing about dogs."

"Fucking the dog? That's what they call it."

"Call what?"

"Sitting around... fucking the dog! It's a technical term."

"It's just so crude."

"That's $65 an hour straight time, Milt."

"Karen said Ashley finished a year early too."

"You'd get time-and-a-half overtime on top of that."

"They are just so proud of her."

"Tiny says Teeny makes $100 an hour working overtime. And when he's up north he's only working in the camps."

"Not that your father and I aren't proud of you."

"That's 10 times what Randy will ever pay you."

"We know you worked really hard on your arts diploma."

"Worked hard? He took five years to get an arts diploma!"

"You could have gone to medical school, hon. If you just applied yourself more."

"He didn't have the grades for that, mother."

"I sure hope Roger's gout clears up soon."

"It's probably not too late to finish the instrumentation. It's good money"

"With the wedding coming up. He'll want to walk her down the aisle."

"Wait, what?"

"I said you should have stuck with instrumentation, like Teeny Schmautz."

"No, the other part."

"Roger's gout?"

"No, no. A wedding?"

"Oh yes. They're planning on getting married in the fall back home, it's so pretty by the lake in the fall, just after harvest. Everyone in town is just so excited."

"Maybe you can get your ticket quicker because you got a five-year head start."

"Who's getting married?"

"Ashley and some doctor fellow from Edmonton."

"Ashley D.?"

"Yes, hon. She brought him home to Chaff Days this year. Really handsome, tall fellow. Seemed nice."

"Good money in instrumentation."

"They're a cute couple. They even let him drive the new S800 in the parade, to sort of initiate him into the community."

"You should see them new S800s!"

"He said it was just like driving his BMW. Oh, did we laugh at that."

"They've got a hydrostatic clutch, supposed to last 10,000 hours."

"Do you remember his name, hon?"

"Who's that? Tiny Schmautz?"

"No, the Dukowski girl's fellow. They had him driving the S800 in the parade there."

"That fella couldn't drive a hot stick through fresh snow, had the hydrostat smoking all the way down main street."

Fig. 12. John Deere S800 Combine Harvester

"He was a real nice fellow."

"That Dukowski girl wouldn't be hanging around that skinny doctor fella if he wasn't loaded."

"Anyway, I'm sure you'll think of something, hon."

"He's had five years to think. He needs a job."

"You could have gone to medical school, hon. If you just applied yourself more."

"He should have stuck with instrumentation. $100 an hour to fuck the dog."

"Oh my, hon, are you all right? Pull over, hon, Milty's carsick, poor thing."

"I'm not pulling over. We're making good time."

"What's wrong, hon? Are you going to puke? Hon, I think he's going to puke."

"He's not going to puke. This is the flattest, straightest road on earth. He's not carsick. He's fine."

"He doesn't look fine."

Milton's mom rummaged through a pile of trash on the floor of the back seat of the car and found half a bottle of old Diet Coke.

"Here, drink this, hon. There's no water."

"I'm fine. I just need some air."

Milton opened the window next to his head. The fresh air helped, but it also picked up about 200 poems worth of loose papers he had in an open box and sucked them out of the car.

"Oh Milty, your art! Hon, pull over, Milty's art?"

"That ain't art, it's just a bunch of paper. It'll biodegrade, he's fine."

Milton decided that second, in the back of that car, to make it his sole purpose in life to get to Montreal as soon as he could.

He got his old job back at Uncle Randy's. But, Uncle Randy would only ever give him two- or three-hour shifts at a time, and refused to pay him the actual minimum wage and instead paid him $5 per hour in cash—"the tax man would take more than that anyway"—so it took a while for Milton to get enough to get away.

Within six months, the week before Ashley D. got hitched to Dr. Jerkface McClutchsmoke on the shores of Lake Diefenbaker, Milton hitched a ride to Regina with "One-eyed" Rick, the local courier who ran freight for several farm-supply stores along Highway 42. There he used 35 five-dollar bills (Uncle Randy took the $5/hour cash very literally) to buy a one-way bus ticket to Montreal.

Fig. 13. Freedom

THREE

UN
CANADIEN
ERRANT

Adieu

Thirty-seven hours later, Milton stepped off the worst smelling bus in North America, into the most romantic city in North America.

He slung his 80-pound duct-taped sack over his shoulder, found a tourist map screwed to the wall in the bus station, made note of the general direction he was going, and headed towards the door.

He was home. His destiny of greatness, fame, fortune, immortality flashed before him. His chest puffed up, the 80 pounds of his entire life slung over his left shoulder was as light as a feather, he was finally here, to sit on his throne, the Fresh Prince of...

WHAM!

The cold hit him square in the face.

On the Prairies it gets cold. Like 50-below-Celsius-with-the-wind-chill-whipping-off-the-Lake-in-the-dregs-of-February cold. It gets so cold your nostrils freeze shut, and it burns to breathe. But it's a dry cold. If you wear enough layers and plug in your truck's block heater, you might survive.

Montreal cold, though, is an entirely different thing. It might only get to 30 below, but it's a damp, biting cold. The wind whipping off the fleuve is like being hit full force in the face with a boat paddle. The humid frozen cold leaks through even the thickest, most air-tight clothes, through your skin, and into your bones. Every cell in your organism screams.

It was this boat paddle that greeted Milton when he took that first breath.

WHAM!

The door greeted him second.

"Mon tabarnak j'vais te décâlisser la yeule, câlice!"

A local commuter welcomed Milton with a local greeting and a shove of the door. The door swung back and hit Milton square in the face, leaving a bright pink mark that would grow into a bruise throughout the day, perfectly bisecting his increasingly frozen face, causing his eyes to water and the tears to freeze as he staggered out onto Berri Street.

The 80 pounds hanging off his shoulder started to feel like it weighed closer to 280. Milton buried his head into the wind and started trudging uphill. He'd figured, from his glance at the map, to walk a block uphill headed north, then a block westward, then another block north, as he worked his way diagonally towards the room he was renting unseen from Craigslist, on avenue de l'Épée.

He forgot to pack a toque, so he dragged his sweater up over his head and zipped his jacket up as far as it would go. He looked ridiculous, but by block two he didn't care, he'd meet the elegance of this city tomorrow. Today he was dying.

• • •

Clueless

Milton didn't know a lot of things he probably should have.

Obvious things, like taking a cab from the bus station

would have been $12 well-spent. Like Montreal was a French city and a basic grasp of the language would have been an asset. Like a hundred other things. But, most of all, in this exact moment, he didn't know that the *Mont* part of Montreal meant mountain, and the *real* part meant Royal and that Parc du Mont-Royal, traversed by avenue du Parc, the street he was trudging up, was Mount Royal Park

Montreal the mega-city is spread across the Hochelaga Archipelago—a bunch of islands at the confluence of the St. Lawrence and Ottawa rivers. The two biggest islands, Île Montréal and Île Jésus, make the shape of a pair of lips, with the heart of the city—the crooked cobblestone streets of Old Montreal, the student ghetto around McGill, the palatial mansions of Westmount, the Jewish delis and bagelries and smoked meateries of The Main, the sex clubs and dive bars and fancy shops of rue Sainte-Catherine, the tourists flocking to the former site of the Montreal Forum (the hallowed former home of the formerly hallowed Montreal Canadiens) only to find it's been turned into a shopping mall on avenue Atwater—is on the bottom lip, Île Montréal.

The topography of the bottom lip was created by a long dead volcano that rises above the city just northeast of downtown, like a bee sting on a fat lip. It's all uphill from downtown and downhill from uptown towards les banlieues, with the most mountain-like part in Parc du Mont-Royal.

In terms of things that make Montreal magical, Parc du Mont-Royal is near the top of the list. In terms of things that make carrying an 80-pound bag several-teen blocks in the freezing cold something that could be mistaken for actual hardship, Parc du Mont-Royal is also at the top of that list.

But Milton was a man now, a poet-man, and this was man-making hardship. He was his great-great-great-great-grand Janne/Johnny crossing the Atlantic. He was that Norwegian fella Sir Edmund Hilroy, crossing the North Pole with his coil-bound scribblers. He was Sir Benjamin Franklin, reaching

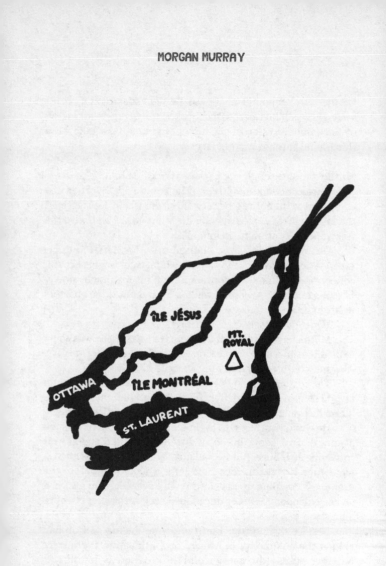

Fig. 14. The Hochelaga Archipelago

for the Don Beaupre Sea. He was Bernie Federko on a break-away. He was John George Diefenbaker, the George Washington of Saskatchewan, crossing his eponymous fake lake on a third-hand three-car cable ferry.

Milton's trek through the park nearly killed him.

It was only a kilometre, but he could have sworn it was equivalent to the entire length of Ellesmere Island. He staggered the last few feet across avenue du Mont-Royal and onto the sidewalk in front of a McDonald's.

Out of the wind he collapsed onto his deflated duct-taped sack. He lay there for a long while, catching his breath, collecting his thoughts, contemplating his manhood, slowly freezing to death. A woman walked by and put three quarters in his hand.

"Quel dommage, c'est terrible!"

Milton had lost his will to go on. He was sure he was going to die there, in a pile, on the sidewalk in front of a McDonald's. Another stranger handed him a couple nickels.

The custom of giving new arrivals loose change struck him as odd, but also a bit delightful. What a kind and generous place, he thought, as someone handed him an entire loonie.

He was trying to get to avenue Bernard, which intersected avenue du Parc some unknown distance on, and then follow it to avenue de L'Épée. But he had no idea how far it was, no idea what time it was, no idea how long it would be before the numbness creeping up his shins would overtake him entirely, so he schlepped his giant duct-taped sack across the street to a bus stop.

Besides the 37-hour busathon from Regina, Milton had ridden the bus plenty in Moose Jaw. Mind you, there were only two buses—the uptown and the crosstown—but he was confident he could figure out one measly Montreal bus ride. After all, he was Dr. Zhivago. He was Ruth Bader Ginsberg.

• • •

The 80

The bus shelter had a sign with a schedule and a simplified map for Route 80, the only bus that stopped there. Of course, the sign was entirely in French and the times were written the French way, 17h15, which made no sense to him, but he didn't know the time, so it didn't matter anyway.

He sat in the bus shelter and waited and waited while the numbing cold crawled up his legs and began biting his ass.

A bus approached, it was the number 80, and it whizzed right by, slopping slush onto the glass front of the shelter.

A while later, closer yet to frostbite and assured death, another bus whizzed by, slopping another glop of slush onto the glass front of the shelter. A few minutes later another. Then another.

Seven busses in all passed the bus shelter where Milton sat freezing to death, before someone else, an early-twenty something with plaid flannel jacket, skinny jeans, and vintage glasses, walked into the shelter to wait.

"Juh'excuse mawh?" Milton asked.

Vintage Glasses dug the headphone out of one ear.

"Yo, what's up."

"Oh, thank god, you speak English. How do you get the busses to stop?"

"Huh?"

"Stop. The busses. They keep going by?"

"I dunno, man, just, like, stand here and they stop."

"But, I've been here for like an hour and they just keep going by, though."

"I guess maybe they don't stop if it looks like you are spending the night in here?"

"Oh... I'm not... I'm just... I just moved here... From Saskatchewan."

"Right on, man."

Vintage Glasses put his headphone back in.

The next bus was along in a couple of minutes and it stopped and opened the door. Vintage Glasses hopped on and scanned a card over a reader. The door was about to close.

"WAIT! I'M... WAIT!"

Milton hauled his giant bag up the three steps and stood beside the driver, who looked him up and down and shook his head.

"Tabernak."

"Does this bus go to Bernard Street?"

The driver just stared at him.

"How much is it?"

Milton shook a handful of change at him.

"Deux-dollars-et-vingt-cinq."

Milton had no idea which question that answered, if either.

He started dumping small coins into the farebox until the driver slammed on the gas, knocking Milton backwards. Milton swayed and staggered his way to an open pair of seats and sat down next to the window and dragged his bag up on the seat next to him. It sat there like his only friend in the world.

• • •

Culottes

His concentration on street signs was broken when the old woman sitting behind him tapped him on the shoulder.

"Monsieur, je m'excuse, monsieur?"

Milton turned to get a face full of dirty underwear.

"Monsieur, vos culottes sont tombées de votre sac."

Disgusted, Milton pushed the underwear away.

"No thank you!"

"Non, monsieur, it is yer panties. Dey fall from yer sac, juste la."

The old woman pointed to Milton's bag.

Milton looked at the underwear again and they were vaguely familiar. Same brand as he wore, same... Oh god! Could it... Same frayed waistband, same hole in the hip where he put his thumb through pulling them on. He grabbed them out of the woman's hand.

"Merci."

Oh god.

He lifted up his bag and saw the gaping hole. *Catcher in the Rye* plopped out on the seat next to him.

His head went hot with embarrassment and the entire movie of the day rewound in his head, he saw now the Hansel and Gretel trail of books and undies he'd left behind him, as he dragged his giant bag through the frozen hellscape he'd just survived. He realized now that the sense of getting stronger, as he walked through the park, was a fiction. The bag wasn't feeling lighter because of some inner super-human strength he'd mustered through sheer will and brooding masculinity; it was feeling lighter because it was getting lighter. Because all his things had fallen out along the way. He wasn't Holden Caulfield. He wasn't even John Hinckley Junior. He was just Milton Ontario.

He cursed mildly at himself, turning the bag over to see what had escaped. Most of it had. There was still his 44-pounds of 98-year-old Underwood No. 3 typewriter, his 1954 Regentone portable record player, one plaid shirt, three well-worn band t-shirts, one change of underwear, three socks, one pair of relaxed-fit Costco-brand blue jeans, two Leonard Cohen records, and maybe five books, including the hardcover *Critic's Picks Annotated Edition* of *Ulysses*, which weighed nearly as much as the typewriter.

The remnants were still there because they were wedged in one end by the *Ulysses* and held there with three wraps of duct tape. It was less than half his stuff remaining, but they were the heaviest things, so the bag still weighed over 60 pounds.

In the course of rolling his eyes towards the heavens to curse god, he caught a glimpse of the sign zipping by out the window: avenue Bernard.

"Frig!"

Everyone on the bus looked at him, then to their neighbour and shared a quiet laugh at the raggedy Anglophone losing his mind on the bus.

Milton pulled the Next Stop cord.

Fig. 15. Son sac

PART TWO

MONTREAL I

FOUR

SEPT-
CENT-
SEPT

Toc-toc-toc

At 00h37 there was a loud banging on the door of the third-floor apartment at 707 avenue de l'Épée. Every light in the place was on but no one was awake.

Two people, one of whom actually lived there, were asleep on couches in the living room, while the TV blasted a Super Putty infomercial. Another uninvited guest was sleeping on a small love seat in what was once a nice dining room but was now a sparsely furnished sort of lounge down the hall next to the kitchen. The only person in an actual bed was Georgette Poule, a 29-year-old chain-smoking puppeteer from Lille, back in Old France.

Georgette was on the lease. It was her Craigslist ad, "Furnished room for rent Mile End," Milton had responded to. It was her "bring cash" message that Milton took as confirmation that the room was his. Now, three hours after getting off the number 80 two stops too late and having, in the freezing cold, to scale an eight-foot fence topped with razor wire, traverse a handful of train tracks, walk a mile one way, walk two miles the other way looking for an opening, and then scaling another eight-foot fence topped with razor wire—tearing the clothes he was wearing and what was left of his hockey bag to ribbons—it was Georgette who was roused out of bed by his banging on the door that was right next to her room.

"Putain! Merde! Qu'est-ce qui se passe? Connard!"

After a great struggle to unwedge the old crooked door that dragged across the worn-out wood floor, and a great deal more cursing en français, Georgette swung the door open to find Milton.

He looked like he'd just survived Napoleon's invasion of Russia: grubby, bloodied, bruised, frozen, in tatters, still wearing his sweater, or what was left of it, for a hood.

"Mon dieu! Ta gueule! Putain!"

Milton stared at his shoes; blood dripped from various razor wire cuts onto the floor.

"Uh... um... hello. I'm... Uh... Milton... Ontario... Your new roommate."

He stuck out his hand.

"T'es quoi—? Get 'way!"

"From Saskatchewan."

"Go the fuck 'way, or I call police! Dégage! Connard!"

"No. I live here now. I emailed on Craigslist."

He attempted to step into the warmth of the apartment. She slammed the door and leaned all her weight against it, trapping him partway. This was the closest Milton had ever been to a grown woman.

"NOIIDEEE! NOHDEEE! WAKE THE FUCK UP! PUTAIN! IL Y A UN SANS-ABRI FOU QU'eSSAYE DE CASSER LA BARAQUE! NOHDEEEE!"

"Uh... My name is Milton."

"Dégage! Connard! NOHDEEE! WAKE THE FUCK UP! CALL POLICE!"

"I'm from Saskatchewan."

A man emerged from the living room across the hall, rubbing his eyes and trying to sort out his hair and his twisted plaid shirt all at once.

"What the hell, Georgie?"

"RUDDY! CALL POLICE! A 'OMELESS MAN IS BREAK-ING IN TO OUR FLAT!"

Ruddy was useless in an emergency.

"AAAAAAAAAGH! AAAAAAAAAAAAAAAAGH! WHAT-DOWEDO?! WHATDOWEDO?! AAAAAAAAAGH! AAAAA AAAAAAAAAGH! DON'TLETHIMIN!! AAAAAAAAAAAGH! OHFUCKOHFUCKOHFUCK!!! AAAAAAAAAAAAAGH!"

He ran down the hall, locked himself in the bathroom, and kept screaming.

"Ah, putain!"

Another man emerged from the living room. He was in a stretched and stained Molson Ex t-shirt—the kind you get free with a case of Molson Ex, but customized with a sloppy "S" drawn with Sharpie between the Molson and the Ex—faded boxer shorts, and filthy work boots. He was the hairiest human Milton had ever seen.

"Another satisfied customer, eh, Georgie?"

He bawled with laughter.

"Nohdee, connard! 'e is trying to break in! Stahp 'im! Call police!"

"Nobody's calling the cops, I've got weed growin' on the balcony."

Another woman appeared.

"Oh my god, you guys! What's with all the yelling?"

"Nudding. Just a lovers' spat between Georgie here, and some hobo fella she was diddling."

"Oh my god! You slept with that!? He's disgusting! Georgette, how could you! Ew-ew-ew-ewwwww!"

"Ta gueule! Jamais! Putain!"

"Christ, b'ys! Will everyone just shut up!"

"I'm Milton Ontario. From Saskatchewan."

"Nohdee! 'elp me! 'it 'im! Nohdee! Putain!"

Fig. 16. Molson sEx

"That's enough, now."

The hairy guy clomped to the door where Georgette had Milton trapped.

"Look, b'y, if she's done givin' ya the business, then the business is done, go on home out of it now."

"I'm Milton..."

Milton tried to wriggle a hand free.

"From Saskatch..."

Before Milton could get the final syllables out Noddy clocked him with a right cross square on the jaw.

Time stopped.

The world went black.

Milton fell backwards and nearly down the one, long, three-storey flight of stairs, but he was saved by what was left of his giant bag that was wedged on the landing. Georgette pushed Milton's leg out the door with her foot, closed the door and bolted it.

• • •

Bienvenue

Milton was awoken by a scream early before sunrise. He'd spent the night, jaw burning, bleeding, sleeping on top of his giant bag in the cold stairwell outside the door of what he'd thought was supposed to be his apartment.

"HESSTILLHERE!!!HESDEAD!!!YOUKILLEDHIM!!! AAAAAAAAAAGH!!!"

Ruddy had spent the night in the bathtub to avoid the hobo murderer lurking in the stairs. He got up when he thought the coast was clear to go back to his own apartment and his own bed before he had to be up at 6:00 to serve coffee at Java Jean on Bernard and Esplanade.

Milton tried to blink the sleep out of his eyes and the stiffness and misery out of the rest of him as the same four faces he met last night leered through a small crack in the door.

Ruddy took off back down the hall to the bathtub.

"Oh my god! He's too disgusting! Oh my god! Georgette! Why! Ewwww!"

"Ta gueule! I'm calling police!"

"Holy Christ on the Cross, will you all just cool it. Buddy, whaddayat sleeping in the stairs? That's a sure way to get another smack."

"No. No. No. Please, no. You don't understand."

"Nah, b'y. I understand just fine. But she's done with ya, and good thing too, I'spose. Looks like she scratched the shit right outta ya. But it's over now. Done, that's it. Put your pecker away and go on home, b'y"

"NOHDEE! Shut up you asshole, I did not sleep with this boy. I would never! 'e's not my type. Connard!"

"Well ya got yourself a level 17 clinger, Georgie, and he keeps waking me up in the middle of the goddamned night. I oughta give yas both a smack."

"No, no, no. That's not it. It's not... I'm not... I never... We never... I'm your new roommate."

"Whowhatnow?"

"Your new roommate. I answered the Craigslist ad a few days ago."

"For Chrissakes, Georgie! He's our roommate."

"My name is Milton Ontario, from Saskatchewan."

"Buddy, you look like you just crawled out of a bum's asshole."

"Ah, Connard! I thought you were coming 'ere yesterday. J'ai besoin d'une cigarette."

"Yeah, sorry, I got a bit lost."

Noddy, the hairiest man alive, helped Milton up and into the apartment. Georgette sat down on an easy chair in the living room and lit a cigarette. Ava, who'd been sleeping on a tiny love seat in the lounge, threw her hands up and declared to no one, "This is crazy, he looks like a bum!" and went back

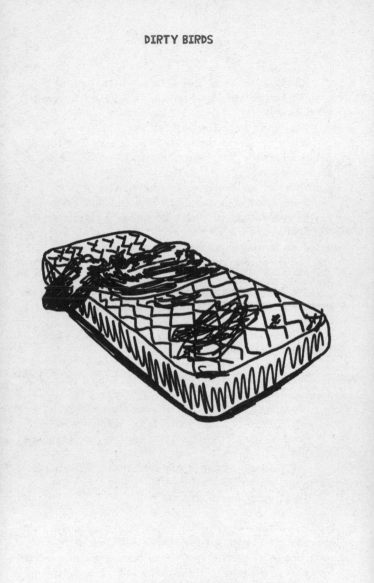

Fig. 17. Furnished apartment

down the hall to her loveseat. Ruddy was still having a moment in the bathtub.

Noddy grabbed Milton's bag and hauled it down the hall towards Milton's new room.

"Jesus, b'y, you bring your brick collection with ya from Ontario? This is yours, it's got some shit in it, a bed, and a lamp, and shit—the bed sucks balls, but it's probably better than sleeping in the stairs. She's all yours. I'll chase Ruddy out of the shitter so you can hose yourself off. Jesus, you look like my Granddad's withered ballsack, and he's been dead for 30 years."

Milton thanked him, Noddy disappeared to "chase Ruddy out of the shitter." Milton collapsed on the bed, and it did suck. A broken spring dug at his kidney, another stabbed into his shoulder. He immediately fell into a very deep sleep.

• • •

Marde

Milton woke up sometime the next afternoon when he rolled his bruised jaw onto a sharp, broken mattress spring. The pain shot across his face, through his head, and smacked into the back of his skull. He rolled onto his back and let his jaw throb.

He lay there for a long time, accounting for his past 60 hours. They had been the hardest of his entire life. He thought of his great-great-great-great Grand Janne/Johnny crossing the Atlantic. He thought of Sir Edward Hilroy, of Benjamin Franklin, of Bernie Federko. He thought of John George Diefenbaker.

He figured the hardship of the past 60 hours was probably enough to net him poems for years. And maybe, maybe, if he played his cards right, he could turn them into a novel someday. A bestseller about overcoming hardship and triumphing in the face of tremendous adversity. He'd have to change the names of the characters, and maybe accentuate some of the details for dramatic effect—call himself Morgan, say he grew up in the middle-of-nowhere in Texas, have him move to Paris or Rome to give it a more cosmopolitan feel, make it less provincial, less Canadian, increase his chances of sales in the States and overseas, have it end with Morgan saving the day, getting the girl, getting the sudden-onset penile hypertrophy, growing a beard, selling the movie rights, living happily ever after.

Milton's Oscar acceptance speech for best adapted screenplay was interrupted by his bowels performing a double backflip in the pike position.

Ever the bashful shitter, Milton had been too shy to go on the bus, or at the 18 Tim Horton's they'd stopped at between Regina and Montreal, or the bus station, or the drug-den McDonald's he collapsed in front of after surviving his trek through the park, or in the abandoned late-night railyard he got trapped in. He'd clenched for several days straight. A rectuming was nigh.

His new apartment was the top floor of a ubiquitous Montreal three-storey row house—one of thousands of massive, narrow, long, brick buildings squashed together with three front doors to three separate apartments.

All these thousands of apartments were arranged more-or-less the same. Kitchen in the back, living room in the front, bedrooms of some sort, usually three or four, in between, and a bathroom somewhere in the middle.

Not that Milton knew any of this. He'd never been to Montreal, let alone a Montreal row house. He didn't know the bathrooms were always somewhere in the middle, amongst the bedrooms. He waddled back to the kitchen holding his throbbing jaw and his fast-approaching shit, then back down the hall past four closed doors to the living room and the door to the stairs he'd spent the night

Fig. 18. Morgan Murray by Milton Ontario

on, then back, before he started checking doors. Behind door number three was the bathroom, and he made it just in time.

Sept-cent-sept was an 8-1/2. In Moose Jaw, they measure apartments in bedrooms. In Montreal they measure them in total rooms, or portions thereof: living room, kitchen, dining room/lounge, some weird tiny storage room with a washing machine that almost worked, and four bedrooms added up to eight, plus a "1/2" to tell you it has a toilet. It's not clear whether the "1/2" refers to a bathroom only counting as half a room somehow, or if it's just a way of indicating there is a room suitable for both number one and number two.

While Milton two'd in the 1/2 he looked around his new place for the first time.

The bathroom might have been nice once upon a time. The floor was covered in tiny white hexagonal tiles, the walls were covered with white glossy rectangular tiles, the tub was an ancient cast-iron clawfoot tub that looked heavy just sitting there, the shower apparatus was sleek, curving chrome pipes and spigots and porcelain handles, and a shower curtain hung from chrome hooks on a chrome ring like in cartoons.

It might have been nice once upon a time.

But the grout lines in the tile had long gone black with dirt. The once-clear shower curtain was now the opaque grey of unbrushed teeth, and three of the eyelets that hooked on the hooks that hooked on the chrome ring were torn out, so the curtain slouched. All the sexy chrome had brown-grey flecks of rust starting to eat through the solid coating of scummy grime. The mirror above the likewise-disgusting porcelain pedestal sink was criss-crossed with cracks. There was a dust ball the size of a softball under the rusting radiator.

It might have been nice once upon a time.

• • •

Deux solitudes

Avenue de l'Épée runs along the imaginary border of the Mile End neighbourhood of the Plateau region of Montreal—the crosshatching of small residential streets and commercial avenues stretching from downtown in the southeast, along the eastern slopes of Mont-Royal, to the train tracks that run alongside avenue Van Horne in the northwest.

It had long been home to Francophones, Hasidic Jews, and émigrés from Greece with their wide array of bakeries and fruiteries and diners and smoked-meat sandwich shops. Its favourite sons were brilliant men like Mordecai Richler and Leonard Cohen.

But the Plateau was now being overrun by trendy fair-trade cafés, gourmet grilled-cheese sandwich restaurants, and yoga studios catering to an endless supply of young Anglophones and their endless supply of asymmetric haircuts, plaid shirts, and fixed-gear bicycles that were locked by eights to every pole and post in the neighbourhood.

A lot of these Anglophones are students at one of the two big English universities downtown: McGill, Canada's best attempt at a Harvard, and Concordia, Canada's best attempt at a Kazakh National Research Technical University.

But many more of the Anglophone expats are refugees escaping the beige infinite flatness of Upper Canada. Of Oakville and Scarborough, of Uxbridge and Etobicoke, of Milton, Ontario.

Scores upon scores of them flock here, like Milton Ontario, to be part-time writers/part-time waiters, part-time painters/part-time bartenders, part-time musicians/part-time baristas.

They flock here to live four and five to a rundown Mile End 8-1/2 third-floor walk-up. Flock here to learn the banjo and start noise bands and write poetry. Flock here when Berkeley didn't pan out and McGill was their safety.

They flock here seeking asylum in the perpetual twenty something adolescence allowed by a cultural-linguistic Anglophone bubble in the middle of North America's most cosmopolitan French city and the largesse of the depressed rents that go along with a permanent state of political rot.

This differentness, from Brampton and Burlington and the cheap rent, is the appeal of Montreal to the skinny-jeaned, horn-rimmed, pour-over hordes of Upper Canadian Anglophone suburbanite refugees. It is very much another country. It's as far away as you can get from the fifty shades of beige of Mississauga and Pickering and still get home for the odd weekend so mom can do your laundry.

But it's summer camp.

It's not real.

Not even for the lot of them too old or so done with their first comp. lit. degrees. The ones who at any other point in history would be well into their middle-age. The 19-year-olds, the 29-year-olds, the 39-year-olds going on 21, have all come to get-on and hangout and hookup and get a deal doing it.

That it's on some of the most politically and historically fraught lip-shaped islands in creation doesn't matter one bit.

That they've created an island of English sameness in a sea of French differentness—which itself is an island of French sameness trying desperately to survive in a sea of English differentness—doesn't matter one bit.

That they are occupying the heart of the largest city in Quebec, which itself is occupying the heart of the unceded territory that has been home to the Kanien'kehá:ka (Mohawk),

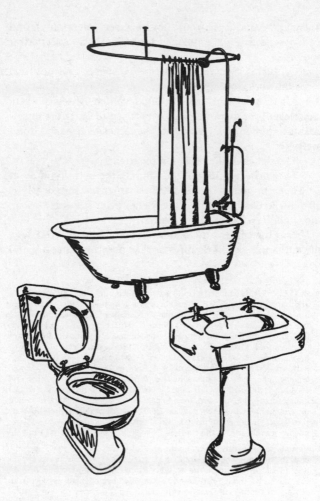

Fig. 19. 1/2

Abenaki, Wyandot (Huron), Anishinaabeg (Algonquin), and St. Lawrence Iroquoian peoples for milennia, doesn't matter one bit.

Centuries of complex historical, social, and political forces at work don't matter.

All of the land stolen, blood spilled, tricks played, and clever bureaucratic manoeuvres used to settle the unsettleable argument over who gets the riches of the land don't matter.[16]

The riches of the land don't matter.

The social tyranny of the Church, the petty tyranny of Le Chef, the petty racism of pure laine, the provocations of "Vive le Quebec Libre," the Richard Riots, Refus Global, the Quiet Revolution don't matter.[17]

The uprisings and mailbox bombs and martial law, the kidnappings and manifestos read on prime-time TV and

[16] In 1535, French Explorer Jacques Cartier sailed up the St. Lawrence River and happened upon a St. Lawrence Iroquoian village called Hochelaga on the side of a giant hill on the bottom lip of an island known to the Kanienkéha:ka Nation as Tiohtià:ke. Since the end of the last ice age, Tiohtià:ke has been a hotly contested and economically important territory that different nations—both from North America and Europe—have met on, traded at, and fought over. Violence most recently broke out in this region over the summer of 1990. The Oka Crisis was a 78-day armed stand-off between members of two Kanienkéha:ka communities and the Canadian Forces, RCMP, and Sûreté du Québec (Quebec's provincial police force) over the proposed expansion of a golf course and condo development by the town of Oka, Quebec on disputed land claimed by the neighbouring community of Kanehsatà:ke. Two people were killed, one from each side, in the conflict.

[17] Various social, political, economic and cultural forces, like the Catholic church, the long-serving premier Maurice "Le Chef" Duplessis (1936-39 and 1944-59), and a simmering nationalist movement based upon French racial purity did much to keep Quebec a primarily agrarian society until the 1960s, allowing urban Anglophones to accumulate a lot of the province's wealth. A series of provocations, including a hockey riot, an art movement, and a speech by French president Charles de Gaulle, set off the Quiet Revolution under Prime Minister Jean Lesage that saw the modernization of Quebec society and the birth of modern separatist movements.

bodies found in the trunks of cars at airports don't matter.[18]

Separatist governments, referenda, 0.6 per cent, "money and the ethnic vote" don't matter.[19]

The compromises and betrayals, the triumphs and heartbreaks, the history of sorrow and disgrace blotted out by rah-rah hockey games that have replaced rah-rah wars and the urgency of survival in a place that has winter two-thirds of the year, which have netted us this complicated country don't matter.

Nothing really matters because the struggle is not survival. The struggle is lugging a heavy bag through a park in winter without a toque to a room you're renting sight-unseen from Craigslist for $250 per month with three others while you flit through your twenties pretending to be a poet.

And maybe real life will happen later. Maybe war or revolution or plague or famine or poverty will show up and demand more than barely rhyming free verse and home-recorded noise albums of all the wandering twenty-thirty-something teenagers in the Plateau. But until it does, asymmetric haircuts

---

[18] Throughout the 1960s the militant Quebec nationalist group Front de libération du Québec (FLQ) carried out a series of attacks on Federal institutions and Anglophone neighbourhoods and businesses in Montreal, killing several and injuring hundreds. In October of 1970 they kidnapped British diplomat James Cross and provincial labour minister Pierre Laporte. The Quebec Government requested federal military intervention and invocation of the War Measures Act—effectively martial law. Laporte was found strangled and stuffed in the trunk of a car at a regional airport a couple of days later. Cross was released after 62 days when his kidnappers were given safe passage to Cuba. Laporte's killers were eventually found hiding in a hole on a farm. By 1982 all the kidnappers had either returned to Quebec or had been paroled, and many have continued to be politically active.

[19] There have been two referenda in Quebec on the subject of sovereignty from Canada, led by separatist provincial governments. The first in 1980 was defeated 60 to 40 per cent. A second in 1995 was narrowly defeated 50.6 to 49.4 per cent. After the defeat, Quebec premier Jacques Parizeau blamed his side's loss on "money and the ethnic vote."

and fixed-gear bikes and scavenged freegan gluten-free lentils and endless online petitions are acts of rebellion. Are acts of courage. Are acts of resistance against the infinite flatness. Until it does, the only thing that matters is that nothing really matters but feeling good and taking the long way to the realization that barely rhyming free verse and home-recorded noise albums matter least of all.

And Milton sits at the very heart of this, taking a shit, taking in the soap scum and toothpaste crust built up on and spilling down over what was once, a lifetime ago, fine craftsmanship, and all it looked like was filth, decay, neglect, and the half-hearted dreams of tens of thousands of adultescent dilettante part-time rock flautists/part-time florists. And all he could think of was where he might find a roll of toilet paper.

He finished, used the last three squares of toilet paper on a roll that had rolled under the rusty radiator, flushed, and felt a thousand times better.

A thousand times better until he saw himself in the cracked and dirty mirror. He saw someone he didn't recognize. He scrubbed at the mirror with a dirty old t-shirt he found tossed in the corner and got it slightly cleaner, but it did nothing for his face.

A thin dark bruise split his face in half; his jaw was deep purple; both eyes were bloodshot and ringed by black (either bruises or exhaustion or both); he was covered in dirt, scratches, and dried blood; his lips were split and swollen from the cold.

He leaned in closer and poked at his various wounds to see if they were real. They were. He winced. The smell of his three days without a shower overpowered the three days of shit he'd just flushed.

He turned on the shower.

• • •

Sa chambre

Milton towelled off with the old dirty t-shirt and went back to his room. He put on his last pair of underwear, his one remaining pair of pants, one of his last few shirts, and the last pair of socks he owned and sat on his disgusting, busted old mattress on the floor in the corner.

His room was small, really small, and windowless, really windowless.

Milton could stand in the middle with his arms out and touch opposing walls with the tips of his fingers.

Next to the mattress was a shaky and swollen pressboard table. There was an ancient lamp—not an antique, just old— on the table that hummed when he turned it on.

The ceiling light, a single bulb, was covered by a sheer red scarf with some kind of flowers on it, the kind of thing your aunt buys at the Farmer's Market, which bathed the room in a pervy red light. The corpses of hundreds of dead flies could be made out through the fabric. Milton would have ripped it down, but the entire apartment had luxurious 12-foot ceilings and there was no way he could reach it without a ladder.

The walls were painted a faded orange, almost peach colour. Except for the wall above the bed where the paint had peeled off in a circle roughly the diameter of a garbage can, exposing bare plaster. Milton rubbed more paint off on the edge of the circle and tapped at the rock-hard plaster. He tried not to imagine what it was that might have caused it, but he figured there was a body concealed in the wall that had decomposed and leached body slime into the plaster, ruining it for paint forever.

Directly across from the mystery circle was another door. This door once led to the bathroom but had been nailed shut and painted over hundreds of times. Its only vestigial function, as Milton would learn, was to improve the conveyance of bathroom sounds into Milton's room.

His room was clearly a converted closet that Milton was now paying $250 per month for, plus internet.

He tore the surviving duct tape off his bag and unpacked his things. He piled what clothes were left in one corner. He piled his last few books next to the mattress.

The biggest ones had survived the trip, ones like *The Collected Letters of Thomas Mann*—who Milton had never heard of, but it was the only non-welding textbook on a folding table of "Free Books" in the PUS Student Centre one day, and he'd yet to open it to notice that it was 1,572 pages of German letters from the renowned German author to various German lovers, friends, and acquaintances—and the *Ulysses Critic's Picks Annotated Edition*, which, for all its indecipherable Irish ravings and incomprehensible critical essays by literature professors, might as well have been in German. He set these two behemoths on the floor next to his bed and piled tattered copies of *Beautiful Losers*, *The Apprenticeship of Duddy Kravitz*, *Gone with the Wind*, and *Down and Out in Paris and London*, and a notebook full of drafts of poems on top of the pile.

Two Leonard Cohen records survived the trip: *I'm Your Man* and *Death of a Ladies' Man*.

The last things he dug out of the bag were his typewriter and record player. Despite the hellish trip, the two antiques were indestructible. He hoisted them both out of the bag and set them delicately on the table. He stood back to admire his new home, which looked more like a cell, a metaphor he played with in his head for a moment and how it added to the rich experience of harrowing hardship he'd just been through and all the poems he could write about it, until he was interrupted by the pressboard table crumpling to the floor under the weight of the testaments to early 20th-Century American manufacturing.

He reassembled the rubble and his pile of books to make a makeshift short table that was just the right height to work at if he sat on the floor, which saved him having to worry about finding a chair.

• • •

8-1/2

After he had his cell arranged, he decided, since no one was home, to snoop around.

He tapped gently on each door before opening them a crack to look inside.

Directly across from him was Noddy's room. It was a long narrow room that ran the length of the hall from the front door to the dining room/lounge. In the back corner was a bare double mattress sitting on the floor with a knot of tie-dye blankets on it, empty beer cans and filthy dishes, and dirty free-in-a-case-of-beer t-shirts were strewn everywhere. In the middle of the room was a carpet with a rusted barbell and two gold, dented plastic, 25-pound weights on either end. There was a big window looking into a sort of courtyard between this building and the one next to it.

The walls were mint green and decorated with a number of posters depicting—clockwise from the door—*Scarface*, a woman's ass in a thong, *Dazed and Confused*, and a woman in a bikini washing a mid-80s Chevy Camaro with her butt. There were several wilted potted pot plants on the floor beneath the window.

The door at the end of the hall, next to the front door, was Georgette's room. The room was probably a den before this place was turned into a halfway house for Lost Boys and Girls. There were massive French doors leading to the balcony, overlooking avenue de l'Épée, but the maple trees along the street threw the entire room, which was painted a deep purple, into shade.

Fig. 20. Decor

It was decorated with all kinds of scarves and beads and smelled of perfume, incense, cigarettes, and dirty laundry. There were dozens of wine bottles with candles stuck in their mouths, and wax dripped down their sides. An accordion peered out from beneath a pile of clothes on a chair in the corner. Several grotesque-looking puppets were hanging by their strings from a nail on the wall next to a large dresser with a mirror. The top of the dresser was buried in bottles and tubes and canisters of creams and oils and waxes and nail polishes, and several sex toys of various sizes, colours and configurations, which Milton, having never seen such things in the wild, mistook for more scented candles.

Next to Georgette's room was the living room. It was big, and built around a large, elaborate mantel. The fireplace itself was boarded up, but there were half a dozen wine-bottle candles on the hearth. Highball glasses overflowing with cigarette butts and empty wine and beer bottles decorated the mantel, the coffee table, and the patch of floor where an end table should have been. Another sheer red, vaguely tribal scarf hung above the mantel. In the corner directly opposite the door sat a massive yet small tube TV on top of a milk crate. Three couches, all older than Milton, were aimed towards the TV from across the room.

Milton would learn that the entire apartment, except for the scarves, which were all from Georgette's personal collection, was furnished with things found on the street.

Back towards Milton's room, between the living room and the bathroom, was another bedroom. He assumed it belonged to Ruddy or Ava, but it looked unlived in. There was a mattress leaning against the wall, an empty clothes hamper, a desk with nothing on it, a dresser with nothing in it, nothing on the yellow walls, and a closet door behind piles of large moving boxes was locked with a padlock.

Down the hall past the bathroom and Milton's cell was the dining room/lounge. It had an incredible built-in china cabinet, crown moldings, and stained-glass windows on the back wall, but the cabinet was empty and several of the doors hung crooked and half-open. There was a wobbly chrome and Formica kitchen table with an old record player, a pile of records and another highball glass overflowing with cigarette butts on it. The table was flanked by mismatched chairs on either side. Opposite the table was a really small love seat. Everything in the room was dwarfed by the grandeur of the once-luxuriant space, a fact that double-underlined and highlighted the cheapness of the garbage furniture and garbage people who had let this place fall apart.

Through a swinging door that didn't so much swing as stutter, was the kitchen. Like the entire apartment, the floors were narrow maple hardwood, with the varnish long worn away. Everything in the kitchen was coated in a fine grey sheen of greasy dust.

The kitchen was laid out almost as though they forgot to add a kitchen at first. The stove was next to the small cabinet holding a large, stained, stainless-steel sink. The sink was right in the way of the door, and the stove stuck out in the middle of the room, so you had to manoeuvre around it. Beside the stove was a doorway to the storage closet/laundry room/second bathroom—i.e. a small room, about the size of Milton's, with a washing machine, a toilet, and a pile of junk shoved in one corner. Beyond that was a fridge that stuck out like the stove and blocked access to the cabinets which ran along the back wall of the kitchen. That was it for the cabinets, a whole 6-feet-or-so of counter space, partially blocked by a fridge. The wall opposite the sink, stove, and fridge had a small wooden table that wobbled mightily, and a window leading to a fire escape.

Milton hadn't eaten since the day before, so he poked his head in the fridge and helped himself to some kind of foul-smelling cheese that was marked with a big, bold "G".

Having shat, showered, and gorged himself on someone else's expensive French cheese, Milton felt brand new. He still looked like he "crawled out of a bum's asshole" but he was ready. Ready for Montreal. Ready to embrace his destiny. Pursue immortality. Ready to leave the apartment.

• • •

Le Mile End

Rue Bernard is shops, restaurants, cafés, and theatres clear across avenue du Parc to boulevard Saint-Laurent—the Main. Parc was the same from Bernard down towards the park, but the flavour of the businesses in either direction was a little different.

Running east-west along Bernard were vintage clothing stores, artisan cheese shops, high-end ethnic restaurants— everything from Brazilian to sushi—pretentious single-brew coffee shops filled with pretentious single-brew drinkers huddled behind MacBooks, the city's foremost puppet theatre, yoga studios with ample stroller parking, a grocery store with valet parking, the other smoked-meat place—Lester's, the antithesis of the ubiquitous tourist trap Schwartz's a few blocks southeast on St. Laurent—and the world's top independent publisher of English graphic novels.

Every inch of the several blocks of Bernard from the Outremont Metro station to the west and St. Laurent to the east, which are crisscrossed by tree lined residential streets, is drenched in yuppie pretense.

The artisan cheese shop, for instance, had 132 varieties of hard cheeses (in addition to their 137 varieties of soft cheeses), including 14 different gruyères, but not a single cheddar. Not one.

The luxury grocer didn't sell frozen TV dinners, but sold individually wrapped grapes from France. Not wrapped bunches of grapes, but single, seedless red and green grapes

Fig. 21. Gourmet grape

wrapped individually in cellophane, each with a tiny list of ingredients, and a barcode to scan each grape at the cash. Individually. They were ten cents each.

Parc, on the other hand, is another world entirely.

Instead of trendy grilled-cheese cafés and the latest Yelp darling boutique poutineries, it is full of dumpy diners cut right out of, and still serving food from, a 1950s dumpy diner catalogue, and butcher shops without names or signage, only carcasses hanging in their windows.

There is a hardware store, a dollar store, an almost-a-dollar store—also without any signage—a stationery store that sells only the cheapest pens and paper, a clothing store called, simply, Vêtements, which according to its window display deals primarily in women's lingerie, baby clothes, and Jewish religious outfits.

Side-by-side-by-side were two competing fruiteries and a discount grocer, all selling versions of the exact same things in unnecessary quantities for unreasonably low prices in attempts to undercut the others—five half-bad pineapples for $7, four pounds of three-quarters-turned grapes for $2, 12 pounds of bruised plums for $5.

These fruiteries, plus the hardware store, were almost entirely responsible for supplying the ingredients that set off the 2006 artisan micro-homebrew toilet brandy blindness outbreak in Mile End.

The Mile End stretch of Parc is anchored by a YMCA on the corner of rue St. Viateur (of bagel fame) and, a few doors down, a former Anglican church-turned-library. Every building along this stretch is guarded by a thousand fixed-gear bicycles chained to every pole, sign, post, railing, and picket.

. . .

Livres

Between the massive red brick YMCA and the massive red brick church-turned-library, sitting tucked almost invisibly between the dépanneurs (a French word for "mob front" that sells cigarettes, chips, and lotto tickets) and Greek drycleaners, is a misplaced row house that was home to Mile End's oldest bookstore.

The store takes up the living and dining rooms of the first floor of an old row house. It's a cash-only kind of place—all books were $2—operated by two ancient French men: Guillaume Vautour and Gweltaz Mouette.

Guillaume owns the building. He inherited it in the 1950s when his mother died. It would be worth more than two million dollars if he were to sell it, or it could bring in several thousand dollars per month in rent, but instead every inch of all three storeys are jam-packed with books and old newspapers and boxes and piles of all of Mother's old clothes and kitchen appliances, and rats. Lots of rats.

In a rotting, unmarked cardboard box on the third floor, amongst a bunch of old, mouldy shoes, is Maurice "The Rocket" Richard's[20] 1946 Stanley Cup ring that Guillaume's father, Georges, took off The Rocket's finger himself in a bar fight on rue Ste-Catherine.

That ring is worth more than the entire building and all of its contents. But Guillaume doesn't know it's there. He hadn't been upstairs for years because of his bad knees, and back, and hip, and the gout, and the uncorrected hernia, and his feet had only gotten flatter since the war.

Neither would the city garbage collectors find it when they took The Rocket's ring, and 27 garbage truck loads of other assorted treasures, to the city landfill after the house was repossessed due to unpaid taxes after Guillaume died in 2011.

---

[20] Maurice "The Rocket" Richard (b. 1921, d. 2000) was a beloved goal-scoring machine for the beloved Montreal Canadiens from 1942 to 1960.

Guillaume sleeps in a room off the kitchen in an old recliner smooth with decades of grime.

On random afternoons he props open his front door with an old wooden chair and balances a handwritten "livres" sign on the seat and sits in his living room, surrounded by piles of French and English books, chain-smoking unfiltered cigarettes, yelling very racist epithets about immigrants and Anglophones at Gweltaz while the two of them remove "Propriété de la Bibliothèque Mile End" stamps from the edges of paperbacks with 100-grit sandpaper.

Guillaume doesn't particularly like Gweltaz. Gweltaz has the annoying habit of humming while sanding the books, he dresses like one of the Tweedles, and he suffers some kind of speech affliction that Guillaume attributes to a weakness of character. After 25 years of Gweltaz just showing up, Guillaume still doesn't know his name. But he shows up every day, sands books for hours for no pay, gives Guillaume half his lunch, and never says a word, just hums, while Guillaume educates him on the existential threat minorities pose to the "pure laine Québécois comme nous."

The other reason Guillaume keeps Gweltaz around is that his arms are long enough, slender enough, and supple enough to fit through the after-hours book-deposit box slot at the library.

Stealing library books is technically theft, but it makes for the perfect, low-overhead business.

Each morning before the library opens, Gweltaz, who lives in an apartment up the street, fishes whatever books he can out of the after-hours book-deposit box. Then the pair spend the day sanding the stamps off the new inventory while Guillaume rattles on about the travesty that are turbans in the police force and Gweltaz hums Wagner.

And because Guillaume owns the building outright and doesn't bother paying any kind of taxes—he learned long ago that city hall was so corrupt that they wouldn't pursue tax delinquents unless someone complained about the stink of a rotting corpse—what meagre sales they do have are pure profit, and keep him well-stocked in unfiltered cigarettes and sherry.

They shouldn't have been able to get away with it once, let alone several times per week for 25 years and counting, but the circulation department of Réseau des bibliothèques publiques de Montréal were never able to figure out why their Mile End branch had such low return rates, such high loss rates, and so many appealed fines.

It got so bad in the 1980s that a branch manager was fired because of it. But the losses weren't because of a lack of managerial oversight, a failure of lending policy, overdue fine structures, or not enough Propriété de la Bibliothèque Mile End stamps. They were solely because the after-hours book deposit box slot placement on the converted church was the ideal height and angle for Gweltaz's spindly arms, and in a surveillance-camera blind spot.

On a good week, if he felt like being open more than a few days, Guillaume might sell 50 books for a couple bucks apiece. But sales had been picking up with the influx of the "maudit Anglais et leurs vélos" in the neighbourhood. So, he started pricing the English books at $4 each.

And every so often, about once a week lately, a hayseed from some Saskatchewan backwater with their face arranged in the wrong order would move to town to pursue some hare-brained poetry dreams, and having lost most of their book collection in transit would stumble upon livres while in search of vêtements and would buy 20 English paperbacks and pay with a $100 bill, which Guillaume would snatch from his hand and then shake his cigarette angrily and yell "Pas de change! Pas de change!"

It was still quite cold, but the sun was shining, and the streets and shops and cafés were all crowded with people—who all apparently had nothing better to do on a Thursday afternoon—and Milton had never felt so alive.

His new neighbourhood was positively brimming with life, and so was he. He practically skipped all the way home, humming to himself the tune that the elderly book salesman was humming—the overture from *Rienzi*—while he happily and lovingly refurbished old books with his colleague as they discussed, he was certain, Continental Philosophy.

Milton returned with 20 books crammed into a couple of sacks of half-rotten fruit and day-old bagels, a ream of so-cheap-it's-almost-transparent typewriter paper, three pens that cost a whopping 50 cents, three coil-bound notebooks that cost a dollar, a six-pack of white briefs—Vêtements didn't carry boxers—a two-pack of synagogue pants and shirts, and 24 pairs of white tube socks. All told, he spent $15 on food and clothing, and $100 on books.

• • •

La viande de cheval

When Milton returned to Sept-cent-sept the stairwell smelled of burning rubber, and thick, greasy black smoke hung near the ceiling.

Something that sounded like French Enya was blaring from behind Georgette's closed door.

Milton nodded unnoticed "heys" at Ava and Ruddy on his way past the living room. They were arguing about Marx and smoking weed out a slightly open window.

"No, you don't understand! It doesn't matter how great his ideas might be, if they are impossible to implement because of the frailty of men's egos, then it doesn't matter."

"But the Russians, the Chinese, the Cubans—none of those were ever true Marxists. Don't blame Marx for their bullshit."

"Like, imagine a toaster, right? If that toaster doesn't make toast, is it still a toaster? No! It's a pile of junk you throw away."

"What are you talking about? Toaster?"

Milton dumped his new books and clothes on his mattress and took his half-bad fruit and bagels to the kitchen.

Smoke was pouring out of the partially open stuttering door. Noddy was inside singing and frying something on the stove.

"*Oh, Sonny don't go away...* Hey, b'y. Whaddayat?"

Milton couldn't make out a word of whatever he just said.

"*Your daddy's a sailor who never comes home...* Want some horsemeat?"

"Sorry, some what?"

"*I'm feeling so tired, I'm not all that STTTTTROOONG GGGG!* Horse, b'y."

"Uh... Did you say h-h-horse?"

"Yes, b'y. They pretty much give this shit away at the butcher, cheaper than rabbit even."

"Rabbit?"

"And it's good. Better than beef, not as good as moose, b'y, but better than seal."

"Seal?"

"*I'm not all that STTTTTTROOONGGGGG!* Yeah, b'y. I'm a lousy townie, so I don't like the texture none. Tastes like my arse. Want some?"

Noddy held out a frying pan of ground horse that was still spitting grease and smoke.

"Uh... no, thanks."

"Bullshit, you're having some, I insist. My treat. I doubts they got anything this good in—where ya from in Ontario?"

"Saskatchewan, actually."

Noddy took two bowls out of a pile of dirty dishes in the sink, shook them off, and divided the meat half in each. He

Fig. 22. Primal cuts

dug his hand in the six inches of brown water in the sink and found a fork and a spoon, wiped them on his off-white Bud Light t-shirt, stuck one in each bowl and held out the bowl with the spoon to Milton.

"It's lean, not like pork, good for you."

He took cans of Coors Light from a box on the window-sill and slid them into either pocket of his plaid cargo shorts, handed one to Milton, and clomped down the hall in his work boots.

"*I'm not all that strrrrrrrrrOOOOOOOOONNNNNGGGGG.*"

This was a regular thing, Noddy having a bowl of fried ground horse for supper. At least five nights a week he'd fry it until the smoke alarm would have gone off, if the smoke alarm had batteries in it, and then eat it with a spoon and chase it with two or three or maybe six, sometimes eight or twelve, warm Coors Lights. That's it. Never a vegetable, never a starch, only ever fried horse and warm beer.

Milton held the dirty bowl of ground horse meat in his hands and stared at it like he was waiting for it to tell him something.

In the living room Ruddy and Ava were still arguing over the ontology of toast.

"No! It doesn't matter if you are putting jam or butter or the tears of angels on it, it's not toast. The toaster didn't toast it. It's just bread. The toaster isn't a toaster."

"Then who's supposed to be the toaster? Lenin?"

"No, Marx."

"I thought he was the peanut butter."

"No. There is no peanut butter. There is no toast. It's still just bread."

"So, who is the bread then? Trotsky?"

"Us, the people, the Russians, the Chinese, the Cubans, the workers of the world. We're all bread."

Noddy had sat down between them, turned the TV on

to a Quebec Hockey League game. It was 1-0 for Thetford Mines Home Hardware Pelles Volantes over Rapide Lube Monstres de Huile de Jonquière in the first period.

"Don't lump me in with those fascists!"

Noddy kept turning the volume up to drown out the toast talk as he washed down mouthfuls of fried horse with mouthfuls of warm Coors Light. Ava and Ruddy just yelled louder at one another.

"God! Nooo! If Marx's chauvinist utopia my-dick-is-bigger theory doesn't transform society, us, the workers, the bread, into toast, then it's not a toaster. It's just scrap metal."

"Jesus! You're both toasted. Shut yer yapping and make room for... uh... buddy here. The game's on."

Milton came in and sat down at the end of the couch farthest from the three of them.

"Oh my god! It's you! How's your face, that looks really bad."

Ava punched Noddy in the arm.

"You're such a jerk, Noddy, gawd!"

"Sorry fer smackin' ya, buddy, don't mean nothing by it, George was just having a moment, and I figured you could take 'er better than she could."

"I'm fine, it was just a misunderstanding, all good."

Milton pawed at his horse with his dirty spoon.

"Or Ruddy, here, screaming like a little bitch in the bath-tub all night."

"Shut-up, Noddy, I was on shrooms."

"What's your name?"

"Me? It's Milton Ontario."

"Oh cool, I'm from Timmins, Ava is from Etobicoke."

"Oh, no, sorry. I'm from Saskatchewan."

"I don't know where that is, I'm not familiar with Milton."

"No, I'm not from Ontario, I'm from Saskatchewan."

"Wait, like Saskatchewan the place?"

"Yeah."

They all shared a laugh. Milton wasn't quite sure why.

"I can't believe there is a Milton there too. What are the chances?"

"No, no. That's my name. Milton."

"Jesus, b'y, get your story straight."

"I'm Milton Ontario, that's my name, like the town, yeah, but not, it's just my name. I'm from a little town in the middle of nowhere in Saskatchewan."

"You're named after a suburb?"

"No, I'm not named after the town. I'm named after the kicker."

All three of them looked at Milton like he had a second head.

"You don't know Doug Milton?"

"Doug who?"

"Doug Milton! He kicked the winning field goal for the Riders in '82."

"82? Never heard of him."

"So, this Doug guy then, he's from Ontario?"

"No. That's just my last name."

"Like the province?"

"Yeah. I guess. My family is originally from Finland, they were called Alatalo, or something, but it got changed at the border."

"So, you're not from Ontario."

"Jesus, Ruddy, b'y, try and keep up."

"No, I'm from a tiny town in Saskatchewan."

"What's it called?"

"You've probably never heard of it, it's like 100 people. Called Bellybutton."

"That's the name of the town? Oh my god!"

"I can't say much, my nan is from Dildo, but that's a pretty stupid name, b'y."

"What, my name?"

"Well, that too, but your town, Jesus."

The four of them continued to make get-to-know-ya small talk while Milton poked at his congealing bowl of horse and Noddy chewed loudly with his mouth open, guzzled warm beer, and turned the hockey game up louder and louder until the Anglophones were shouting over the French announcers and the French Enya blasting from the next room.

• • •

Les colocs

Ruddy and Ava brought Milton up to speed on the roommate situation.

Noddy dated Ava on-and-off, mostly off, for most of last summer. At some point, in some kind of VennDiagram/*Threes Company* sort of situation, Ava started dating Ruddy from her band Spigot—a two-piece noise ensemble, Ava on recorder, Ruddy on laptop drum machine. But even when her and Noddy were all the way off, even after the summer had ended and she was back in school, double-majoring in Eastern Religions and Centrally Planned Economics, even when Ruddy dumped Ava for a guy named Crane in his other band, Narc Wolf—a three-piece grind-core noise band—Ava kept coming around the apartment with Ruddy just to hang out. Not to hang out with Noddy, just to hang out.

Ava and Ruddy would sit in the front room, smoke pot, burn incense, pet the downstairs neighbour's cat who was always upstairs, drink tea, eat the communal long-grain brown rice, and get into arguments about third-wave Marxo-feminism with anyone in earshot.

Neither Ava nor Ruddy actually lived there. The unused bedroom belonged to a fourth roommate named Andy, or Andi, or Andie, or André—Milton wasn't sure. They were never around. They'd all but moved in with their boyfriend or girlfriend in some other 8-1/2, but commitment issues kept them paying rent to store their stuff at Sept-cent-sept.

Georgette was from Lille, in France, but had moved to Montreal to work at Place des Poupées: "the best puppetry theatre in the North America." She had studied puppetry at Les Beaux-Arts, part of the Sorbonne in Paris, for seven years, and now was an apprentice prop mistress, making the tiny props for the puppet shows. It barely paid anything, but it kept her in menthol cigarettes, red wine, and vaguely tribal scarves she hung all around the apartment.

Ava explained Georgette's music code. If it was French Enya turned up to 11 she was in having sex with Larry, a 52-year-old married Anglophone insurance salesman from Repentigny. If it was the Rolling Stones, it was Chris, a med student from Brampton.

It sounded salacious and complicated to Milton, but the way Ava and Ruddy explained it, while Noddy held two fingers up to his mouth and flicked his tongue in Ruddy's ear, it was a normal thing for normal adults to do, and that sometimes Larry and Chris would come hang out too. They were both kind of square, but Larry would bring foreign beer, and Chris would bring good weed.

When his bowl of horse was empty, Noddy started to tell Milton the highlights of his story. But he only made it as far as he was 41 and had left St. John's and his decade-long gig DJing at the Sea Horse, a strip club, "the classy one," a year and a bit before Milton showed up at Sept-cent-sept.

He talked a lot about the "girls" at the "Horse" and how he "looked after them" with a sort of big-brotherly pride. He was all of five-foot-four and 150 lbs, but he still talked as if he were their protector. There was a subtext to his story of out-of-control alcoholism and coke-binges he referred to as his "glory days."

There was some debate around the apartment, behind his back, as to why Noddy left St. John's. Everyone was convinced he was on the run from something or someone.

His name probably wasn't even Noddy.

Noddy rarely went out. He'd come home from work and just lounge around the apartment in work boots and cargo shorts with a juice glass full of vodka, or a warm Coors Light in each hand, with the hockey game on in French—which he swore he spoke fluently but no one had seen a lick of evidence of such—and blow his roll-your-own smoke out the half-open window, most of it blowing right back in, and go on loudly, and at length, about the "girls" and unrelated "tits" and "pussy" and "pieces of ass" from St. John's he'd been into in his "glory days."

After the unwatched game would end, he'd go into his room and blast Poison or Ratt until he'd either fall asleep or Georgette would bang on the wall and yell "Nohdeeee! Putain! Shuddafuckinmusicup!"

The French Enya wound down around the same time as the hockey game. Noddy, several warm Coors deep, didn't bother turning down the recording of a French hockey radio call-in show that came on after the game, and insisted instead on telling stories about a particularly "sick piece," who was one of "his" dancers "back in Town."

Georgette emerged from her room wrapped in a scarf, "Nohdee! Connard! Turn it DOWN! Putain!"

"Sorry, Georgie, couldn't hear it over Larry railing ya."

Ava, Ruddy, and Noddy all yelled in unison: "Hey, Lar!" Noddy added, "how was your nut?"

Larry flatly responded "Hi guys" back.

"Ta gueule! You are a disgusting!"

This delighted Noddy greatly.

Then Georgette turned her attention to Milton.

"New boy, you are not dead, that is good. Do you have my money?"

Georgette did not take kindly to being given $250 in fives. She was still cursing when she slammed her door.

"They're probably gonna fuck on all that money like Donald Duck's uncle there, what's his name? Darkwing?"

They all fell silent as they watched the radio-on-TV in a language none of them really understood for a while before Ava yawned and said: "I'm bored, let's go out."

"Robin is having that potluck thing tonight. Owly and Hawk are playing after the soup is gone."

"I could have soup. Noddy, you want to come?"

"Yes, b'y!"

Noddy belched. He could barely keep his eyes open from drunkenness and waking up every day at 5:00 a.m.

"What about you, new guy?"

"Sorry, what is this?"

"Oh my god! He says sorry like such a hoser! Adorable!"

"A potluck. A house show. A party. You'll meet people. Might even get laid or whatever you're into."

"Yeah, sure, I guess."

FIVE
POTLUCK

Pain aux courgettes

"Could you pass the zucchini loaf? Thanks. The whole thing is just a flimsy representation of Owly's dick. The phallicness of it is overwhelming, but the whole thing is just so flaccid. You know? How's the soup?"

"The soup? It's, uh. It's great."

It wasn't. Milton lied. It tasted like the contents of a sink trap cooked in a broth of trash-can water. It was vegan.

"And I mean, sure it's a giant paper-mâché penis on the back of a truck, but, like, it totally ignores the whole fact the military-industrial complex is so 1982. It's been replaced by the media-postindustrial complex, which is far more complex, not to mention narcissistic, than intercontinental ballistic missiles. It's just a bad Cold War dick joke that nobody gets. Were you even born yet when the wall came down?"

"Me?"

"Yeah."

"The wall?"

Milton had no idea what the hell they were talking about. He was just a zucchini loaf intermediary nod-along between the two of them—a guy dressed not unlike Where's

Waldo, and a girl with the most arresting, deep brown eyes he'd ever seen.

"Yeah, you know. The Wall."

"Oh, *that* Wall. Yeah, I was like seven."

"So, like, you don't even remember."

"Yeah. I remember. I was seven."

"But to make such an ordeal of it! Wren's been filming the whole thing. He's got Pochard and Booby down there every day, for hours, shooting the whole thing on film."

"On film? Fuck off!"

"No, it's true. 35mm. He says he's going to make a doc out of it. I laughed in his face. In. His. Face. I told him no one wants to watch some asshole making paper-mâché dicks in their bathtub. But apparently he's cutting it now and is going to try and take it to Telluride."

Milton thought it didn't sound so bad.

"Ha, so he can fuck the girl from *Degrassi* again? Good luck."

"Could you pass the zucchini loaf?"

They were sitting on the cold cement floor of a building in the heart of St. Henri, an old working-class neighbourhood that was being invaded by freegan, anarchist, Anglophones studying Russian at Concordia, and young marketing executives in their 16-foot ceilinged, exposed-brick warehouses-turned-condos who found the whole Plateau thing so last year.

This particular squatters' co-op used to be one of the biggest furriers in Canada. The blood of thousands of critters was spilled on the cold cement floor that Milton and a couple dozen of his new closest friends all sat on sipping hot garbage vegan soup from chipped mugs that said things like "I hate Mondays" and "World's Best Dad" on them.

Milton was sandwiched between two Ontarians. They had a mutual friend who knew someone from *Degrassi*.

"The original?"

"No, the shitty remake."

"Really? Bullshit, no way."

"That's what he was telling everyone when he got back."

"Do you like the soup?"

"Yeah, yeah. It's good."

It still wasn't.

"Uh, what kind is it? I am getting some, um, is that turnip?"

"It's rutabaga and kale in a parsnip broth. Mag found a twenty-kilo sack of rutabaga in Chinatown."

"That's a lot of rutabaga. Must be cheap to get them in bags that size."

They both laughed at Milton. Partly in a semi-offensive patronizing way, and partly in a fully offensive "what a stupid asshole" way.

"No, she found them..."

"..."

"...Like dumpstered them."

Milton swallowed a mouthful of garbage soup hard.

"Dumpstered?"

He really wished he could take that question mark back.

"Could you pass the zucchini loaf? Thanks."

"Did you see the film he took to Telluride though? It was hideous!"

"No. But I heard it was a real bag of shit. Who scored it?"

"He did. Him and the girl from *Degrassi*."

Milton laughed along as hard as he could, searching his memory of anyone from any of the Degrassis.

He had nothing. He looked around for Ava or Ruddy or even Noddy, any familiar face. Ruddy and Ava were probably off smoking someone else's pot, and Noddy was sitting in one of two chairs in the room, talking to a girl sitting on the floor next to him. He was yelling something about the "badassity of AC/DC."

• • •

Fig. 23. Trappings of an anarchist potluck

Oiseaux sales

"What did you say your name was?"

Milton's freegan gastronomic faux pas (plural) hadn't been enough to scare the girl with the eyes off completely. She was cute, albeit so far out of his league it wasn't even the same sport.

"Uhm. Milton."

"Have we met before?"

"No. I just moved here. To… Uh… to write poetry." Shit.

"I mean. I do write poetry. Well I do. Sometimes."

"When did you move here?"

"Yesterday."

"Wow, brand new!"

"Where'd you move from?"

"Saskatchewan."

"Oh no way. Cool."

"Where are you from?"

"The GTA."

"Is that here?"

"No. The GTA. The Greater Toronto Area."

"Oh. Okay."

"I'm from Newmarket."

"Sorry, what was your name. I didn't catch it."

"I didn't say it. It's Robin."

"Like the hood?"

"I guess." She gave him a look. "What kind of poetry?"

"Poetry?"

"What kind of poetry do you write?"

"Oh, you know. Poetry."

"What about?"

"Life and stuff."

Life and stuff, what a damned fool.

"Okay. What about life?"

"Oh, I don't know. Like life. You know?"

"Do you have any with you?"

He did. A pocket full. Always.

"No. Sadly."

"What was the last one you wrote?"

It was about paper-mâché penises.

"Uhm, I think it was about mortality."

"Cool. Who are your poetic heroes?"

Don't say Leonard Cohen.

"Yeats, Keats, Frost, Whitman, you know…"

"Milton?"

"Oh yeah, he's good. Leonard Cohen."

Shit.

Robin smirked.

"Leonard Cohen, eh?"

"Yeah, 'Anthem' is probably *the* great Canadian poem."

"Ah, right, with the cracks and everything. Classic."

"And what do you do?"

That makes you so damned special.

"I make films."

"Any with the girl from *Degrassi*?"

"No, not *those* kinds of films."

Without even the slightest hint of a guffaw.

Milton began to sweat even more than he already was. Maybe she thought he thought she made *those* kinds of films. There was a lot of that in Montreal—aspiring part-time film-makers/part-time baristas who made porn because it paid. Maybe she thought Milton was a perv.

"What kind of movies? Porn?"

"Documentary."

Straight-faced.

Milton laughed at his own bad joke hoping to make it seem like he was doing this on purpose and maybe peer-pressure her into a tension-breaking pity laugh. She wasn't having any of it.

"Anything I might have seen?"

He caught a glance of Noddy humping his chair across the room, and no one was laughing at him much either.

"*Dirty Birds*?"

"I beg your pardon?"

"*Dirty Birds*, it was a short I made that came out last year about the landfill gulls of Calcutta."

"Oh, cool. I haven't seen it. So, you've been to Calcutta then?"

"Yeah, I lived there for three years while we were working on the film."

"Wow. Three years! How long is this movie?"

"It's about seven minutes."

"Oh... Did you like it?"

"The film?"

"Uh. No, Calcutta?"

"Oh, yeah. It was pretty harsh. Poverty on a level most Westerners just can't comprehend."

"Sort of like St. Henri, eh? Haha."

Stone-faced.

Thankfully the chair Noddy had been humping, which wasn't much of a chair to begin with, buckled and shattered into splinters underneath him. The entire room of floor-sitting garbage-sippers went silent. Noddy burst out laughing. Milton started to laugh and looked at Robin. Nothing. He stopped and shook his head disapprovingly.

Robin talked about *Dirty Birds* like Milton's uncle talked about his bowel movements: matter-of-factly and to no one in particular. He was fascinated. This must be how artists, real actual artists, talk.

She'd won some award for it, something French that Milton never heard of, something about eggs.

"It's all an elaborate allegory."

"For the poor?"

"No. That's what everyone always thinks, but I want to

challenge the conventional correlation between gulls and the poor and garbage and landfillscape; I want to give these birds agency. Everyone is too hung up on the poor."

"Too hung up?"

"Yeah, especially in Calcutta where the poverty is so blatant. So in your face."

"In your face?"

"The West just fetishizes it. It's perverse."

"Perverse?"

"I wanted to challenge that. No one is talking about the birds of Calcutta—the gulls. They are so beautiful, and so miserable, yet so utterly overlooked. It'll break your heart."

"Overlooked?"

"Everyone is searching for some obvious connection between the filthy poor and these filthy birds, but it's much more complex and nuanced than that. These beautiful birds are creatures of flight, free, unbound. But, like the people they share the landfillscape with, they are bound by gravity, desire, yearning, and appetites. They're descendant from completely different prehistoric contexts, yet they have to muck about, fucking, fighting, living, dying in the same garbage pile as man."

"You mean they're like dinosaurs?"

She rolled her eyes hard and long, searching the room for someone interesting to talk to, stopping on Noddy—his beer t-shirt off, showing a crowd of uninterested anarchists his Newfoundland gang tattoos: WHITEFISH in Olde English letters across his chest, a knife through the letters, tattoo blood running down his beer gut and into the top of his cargo shorts.

"Where can I see it? Is it online anywhere?"

"No, not really. I'm talking to the BBC who may include it as part of a new series they're doing."

"Oh, wow! That's great!"

"They are such a bunch of assholes though. They treat filmmakers like trash."

"Like dirty birds?"

Nothing. She'd moved on to ignoring his jokes altogether.

"I spent three years living in a landfill in Calcutta, and they want my film for nothing! I told them to go to hell."

"Well you don't smell like it!"

"What?"

That caught her attention.

"Like you've been living in a dump for three years."

"Oh."

Still nothing.

"Anyway, I'd really like to see your *Dirty Bird*. Sometime maybe you could show it to me?"

"Excuse me?"

"Uh… Your film."

Milton wanted to drown himself in his "Teacher of the Year" mug of garbage borscht.

"Hah! Yeah, maybe."

Now she laughs.

"Could you pass the zucchini loaf? Thanks."

• • •

Cool Ranch

Their awkward conversation eased awkwardly into awkward silence as Milton slurped the last of his trash bisque and Robin sopped up the dregs of hers with the stale zucchini loaf that someone had made with gluten-free rice flour they'd found in a dumpster in Westmount—where the good scores are. The flour had obviously turned. If flour could do that.

"What'd you bring?"

"Me?"

"Yeah, what'd you bring for the potluck?"

"Oh. Uhm…"

Milton searched the dimness of the room for a good lie. He was stuck between admitting to bringing Cool Ranch

Doritos or admitting to bringing Noddy. Both were horrible mistakes. Both were the worst social missteps he could have made, save for telling some brilliant filmmaker girl with the most arresting deep-brown eyes that he wanted to see her dirty bird. He contemplated ripping off his pants and doing the helicopter across the room to distract Robin from his severe social ineptitude. He was pretty sure that wouldn't be nearly as bad as having brought Doritos and Noddy.

"I brought some, uh, chips. I was busy. I didn't have time to, uh, make anything, and the vegan bakery by me was closed, and I was really rushed, and I didn't know it was a potluck until it was too late."

"Oh, those plantain chips? Those are really good."

"They are!"

Noddy wasn't quite helicoptering around the room, but he was lying on his back with his legs folded as close to behind his head as he could manage, with a lit lighter inches from his ass, his face all screwed up red from extreme concentration.

POOF!

Milton buried his head in his hands. Noddy burst out in obnoxious laughter, drowning out the mini drum/didgeridoo circle that had formed in the corner. He hollered something about "sharting" and Milton wanted to die.

"Who brought that asshole?"

"Do you know him?"

"Him? No."

"Could you pass the zucchini loaf? Thanks."

Milton had given up any hope of ever impressing Robin. He had given up any hope of even making her laugh, even a little bit, even by accident, at one of his terrible jokes. He was so relieved when Where's Waldo, who'd drifted off mid-*Dirty Birds*, returned and waved a joint over Robin like a magic wand and invited her outside. She leapt up after him, leaving two empty person-sized spaces on either side of Milton in an otherwise crowded room.

To Milton's right, a group was engrossed in conversation about something post-colonial, and to his left, a group was chatting about farming—something he actually knew some-thing about.

He scootched over to try and join the farm circle. His entrance, like his night, was awkward and ill-timed and resulted in his being more of a lurking eavesdropper than a participant. Which was fine, the conversation wasn't actually about farming.

Two of the freegans had heard that land in Belize or Bolivia or Bulgaria was dirt cheap, so they'd saved up some money—about $1500 it turned out, though it wasn't entirely clear how they may have gotten it—and were going to ride their bikes south until they found some affordable farm land, upon which they would grow pot—all for their own use, of course.

Milton gave up on the farmers and picked his asleep legs and ass up off the bloodstained cement floor and went look-ing for his Doritos.

In the kitchen, a girl with just one long dreadlock was standing on a bench holding Milton's Doritos and screaming something about "Monsanto and factory farms are mass pro-ducing genetically modified corn that doesn't even resemble food anymore, but is just a chemical cocktail designed to cause learning disabilities and lower brain function in children! What monster brought this mind-control poison into this home? Who!?"

Noddy walked in with his arm around a girl.

"Cool Ranch! Deadly, b'ys!"

He grabbed the bag of Doritos out of Dread Lock's hand, opened it, and started stuffing handfuls of chips in his face.

Rather than sticking around to witness a murder, Milton decided to do a lap around the large open kill floor.

Past the anarchist pot farmers, past the anarchist post-colonial agitators, past the anarchist digeridoo drum circle, past the pile of sleeping bags and foam mats that the 12 people who lived here all slept on, on the bloodstained floor. There was nothing much for him in any of these groups so he followed a smattering of people spilling out into a stairwell.

He made his way past Ava and Ruddy and three or four others sitting on the steps smoking— "It doesn't matter if it's a bagel or rye or toxic sludge Wonder Bread, it's still not toast!"—and out into the street.

• • •

La graine fusée

Robin and Where's Waldo were leaning against the graffitied brick façade of the vermin abattoir, them and four others shivering and smoking and drinking homebrew brandy out of the same mugs that previously held their garbage soup.

They were still arguing loudly, drunkenly, highly about art. They yelled and shook burning joints in one another's faces, and then passed the joint to their opponent, who would take a puff and shake it right back at them.

Milton couldn't be sure, because he wasn't sure what a *simulacrum* was or what the "male appropriation of the female gaze manifest in representations of phallic maleness, you idiot" truly meant, but it sounded like a continuation of the debate about the giant paper-mâché penis that their friend Owly had made and was driving around town in the back of a military truck like an intercontinental ballistic dick missile.

"Nah, Rob, Owly's laying bare the notion of the dick as the organizing meta-narrative of modernity. The thing, his dick truck, isn't just about the obvious shit like the Cold War and all that. He's also driving around through all the suburbs, playing his corny ice-cream truck music, saying to everyone, 'Look at it, look! This is your god! Isn't it stupid!' It's an idol, Rob, a monument to the inherent absurdity of our dick-centric hegemony."

Milton understood about every fifth word of that.

"Give me a break! He's saying 'Look at my dick, isn't it big, aren't I clever?' It's such a tired trope, man. As if every building ever built, every car ever made, every anything ever done wasn't some guy waving his dick at the world saying 'Behold!'"

"I've never—"

Milton felt invisible, but as soon as he opened his mouth, everyone who was arguing about something else stopped to see how he was going to go about fitting both his feet in his otherwise normal-sized mouth.

"—seen this dick truck."

He was going to say he'd never waved his dick at anyone, but saved it at the last second. Her heart swelled with pride.

"Well, it's your lucky day."

On cue, ice-cream truck music became audible and an ancient looking military truck carrying a giant penis rumbled into view.

"Ho-leeee Christ! Look at the size of that cock!"

Noddy had found his way outside.

"Look at 'er, Milty, b'y, look! Ain't she a beaut!"

The truck was being driven by one of Pochard or Booby, while Wren, the filmmaker, sat in the passenger seat. In the back the other one of Booby or Pochard pointed a giant film camera at the artist, Owly, who was riding the dick missile Dr. Strangelove-style, cowboy hat and all.

The truck, a 1950s military transport truck of some kind, was deafeningly loud and spewed choking black diesel smoke over the smokers gathered on the sidewalk outside of the furrier. It jerked to a screeching, squealing halt and Owly slapped a large button on the shaft of the giant penis and it ejaculated confetti and glitter.

Fig. 24. Intercontinental ballistic dick missile

"Greetings, cock-watchers!"

Owly jumped down and started hugging and high-fiving everyone on the sidewalk. The film crew followed him with the camera and boom mic.

He gave Milton a big hug and told him he loved him. Milton, instinctively, said "I love you too."

Noddy was even more effusive. He picked Owly up with a giant bear hug.

"Is that your dick, man? It's fuckin' deadly, b'y. Wicked! Let me buy you a beer."

Noddy dragged Owly into the building and up the stairs to his dwindling stockpile of warm Coors Light and Cool Ranch Doritos. The film crew followed behind.

In the shadow of the massive dick missile Milton turned to Robin.

"So that's it then?"

"That's it."

• • •

Chanter la pomme

For the rest of the night Milton followed Robin around like a lost puppy and lurked on the edge of all of her conversations—almost always arguments about art, almost always arguments about Owly's dick art, almost always arguments with Where's Waldo and, now that he was there, Owly.

Every so often the arguments would get political and she'd yell in violent agreement with the other freegan anarchists about what a dick Cheney is and what a buffoon Bush is.

In between mugs of homebrew dumpster brandy or on smoke breaks, Milton would try to make conversation.

"Where did you grow up?" "What did you study?" "What do you want to be when you grow up?"

He managed to piece together that Robin grew up in Newmarket but left home at 16 to study Romance Poetry at

Oxford. It didn't take long for her to figure out that Oxford was "the most patriarchal petri dish of penis envy you've ever seen."

"If you think bozo here driving his dick around town on the back of a truck is bad, you should sit through a seminar on Byron."

So she dropped out midway through her second year and moved to Calcutta to make *Dirty Birds*, because "dump gulls and Calcuttan slums are matriarchies."

Now she was back in Montreal for a few months working on getting her next film underway. In the meantime, she cooked in a freegan food co-op soup café in the Plateau and went to parties to argue with "dicks about dicks, mostly."

She was fascinating. Milton had never met anyone quite like her. She was loud and smart and used words in drunken arguments that were as long as his arm. He was already in love when she, well into the night, sitting next to him in the dark corner of the slaughter floor-squatter dorm, asked: "So, Milhouse the poet, what are you working on now?"

He wasn't sure if she didn't know his name, or had already given him a pet name, but he didn't correct her, he just reveled in the fact that she, the first person in his entire life, believed him when he said he was a poet.

"Poems."

"Yeah, about what?"

There was a pocket-sized notebook damp with ass sweat in Milton's back pocket that was full of scribbled bits of an epic poem he was working on about how much he hated the band Nickelback. He usually typed free-verse love ballads on his Underwood into the wee hours, but in between these fevers, lying awake at night imagining his life as a poet, he added verse after verse to "Greaser Fire" (working title).

```
chad •r brad
•r whatever y•u g• by c••l dad
you crisc• headed hipster
y•u scratchy v•iced lipster
y•u c•uldnt make it as a deaf man
but wed all be better •ff if that was
the case man
case l•t
case l•st
l•t cast
bad taste
l•st cause
cause
cuz
```

But he didn't dare tell Robin this. Next thing he'd know, she'd be shaking burning cigarettes inches from the end of his nose telling him to put his dick back in his pants.

"Mostly about pop culture... and the patriarchy."

He wasn't sure what exactly "patriarchy" meant, but he had heard it at least 40 times throughout the night.

"Λ(wo)men to that, man."

Milton's knees went weak and his head got light as a cocktail of hormones coursed through him. It was the first openly friendly thing Robin had said to him all night. At last, he had broken through her defences.

She reached out and touched his shoulder.

Images of their lives together filled his head: him writing her poems, her making films, him making her breakfast, her making films, him picking their children up from school, her making films.

Before Milton figured out a way to parlay a positive affirmation and clumsy pat-pat into smooching in the corner of the critter kill floor, several gunshots rang out, crack-crack-crack-crack-crack. Followed by screaming and people running.

Milton squealed next to Robin. She started but didn't make a sound, so Milton tried to play it cool. Noddy, across the room, burst out laughing.

"Bahahahahaa!"

Owly had brought some firecrackers and loaned them to Noddy to incorporate into his farts-on-fire routine. He was thrilled by the outcome. Especially when a jug of something made in a bathtub out of dumpstered plums that smelled like sewer gas and tasted like asshole, and was, it turned out, highly flammable, was kicked over in the excitement.

Everyone crowded out into the street while black smoke and the stench of chemical fire and burning mink blood poured out of the windows and down the block.

Noddy crawled on Owly's giant dick missile and the two of them and the film crew took off before the cops showed up. Dozens of others fled on their fixie bikes.

Milton followed Robin and a half-dozen hangers-on hanging off her every word down the street back towards the tunnel that crosses from dirt poor St. Henri into filthy rich Westmount.

It was late, after 2:00 a.m., but the party had ended prematurely. Elaborate plans of seduction and intrigue that had been cultivated all night were uprooted. Audibles were called. It went from a chess match to a cock fight. An arms race.

This guy had some rye left for her, this other guy had some cigarettes, this other other guy knew the way to the one 99-cent pizza-by-the-slice place in St. Henri that was still open.

Milton had nothing to contribute, but he was the last one talking to her at the party. The last one she called a poet, unironically. The last one whose shoulder she touched, maybe on purpose.

Robin, beautiful, perfect Robin. The matron saint of organic, freegan, trash-eating-dump-seagull-documentary-filmmaking neo-Marxist fifth-wave feminists. Saint Robin of Whole Grains, would revert to frat boy after an abbreviated night of too much dumpster plum liquor: 99-cent pizza-by-the-slice, after slice, after slice; laughing too loud; belching too often; swearing constantly; bumming change to dip into the Dep to buy the cheapest cigarillo.

Robin and her suit of suitors sat on a curb next to a park full of homeless people trying to stay thawed through one more miserably cold night, while she sucked on a brown tube full of all that is wrong with the world and railed against "Donald 'motherfucking' Rumsfeld" and "Karl 'motherfucking' Rove."

And she knew all the half-dozen look-a-like hangers-on were there for her. Were watching her. Were dangling off her every. single. word. Were lapping up every last drop of rotten cigarillo. Were oblivious to the cliché-ness of her impotent rage. Because they were all rehearsing scenarios that started with a four-alarm-firecracker-fart-fire and ended in her pants.

And on this particular night, Milton thought he was the particular hanger-on who was closest to getting in because she was punching *his* shoulder and blowing her rotten smoke into *his* eyes and squeezing *his* cheek (!!!) when she spouted off some two-bit CNBC line about the hopelessness of The Surge.

And maybe, just maybe, just this once, it was going to happen for Milton. And maybe, just maybe, all these other hangers-on would clue in and take off and Milton and Robin could get out of here.

"Want to get out of here?"

Is what he wanted to say.

But he didn't. He just laughed and nodded along with the rest of them.

When all the pizza was eaten, and all the cigarillos smoked, and the last of the party plum poison was drunk, and there was no reason to keep sitting on that curb, outside that park, in the frozen armpit of the city while the sun started coming up, Robin got to her feet.

"Thank you, boys, for a night."

One after another the suitors played their last cards: offers of walks home, of invitations to "nightcaps" back at their places, of going for just one more. But she said no thanks. She said she was going home. She said good night, go away, see you later, and disappeared around the corner. Leaving six dudes who didn't really know or like each other— sworn enemies—to walk as a pack through the tunnel and up the hill towards Vendôme metro to catch the first train of the day back to Mile End. Defeated.

In the arms race for Robin they all forgot one key thing— Robin wasn't a country or a colony or a sparsely populated tropical island or a prize of any kind. She wouldn't be won so easily, and she certainly couldn't be conquered.

The half-dozen hangers-on rode the metro in silence, transferred at Snowdon in silence, got off at Outremont in silence, climbed the stairs into blazing, sobering daylight in silence, and scattered into their home turf, back to their shitty bare mattresses in their shitty rooms in their shitty shared 8-1/2s to sleep it off. In silence.

SIX

SPECTACLE DES OEUFS

Cherchez la femme

The next weeks blurred together into a rash of long nights that bled into early mornings that ended with Milton curled up under a ratty towel and his winter coat, with a ball of dirty laundry for a pillow, on the bare, filthy, fifth-or-sixth-hand mattress in his windowless room.

He tagged along with Noddy or Georgette or Ruddy or Ava to every house party and potluck, every secret music show of bands no one had ever heard of, every pay-what-you-can fringe festival vaudeville burlesque extravaganza, every art student term project exhibition, every Free-First-Tuesday-of-the-Month at Musée des Beaux-Arts, every Free-Second-Wednesday-of-the-Month at Musée d'Art Contemporain, every half-off showing of *Elephant Man* at Cinema du Parc, every poetry reading at every out-of-the-way St. Henri freegan co-op coffee shop, every two-drink minimum open mic bilingual comedy night in dive bars in Notre-Dame-de-Grâce, every work acquaintance's bowling birthday party in the far-flung banlieues, or entire nights spent wandering from 8-1/2 to 8-1/2 pre-drinking for parties that never happened.

To the outsider, it looked like he was being social and having the time of his life. Becoming fully immersed in the underemployed Anglophone Bohemian art student expat caste. Mixing in with the thousands of Normcore asymmetric haircut GTA refugees, and the usual bit of alcoholism that goes along with it. But really, it was all just an ongoing search for Robin.

Not that he ever needed help nor excuse to imagine impossible happily-ever-afters for himself and the unsuspecting subject of his infatuation, but the intense regime of sleeping all day, and going out all night, the endless unoccupied and unencumbered hours, the lack of any responsibility whatsoever— the vacuum of obligation, connection, and preoccupation that his life had become—was filled almost entirely, as it had been by Ashleys for most of his childhood, with daydreaming of, with fantasizing about, with obsessing over Robin.

While out at the hundred different variations of bemused late-onset teenagers moping about in coffee shops and bars and art galleries and Leninist bike repair co-op noise band concert venues and under-furnished living rooms and kitchens, he was always watching the door, or checking over his shoulder, or approaching chestnut-haired girls with their backs turned.

While at home, when he wasn't sleeping off the night before, he filled pages and pages of cheap paper from the Greek papeterie with brooding, lovesick poems that swung between enraptured and enraged, depending upon how cold the trail for his unrequited new true love had been the night before.

He had only ever met her the one time, at the anarchist freegan potluck in the vermin abattoir. They talked, she was engaged, but slightly aloof. Cold even. She travelled in and out of conversations with Milton.

There were moments he was sure they were plumbing their deepest depths in the way that welds two souls together. And other moments where she didn't seem to give a shit. And others yet when she was drunker and higher and called him a poet. And meant it. And touched his shoulder. And maybe meant it. And others still when she laughed at him for being a poet, for being in the same room as her, for being on that curb beside her in front of that Dep in that rundown neighbourhood at that late hour of the early morning, dumpster borscht, bathtub brandy, and cheap cigarillo on her breath, her eyes glassy and distant, on the run from imaginary police after imaginary fart-firecracker-fire fights.

He replayed every moment of that entire night over and over. He rehearsed better things to say in conversations that happened weeks ago. He mulled over the meaning of every look, of every inadvertent touch, of every joke made at his expense that no one laughed at. Was it contempt or curiosity, or maybe even connection, behind the teasing? Did she feel it too? Was she lying on a bed of broken springs and mysterious stains fully clothed for warmth staring into the darkness where the odd-shaped hole in the paint was, wondering what he was doing just then? Wondering if he was wondering too?

Of course not.

She didn't care. She went to Oxford. She dropped out of Oxford because she's above that shit. She spent three years in a Calcutta dump, filming seagulls for a seven-minute mostly-silent black-and-white film about seagulls in a Calcutta dump. Not a film of Calcutta dump seagulls that was a metaphor for anything, not a suggestion of anything, just dump birds for their own sake, she swore. An honest-to-god, earnest-to-Jesus, meditation on dump birds. She hung around real artists who made real art. She argued loudly about the merits of her friends' paper-mâché dicks.

She didn't hide. She was perfect and real and immediate and present. If you bored her, her eyes told you, her body told you, her mouth told you, her getting up mid-sentence and walking outside to smoke a joint with Where's Waldo told you. There were no airs or pretense or bullshit. She

didn't hide behind a veil of irony and sarcasm and disconnected smart-assery like everyone else trying to be someone
else. Trying to be poets. Trying to be artists. She *was* an artist.
A maker. A creator. Not a critic, a pretender, a hanger-on, a
faker, a hater. She was so sure of everything she did and
everything she said. She was a goddess. She was beautiful.
Her eyes. Her cheeks. Her hips. Her lips. The faint curves of
so much more hiding under the old military surplus winter
jacket she wore that night.

She was perfect.

```
the wind blew you
next to me
i could feel your soul
when you blew
your smoke
in my face as a joke
that night
we met
that night we fell
fell into the well
of your eyes
your heart
of forever
```

She was cruel. She asked Milton to open up, to share his
insecurity and deepest secrets, to share his poems, his art,
his soul. And what did she offer him in return? A tease. A
touch on the shoulder. A face full of cigarillo smoke. How
dare she!

```
that name
is not my name
my name is not
milhouse
that is much more lame
name than milton
```

It was her fault that he was alone, even when he was out
with people. She became the key to his happiness, the one

thing in the world that made sense to him. But he didn't know where she was, didn't know what she thought of him, didn't know how to find out, didn't know how to find her.

He nonchalantly asked Ava and Ruddy if they knew her. And they did. He asked them if they knew where to find her. And they didn't.

"She's around."

He caught a glimpse of her a couple of weeks after the potluck. He was riding the 80 bus downtown to take a metro to a poetry slam in Hochelaga, she was riding her bike uptown through the Park. He got off at the next stop and ran uphill three blocks as fast as he could before his lungs gave out and he collapsed in a heap on the sidewalk, in front of the same crack den McDonald's he'd collapsed in front of when he first arrived. Someone threw a quarter at him while he lay there, chest heaving.

She was long gone.

• • •

Cultivez votre pécule

It was more than a month before he saw her again at the crack of dawn in the lobby of a giant downtown bank.

The bank was a title sponsor of the annual Festival Toute la Nuit—an all-night mish-mash of art things scattered around the city. It all wrapped up with a free breakfast at the bank—a 10,000-egg omelette cooked in a cartoonishly giant pan balanced on top of a dozen propane burners. All to cleverly launch the bank's new advertising campaign: Cultivez Votre Pécule/Grow Your Nest Egg.

20 "chefs"—signified by their hats, not their credentials, including the bank manager, his wife, their 15-year-old daughter, seven bank employees, three of their spouses/partners, two accounting interns (who were quite drunk after sharing a bottle of vodka in a paper bag on the curb outside of Place-des-Arts after leaving the modern dance show that

was happening for 12 hours straight inside), the chairwoman of the festival planning committee and her husband (who was still dressed as a clown having just completed a marathon juggling performance with his juggling troupe in a 24-hour doughnut shop on St. Laurent), Gilles "Pépé" Papineau, the morning show shock jock and flaming racist from 108.4 FM La Bouche, who was doing a live spot from the scene, and two line cooks from Saint-Hubert, a popular chicken restaurant—stirred the pool of egg slop with canoe paddles.

Dozens of volunteers in green vests attempted to corral the throng of thousands of half-drunk and over-tired all-night art festival-goers that packed themselves unsafely close to the giant vat of bubbling eggs.

"S'il vous plaît, faites la queue! Derrière la ligne! S'il vous plaît! S'il vous plaît! S'il vous plaît!"

They cried, begged, pleaded with the unmoving, ever-growing mob.

"S'il vous plaît! S'il vous plaît!"

There was also an official adjudicator from *The Guinness Book of World Records* counting the empty egg containers in a mountain of empty egg containers near the giant pan and examining evidence of broken eggs on the floor around the pan.

The reigning world record for largest omelette was held by the Tuscaloosa Breakfast Festival, which, in 1998, attempted to make a 10,000-egg omelette, but due to premature breakage, spillage, and wayward eggery (the technical terms coined by the very same Guinness adjudicator) managed to only make a 9,876-egg omelette.

The Toute la Nuit organizing committee were sure the record was theirs as they ordered 1,000 dozen eggs to ensure they wouldn't fall short of the 10,000-egg mark.

A record-breaking 10,000-egg omelette to be shared with festival-goers free of charge as the exciting conclusion to an all-night art festival and exciting launch to a retirement savings plan marketing campaign sounded like a good idea to the organizers, the bank higher-ups, and the slowly sobering festival-goers.

Who doesn't like garish publicity stunts and free breakfast after a long night secretly drinking in performance art shows that make no sense in all-night fast-food joints and half-closed art galleries?

However, none of the 20 culinary dilettantes pawing at the puddle of eggs had ever attempted to make a 10,000-egg omelette before. Only a few people on earth had ever tried it. And no one from the Montreal team called any of them to learn about how long it takes to actually cook an omelette that size nor how unappetizing a swimming pool-sized pan of eggs looks, and sounds, and smells—especially smells—nor the effect that thousands of drunk and tired people crowding into the lobby of a downtown bank will have on the temperature and smell, *the smell*, and general ambiance of the room—a B.O., egg fart, and whiskey morning breath stinking mosh pit.

The plan had been to make a great show of dumping the 10,000 eggs they'd spent the previous three hours cracking into five-gallon buckets into the giant skillet right at 6:00 a.m., to great fanfare and snapping of photographs by all the major papers—maybe even one of the nationals.

They'd then vigorously stir the eggs with the canoe paddles for the 10-15 minutes it would take for them to cook—just slightly longer than a normal omelette, they figured—and then jubilant festival-goers would, in an orderly queue, file by with their bank-branded paper bowls for a scoop of eggs and a small foil container of milk supplied by Les Producteurs de lait du Québec. The festival-goers would make their way to the food court of the conjoined shopping mall, quickly eat their eggs and clear out for the next wave of omelette eaters.

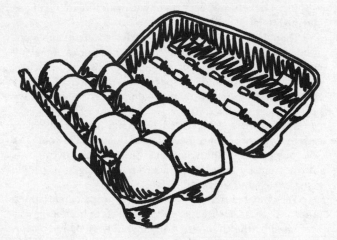

Fig. 25. Votre pécule

Records would be broken. Priceless media exposure would be won. Scores of high-rate, low-interest retirement savings plans would be sold. Everyone would be home, satiated, and gleefully asleep by no later than 9:00 a.m.

By 5:00 a.m., long after most of the festival performances had wrapped up, the first few thousand festival-goers assembled outside the doors of the bank. Every new group of two or three rattled on the doors of the bank trying to get in out of the cold.

Inside, dozens of volunteers cracked the last few hundred eggs into buckets and beat them with paint-mixing paddles attached to large drills.

Though banks invented and perfected the queue management post-and-stanchion system over centuries of making people wait in lines, this particular bank on this particular day was woefully underprepared for the mob of hangry zombies that poured through its doors nonstop after they opened shortly after 5:30 a.m.

The crowd quickly filled the bank lobby beyond its capacity, yet more continued to push in out of the cold. The S'il vous plaît's of the volunteers in their green vests was drowned out by the yelling, in several languages, of people being jostled and squeezed.

The crowd closed in around the frying pan and flaming propane burners. Entire five-gallon buckets of beaten eggs, as was noted by the Guinness Adjudicator, were dumped over, making the floor slick and sending people falling and sliding into one another.

A few shoving matches and at least two fist fights broke out. There were rumours that someone close to the ATMs had been stabbed.

An elderly woman who had earlier spent most of the night watching her granddaughter, a 21-year-old textile student from Université de Montréal, knit a 22-foot long single wool tube sock in a metro-station tunnel, fainted from the heat and overcrowding and had to be crowd-surfed from the front of the mass to the paramedics waiting in the rear.

The throng spilled out of the bank in through a narrow doorway that had been opened into the neighbouring mall food court. And they just kept coming.

The volunteer security force called for police backup around 5:45 a.m., and the Montreal police, not unfamiliar with its share of hockey riots, and ever vigilant against potential race riots, especially with the huge number of Anglophone free food lovers that were in the crowd, sent 300 officers in full riot gear.

The chief of Service de sécurité incendie de Montréal, a cherub-like lifetime firefighter named André, showed up with a small army of first responders and fought his way to the front of the crowd to issue the bank manager and festival chairwoman each tickets for fire-code violations, and threatened to "fermer le tout!"

Had the bank manager not been a close personal friend of the mayor and the chief of police, the entire event would have been shut down. Instead, the riot police merely broke up the scattered fights, shepherded as much of the mob as possible into the mall and adjacent metro station, and began turning away latecomers.

The chaos receded into monotony as 12,000 people waited for 10,000 eggs to solidify.

They began lying on the floor, huddled together in packs of threes and fours. Sleeping on friends and backpacks as the dawn broke.

The marbled lobby of the head office of Montreal's biggest bank on the launch day of the biggest publicity campaign in its history was transformed into something that looked like a Red Cross emergency shelter.

Victims of a night of revelry and ill-conceived contemporary art exhibitions—the well-heeled, the unencumbered, the childless, the bohemians, the students, the swarms of twenty-something teens—gathered for warmth and shelter and their daily ration of lukewarm egg goo.

• • •

Toute la nuit

The night had begun with Noddy, Ruddy, Ava, and Milton walking down to see Georgette's puppet theatre company, Place des Poupées, an all-night Victor Hugo puppet-show marathon.

It began with *Cromwell*. The epic lyrical play about the English politician/warlord/only-commoner-to-be-Lord Protector, Oliver Cromwell.

The play was so long and complicated—6,920 verses, 79 characters, countless extras—that it was 129 years from when it was written before it was finally produced. This was the first time it had been staged with puppets.

Georgette had explained that they needed 13 puppeteers to pull off the four-hour play with 39 puppets—nearly every single one in their inventory.

High-end puppets cost thousands of dollars each, so the company would reuse puppets from show to show. It's rarely an issue, just repaint the grey moustache of King Lear brown and call it Cromwell.

However, the number of puppets needed for this show required them to get creative with their puppet recycling.

The Lion from *The Lion, the Witch, and the Wardrobe* became Member of Parliament "Death-to-Sinners" Palmer. The skeleton from their Halloween production of *The Nightmare Before Christmas* became Barebones the Leather Dealer. They had no other choice but to make the parrot from their production of *Aladdin*, Lady Falconbridge.

Cromwell's four jesters—Trick, Giraff, Gramadoch, and Elespuru—were played by puppets who were previously Montreal Canadiens legends Rocket Richard, Boom Boom

Geoffrion, Toe Blake, and Jean Beliveau respectively. They had been created especially for a 2005 show, *On a tué mon frère Richard*, about the 1955 Richard Riot.[21]

To add local flavour, the four Canadiens puppets were left in their uniforms for *Cromwell*.

That it was part of an all-night city-wide arts festival, and likely because it was free, four hours long, started at 10:00 p.m., and was a 181-year-old lyrical play by a French poet about a British shit-disturber, there were seven people in the audience when *Cromwell* started.

Half an hour into the first act it dropped to six when Noddy, who'd brought a case of Coors Light, drank his last beer, belched, said "fuck this shit," and loudly, clanking beer cans and tripping over the legs of everyone else in attendance, left the theatre.

Milton didn't understand a word of it, and he was pretty sure Ruddy and Ava didn't either. But they were there in support of Georgette, so they sat through the first act, passing a bottle of cooking sherry between them that Ruddy had brought, grimacing with every sip.

By the second act all three of them were asleep, with Milton snoring the loudest. They were awoken by the house lights when they came up for the intermission after Act Three. It had already been nearly three hours, so they thought it was over and left. Headed for the bus to take them downtown to wander amongst the galleries and all-night diners/performance venues and bus shelters/concert-halls for the night.

Georgette was royally pissed that they didn't stay through the entire play, let alone the entire Hugo marathon. She let

---

[21] The Richard Riot was an outburst of violence, destruction, and looting by hockey fans, incensed over the suspension of their idol Maurice "Rocket" Richard for the final two games of the regular season and all of the 1955 play-offs for cracking his stick over the head of Boston Bruin Hal Laycoe and punching out a linesman. The riot is regarded by many as an inciting incident in Quebec's Quiet Revolution.

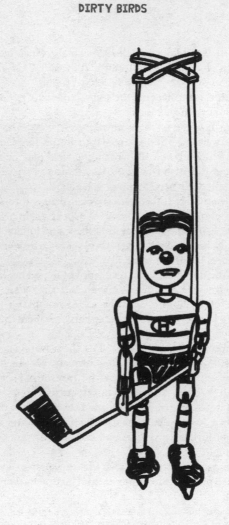

Fig. 26. Bernie "Boom Boom" Giraff

them know with a barrage of "Putain!"s and "Connard!"s when they were all back in the apartment the next day.

The rest of the night blurred together into a lot of wandering around lost and cold, standing on street corners, in hotel lobbies, and metro station entrances trying to decipher a very artistic but otherwise incredibly useless map of venues and events. Ava and Ruddy were bent on seeing as much as they could, with a focus on being seen.

The range of things they saw ran the gamut from an art studio complex by the old port (i.e. an abandoned warehouse) where 100 artists gathered to make art for 24 hours straight, to a small independent theatre hosting a karaoke slow-dance-sock-hop-a-thon.

In a heavily graffitied alley in a particularly seedy part of town, a dance school hosted a multimedia performance that featured 12 naked dancers—six men, six women—dancing in the 22-below cold while video of a re-enactment of Napoleon's march to Moscow was projected on their bodies. The twenty-minute piece was set to run every hour on the hour, but had been cancelled by the time Ava, Ruddy, and Milton arrived at 1:00 a.m. after two of the dancers were hospitalized with frostbite and the projector had been stolen.

In the lobby of the Musée d'Art Contemporain a performance artist from Newfoundland was splitting frozen codfish with an axe like they were firewood while reciting, or more like screaming, the 1949 Terms of Union with Canada.

It only took him a few hours to go through all of the 500 pounds of frozen fish he'd brought, so by 2:30 a.m. he was just pulverizing thawing fish parts with his axe while completing his fourth lap through article 46: "Oleomargarine or margarine shall not be sent, shipped, brought, or carried from the Province of Newfoundland into any other province of Canada."

The smell of fish entrails hung thick in the air. No one watched for very long.

Ava, Ruddy, and Milton spent the longest time sitting in a dark corner of a ballroom in Casino de Montréal, located in the former French pavilion for Expo 67 on Île Notre Dame, watching a silent rave.

To avoid having the noise impact the Casino's clientele of elderly addict gamblers and tourists, the rave was silent. The dancers wore wireless headphones connected to the DJ booth.

The Casino, in good capitalist form, found a loophole in the Toute la Nuit free-for-all policy by allowing anyone into the rave for free, but charging $20 each for headsets.

Instead of dancing, Milton, Ruddy, and Ava sat in a dark corner, coming down from their cooking sherry drunks transfixed by the sight of hundreds of ravers whacked out on ecstasy and $12 vodka-Red Bulls, throbbing in unison in complete silence.

Eventually it put them all to sleep until they were woken, again, by the house lights coming up when the party ended at 6:00 a.m. with an announcement about a free breakfast at a downtown bank.

"Breakfast?"

"I could eat."

"Let's go."

• • •

Je m'excuse

Several hours later, Milton was laying on the hard marble floor of the bank, staring up at the cheap pot lights, crossing and uncrossing his eyes, making the lights double and dance back and forth, waiting for the 10,000-egg omelette to cook.

The aid-worker/volunteer/security force in their green vests circulated through the crowd waking people up, telling them they'd have to leave if they were going to sleep, and telling others the eggs would be ready any minute now.

It was 9:30 a.m., with the bank due to open to real customers in half an hour, when word spread through the mass that the omelette was finally ready.

What had been a peaceable crowd for the previous few hours—after the initial throng had calmed and the drunkest of the scrappers had been hauled off to jail—stirred slowly back to life, rose to their feet, and again began squeezing in towards the free eggs.

The riot police, who had all been sitting slumped in a pack, or pacing eagerly in the back corner of the bank, juste au cas où, also came back to life.

The vest brigade broke into their chorus of "S'il vous plaît," but the long wait had sapped most of the life, and most of the drunken unruliness, out of the crowd and it was more of a lumbering, half-asleep, undead mass pushing towards the source of the egg stench.

Through the dopey madness, across a throng of thousands, on the opposite side of the bank, Milton saw Robin.

She was with Where's Waldo from before, and Owly of paper-mâché dick-missile fame, and some others Milton didn't recognize.

She laughed easily and despite her probably having been up all night watching puppets perform *Les Mis* and some angry Newfoundland separatist eviscerating putrid fish with an axe, she sparkled.

All of Milton's guts, his hopes, his dreams, his visions of Nobel prizes and Oscars and perfect children running through meadows of daisies leapt into his throat.

He'd been replaying the night they met over and over on an endless loop for weeks, but now he clammed up. He'd been up all night. He smelled like fish and eggs and silent casino rave. He wanted very much to find the right way to get over to her, make it look all nonchalant, say just the right thing to make her laugh, make her eyes light up, make her fall madly in love with him.

But the lines he had been rehearsing were re-writes of that first night. All his dreams were of a vague future. He was utterly unprepared for this moment.

Of all the dozens of hip parties and hot music shows and trendy art happenings that he'd been to in search of Robin for the past several weeks, it was at a botched pre-dawn free breakfast in a bank lobby that he inevitably ran into her.

But you don't get to choose your destiny; it chooses you. So, if it was to be today, it was to be today. Here. Now. He had no choice. It was his destiny. He had to act. He had to remind himself of the steely-eyed courage he'd forged on that long walk through the park. He had to remind himself that he was Edmund Hilroy, Benjamin Franklin, John George Diefenbaker!

He psyched himself up. He felt himself grow taller. More handsome. Stronger. He was ready to grab his life by the horns. Show it who's boss. Sweep it off its feet.

He still didn't know what to say, or how to act cool, and he especially didn't know how to get over to her through the throng of hangry zombies.

There were hundreds, maybe thousands of people, and a swimming-pool-sized frying pan of goopy eggs between him and her. He was going to try to work his way over to where she was. He was going to try to get her attention in the meantime. Make eye contact. Maybe wave in an aloof but earnest way. Not too earnest. Not too aloof. Like you would wave at a neighbour across the produce section in the grocery store. If that neighbour was the love of your life and she didn't know it yet. Maybe just a nod. Or a nod and wave. But one of them up-only nods, where your eyebrows carry your entire head upwards in warm, friendly recognition. Can't be too eager though. Can't let the brows go too wild. Can't look too surprised or excited. Can't snap the head back too hard. Can't get whiplash in the lustful excitement of seeing your future walking around right in front of you.

He told Ava and Ruddy he was going to the bathroom and began elbowing his way through the crowd. He kept his eyes locked on Robin as he pushed his way through the mass of bodies.

"Je m'excuse. Je m'excuse. Je m'excuse. Je m'excuse."

The thought occurred to him about halfway there that maybe he could show her a poem. Maybe read it to her. Or just give it to her.

"Je m'excuse. Je m'excuse. Je m'excuse."

He felt for a wad of paper, sweaty and creased, in his back pocket. There were at least a dozen poems, all about her in one way or another. Maybe there was one in there that would be just right. Maybe she'd respect him more if she knew he was a serious artist too. Maybe there was one poem that was vague enough to not totally creep her out.

```
children sweep like a flock
of dump seagulls
without their sea
with their landlocked
landfill pantomime dreams
and they dont even want
children
seagulls
parasites
circling the garbage trucks
looking for a free meal
```

"Je m'excuse. Je m'excuse. Je m'excuse."

As Milton got closer to the bubbling egg pan, the crowd grew thicker and his "Je m'excuse" began to lose its effect.

"Je m'excuse."

He began having to shove his elbows into the smalls of people's backs and throw his shoulder with all his weight into narrow openings between people to get them to move. He slowed to barely moving at all.

Eyes still locked on Robin. Mind racing through the inventory of poems he had in his pocket, trying to write a scene that began with some cool chit-chat, segued effortlessly into him unfolding a poem from his pocket and whispering it into Robin's ear as they became an island of two people falling in love while a stream of undead flowed past them towards some free tepid omelette soup.

Having fought his way to the last row of people between him and the omelette, he threw his weight into a barely perceptible gap between a guy and a girl who were jockeying to be among the first to get their paper bowl of egg slop.

Just as he did, though, his concentration was broken by Robin's eyes. She saw him. He saw her. They saw each other. He could have sworn her eyes lit up. He could have sworn she flashed a barely perceptible smile that confirmed she had feelings too, that confirmed soon she'd be Mrs. Milton Ontario.

In the midst of imagining what song they'd have their first dance to at their wedding reception in the Bellybutton Legion, someone tried to push past him going the other way. The two pushes acted as a force multiplier and knocked the girl Milton was trying to get by off balance. Standing, as she was, in a puddle of eggs that were spilled in the first act of the breakfast gong show, her feet slid out from under her and she barrelled into the ankles of one of the riot police.

This set off a chain reaction causing several riot police to fall like dominos, the last one crashing into the frying pan handle—which served no functional purpose—sending the 10,468-egg omelette, as the Guinness Adjudicator had certified, sloshing through the air, blanketing Robin and a few hundred bystanders in goo, which settled into a 6-inch layer on the floor of the bank.

The commotion also knocked over a number of the propane burners, setting fire to the mountain of emptied egg cartons and paper bowls waiting to be filled.

• • •

Niveau trois

Riot police are trained to perform a number of escalating crowd-control measures. These range from Level One: Non-Active Deterrence—i.e. standing in a position that is visible to a potentially volatile crowd to dissuade them from notions of violence and chaos—to Level Five: Active Suppression with Lethal Force—i.e. shooting people.

Within each level there are a number of sub-levels depending upon the circumstances. Level Two, for instance, is Active Deterrence, meaning the officers place themselves between the crowd and their target. If the presence of the officers isn't enough to calm or disperse the crowd, the commander can escalate to Level Two-B: Non-Engaged Active Deterrence, to include a highly choreographed and exhaustively practiced series of manoeuvres that include marching, stomping, slapping their clubs on their shields, and chanting "Cesser et se disperser!"—very much similar to the haka dance that has made the New Zealand All Blacks rugby team one of the most feared in the world.

If the dance routine fails, they might then begin moving towards the crowd with the intent of taking away their space and scaring them off.

Level Three, initiated in the bank lobby when Inspecteur Lebarbare began shouting "Niveau trois engage!" after Milton precipitated the synchronized riot police tumbling routine, is Active Non-Lethal Suppression and Detention. That is riot police-speak for "commence beating the shit out of rioters with clubs and arresting as many of them as possible."

Riot police, however, are trained and equipped generally for outdoor riots. Wielding large shields and swinging clubs is most easily done in open spaces and on solid ground. The bank lobby was enormous, but it was crowded, and the solid ground was buried in sloppy eggs. So as they began to push out from the centre of the bank in attempts to push the crowd outside, and as they began to swing their clubs, and as they attempted to grab those nearest the centre of the rapidly escalating riot and bind their hands with plastic handcuffs, they slipped around on the omelette mess, and the entire scene devolved into a very sloppy wrestling match.

It was a scene that would later be recreated for a completely different effect at several rue Sainte-Catherine strip clubs with the always popular "spectacle des œufs," daily wrestling matches featuring scantily clad women rolling around in kiddie pools full of scrambled eggs.

Milton ended up on the floor in the original dominoing, so he avoided being clubbed immediately. He managed to fight his way to his feet and join the throng of people fleeing the swinging batons. He did get hit on the side of the head and the back of the shoulder with a club, which left some serious bruises, but he managed to escape.

Montrealers never shy away from a chance to have a proper riot. As the egg zombie horde spilled into the streets, they started smashing windows, flipping over and setting fire to cars, looting jewelry stores and Baby Gaps, and climbing light poles draped in Quebec flags singing Montreal Canadien fight songs.

The crowds and trail of destruction spread quickly in all directions and the 300 heavily armed riot police could do little to stop them, still trapped inside the bank, slopping around in the egg goo trying to disperse the crowd and make room for the fire department to put the burning pile of cartons and paper bowls out.

The chief of police had to call in reinforcements from multiple other police departments to assist. But even then, smoke could be seen rising from downtown for the rest of the day.

Milton got out of the bank and wandered around the chaos looking for Ava and Ruddy, or, and mostly, Robin. He couldn't find any of them, and decided, as the number of police began to grow, to go home out of it.

The buses and metro had been shut down while the rioting was going on, so Milton had to hike all the way back over the mountain in the freezing cold to get home.

He got back to the apartment late in the afternoon, and found Ava sitting on the step smoking a cigarette.

"You okay?"

"Yeah. You?"

"Yeah. I'm fine. What happened to the side of your head?"

"Club, I think."

"Ouch."

"Why are you here?"

"Looking for Ruddy, I thought he might show up here. Have you seen him?"

"No. I just walked back up here from downtown. I was looking for you guys."

"Argh. Mind if I wait here with you?"

"Yeah, sure."

Upstairs, Georgette was sleeping off her Hugo marathon, and Noddy had gone to work. Ava and Milton turned on the TV and watched news coverage of the riots. Shots from the Channel 11 Traffic-copter of packs of people being chased from burning car to burning car by packs of police. Live shots of people climbing out of broken store windows with their arms full of electronics and diapers. Live reports from reporters reporting live from the scene.

"I'm at this intersection where rioters have just done that thing and police have responded in this way. Back to you in the studio."

The sound of the sirens on TV woke Georgette.

"Putain! Ta gueule! A riot! Mon dieu! C'est fou! Merde!"

Noddy came home from work not long after.

"Fuckin' metro's closed because of this bullshit! Cost me 40 bucks to take a cab. There's cops everywhere, b'ys."

The riot on TV was by far the most interesting and exciting performance any of them had seen that night or day. But it was difficult to compute that the burning cars and water cannons and tear-gas grenades were happening live, just down the street, where they had been a few hours ago.

It looked more like something that only happens on TV. That only happens somewhere else. But, having been there, having been trampled, having been skulled by a baton, having escaped the clutches of police, having run through the streets that were now on fire, it made the entire situation somehow something else. It was almost more real. Almost.

It was more than just a spectacle on the News. It was a spectacle they had witnessed, they had lived through, they had survived.

But they survived it in much the same way a bumpkin survives a long walk through a cold park. They'll burn the sound of sirens and the smell of smoke in their memories, they'll tell the story, they'll turn it into their shitty art. They'll think of themselves as somehow courageous, as somehow something.

When, in the end, it's barely even that. A free-breakfast clusterfuck of a riot is as close as any of them will get to a cause. And what a cause.

It was all fun and games until the riot police started bashing skulls in, then it was still just more fun and games.

"Look at them fuckers go, b'y! Gonna be some sick deals on Craigslist this week."

• • •

Fig. 27. Unmaking an omelette

Provocateur en chef

The four of them watched the news play and replay high-lights from the riot well into the night. Around 10:00 p.m. a serious-looking anchor sitting at a serious-looking news desk came on.

"Channel 11 has just gotten security video footage of the incident that incited the outbreak of violence at what was supposed to be a celebratory breakfast for art festival-goers at the downtown headquarters of Banque de la Nouvelle-France. This footage has just been released by police, who are asking for the public's help in identifying those involved with starting the ugly incident, which has since spread throughout the downtown."

Grainy black-and-white security video from inside the bank came on the screen. A short clip played showing a massive crowd milling about a massive frying pan full of eggs that was being stirred by 20 people in chefs' hats with canoe paddles, surrounded by riot police.

"The chief of police has told reporters that the riot squad was dispatched around 6:00 a.m. this morning to the scene of the free breakfast that was the culmination of the Festival Toute la Nuit to assist event organizers with crowd control."

On the video the crowd was dense and restless but contained, when suddenly several police officers toppled over, knocking the pan over, spilling the eggs, starting a fire.

"This footage is from after 9 o'clock this morning. Police have told reporters that the crowd was subdued until this point, when an unprovoked attack on police took place and the scene, as you see, was quickly plunged into chaos."

They replayed the video in slow motion and zoomed into the part of the crowd where the "unprovoked attack" came from. They put a halo of light around the area of most interest.

"Now pay close attention to the highlighted portion of the video. It clearly shows... RIGHT THERE! An unidentified man throwing this young woman into the line of police officers. Watch it again…"

The highlighted portion showed a grainy black-and-white man bumping into a grainy black-and-white woman, and the woman bumping into the line of grainy black-and-white riot police.

They played it again, from another angle.

"As you can see, from this alternate angle, the woman is standing there, minding her own business, when this man… RIGHT THERE! Throws her towards the police barricade."

The alternate angle showed the same grainy blur, just from the side instead of the back. The shapes of distinct people were barely discernable.

"At this hour, the man who incited this terrible scene remains at large. The police are asking for the public's help in bringing him to justice."

They put a blown up still image from the grainy video on the screen along with the number for police, all under the headline "Riot Provocateur Remains At-Large."

It wasn't easy to tell the man in the picture was Milton— the graininess and blurriness and black-and-whiteness of it all—but every head in the room watching with him snapped around.

"Hoooollllyyyy fuuuuuuu-ck!"

Milton went beet-red with embarrassment.

"O.M.G! Milton!?"

"What?"

"C'est toi?"

"I… dunno… Maybe? I was there. I got bumped."

"Bahahaha! Milton Most Wanted! Fuckin'-eh buddy! Nice! NICE! Yis, b'y!"

"I cannot believe it! Oh. My. God!"

"Putain!"

"Am I gonna get in trouble?"

"Nah, b'y. Look at that ugly fucker. Can't tell if that's a

Fig. 28. Breaking news

super-criminal or a bag of dicks. No one's gonna know it's you."

"Should I turn myself in? It was an accident, I got bumped."

"Fuck that, b'y. They'll eat you alive. An Anglo!? They'll string you up from the tower at the Big O. You're fine. No one knows you, that picture is junk, b'y."

"The police are offering a cash reward for information leading to the arrest of the Riot Provocateur."

"Or maybe I'll turn you in. Make a buck. Hehehehet."

"Somebody is going to! Somebody knows! Somebody saw! I'm going to go to jail!"

Milton began pacing across the room.

"Milty, b'y."

"I'm going to rot in jail for the rest of my life because of this. I was just trying…"

"Why were you even over there? You said you were going to the bathroom, they were, like, behind us."

"I can't go to jail! I'm not built for it!"

"Milt!"

"Oh my god, Milton, did you do that on purpose?"

"I can't. I can't. I can't!"

"Putain!"

"Milton!"

Noddy grabbed Milton by the shoulders.

"I can't! I'm too young to go to jail. I'm not tough. I can't!"

"MILTON!"

Noddy slapped him in the face.

"No one is going to jail. No one is going to snitch on you. Are they?!"

"But…"

"Are they?!"

"No, mon dieu, those pigs deserve that!"

"I won't say anything. It was just an accident. Right?"

"We've all got your back. You aren't going anywhere.

No one in this town knows you. No one knows it's you in the video besides us. So just chill the fuck out, b'y, it's fine."

"Ok."

"It's fine."

"It's fine. Ok."

"Your ass would be destroyed so fast in prison anyway, b'y, nobody wants that. Bahahaha."

"Ta gueule! Nohdeeeeee! Connard!"

Milton gradually calmed down, and they all stayed glued to the news. The video of his grainy blob shape bumping into the girl's grainy blob shape bumping into the policeman's grainy blob shape played every half hour. They called it the Omelette Riot and had dubbed the grainy grey blob of Milton the Provocateur en chef.

Sometime in the middle of the night, Milton fell asleep on the couch in the glow of the riot coverage. Georgette and Noddy had already gone to bed, Ava was sleeping on her usual tiny love seat down the hall. No one had heard from Ruddy. Or Robin.

• • •

Le voyou

Ruddy woke Milton up at around 7:00 a.m. the next morning with a slap on the leg.

"Milty!"

"What! What?"

"I got arrested!"

"What?"

"They got me. Fuckers. I didn't do anything. I was just trying to leave the bank when some asshole cop grabbed me, cuffed me, and put me in a van."

"What?"

"Yeah man. They had nothing. I didn't do anything. But they kept me in 'the shoe' overnight! But I'm out now, 'cause I didn't do anything. Just got a bullshit ticket for $500! Like

I'm fucking paying that! Bullshit! My dad said he'd sic his lawyer on them."

"What?"

As each of the others woke up to Ruddy's tales of doing hard time, his story grew and grew.

Noddy was impressed with Ruddy for surviving a night in "the can."

"I thought for sure you'd be somebody's bitch before they even closed the door behind ya."

Georgette didn't really care.

"Ta gueule! Pourquoi es-tu toujours là? Rentre chez toi! Va-t-en! Putain!"

Ava was the last to wake up, and the happiest to see Ruddy.

"Oh my god! I thought you might be dead! I couldn't live without you."

They were supposedly broken up at the time, but that didn't stop Ava from burying her tongue down Ruddy's throat.

"Never leave me!"

Ava got the full story out of Ruddy.

When the riot broke out, he curled up into the fetal position and started screaming near the exit of the bank. To get him out of the way, keep him from getting trampled, and to pad their arrest stats, the police threw him in the paddy wagon and put him in jail.

In jail he curled up into a fetal position in the corner of the holding cell and began screaming, which annoyed both prisoners and guards and led to his being thrown in solitary confinement, or "the shoe," as he called it, overnight.

They let him out in the morning with a ticket for contravening the city's noise by-law, which they gave to everyone they arrested. But while most of the arrested rioters, looters, car burners got the minimum fine of $75, Ruddy's ticket was the maximum possible, $487, because he made such an annoying racket in the jail.

"The food, the people, the conditions in there, the shoe! It's all so medieval and vile."

"Oh my god."

"Yeah, you're a real hard ticket, b'y."

"It was rough, man."

"Not nearly as hard as Milty 'ere. Buddy's on the run. Montreal's most wanted. Right here, b'y. That's hard as fuck."

SEVEN
S&M

S&M Construction

Milton never turned himself in. The police never showed up to arrest him. The cash reward went unclaimed. The fires were put out. The furor died down. The eggs were hosed off the walls and floor of the bank. The Cultivez Votre Pécule/Grow Your Nest Egg promotion was shelved. Life returned to normal and Milton returned to the trail of Robin.

He continued searching for her at every music show and art exhibit and poetry slam he could find. He didn't know if she survived the riot. He hadn't even seen that she was on the receiving end of the full force of all 10,468 eggs. He didn't know if she had been arrested, or clubbed, or hurt in any way. He wanted to ask Ava if she knew anything but didn't want to seem too eager or too weird or too stalky about it, so he just continued looking everywhere for her.

Gradually, though, despite his best efforts to find ways to get into things without having to pay, his savings dwindled. He had been in Montreal for two months and had burned through all the $5 bills from Uncle Randy's, and maxed out his Visa.

He was living off two-for-one half-rotten pineapples from Fruiterie du Parc and day-old bagels from St. Viateur's.

It wasn't complete destitution. Of whatever he had, some went to rent, some went to food, and most still went to cover for shows and poetry readings, whatever English books Guillaume et Gweltaz stole from the library, and cheap typewriter paper he got from the stationery store down past the Library. But the quality of the shows and poetry readings and the quantity of books and paper was dwindling to the point he was only able to afford Pay-What-You-Can events put on by students, paying with metro transfers and change he'd steal from Noddy's bedside table.

It wasn't complete destitution, but it wasn't far from it.

He was having the time of his life, but with only 73 cents left to his name, things were starting to look bleak. He'd soon have to start looking for work.

But on the eve of Milton's birthday, Noddy saved him.

Sort of.

Noddy had had a tough time finding work when he first moved, or fled, to Montreal. His one skill, Newfoundland Strip Club DJ, was the one he wanted to avoid using most. So he bought a Y membership and a got a library card, and swam and read for weeks on end until he met Ava at a bus stop. She was a student with a streak of pink in her bleached-blonde black hair, and she found Noddy's accent worldly. Best of all, she had a line on a summer job as the head of a house painting crew for College Painters, a company renowned for hiring half-assed college kids to do half-assed paint jobs for full price.

She gave Noddy the job, though he claims, "She gave me more, if you know what I mean... sex... I nailed her... on that couch... and that chair... nutted right where you're sitting, b'y."

The work suited Noddy fine. The pay was shit, but it was all students on Ava's crew, except for him and Sam Wrybill—

an illegal immigrant from New Zealand who says he defected because of that country's fascist government and would claim refugee status if it weren't also for this country's fascist government and as soon as he got enough money saved up from the array of under-the-table, cash-only, below-minimum-wage jobs he was eligible for, and capable of, he was going to hitch to Mexico and get into the coke game and "fuck all y'all, mate"—so the summer was spent drunk and hooking up with college kids or hungover and slopping cheap paint on expensive houses.

When the summer ended and the students went back to school, Noddy and Sam, now out of work and drinking mates, decided to start S&M Painters.

S&M Painters went gangbusters. Without any talent, tools, expertise, or more than three months' experience between them, Noddy and Sam got contract after contract.

It may have had something to do with the fact they charged a quarter of what the work was worth if done by someone who had half a clue. And when a client, over afternoon beers, bemoaned the lack of available carpenters in town, Noddy offered S&M's services.

"I thought you just painted?"

"Nah, b'y. We paints, renovates, does kitchens, bathrooms, decks, landscaping, whatever ya got. We got a good crew, real cheap."

"I've got a place..."

And like that S&M Construction began restoring 200-year-old two-million-dollar homes in Westmount for the lazy son of a millionaire.

The first morning Noddy, on his bus-metro-bus ride to the jobsite, stopped and bought a hammer, a saw, a tape measure, and a tool belt to hold them all—just like he'd seen on TV. The next day he bought a bigger hammer, a crowbar, and a radio.

Fig. 29. Weapons of mass destruction

All day, every day, except Sunday, Noddy and Sam could be found tearing the guts out of one of Montreal's oldest mansions.

When asked by the client about permits, Sam screamed through the dust: "That's how the fucking fascists control you mate, don't fall for it."

When asked about the piles of rubble being coated in a thick layer of dust that certainly contained asbestos, lead, and formaldehyde, Noddy shrugged and coughed something about: "I come from a long line of coal miners around Buchans, b'y, I'se got lungs on me like a crab trap," and that Sam was "one of them Aussies, they's all from criminals down there, they don't mind a bit of dust."

When asked about when the work of putting it all back together again would start, Noddy put a reassuring hand on their shoulder and said: "Now, just leave that to the experts, b'y, got to crack a few eggs when you're after making an omlette."

It was two months before Noddy bought a broom on one of his commutes.

On the eve of Milton's birthday, as he toasted a day-old bagel on the stove for his supper, Noddy poured himself a juice glass of gin and asked: "What are ya at tomorrow?"

"I don't know. Nothing, I guess."

"Want some work?"

"Uh... okay."

The pay was 50 bucks per day, cash. They were leaving at 5:15 to be there by 6:00—someone was meeting them there.

"Wear something warm."

• • •

S&M Destruction

If you are up before the sun it means you are either unemployed or employed in some of the worst shit work. The unemployed watch the sunrise from the back. Stumbling back to their apartments after long nights out. Labourers, bakers, candlestick makers, and ex-strip club DJs playing at contractor are up before dawn, staggering through their houses in work boots with a couple of soggy tomato sandwiches in an old grocery bag.

Noddy beat on Milton's door at 5:25.

"Time to go!"

Milton was cold and itched all over. He'd fallen asleep under his winter coat and gnatty towel he had stolen from the dryer and been using as his blanket, while reading *The Sun Also Rises*, between two and three. He'd gotten, at the very most, three hours of sleep. His eyes burned like a smoldering fire that no amount of rubbing would put out.

Noddy handed him a radio and stomped out the door towards the bus stop.

Noddy was one of them morning assholes. He wanted to talk on the bus ride, but instead of the usual banter about how cold it was, or about the hockey game he half-watched the night before, or about "legs" or "bush" or "jugs," he wanted to talk about the Newfoundland cod moratorium and Russian trawlers and whothehellknows. Milton just wanted sweet, sweet death.

A bus, a metro, and three-quarters of the way through the history of the North Atlantic codfish, they got to where they were going—a giant three-storey stone house—fifteen minutes late.

Noddy didn't have keys. Sam was bringing them, so they sat in the dark, in the freezing cold, on the front step for the conclusion of Noddy's treatise on overfishing. Milton had tuned him out long ago and sat freezing, staring covetously across a park at a Java Jean's, slowly filling with morning commuters.

With these work arrangements having been negotiated after everything was closed the night before, and his lack of money to get anything anyway, Milton hadn't brought along any soggy tomato sandwiches. He would have killed a man for a sandwich right then. A hot chocolate maybe. A few doughnuts. Hell, even a plain scone.

He offered to run over and grab some coffees and snacks, "for the crew," but Noddy assured him that work was set to start at any second and assured him he could procure a lunch at a nearby burger joint when the time was right.

In the meantime, all he had to do was clear the basement of rubble from the previous months of S&M's handiwork.

There were a "few" bags and boxes and piles of lumber and concrete and "shit" that needed to be hauled up out the basement and taken to the dump. A "guy with a truck" would arrive any minute now to take it away. Blah, blah, blah... Any minute now.

"Here, wear these here gloves."

There was a hole in the right index finger.

Milton's toes burned with cold inside of his old, ironically vintage-running shoes, and the end of his nose was solid and purple, and clear snot dripped off the tip and froze in a pile on the ground. It was so cold he couldn't feign interest in Noddy as he transitioned to a dissertation on Victorian-Anglophone Architecture in Westmount.

The 'any minute now' of Sam's arrival was about forty-five minutes later. He'd stopped to get coffee, and there was a line-up, and, and, and.... He didn't know Milton was coming, "Good to meet you, mate," so he only got two coffees. One for him and one for Noddy.

While they sipped their steaming coffees and made small talk, Milton dreamed of bludgeoning them to death there on Greene Avenue, in front of all the bourgeoisie out taking their dogs for a shit.

Sam said the truck guy, whose name he couldn't remember, would be there any minute now.

Any minute.

He'd found this guy on Craigslist: "Truck for hire. Fare rates," and a phone number. There were a "few" loads, so he was going to come early to get a good start, maybe bring a helper. 100 bucks cash for the half day. The guy with the truck was worth four times what Milton was.

It better be a big damned truck, he thought.

Sam dug a mess of keys out of his pocket and started trying different keys in different locks at random in a I've-had-coffee-and-am-warm-so-I-am-in-no-rush-to-get-this-door-open-let-me-stumble-fuck-around-with-these-500-keys-for-a-while-while-the-frostbite-climbs-up-your-legs-and-you-lose-feeling-in-your-balls way. Half-a-million keys later, they got into the giant mansion that had been ransacked by a couple of amateur demolition technicians.

Not that being inside made much of a difference for Milton's frostbite. An overzealous swing of a sledgehammer severed a gas line last month, so the heat had been shut off in the giant old house for weeks. Any hope Milton had of warming up would have to wait until lunch when he would be found floating face down in a vat of coffee.

Of course, the truck and its high-priced driver weren't there for 6:30 a.m. as promised, nor 7:30 a.m. by the time Sam remembered that the key for the inexplicably locked inner porch door was in his other pocket and they got out of the biting, kicking, screaming, clawing at your eyes wind for a few minutes.

The truck wasn't there by 7:45 a.m. when Noddy had Milton sweeping bedrooms on the third floor that they hadn't demoed yet.

"It's good to keep a jobsite clean, it shows professional-ism."

So clean that there wasn't a sign of any tools even, other

than the two tools currently screwing an Ikea kitchen cabinet upside down over a toilet hole in a downstairs bathroom.

Professionalism.

By 9:00 a.m., and still no truck, Milton had added another couple giant contractor-sized garbage bags worth of dust and demolitia to the contractor-sized garbage bag mountain in the basement awaiting the still-unseen Manwith Truck.

Noddy and Sam had just torn everything they could tear out of the house and thrown it down the stairs into the basement. The stairs were buried by shards of drywall and old trim with three-inch-long finishing nails sticking out of them. To get into the basement you had to slide down the rubble stairs, careful not to have one of those three-inch-long finishing nails tear you a new one.

By 9:45 a.m. Milton was hefting one end of a cheap-looking tub surround into place while Sam hefted the other end and Noddy blazed drywall screws through the no-longer-watertight plastic sheeting, screwing it to the wall surrounding a filthy tub with a leg-length, pinky-wide scratch—a casualty of "some serious demo" that would "probably buff out."

Milton's suggestions of levels and caulking and taking half a damned minute to get the thing in straight and not filling it full of screws that rust easily, let alone screws at all, were rebuffed with Noddy brandishing his Philips-head screwdriver—also known as *the* screwdriver—crotch height and saying something about "I got your caulk right here, b'y."

By 10:30 a.m., with the tub thoroughly surrounded, it was coffee-break time. Noddy lit a cigarette and dumped a bottle of stale water into a busted kettle on a busted stove while Sam pulled a box of rubble up next to the radio and shook a day's worth of dust out of a filthy mug.

"Tea?"

"I... uh... yeah... Please."

Thank God!

"Got a cup?"

Noddy shook the dirt out of his dirty mug and dug a bag of Red Rose out of a bag of Red Rose and dropped it in.

"No…"

No one told Milton about BYO-mugs, or food, or any of this.

"Sorry, brah, have a look around, but I don't think there are any others."

They weren't brahs. There were no others.

"You can use mine when I'm done."

By 10:35 a.m. Milton was sitting on a pile of rotten, asbestosy lumber watching Sam and Noddy warm themselves with tea while Sam went on about what a "fascist bitch" his girlfriend, a student from the summer crew, was, "always on the computer, always giving me shit," always, always, always.

By 10:40 a.m. Milton was wiping Noddy's mouth off the grimiest mug you've ever seen and digging a Red Rose bag out of the Red Rose bag and pouring the last few precious mouthfuls of hot water left in the busted kettle into the filthy mug.

That half cup of tea. That tea. That tea! Was the sweetest thing Milton had ever tasted. He drank it, scalding hot, all in one gulp. Scorching the roof of his mouth, and his tongue, and all the way down his gullet. A burn that itched and screeched for the rest of the day, and a few after. A burn that made everything he'd eat for the next two weeks taste tinny and bloody and sandpapery. A burn that kept him from going hypothermic or postal or both at that precise moment. Sweet heavenly boiling hot tea. Manna from heaven. Sweet, sweet manna from…

"Back at it, b'ys."

• • •

Dans les chiottes

Still no Man with Truck by 11:30 a.m., as Sam and Milton watched Noddy overtightening the bowl nut on the brand-new dual-flush low-flow Jet Flush JF250 toilet, which was worth about $500.

Not by 11:31 a.m. as Sam and Milton watched the tank shatter and fall in two heavy halves on either of Noddy's feet, adding insult to stupidity.

Not by 11:32 a.m. as Sam and Milton dove for cover as Noddy picked up what was left of the $500 toilet and threw it, Olympic Hammer Throw-style, through the freshly dry-walled partition wall between the bathroom and the hall linen closet leaving, as you might suspect, a $500-toilet-sized hole.

Not by 11:33 a.m. as Sam and Milton, laughing to themselves, hid behind a lineup of brand-new still-in-the-box kitchen appliances like it was some kind of foxhole while Noddy hurled obscenities and the entire contents of the toolbox, one tool at a time, through the $500-toilet-sized hole in the freshly dry-walled partition wall between the bathroom and the hall linen closet. Laughter that got a bit too loud as evidenced by the 6-inch C-clamp that smashed into the side of the stainless-steel fridge, right next to Sam's head, leaving a noticeable gash in the side of the fridge. Just another thing to "buff out" later.

Out of tools to throw, but with plenty of obscenity left, Noddy left the house, leaving a trail of slammed doors behind him.

"Holy cow!"

"He'll cool off. Happens all the time. Yesterday it was a closet shelf."

"All the time?"

"He's got a bit of a temper. Y'know. It's why he's here, in Monty-Hall? Temper got himself in some hot water back in Newfoundl'nd. Right, mate?"

"Uh... Right..."

Noddy resurfaced a few minutes later with a cooler head, and a tall cup of piping hot coffee.

"I can't believe that toilet was faulty like that. Shit's not supposed to happen. Have to take it back and shove it up their fucking asses."

"Even the shitters these days, even the shitters, are just disposable pieces of plastic corporate shit meant to keep us subservient to our corporate overlord masters, mate. Fuck all that shit. Let's go install the bar in the rec room."

By noon Noddy was smoking cigarettes on an upside-down pail watching Sam watch Milton trying to assemble an Ikea bar. There was only one Allen key, so Noddy barked orders, Sam handed odd-looking screws, Milton screwed.

The noon-hour newscast over the radio was the lunchtime bell.

"Enough of this shit, let's have lunch."

Milton had never been so happy to hear about a Guatemalan mudslide, low-pressure cold fronts, or backups on the Décarie southbound. Never in his life.

His stomach, unamused by the splash of lava tea, had been eating itself for hours. Gnawing its way up his esophagus towards his head to look him in the eye and ask him what his problem was.

Milton thought about how he might navigate the situation at home with Noddy if he just walked out and never came back. If he said eff all of this Two Stooges Construction Company, eff the imaginary Man with Truck, eff all this and went home for a day-old bagel and a half-rotten pineapple and a nap and a shower and then down to Java Jean for as much of a bucket of something hot he could get with his 73-cents and whatever change Noddy had left in the ashtray on the table beside his bed. Maybe he would even find Robin, it was his birthday after all.

The only catch was Noddy would be home stinking of asbestos and ass sweat, frying horse meat, by 6:00 p.m. and would wonder where he'd run off to and would probably want to put him through the partition wall between the bathroom and the hallway linen closet, so it was probably best to just go find that burger place and pray his credit card would work and drag his bleary-eyed ass back here for the rest of the afternoon.

Hamburger.

The Red Rose blisters on the roof of his mouth, and his tongue, and all the way down his gullet were watering at the thought of it.

Hamburger.

It'd be enough to save him. Enough to save this shitty birthday. For the sake of everything good and redeeming on this earth, on this bitterly cold day, for all those buried in mud in Guatemala, for all of that, there was that hamburger across an empty park, buried in winter, and half a block down.

Hamburger.

Just half a block...

BANG.

Outside, a 1980-before-Milton-was-born two-tone rust and blue Ford F250 quad-cab pickup truck with a snow plow on the front had just climbed the sidewalk, and punted a metal garbage can end-over-end into a BMW parked in the driveway of the house next door, setting off its alarm.

MWRAMP-MWARMP-MWARMP.

"Truck's 'ere."

Lunch was going to have to wait. Milton wanted to cry/die/murder everything.

• • •

Fig. 30. F250

Les éboueurs

Two ancient men got out of the truck. The tall one with the toque perched on top of his wrinkled raisin of a head, whose clothes just sort of hung off him, was the driver. He unfolded himself out of the truck, stomped over to presumably survey the damage to the BMW and leave a note under the windshield wiper with his insurance information. Instead he kicked the garbage can into the side of the BMW again and turned to shake his fist and scream something at his sidekick: a short prune of a man who couldn't zip up his coat.

The screaming raisin, Milton would eventually decipher, was called Johnny (for Giannis). He was the leader, the driver, the brains, the toque, the mouth, the bottomless pit of spectacularly humourless in-your-face rage of the tandem.

The prune, Peter (for Panagiotis), said nothing, did nothing, contributed nothing. Everything you could want in a loyal sidekick.

They were both Greek, Milton assumed. Not that that means anything other than they spoke no English nor French other than, "you guy..." point, point, nod, shake head, shake fist, Greek slur, Greek slur, Greek slur.

Noddy met them on the sidewalk and played curse-charades, "GO AROUND BACK! BACK! BACK! FOR FUCK-SAKES!" and convinced them to pull the truck around back, where Milton would help them wrestle load after load of junk and toxic dust out a narrow window, across a snow-buried yard, and into the antique truck that was really just chunks of rust and dents stuck together with peeling duct tape and wire.

Johnny pulled into the alley that was built for a vehicle about a third the size of the massive truck, and pulled off an impressive 37-point turn that included his crushing several more garbage cans, scraping a gash in the side and busting out a tail light of a Mercedes parked two doors down, and culminated in his snow plow ramming through the fence across the alley.

Once parked, Johnny and Peter both got out. Johnny jimmied some wires holding the tail gate closed and swung it down to make loading easier. Then scowled at Milton, screamed "you guy!" and some Greek curses, and pointed to the junk and then the truck.

The two of them watched, in the bitter cold, for half an hour while Milton pushed junk out the basement window, wiggled his way out behind it, dragged it through the snow, and heaved it onto the back of the truck.

With a full load, Johnny started slamming the tailgate shut repeatedly, hoping it would catch enough to allow the wire he'd rigged up to hold it shut. In the slamming, the tailgate was forced out of alignment, and, in the most active thing Milton saw him do the entire day, the mute Peter grabbed the edge of the tailgate to shove it back into alignment mid-slam.

Naturally, Johnny slammed Peter's hand in the tailgate with all of his might. His hand could have been broken, but Peter didn't make a noise. He just grimaced and rubbed it and looked at Johnny like he'd just killed his puppy. Johnny didn't skip a beat, but added some angry Greek cursing directed at Peter to the mix.

Eventually the tailgate got wedged sort of shut and the two of them piled into the truck. Milton was supposed to go with them to unload, as obviously they weren't going to do it themselves, but they both slammed their doors before he could crawl into the back of the extended cab.

Johnny had it in gear and was ready to go when Milton tapped on Peter's window. Peter's face, upon realizing his mistake, looked more distraught than when Johnny almost ripped his hand off. He opened the door and a stream of Greek slurs poured out from Johnny at them both. Milton pulled up on a little lever at the base of Peter's seat and had to fight to get it to tip forward so he could climb in and sit on the tiny bench seat that held about half his ass and had no seatbelts.

Before Peter was all the way back in, Johnny floored it and they took off down the alley, scratching a long, deep gouge in the brick wall of the million-dollar mansion across the alley.

• • •

Poubelles

Johnny wasn't built for reliability or kindness or hard work or any of that. Johnny was built for one thing and one thing only: speed.

Red lights: he didn't give a shit.

Speed limits: ditto.

Punk kid in a Civic looking to race gramps in the rust bucket of a truck: eat dust.

Garbage cans in alleys: bugs on the windshield.

Milton dug his nails into the dirty back seat of that old F250 while Johnny careened, ricocheted, sped, bounced, slammed, scraped, skidded, and swerved his way around town. Milton had never been so afraid for his life.

For the next several hours the three of them fell into a routine. Johnny would scratch and dent and wedge the truck into the back alley. He and Peter would watch Milton break his back crawling in and out of the basement window with armloads of asbestos. They'd go through the dance of the tailgate—slam, slam, slam, slam, hand, crunch, curse, slam, slam, slam. And then they'd speed around town breaking every traffic law imaginable looking for dumpsters.

When they found a dumpster Johnny would back the truck into it at high speed. All three would pile out of the truck, and Johnny and Peter would watch Milton unload the contents of the truck into the dumpster. All the while a constant stream of angry Greek instructions, demands, and curses streaming from Johnny, while Peter kept mute.

After the third or fourth trip, Milton had blocked the endless Greek epithets out. So he was a little surprised when the cursing stopped, and the doors slammed, and the truck fired up and took off with him still in the back on a pile of shifting nail-riddled, asbestos-y garbage.

They tore out of the loading dock of a downtown Federal government office building just as a pair of armed security guards and their attack dogs arrived. Milton grabbed the sideboard of the truck box and hung on for dear life as Johnny slammed through a closing chain-link gate, sending the gate cartwheeling into a busy street, and squealed around the corner.

The dogs followed the truck, which the guards were sure was full of stolen government property. Milton laid down flat on the garbage, nails digging into his skin, as gnashing killer-dog teeth nipped at his heels as they dangled off the end of the truck.

Johnny sped up and weaved in and out of traffic for several blocks until he was satisfied they'd lost the dogs. He spotted a dumpster behind a Chinese restaurant, slammed on the brakes, sending Milton crashing into the back window, wheeled around, and backed into the dumpster with a loud crunch.

Johnny and Peter both got out of the truck and came back to survey the damage.

Or something.

Milton was laying on the pile of garbage, bleeding out of several nail holes, face bruised from bouncing off the window, breathing heavily. Johnny began, or continued, shouting.

"You guy!" Curse. Curse. Curse. Pointing to the dumpster.

"Are you crazy! You almost killed me!"

Curse. Curse. Curse. Point. Point. Point.

"Forget this!"

Milton crawled out of the back of the truck and dusted the asbestos and debris off his torn clothes.

Johnny increased in volume and frothiness. He was clearly extra pissed that Milton had somehow been responsible for getting busted by the Feds. He was pointing with extra violence at the dumpster. Demanding Milton empty the truck. Milton refused, as he doubled over to catch his breath.

"Empty it yourself, you old fart. They sicced dogs on me! Jeez!"

Johnny didn't take no backtalk. This was why he and Peter got along so well. He grabbed Milton by the back of his collar, stood him up, and kicked him in the ass with his heavy winter boot.

Curse. Curse. Curse.

"Get off me! Don't!"

Johnny reached in the back of the truck and grabbed a piece of 2x4.

"Yeah, you empty it!"

Johnny wasn't about to empty anything. He swung the 2x4 at Milton's head. Milton ducked but couldn't duck the follow-up blow that came down on top of his shoulders and dropped him to the ground. He rolled onto his back and Johnny stepped all his weight onto Milton's chest with a big dirty white winter boot and pressed the 2x4 into his throat.

"Αδειάστε το γαμημένο φορτηγό ή θα σας σκοτώσω και θα σας βάλω στον κάδο! Εσείς λίγο σκουλήκι!"

Milton wasn't sure what the angry words Johnny spat on him meant, but he guessed, by the look in Johnny's eye and the weight he was leaning onto the 2x4, that he best empty the truck before it was him going into the dumpster.

He tapped Johnny's boot in surrender and Johnny let him up.

Johnny didn't prove entirely unreasonable, though. Or at least he was willing to let bygones be bygones enough to not leave Milton behind that Chinese restaurant. No more than they tried to leave him anywhere. Peter slammed the door on Milton before he could get in. Milton tapped on Peter's window. Peter got out, Milton climbed in, Johnny took off before Peter could get all the way back in.

Back at the mansion, after Johnny got the truck wedged back into the alley for the next load, Milton found Noddy and Sam upstairs taking turns electrocuting themselves trying to install a light fixture.

"I'm not riding with them anymore!"

"OUCH! Fuck! What's the problem?"

"Those two idiots tried to kill me!"

"Oh, g'wan b'y, they're harmless old fucks."

"Yeah right! We got chased by dogs! And then the tall guy hit me with a 2x4! I'm done. You don't pay me enough for this!"

They could hear Johnny yelling from outside.

"He what?"

"Some security guards sent dogs after us, and he takes off going 100 miles an hour while I was still in the back of the truck, and when we got away I told him off and he hit me with a 2x4 and tried to choke me."

"I always figured you liked the wood, b'y. Bahahaha!"

Sam thought Noddy was hilarious.

"I'm not kidding!"

"Just calm down, I'll go talk to him. Here, hold this."

Noddy stepped off the new dishwasher they had turned on its back and were using for a step stool and handed the light fixture to Sam. It sparked.

"OUCH! MOTHERFUCKER!"

Milton watched Noddy confront Johnny and Peter through the basement window he'd been crawling in and out of all day. They didn't speak English, so far as Milton could tell, and Noddy didn't speak Greek, so far as Milton could tell. Noddy mimed something that looked like jerking off and dogs barking, Johnny screamed, spat, and cursed, and Peter looked at something up a tree down the street.

They reached some conclusion when Noddy started patting Johnny on the back and saying loud enough for Milton to hear, "Best kind, b'y, best kind." He fished $20 out of his pocket and gave it to Johnny.

Noddy came over to Milton's window and stuck his head in.

"All right, b'y. All settled. He agreed not to try and kill you again. It cost me an extra $20, which I'm gonna have to take out of your wages, but you should be all good."

"Wait, what?"

"The b'ys can only stick around for another hour, so you've got time for a few more loads. They'll drop you at our other jobsite for the rest of the day."

"This sucks!"

"That's why they call it work, b'y, and not fucking your mother."

• • •

Love Cams Inc.

Milton and the Shitty Truck Mafia managed to move two more truckloads of rubble without anyone getting eaten by dogs or choked out over the next hour. After emptying the last load, they drove 20 minutes into the depths of some kind of sprawling industrial park. Johnny pulled up in front of one of the anonymous looking buildings, one with a generic-looking sign, "Love Cams Inc.", over the door.

He shouted something and pointed to the door. "You guy!" Curse. Curse. Point. Point. Peter wouldn't get out, he was probably worried Johnny would leave him there too, so he just leaned forward and Milton had to contort himself into all sorts of compromising positions to squeeze out of the truck. He still had one foot caught in between the seat and the door frame when Johnny gunned it and sped off. Milton toppled out onto the icy pavement.

"And screw you too," he whispered laying on the ground.

He was on the ground a while when Sam poked his head out the door.

"*Kia Ora*, mate?"

The guy who owned the two-million-dollar mansion S&M were destroying, some guy called Tony, also owned Love

Cams Inc.—a quasi-legal internet porn company. Milton wasn't sure of the whole story. But Tony had hired S&M to renovate the offices of Love Cams Inc., too.

Offices isn't the right word for it, though. They were turning what used to be a metal fabrication shop into a bunch of cubicles. Each cubicle was decorated sort of like a bedroom—there was a bed at least, usually with cheap satin sheets, and a webcam. Lonely internet pervs would drain their bank accounts paying girls to roll around on these beds in their underwear.

"He makes a fortune," Noddy told Milton when he explained it to him later.

For now, though, Milton was picking himself up off the frozen pavement and joining Sam inside.

"Noddy went to a client meeting, so it's just us."

Of course he did.

"We've got to finish painting everything in here. I'm half done this wall."

Sam gestured to a wall that looked the same as all the other walls.

"Did you get lunch?"

Mercy! There is a god after all.

"No."

"There's nothing around here for miles, but you can have this."

Sam held out a grimy, dusty plastic container. Milton pried the lid open and found a half-eaten piece of cold left-over lasagna.

"My girlfriend made me this. She can't cook worth a damn."

On any other day, in any other circumstances, Milton would have gagged in disgust. But he was starving.

"Do you have a fork?"

"Yeah, here."

Sam handed him a clearly used plastic fork. Bits of sauce and smooth lumps of cold cheese stuck to the tines.

"Thanks."

Milton had never tasted anything so good.

Back in the land of the living and the fed, Milton joined Sam in painting for the rest of the afternoon. It was the first time they'd ever actually spent any time together, and while Sam's political views were on the rather extreme end of things—he wouldn't stop going on about the deep state and the dark web and the mind control agenda of "neo-liberal fascists and their so-called 'vaccines'"—he wasn't altogether terrible.

At 5:00 p.m., as it was getting dark, Sam said they were done for the day, except for the 45-minute walk to the nearest bus stop, and the 95-minute bus-metro-bus-metro-metro-bus ride home.

Milton got off the 80 at the Library to check his email. He had a handful of birthday messages from friends and family. Including a message from his best friend in Bellybutton, Cory:

"HBD Bro" with a link to a news article explaining how researchers in the UK had scientifically determined that this exact day was the most depressing day of the year.

"The days are short and cold. You're leaving work in the dark and getting home in the dark. You may not have seen the sun for weeks," said Dr. Morley Brennan of the University of Sussex. "The only way it could be any worse was if it was your birthday today."

Back at the apartment, stuck to Milton's bedroom door, was $30 and a note:

176

All that for $30. The misery, the hunger, the cold, the multiple brushes with death, the getting clobbered by a 6'3" antique Greek raisin, the verbal abuse, the back-breaking labour, the asbestos, the lead, the formaldehyde, the left-over leftover lasagna with another man's fork, the painting sex cubicles. All that for $30.

With travel time it amounted to just over $2.00 per hour. But it was $30 that Milton didn't have, so he stuck it in his pocket and went back down the street to Parapluie de Nouilles to treat himself to $30 worth of MSG to celebrate his birthday.

• • •

Col bleu

Each day with S&M followed a script similar to the first: cut corners, cut fingers, lunch breaks cut short by three-hours-late Craigslist rent-a-trucks, hissy fits, shouting matches, heavy breakable things broken and thrown through freshly hung drywall, never-ending near-misses, lungs full of toxins, sloppily painted webcam sex cubicles, and slowly-destroyed million-dollar homes.

Despite Milton probably being the handiest of the three—he once built a deck and a backyard fence with his dad that was by no means the Sistine Chapel, but turned out better than anything S&M had ever done—his name wasn't on the nine business cards Noddy printed at Kinko's as part of a free sample promotion, so he remained the one and only lowly employee. Which was fine with him. He got the shittiest jobs, but at least he got paid each day.

Besides, Noddy didn't take so kindly to advice or pointers or constructive feedback. Especially while holding the other end of a 300-pound, $1,500-bathroom vanity with double sinks that bounced three times as it toppled down the stairs. So, Milton kept his mouth shut.

He kept his mouth shut when Noddy started cutting the $150 Italian marble threshold six inches too short. Kept his mouth shut when Noddy dragged a washing machine across the freshly laid engineered hardwoods floors—leaving a deep gash the entire length of the hallway. Kept his mouth shut as Noddy stabbed the screwdriver through a newly painted wall looking for a stud and only finding the electrical junction box he'd illegally covered up the day before—Milton could have sworn he saw sparks shoot out of Noddy's ears as he flew off the stepladder, landing hard on the radio, crushing it.

He learned to keep his mouth shut and just smile to himself, making mental notes to include in his semi-autobiographical best-selling novel years later.

With that understanding, things settled into a sort of normalcy, and Milton and Noddy became sort of friends. Only sort of. Noddy was still the boss, but felt he was Milton's mentor, his big brother, his spiritual guide.

Every day, from the rap on Milton's door at 5:15 a.m.-ish each morning, until they dragged themselves back in the door after 6:00 p.m., Noddy would talk Milton's ear off.

He would expound on all the life lessons he'd learned from growing up "poorer than dirt in the Circle" in St. John's (or "Town" as Milton came to know it).[22]

Lessons from having to fight kids twice his age: "One of my mom's kitchen knives or that bat I stole from the gym closed the age gap pretty fuckin' fast, let me tell ya!"

Lessons from the summer spent at a camp for wayward boys because he stabbed a kid six years older than himself in a fight after school one day: "Harder to find a knife or a bat in one of them camps, but they can't lock up every fuckin' rock in Newfoundland, b'y."

---

[22] The Buckmaster Circle neighbourhood of St. John's, a.k.a. "The Circle," is a notoriously rough area of "Town" full of "Hard Tickets," a.k.a. tough characters.

Lessons from doing a year in "juvie" for assaulting a counsellor at the camp for wayward boys with a rock because: "He was one of them rich Townie fucks, thinking he was some grand, coming at me trying to grab my ass n' shit, it was self-defence, b'y. But, of course, the judge didn't think so, he was one of them rich Townie fucks too."

Lessons from dropping out of school at 14 to go to work on the docks: "Me uncle got me into the longshoreman's union, making $20 an hour to unload cargo, if ya know what I mean," Milton had no idea what he meant, other than that he didn't mean unloading cargo.

Lessons from befriending the prostitutes who'd hang around the docks when there were boats in: "You should try it, get right friendly with 'em. On a slow night, they might give ya a deal on a handy. They knows their ways around the gear, b'y."

Lessons from having to fight Russian sailors on the docks who were too rough with the girls: "Those fuckers fight dirty, b'y. They've all got knives and clubs and shit in their boots, and they'll gouge your fuckin' eyes out if you're not watching. The trick is to let 'em beat the shit out of ya pretty good the first time, they won't kill ya the first time. Just take your licks, don't really fight back, and then they thinks you're beat. Then you comes back the next night with half the fuckin' Circle fastpitch team—and take the fuckin' bats to 'em."

Lessons from a few years in prison and how "the Pen" compared to "juvie" and how it's prudent to "Slam some b'y's head in the workroom door on the first day and send 'em to the infirmary and they'll all back down."

Lessons from turning his passion for friendly prostitutes into a career: "I gets out and they wouldn't give me my job back at the Port, fuckers said they can't have convicts working for 'em even though half the fuckers down there done time. So's I went on the pogey and pretty much moved into the peelers and got right friendly with the girls there—

for the deals on lappies when things were slow, right—until the DJ didn't show up for work—'cause he was floating face down in the Gut[23] for not knowing the right way to scrap with the Russians—and they gave me the job. Good one too. Free drinks, free lappies, just hanging out pushin' play on the fuckin' CD player. Did that for ten years."

The only story he didn't tell was why he left St. John's.

In all, it was quite the master class in hard living. But Milton wasn't sure how much of it was true. He googled Noddy and nothing came up. No court reports or news stories about a bunch of Russians being beaten by a fastpitch team down on the docks for looking sideways at prostitutes. Nothing.

One day at Love Cams, while they used razor blades to scrape up paint they'd previously splashed on the floor, Sam told Milton that most of what Noddy told him was bullshit.

"I dunno, mate. I've 'eard all them stories before, and they're mostly bullshit. I'm sure of it. His dad was a politician or something, no way he'd let that hard shit happen."

Milton googled that too, and sure enough, someone with Noddy's intense forehead was the Minister of Fisheries and Labour in Newfoundland and Labrador for three months in the '70s before being thrown out of office for sleeping with his unnamed son's babysitter and into jail for corruption.

When he asked Noddy if he was any relation, Noddy said something about his mom being "some Townie politician's side piece for a while." And though he claims he never met the man, bringing it up set off several weeks of more lessons.

Lessons on Newfoundland history: "Confederation was a fraud, b'y. Everyone thinks the place was bankrupt, but that was bullshit lies that Quebec spy Smallwood told everyone 'cause he was on the take. And even then they didn't have

[23] "The Gut" is a small harbour surrounded by the former fishing village of Quidi Vidi (pronounced "Kitty Vitty") which is now a picturesque tourist trap on the outskirts of St. John's.

the votes to get 'er through! 'Til Joey and his buddies got every corpse laying in every grave in Town to vote for it."

Lessons on politics: "If you think them Russians fight dirty, you should see fuckin' politicians. My dad grabbed some fella by the throat on the floor of the House there one day, and told him if he didn't go along with whateverinthefuck, his family would pay, then he got a buddy with the phone company to change all his family's numbers so he couldn't get a hold of any of them, even his daughter away at school on the mainland. Buddy thought my old man murdered them all, he was right rotted, b'y."

Lessons about economics: "She's rigged, b'y. The works of 'er. The banks own it all. And they own the politicians. And they make the rules. And the rules say they get it all. And they get it all because we give it to them. We walk right through the front door and give them all our cash. We give to them like damned fools. Fuck that, b'y. I've got all my cash in my boot right now. They ain't getting nothing from me."

Lessons on labour relations: "Unions are a racket, b'y, so you gots to get in 'em, if you can. I was in the stevedore union, it was prime dog fuckin'. Never stole so much shit and made so much money in my life. But the big bosses, who steal way more shit than any union ever did, don't like that none so they'll fuck with the unions as much as they can. It's war. I've seen some shit that'd make your skin crawl. A whole shipping container full of union brass sealed up tight and dumped over the side in the middle of the Indian ocean. No one knows anything about it, no newspaper or police would dare say a word about any of it, they're all in on it."

All the while, Sam, Noddy's hype man, would chime in with "fuckin' right," and "the man, man, fuck the man."

It was like Milton was working with the Marx & Engels Construction Company—if Marx was a disgraced ex-con strip club DJ and Engels was a Kiwi anarchist stowaway.

EIGHT

UGLY
SWEATER
PARTY

À la mode

It wasn't particularly safe, and the hours were terrible, and the asbestos or lead or formaldchyde had given Milton a perpetual rash, but working for S&M was mildly entertaining, good material for his future novel, and most of all, money. More money than Milton had ever made.

His work for Uncle Randy or Farmtime was part-time work that paid below minimum wage. S&M paid $50 per day—less made-up deductions like angry truck driver extortion—six days per week, cold hard/warm wrinkled smelling like feet cash.

The supply of $50s allowed Milton to resume his search for Robin.

Several nights per week he'd go out to bar shows and house parties and gallery openings looking for her. Several nights per week he'd schlep back home, alone.

Finally, after weeks without a trace, he got a break in the hunt for his one true love by way of an invite from Ava to an ugly sweater party at Owly's place.

Milton was sure Robin would be there. He agonized over it all week.

One night after work he rode the Green Line way out

farther than he'd ever been, into the heart of Francophone working-class Montreal to Village des Valeurs to find an ugly sweater. He ended up spending that day's entire $50 on 15 ugly sweaters.

The night of the party he was modelling each sweater in front of the grimy, busted bathroom mirror when Noddy burst in.

"Whaddayat, b'y?"

"Trying to pick—"

Milton was distracted mid-sentence by Noddy pulling down his pants and sitting down on the toilet.

"Pick what?"

"Dude!?"

"Wha'?"

"Are you... pooping?!"

"Aw, c'mon, b'y. Everybody shits, don't be such a pussy. Jesus."

"Yeah, but not in front of other people!"

"Well you turned the shitter into your ugly shirt fashion show thing here, what do ya want?"

"You not to... not to poop in front of me!"

"You'll live. What are ya doing with all them ugly shirts now?"

"Seriously!"

When the most earnest grunting started Milton made for the door.

"Aw, come on, man. I'm almost done."

The smell followed Milton out into the hall; he nearly gagged.

Noddy yelled after him.

"Goddamn, b'y. This is a wild one! Enough to curl the hair on your chest!"

Milton had his breath mostly caught when Noddy's head poked out from around the corner, scaring him.

"Left ya a present. Bahahahaha!"

"Gross. You're so disgusting!"

"Really, though. You going on a tear tonight, or what?"

"Ach! It smells like something died."

"Something did die: my ass. If you're going out tonight, I'm coming with ya. I haven't gotten laid in a week. My pecker is going to dry up and blow away if I don't do something about it."

"That's not a great idea..."

"Don't be a dick. You're getting dressed for one of them ugly sweater parties you stupid hipsters have. I'll wear this piece of shit."

Noddy pulled on Milton's favourite ugly sweater of the 15.

"It's a stupid hipster thing. You won't like it. It'll all be students."

"Hey, hey, hey! I like students, b'y. Young and supple minds. If you know what I mean?"

"Yeah."

"Supple. Get it?"

"Yeah, I get it."

"I mean tits."

"That's great."

"And ass."

"Mmhmm."

"And cooter."

"Super."

• • •

Chinatown Centre

When he wasn't riding giant dick missiles around town, Owly lived in a shopping mall, The Chintown Centre, in Chinatown, which was quickly becoming the next frontier in the Anglo-Adultescent invasion.

The Chinatown Centre was on the edge of the country's third largest Chinatown. Next to the city's best Pho restaurant, across from a new ramen place that charged $16 for a Mr.

Noodles but got a good review in *The Mirror* because its decor and entire ethos was trapped somewhere between Ed Hardy, Hello Kitty, and *The Grapes of Wrath*.

The rest of the street was alternating green-grocers and steamed bunneries punctuated by a coffee shop that aspired to all things but making a cup of coffee that didn't taste like lukewarm blood; a bubble tea bar with free fooseball that was *the* bar three bars ago; an ad agency with a messiah complex as evidenced by its insistence on selling branded t-shirts, and that being its most successful line of business; and an unmarked storefront crammed around the clock with old men playing Mahjong.

The sidewalk was filled the entire day with old women ramming wheelie carts full of exotic vegetables into the shins of an ever-increasing crowd of young people migrating by the handfuls from The Plateau to try the new ramen place they read about in *The Mirror*, and drive up the prevalence of aspirational coffee joints and drive down the vacancy rate.

The Chinatown Centre was definitely one of the shittiest malls in the country. Built in the Cultural Revolutionary style—narrow cheek-by-jowl storefronts adorned in asbestos, jaundiced semi-gloss paint, and stained concrete floors— its dozen tiny storefronts crammed L-shape in a too-small building on the corner would, if not for the filthy skylights, receive no natural light at all.

There were three units that kept somewhat regular hours: a herbal medicine clinic that no one ever went to, a novelty legging store that would be closed before the end of winter, and a discount clothing store owned by an old lady who spent the day reading *Les Presses Chinoises*, working through her *Easy Sudoku Bible*, smoking cigarettes, and never selling anything.

In addition to these, there were three units with signage that were never open: two tattoo parlours and a pottery studio.

The rest of the units had big curtains draped behind their clear security gates. Which gave the impression of a ghost town.

Owly, in a burst of miserly inspiration that dwarfed the dick missile as probably his greatest accomplishment, figured out that an entire storefront in the Chinatown Centre could be rented for much less than an apartment of comparable size. It was owned by an absentee slumlord, who only corresponded with Owly through his emissary, Vick. And even then, Vick and his bad breath were rarely seen, only when rent was late, and he left the distinct impression that rent shouldn't be late. Ever.

The lease Owly and his roommate Pochard, the sometimes-filmmaker, sometimes-Russian Lit. grad student at Concordia, signed was an over-copied copy of a 25-year old commercial lease that forbade pets and smoking and unlicensed medical and food establishments, and, most of all, forbade two bachelors in their almost-30s from building elaborate dummy walls out of *Les Presses Chinoises* back issues and one-by-twos to divide the space into living quarters and sleeping quarters and turning a discount storefront into a makeshift two-bedroom bachelor pad and giant papermâché dick-missile studio.

Soon the rest of the vacant units were filled with bachelor pad pottery studios and bachelor pad novelty dragon-etched polymer skateboard studios and bachelor pad abstract conceptual Lego sculpture studios.

Owly and Pochard's unit was about 800 square feet. About 25 of which were spent on a half bathroom—toilet and sink—in one corner. Another 50, which was theoretically an office in which legitimate businesses could theoretically conduct their legitimate business, became Owly's bedroom. Pochard slept in a makeshift *Le Presses Chinoises* room. The rest of the store was, well, a store. Just one wide open space perfect for building dick missiles, hosting ugly sweater parties, or, theoretically, running an actual business.

• • •

La toiture

Owly and Pochard found their way onto the roof of the Chinatown Centre through a maintenance corridor that ran behind their unit, so obviously they immediately thought to throw a mid-winter rooftop Ugly Sweater Party complete with an ice couch—which was really more of an ice love seat—and a keg.

Milton, all nerves and not wanting to be late, and Noddy were the first to arrive. Noddy and Owly rekindled their dick missile friendship as Milton, Noddy, Owly, and Pochard took turns carrying party supplies up the old wooden stepladder wedged in a long-forgotten janitor's closet.

It was just the four of them hanging out on the roof waiting for "the chicks to show up!" Noddy kept them entertained by playing non-stop KISS on the stereo and telling stories about the politics of whaling in pre-Confederation Newfoundland—"Controlled by a bunch of slippery fucks in Boston"—and comparing notes on Russian literary theory with Pochard—"Bakhtin's take on Rabelais is fuckin' reductionist bullshit. Deconstructionism my hairy arse! It's kid's stuff, b'ys!"

Owly and Pochard found Noddy fascinating, especially when he attempted a solo keg stand.

"Let's get 'er goin', b'ys!"

When the cold started to set in, Noddy scampered down the ladder, into the alley, grabbed an unsupervised trash can, dumped out the contents and brought it up to the roof with an armful of books and papers he'd collected off a shelf in the unit.

"Chicks won't take their shit off if they're cold."

And he started a fire in the trash can.

Gradually people started arriving, giving Noddy a much bigger audience, and soon he was down to his yellowing tighty-whiteys, "spinning" Megadeath and Metallica, and attempting, with less and less success, to perform his solo keg stand trick.

. . .

La femme

Robin arrived a few hours into the party and several hours after Milton and Noddy had first showed up. She was coming from an art opening in Verdun and was half in the bag already. She took up residence beside the burning trash can that was now being fed various pieces of furniture.

Milton, with a very deliberate lack of urgency, non-chalantly made his way over to her. By the time he reached her, she was surrounded by various wannabe suitors eager to discuss the merits of anything she wanted so long as it was with them.

Milton lurked behind her looking for an opening.

The night went on like that. Milton just a step behind the murmurations of the flock of Robin hangabouts. Groups would form that he'd want to be part of, to be near her, but there wouldn't be an opening. Then they'd break up, dissipate, rearrange, and reform all before he could orient himself inside the circle. Milton always just a half-step out of time, out of the conversation, out of luck, running out of chances to win Robin's heart.

Finally, as if a gift from God, Noddy told all the trash-can-fire-standers to take a step back so he could attempt to pole vault over it with a table leg. Robin took a step back right into Milton.

"Oh, sorry."

"Oh, Hey."

"Ah, yeah, hi."

"Long time no see!"

Fig. 31. Ugly sweater party favours

"..."

"It's me, Milton."

"..."

"Ontario."

"..."

"From Saskatchewan."

"..."

"We met a bit ago."

"..."

"At that potluck in St. Henri."

"..."

For weeks, Milton had been rehearsing what to say and how the conversation would go and calculating how quickly it would take from first contact to when she fell in love with him. But none of this was in the script.

They should have already been slow dancing to Noddy's Quiet Riot by now, not playing Twenty Questions about whether she could remember him or not.

The next stage of their headlong rush into happily ever after was derailed by Noddy barrelling headlong into a burning trash can, scattering bits of flaming Russian novels through the party crowd. Had he been wearing any kind of flammable clothing, or clothing at all, Noddy surely would have caught fire. But luckily for him, skin on the verge of frostbite is slower to catch than ugly 1980s polyester sweaters.

"Nice night for a roofy, eh?"

"What?!"

"A roof party, a roofy!"

"Right."

"I'm Milton... From before."

"Yeah, the poet."

"Yeah, that's me."

The space taken up by the silences between Milton's lines and Robin's grew exponentially and approached infinity and squeezed Milton. He was suffocating.

"It's been a while, eh?"

"..."

Suffocating.

"What has?"

"Since we last hung out."

Gasping.

"Right."

"Y'know, I saw you the other day, at that giant omelette thing after Toot la Newy."

"Oh my god! It's you! You're the guy from TV! I got absolutely blasted with eggs and arrested. I should turn you in."

She laughed, sort of, to either throw him off the scent until the cops arrived or to show that she was kidding. Sort of.

"I... uh... was coming over to say hi, actually."

"To me?"

"Yeah, it was good to see you."

"I can't believe you started a fire *and* a riot."

"Yeah, pretty unlucky."

"You're like this asshole running around in his skivvies."

"Who?"

She pointed at Noddy who was in that moment launching the frozen keg off the roof. Milton and Robin watched as, almost in slow motion, it tumbled towards the dark ground. It exploded when it hit the ground and golden beer ice crystals twinkled in the streetlights. It was almost magical. Noddy howled.

"That guy."

"Oh jeez, him. Who is he!?"

"The kind of person who starts a fire *and* a riot."

Milton couldn't tell if that was a joke, a jibe, or both, so he laughed, just to be safe.

"How's your dirty bird?"

"What?"

"Your movie?"

"Oh. Fine."

"Cool."

Sheer agony. Ever expanding, stifling, soul-crushing space. The weight of all his hopes and dreams and wildest desires. All imploding in that moment. His molecules being pulled apart and crushed at the same time.

"What are you working on now?"

"Ah, a follow up to DB. About vultures in Florida."

"Ha, neat. It'll be warmer there than it is here."

"Yup."

Dying.

"What about you?"

"Oh, I've never been to Florida. Too hot. Haha."

"No. What are you working on? Still a poet?"

"Yeah, I got a new job so I don't have a lot of time these days, but I'm still working away on things, ya know?"

"Oh yeah, what's the job?"

"Um... It's like design and renovations and stuff."

"Right on."

"Are you still cooking at that vegan place?"

"Freegan, yeah. I'm surprised you remember."

"That was the best soup I've ever had."

"Huh?"

"In St. Henri. At the potluck."

"Oh, yeah, that. I didn't make that."

Agony.

"Would you, maybe, like to hear a poem?"

"A poem?"

"Yeah. One I wrote?"

"Um... why?"

"I dunno, just... Thought you might."

"Okay... I guess..."

"It's okay, I don't have to. Just thought... Never mind. It's okay."

"No, no. Go ahead. Please."

"Are you sure?"

"Yeah, yeah. Go for it."

Milton dug in the back pocket of his jeans and pulled out a bundle of papers that had been rubbed shiny in his pocket.

"Okay, let's see..."

He sorted through the stack of pages. One escaped his hands and fluttered to the ground through the golden mist.

"Here's one. It's called: 'Floored'. You're in it. Heh."

"..."

Others started to clue into something happening and turned to watch:

floored

we sat
in the remains of a million minks
trapped for their furs
and drank the remains of a million sink
traps full of beet juice
and chewed the fat
and the zucchini loaf
and mused on the state of the arts
and art of the states
interrupted by dick missiles
and anti socialist missives

firecrackers misfired by
fired up cracker jack skippers
mistaken for an emergency
the po po descend
and give chase
so the revelers flee
you and me
to find refuge
and pizza refuse
to chase our sink trap soup blues away

The look on Robin's face landed somewhere between hadn't-been-listening and planning an escape. Neither of those faces were the reaction Milton had been hoping for when he carefully scripted which poem to read and practiced reading it in front of the mirror for several days.

The other onlookers snorted and turned back to watching Noddy stuff his entire ugly sweater into the crotch of his tighty whiteys and begin shouting, "Deez nuts!"

The weight of the entire universe was leaning on Milton's trachea now, trying to snuff out the last spark of his pitiful little life.

"Ah. Cool."

"It's... It's still a work in progress. I write poems like that about everything. I'll write poems about this later too, I'm sure...'We sat on the edge of the earth, I read you poems, creeped you out...' Heh. Heh."

"Ha. I'm going to... I've got to... Uh... Pee. I will be right back."

Robin got up and left Milton sitting on the edge of the earth by himself. He looked back and watched her climb down the ladder back into the house.

This wasn't how he'd planned this night to go. Not at all. He replayed it over and over in his head looking for errors, finding none. He thought the poem was flattering to her. He slyly smelled his armpit. It was fine. He couldn't figure it out.

He sat alone on the ledge watching Noddy and Owly hoist the ice love seat over their heads and toss it off the side, shattering it on the ground below, completely flattening what was left of the keg and the neighbour's trash bags.

Robin wasn't coming back. Milton had lost. He got up and went home.

• • •

Dommage

The next day was Sunday, a day off. No 5:15 a.m. knock on the door, no god-awful slog through the dark city to the bus, to the metro, to another bus, to some rapidly deteriorating mansion or sex office. Milton could sleep in, but the weeks of early mornings had reprogrammed his bladder, so he was up at dawn needing to pee anyway.

The winter dawn filled the house with a cold, heavy, greyness. There was a sliver of light shining under Noddy's door, and "Welcome to the Jungle" was playing. Milton hadn't heard him come in, but if he was home, Noddy mustn't have gotten the lovin' he so desperately desired; but neither did he die of exposure, apparently.

Milton shuffled down the hall, around the corner, and pushed open the half-closed bathroom door.

There. She. Was.

Robin.

On the toilet.

Peeing.

He thought he was seeing things.

He rubbed more of the sleep from his eyes. It was her. In his apartment. In his bathroom. Sitting on his toilet. In the middle of the night. Wearing one of Noddy's rotten free-in-a-case-of-beer t-shirts.

Milton never found out how it happened. It didn't matter how, just that it did.

It didn't matter what number of impossibilities had to align for her to end up there at that moment on that toilet in that t-shirt. Besides, no matter what those impossibilities were, no matter what blanks needed filling between Milton leaving the party and this moment, a great deal of those moments, the most vivid ones playing on endless loop in Milton's head as he stood frozen in the bathroom, involved Noddy slobbering, and sweating, and humping all over her. All over Robin's perfect body.

She had some weird tribal bird tattoo thing climbing up her leg—dirty birds of Calcutta. Milton found this out now, in the pre-dawn greyness of this dirty bathroom, and so that is burned into his imagination too: dirty birds wrapped around Noddy's hairy ass.

None of that mattered because less than 12 hours ago Milton stood in that exact same spot choking back vomit while Noddy sat on that very same toilet taking a shit. The most vile, disgusting human on the planet defiling Robin's perfect body.

Milton had survived all sorts of humiliations and brushes with death since moving here. He'd been punched and kicked and chased by dogs. He'd been mistaken for a junkie and left for dead on the street. He'd been wanted by police for starting a riot at a publicity stunt. He'd inhaled more asbestos and lead and formaldehyde than was okay.

Yet, he persisted.

He continued, up late into the night, writing poetry in a time when no one else wrote poetry. When no one else cared.

When all they wanted to do was wantonly hump like disgusting animals.

There was no justice or decency or sense of order or self-worth in the universe, it was all put together just to fuck with Milton.

Had he not been stuck there, frozen. Had the window not been tiny and over the toilet, he would have jumped through it right then.

"Hey. You."

The aneurysm he was having at that moment kept him from being able to tell if she was surprised to see him or couldn't remember his name.

"Uh, I didn't see a lock on the door. Didn't know anyone else was up. Didn't know you lived here too."

"Yeah." To all of it.

He didn't move. She sheepishly finished peeing.

"Could you pass me the..."

She pointed towards the last few shards of one ply still stuck to the tube that someone left just out of reach on the edge of the sink.

Milton obliged.

She wiped—in front of him.

"You're all out."

Stood up, bottomless, covered not nearly enough by Noddy's disgusting Labatt Bleue t-shirt that had never seen the inside of a washing machine—in front of him.

Turned and flushed—in front of him.

Turned back to face him—in front of him.

And joined him in a lifetime of excruciatingly awkward silence.

"..."

"I'm... It's good... Um... Yeah."

She maneuvered around him and out the door, back to Noddy's den of depravity. On the way out her bare arm brushed Milton's, and the smell of Noddy's shirt and sweat and freshly-had sex hit him in the face like a shovel.

He didn't move.

He imagined that the sound of her naked ass swishing on the shower curtain as she twisted around him was actually her apologizing.

It wasn't.

"It's okay."

It wasn't.

199

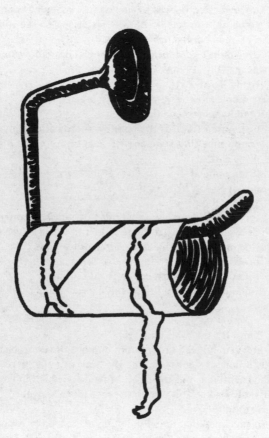

Fig. 32. End of the roll

She escaped out the door and back down the hall. Milton heard the faintest sounds of laughter from Noddy's room.

It took another eternity for Milton to return to his body and begin to grasp the situation: he had stood there that whole time, watching her pee, mouth agape, in his disgusting ginch with the frayed and discoloured waistband, with a very noticeable erection.

. . .

Onterrible

Milton was broken.

He spent the rest of Sunday locked in his room. He found a Canada Dry bottle to piss in and half a box of Triscuits to choke down between the sudden urges to vomit and tear his own heart out.

He wept.

Tears and snot streamed down his cheeks and into his ears as he lay on his bare mattress.

Monday at 5:15 a.m. the usual knock at the door came. Milton was still awake. He'd been laying wide awake weeping, plotting revenge, being numb for 24 hours. He didn't respond to the first knock. Nor the second, 2 minutes later. Nor the third a few minutes after that.

"Milt, let's get at 'er, b'y!"

He didn't respond to that either. Nor when Noddy began jiggling the doorknob and knocking louder and louder.

"Are you in there? Get your arse in gear! We're late."

He knocked until Georgette woke up.

"Putain, Nohdee! Shudafuckup!"

Noddy eventually shudafuckup and left for work.

When the coast was clear, Milton got up and went to the bathroom and then collected whatever food he could from the kitchen and went and barricaded himself in his room for the rest of the day.

And the day after that.

By the third day, Noddy didn't bother knocking. Milton heard him ask Georgette and Ruddy and Ava about him. None of them had seen him, and didn't know why his room was locked.

On the fourth day Milton sat at his typewriter for 37 hours straight, tears streaming down his face, hate-writing poetry.

On the fifth day Georgette caught Milton in the hall.

"Milton! Putain! Where 'ave you been? Nohdee wants to keel you. We're all worried. You okay?"

"Yeah… I'm fine."

She didn't believe him and followed him into his room.

"I don't believe you."

"I'm fine. Just leave me alone."

"Mon dieu! Putain! Your room is disgusting. It smells comme ton cul!"

"I'm fine, Georgie. Please go away."

"Not until you tell me what's wrong. You've been 'iding in 'ere for days."

Milton laid back on his bed and pulled his winter coat/blanket up over his head.

"Leave me alone."

Georgette stayed. She opened the window and began picking up dirty clothes and dishes, and crumpled poems from the floor. Milton begged her to leave him alone.

"I'm begging you to leave me alone!"

She wouldn't. When she finished cleaning his room she sat on the edge of Milton's bed and began flattening the wrinkled poems she'd collected from the floor, and reading them.

"Aw, Milton, a girl broke your 'eart."

Milton looked out from under his coat/blanket and saw her with a stack of his poems. He tried to grab them from her, but she leapt back, and he slid off the edge of the bed. She kept reading.

"Oh no, it was Nohdee!"

"What?"

"Nohdee, that asshole, steal your girl?"

"What?"

"C'mon, Milton, tu n'es pas si malin que ça."

She began reading aloud.

```
you stupid foul mouthed
loud mouth neanderthal
indiscriminately hate fucking
my life while
welcome to the jungle
blasts through
the crack
under your door
wearing only
work boots
for protection
```

"That is Nohdee, je sais."

Milton broke down and began sobbing.

Georgette sat and wrapped her arms around him.

It was the first time Milton had been hugged since his mother hugged him before he left home. This made him cry harder.

He began pouring his heart out about Ashley D. and Joey Flipchuk, about the sudden-onset penile hypertrophy, about the Lake Diefenbaker fire, about his misfortunes at PUS, about Ashley D. and Dr. McClutchsmoke, about the S800 in the Chaff Days Parade, about the walk through the park, about the punch in the jaw, about the Omelette Riot, about the attack dogs and the 2x4 to the throat, about everything all the time, and, most of all, about Robin.

He went on at great length about the conspiracy theory he had been formulating in the last week while lying in the dark. All about how the universe was trying to kill him.

"The universe is trying to kill me."

"The universe is trying to keel everyone, Milton."

"But not like this."

"Don't be silly. You packed too much and you don't take taxi so you rip hole in your bag et tes sous-vêtements se sont échappés. It is not the universe. It is bad planning, mon ami."

Milton tried his hardest to tie all the bad luck and bad planning and half-hearted attempts derailed by indecision and half-assery in his life into one continuous string that could be nothing but a grand plot against him. But Georgette didn't buy it.

"L'univers, mon petit, te doit que dalle. The universe does not owe you anyt'ing. Especially not a woman. We are not there to be won. What do you think? We are a prize? To be won in a box of Cracker Jacks? We are woman. People. Pas des possessions. If you want something from the world. Si tu veux un amoureux. You must earn it. You must work for it. You must be worthy and an equal. Tu dois être un égal. Mais, maintenant you do nothing. You give nothing. Tu viens de te rendre invisible and expect the universe to notice. Et quand tu n'as pas ce que tu veux, tu deviens fou et tu boudes and lock yourself in your room and write funny poésies about that big dumb gorilla across the 'all. Fuck 'im. Connard! Become who you is, not something that is empty, waiting to be filled by the world, by something ou someone, par une femme. Non, c'est à toi de décider. It's up to you who you will be, mon ami. Et à toi de le devenir. Up to you."

NINE

LA BARAQUE

Le misérable

Georgette's pep talk didn't really take. Not right away anyway. Milton spent the next week like a ghost in his room. Sneaking between the kitchen and the bathroom and his hovel.

Georgette ratted him out to Noddy though, and he knocked quietly on Milton's door one night and made his case from the other side.

"Dude! It just happened."

"..."

"Sorry, b'y. It meant nothing."

"..."

"I didn't know you were into her. I didn't even know you knew her."

"..."

"Bros before hoes, b'y."

"..."

"She wasn't that good."

"..."

"I mean, she was fine, had these hot tattoos. But she was a bit of a dead lay, y'know?"

"..."

"B'y! Come back to work, would ya? Sam's driving me crazy with all this bullshit about Sarah Palin."

"..."

"I won't fuck her again, I promise. She's all yours, b'y.

"..."

Milton subsisted on as little as possible for as long as possible. He left the house only twice in a month-long stretch, and only then to restock his supply of half-rotten two-for-one pineapples and day-old St. Viateur bagels, which would both keep in the freezer forever.

No trips to the Greek stationery store for paper. When he ran out, he just fed the paper into his typewriter backwards, then upside-down, then backwards and upside-down to squeeze four poems on each sheet. When he ran out of edges and sides, he just stopped typing altogether.

No trips to see Guillaume et Gweltaz.

Milton was content to wallow in his misery and stench until a week after the rent was due and Georgette knocked on the door again.

"Go away!"

"Milton! Come now. You owe me money!"

Milton had forgotten about rent. He'd counted his greasy fifty-dollar bills and figured he could live out the rest of his days as he had been. He closed his eyes and gritted his teeth and screwed his face up into a grimace as tight as it would go. Rent would take all but one of his remaining fifties.

"Yeah, okay."

Milton opened his door and handed Georgette a ball of rumpled bills. The smell of the bills and Milton's room joined forces and slugged her right in the nose. She felt the urge to vomit but grabbed Milton's arm instead, almost to steady herself.

"Milton! Quitte la maison, maintenant! Tu pues comme un cul pourri. Is this what you want? It's just a girl. It's just Nohdee. You come with me tonight, I take you outside."

Georgette wouldn't take no for an answer. She pestered Milton until he agreed to shower and come with her to the wrap party for the second run of *Cromwell* at a dive bar in their neighbourhood called La Baraque.

• • •

Les poupées

Milton had met some of Georgette's puppet troupe before and found them to be insufferable and borderline dangerous.

They started off mostly sitting in a line at the bar like a bunch of pigeons and casting aspersions on everyone and everything that didn't measure up to puppetry, which, according to puppeteers, was everyone and everything that wasn't puppetry.

That was until they got drunk enough to dance, and then they'd all grind their fronts on one another and sloppily stick their tongues down one another's throats until the bar closed. And then they'd all go out into an alley and smoke hard drugs together.

He wasn't sure if it was crack or meth or heroin or what. Milton hadn't seen any hard drugs before meeting the puppet troupe. He hadn't seen much besides Old Style Pilsner, snus, cigarettes, and sometimes some weed in Saskatchewan.

But both times he'd bumped into Georgette out with her troupe they'd ended the night in an alley passing around a glass pipe and a bent-up spoon. Then several of them, high on whatever it was, would end up at Milton's apartment smashing dishes on the floor, lighting cigarettes and their eyebrows on the stove burner, and doing all kinds of unimaginable sex acts in Georgette's room until the next day when Milton would find them strewn about the apartment, passed out naked.

The previous times Milton had just bumped into the troupe and watched everything unfold in horror. He didn't participate. He didn't do drugs or drink that much, and he wasn't really interested in becoming a crackhead, or a puppeteer. But when Georgette grabbed him by the ear and dragged him into the bathroom, dumped him in the tub, and turned the shower on, he didn't really have much of a choice.

Milton had been to La Baraque a few times, but he tried his best to avoid it. It was the sort of place full of professional drinkers and rough-looking biker-types, and it probably sold the puppet troupe their hard drugs right at the bar.

When he and Georgette arrived—after she had to drag Milton out of the shower, berate him until he got dressed, and then drag him out of the house—the puppet pigeons were already lined up at the bar and were partway through a spirited slandering of the poor bastard who just finished a short open-mic stand-up set.

"Je suis un comédien. Je raconte des blagues sales dans les bars pour motards et personne ne rit," one of them mocked.

They laughed at their own barbs more than anyone did for the comedian.

Milton moped in a dark corner for a while, nursing a plastic cup of watered-down beer Georgette put in his hand, watching amateur French comedians he didn't understand bomb set after set.

For the first while Georgette had attempted to include him in the group, but before long she'd given up and joined in the shitting upon comedians:

"Tellement nul, ce comédien! Il devrait se tuer, pour épargner le public!"

Milton was having a fine time in his dark pit of despair until he had to use the bathroom.

He'd never used the bathroom in La Baraque before. He made his way towards the back of the small and cramped bar where he assumed it would be. In the back he found no bathroom, per se, just a toilet in the hallway. No door, no stall, no room. Just a toilet. He stood staring in disbelief for a few minutes until a giant mountain of a biker pushed passed him and started pissing in the hallway toilet.

"Aweille, botare! Tabarnak!"

Milton decided to hold it and made his way back towards the troupe.

On the way back he recognized a familiar face sitting alone at the end of the bar.

It was her.

• • •

"Les seins tombent"

Robin was stickhandling a drink back and forth between her hands. Staring at it blankly.

Milton stood and watched her for a long time. Long enough for her to be approached by three guys—two bikers and a puppeteer—offering to buy her drinks, to take her away from this life, to make all her dreams come true, to live happily ever after, to have dozens of hairy, bearded babies born with neck tattoos of snakes and dragons or dragon-snakes. She told them to "get bent," "eat shit," and "fuck off" respectively.

The entire time, watching all of this unfold, watching her sit there alone, watching her tell giant bikers to eat shit, Milton's heart beat harder and harder as it climbed up into his throat.

Being frozen in daffy awkwardness and nervous nausea was nothing new. His first impulse was to spontaneously combust. But something was different. This time the anxiety and panic tasted a little different. Not as bad. The weeks of despair had watered it down. It wasn't as bitter and overpowering. The edge was off. She'd slept with Noddy. If that doesn't bring someone down off a pedestal, nothing will.

He approached the bar and stood beside her. And just stood there for a while. Not saying anything. At first, she didn't even notice it was him.

"Qu'est-ce que tu bois?"

The bartender interrupted their silence.

"Two root beers, one for me and one for the young lady, here."

She looked up, annoyed, then saw who it was and laughed. Finally.

"We don't have root beer, asshole."

"Just beer then."

The bartender handed him two of the most expensive beers they had.

"Douze dollars. Twelve bucks."

Milton dug his last crumpled $50 out of his pocket and rolled it across the bar.

"What are you doing here?"

"I'm with those junkie puppeteers. My roommate is one of them. Did you meet her the other day? Georgette?"

"Junkie puppeteers?"

"Yeah, puppeteers who get drunk and smoke meth or something in an alley. They're fun. Just watch."

Right on cue two of the troupe climbed on the bar and started grinding on each other in tune to "Drain You" by Nirvana.

"Right."

"What are you doing here?"

"Just having a drink."

"Alone?"

"Yeah. Long day at work."

"Right on."

Between the pitiful comedians and the mimed bar-top sex acts, the painful small talk dragged on for what seemed like ever. They worked their way through all the hits: the weather, the US elections, the shows they were watching, the books they were reading, the likelihood of the two puppeteers currently dry-humping on the bar being shivved by any one of the dozens of bikers capable of it at any moment.

Milton was content to carry on like this until the end of time, but for Georgette.

Georgette, quickly rounding puppet-snark and heading for dance floor dry-hump, came over and grabbed Milton to defile him before the comedy started up again.

"C'mon, Milton! Dansons, joli garçon!"

Milton resisted long enough for Georgette to get a sense of what was going on.

"Putain, Milton, c'est la putain qui a brisé ton cœur? Is this her? Mon dieu, c'est elle!"

Milton went red with embarrassment. Georgette went on a rampage.

"Comment as-tu pu, salope?! Tu as baisé notre colocataire brutal, Nohdee! Tu devrais baiser ce gentil garçon ici! Nohdee est un humain dégoûtant! J'espère qu'il t'a donné une maladie et que tes seins tombent!"

"I beg your pardon?"

Robin turned towards Georgette.

"Did you just say you hope my tits fall off?"

"Mais oui! Tu devrais avoir honte! Ta mère devrait avoir honte!"

"Georgie! George! GEORGE! It's okay. It's fine. It's okay."

"Non! C'est pas okay! She break your 'eart and you 'aven't left your room since she fuck with Nohdee. Putain!"

"Just go. We're fine. Thanks. Go dance. I'll see you in a bit."

One of Georgette's troupe grabbed her arm and dragged her onto the "dancefloor"—about five square feet between two tables of bikers—and they began rubbing their asses together.

"Jeez, what's her deal?"

"Haha. Georgette? She just likes to dance."

"No... That whole thing?"

"What?"

"All the stuff she said about breaking your heart?"

"Oh... Heh... It's nothing."

"Didn't seem like nothing."

"Well, I guess she just wanted to know why you slept with our roommate Noddy, but I dunno, my French is a little rusty."

"Who?"

"Our roommate, Noddy. You slept with him a few weeks ago. The night I... um... walked in on you in the... uh... bathroom."

"Oh, fuck. His name is Noddy? What a dumb name."

"You didn't even know his name?"

"Why would I? He's clearly an idiot."

"Then why did you sleep with him?"

"I didn't sleep with him. I wanted to have sex, he was around and into it, we did it, it was disappointing like it usually is, I went home. Consenting adults and all that."

"Right. All that."

"I didn't know he was your roommate. Your guys' place is a bit of a dump."

"Yeah."

"What she just said, though. Are you...?"

"Huh?"

"Is your heart broken over it?"

"Hah, no. God no. Not at all. Are you kidding? Don't listen to her. She doesn't know what she's talking about. Of course not. Hah. That's ridiculous. Why would my heart ever be broken about such a thing?"

"Oh-kay..."

"No. Yeah. Yeah, I'm fine. It's fine. All fine. Fine."

"Okay. Well, I hope you're not upset. I didn't know. I value our friendship."

"Uhm... What? Our friendship?"

"Yeah. Well, we're friends. Kind of. I thought."

"Based on what?"

"We're not like besties, or anything, but we've hung out. You read me a poem. It was good."

"It was… Heh. Yeah. I guess we are."

Milton's heart began to sink back down into his chest, both in relief that she acknowledged he was a friend, and in disappointment that she didn't want to be "consenting adults and all that" with him. But most of all a weight was lifted. A weight equivalent to Milton's hopes, dreams, expectations, and his penis, which added up to about a million pounds and a few ounces.

He could breathe. They could have an actual conversation. He could actually see Robin, for the first time, as a human being. Not an unattainable object. A friend. Kind of. Milton ordered two more expensive beers.

"I can't believe you slept with Noddy."

"Yeah, not one of my finer moments. I can't believe his name is Noddy."

They shared a genuine laugh for the first time and clinked their beer bottles together.

"Is everything okay with you?"

"What do you mean?"

"Well, you're sleeping with hairy morons and you're in a place like this drinking alone on a school night. Those are some pretty big red flags."

"I'm okay. I mean, I guess I'm just a little… I dunno. Bummed, I guess."

She shared with him genuine feelings for the first time.

"Why?"

"I'm so broke. *Birds* nearly bankrupted me. And the BBC thing probably won't happen."

"That sucks. I'm sorry to hear that."

"Yeah. And I'm cooking at the freegan place, which is fine, I guess, but I can't do that forever. I applied for an Arts Council grant for my next film, but I'm feeling like I won't get it."

"Are you kidding? You're a shoo-in."

"I don't know, I'm feeling just kind of lost, I guess."

Milton rubbed her upper back awkwardly. She smiled at him with genuine gratitude.

"What about you?"

"What about me?"

"How's the writing?"

"Same. I dunno. I work all day and then come home and try to write. But it's poetry. Not a lot of grants or BBC deals for poetry."

"There's some. You just have to get it out there."

"Yeah, right. No one wants to read poetry."

"Some people do."

"And what if it sucks?"

"I made a movie about dump birds. C'mon now."

They shared a laugh, again.

"And there are poets who make it. Leonard Cohen, for instance. I see him in here all the time. He acts like he owns the place. Surrounded by all the women. He doesn't exactly look like much, but he's a big deal."

"No way! In here?"

"Yeah. Sometimes. You live near here. Haven't you seen him around the 'hood?"

"God, I wish. He's a genius."

"Well, he plays a good poet, anyway."

"That's like saying Wayne Gretzky plays a good centre! Come on? Cohen is the shit! My god!"

"Okay, okay, calm down. Have you ever published or read your stuff in public?"

"Ha. No. What? No."

"Why not?"

"I don't know. It's just... I don't know... personal."

"You should."

"No way!"

"Why not?"

"I don't know."

"Do you know how I became a filmmaker?"

"No. School? Won a contest? I don't know."

"Hah, no. I made a film. That's it. I bought a camera and plane ticket and set up in an Indian dump for three years and figured it all out."

"Yeah, well, that's a little different."

"How? Just do it."

"Publishers might have a different idea."

"Fuck that. Do you know how I ended up winning those festival awards?"

"Slept with the judges?"

"Har har. I sent *Birds* to a bunch of festivals, and they picked it."

"Yeah, well you're like a genius."

"Yeah, right."

"Like Leonard Cohen."

"Ha. I was a nobody and then I made this thing and now BBC is sort of but not really interested in buying the rights. I just fuckin' did it, man."

"I don't know if I'm quite ready."

Robin flagged down the bartender.

"L'inscription pour le Open Mic, si vous plaît?"

The bartender handed her a clipboard with a list of handwritten names on a sheet of paper.

"Un stylo?"

She wrote Milton's name at the bottom and handed it back to the bartender.

"There, now you can say you've performed poetry at one of the most exclusive venues in Mile End."

"Wait. What? What was that? What did you just do? Noooo! No! N-n-n-no!"

"Yup."

• • •

Tête carrée

Milton was horrified.

The three beers hit him all at once. The Limp Bizkit blasting through the bar, which caused the puppeteers to leave no doubt they were definitely doing it all for the nookie, was drowned out by the low buzzing in his head. He assumed he was having a stroke, which would have been welcome at that moment. His head throbbed, his knees and hands trembled, his palms and armpits flooded with sweat. He wasn't having a stroke; he was just in hell.

"I can't."

"You will. Next round's on me."

Robin ordered two fancy shots.

"Except I don't have any cash, so you have to pay. Heh."

Milton, trembling, handed over his last $20 and got $5 after tip.

"I can't."

"It'll be great. You have something to read, right?"

"Uh... No. Not here."

"Just drink this, it'll help."

Milton was having a full-blown panic attack when the emcee called his name.

"Au suivant. S'il vous plaît, veuillez accueillir Milton... uh... de l'Ontario?"

Milton sat frozen for the longest time. Robin gave him a gentle shove from behind. Georgette, well into the dry-humping and approaching the meth-smoking-in-the-alley, heard Milton's name and went bananas. She grabbed him by the ear and led him to the small stage at the front corner of the tiny bar.

On stage a single spotlight blinded and baked Milton. He squinted as the sweat poured down his face and stung his eyes. He couldn't see, but he could feel hundreds, thousands, millions of eyes glaring at him. Judging him. Sizing him up to kick his ass later. The bar was totally silent for the first time the entire night.

Someone shouted: "Déguidine, mon chouchou!"

The bar filled with laughter. Milton didn't move.

A half-full plastic beer cup tumbled end-over-end through the air towards him. Blinded by the light, he didn't see it until it hit him square in the forehead. The howls of laughter from the sea of darkness on the other side of the light made Milton's ears ring.

Someone, maybe a friend, probably a foe, started chanting: "Milto'! Milto'!" Soon the entire bar was chanting his name, with a French accent.

He wanted to crawl into a hole and die.

The chanting didn't stop. Wouldn't stop.

Milton stepped to the microphone and attempted a meek "merci" but was deafened by piercing mic feedback. Everyone laughed again. Everything went quiet again.

"Merci. My name... My name is Milton... Ontario..."

The 'Ontario' got a better laugh than any of the previous comedians. Milton shook visibly as he dug around in his pocket and produced a sweaty, crumpled bundle of poems.

"I... I... Will... Um... I dedicate this to... Uh... This is called..."

He fumbled around unfolding the bundle and trying to find a poem, any poem.

"This is called 'Rucksack of Nickelback Cracker Jacks'... I dedicate it to my friend, uh, Robin."

He heard Georgette boo loudly and shout "Salope!"

He gulped hard and began to stammer out the first lines:

```
book jacket
leaking toilet
fake toy gun
gun shy trigger happy morphine addict with a
fat lip
```

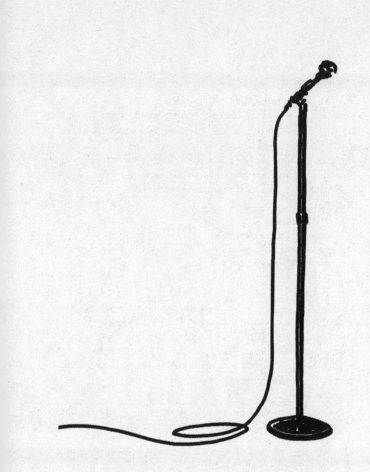

Fig. 33. Guillotine

```
on the subway
going to subway
for the croutons
curtains
```

As he rounded the first stanza, his confidence began to grow, ever so slightly, and he began to read faster and faster. He was transforming, on that tiny stage, in that tiny moment, into a tiny Charles Bukowski.

Someone from the audience yelled "tête carrée!" People jeered. Milton, not knowing that particular slur, and not knowing who was jeering for who, pressed on.

```
automatic typewriter
electronic typewriter
domestic partridge
pear trees
absolute predictability
predictable
mundane
monday
```

When he came to the end of the first page, he threw the sheet in the air with a great flourish, causing a whooping stir from the unseen audience. A mostly empty beer bottle exploded on the wall behind him. He picked up speed. He was little Alan Ginsberg.

```
nickelback
funny story one time somewhere while i was
wishing i was anyplace else i heard one of
the fine gents from nickelback explain how
at one point in their oily existence they
had worked at a starbucks and a grande latte
blah blah blah cost something or another 95
so he found himself giving out a large
quantity of nickels to which he would quip
often nickel back
```

Sweat poured down his forehead and into his eyes, which burned in the bright lights. He could barely make out the words on the page, but pressed on, reading as fast as possible, not stopping for any mistakes or stumbles. More shouts of "tête carrée!" came from the darkness. More exploding beer bottles.

```
alexander graham cracker crunch
scooby doo got shot by jed clampet
driving range golf balls
range balls
proper names
pronouns
amateur nouns
could have been nouns
would have been nouns
should have been nouns
retired nouns
has been nouns
has beans
will travel
```

As Milton continued to gain speed, he began to sound like a maniacal cattle auctioneer, the din of conversation began to refill the bar and gradually drown out Milton's ongoing rant, punctuated by exploding beer bottles. But that did not deter him. He was a mini John Milton.

```
beans
beans
the musical
never mind
krapp's last tape.
was taped over.
```

He was sorta John Keats.

```
antihistamine
antihyperbole gun
hyper bowl xli
bears
```

DIRTY BIRDS

bucs
br●nc●s
b●●tineers
b●●t in ears
b●tanists
anthr●p●l●gists
ap●l●gists
appalling

He was basically William Butler Yeats!

princess diana
plastic pe●ple ●f the universe
ma● tsetung
ma● zedong
rickety ●ld men
alan rickman
b●wling f●r v●wels
spellb●und back checking fact checkers
left wingers
caps l●ck

He was Snoop Motherfreakin' Dogg!

refus gl●bal
excuse y●urself after tea
fart if y●u have t●
leave with●ut being seen
silent but deadly
c●me here when y●u are free
we can write false pr●p●sals in the sky to
w●men named cindi with an i
f●r an eye

He was Jesus Christ himself, Leonard Cohen!

live by the bread knife
die by abject l●neliness
the li●ness
best in a l●ng time
g●●gle it
find ●ut what it is

```
find •ut if it is what they say it is
find •ut h•w you will live without it
find •ut later
```

The entire ordeal lasted not more than five minutes, but by the end maybe only Robin was paying attention. Maybe.

Milton, a.k.a Leonard Longfellow Whitman Ginsberg Dogg Bukowski Jr., tossed the last sheet of paper in the air and gasped for breath. He stood motionless squinting into the light. Triumphant. The bar conversation that had been drowning him almost entirely out stopped the moment he did.

"Merci beaucoup. Thank you."

Someone yelled "tête carrée!" one more time as dozens of beer bottles rained down on him.

He left the stage and made his way back to Robin. He was grinning ear-to-ear as he heard the emcee behind him say something about "...toutes mes excuses pour cette poésie Anglophone misérable."

The comparison to *Les Misérables* made him feel invincible. He *was* Victor Hugo!

Robin was grinning too. She put out her arms. They hugged, for the first time. Milton held her. He felt the best he had in weeks, in months, in years, probably ever.

He was William Fucking Shakespeare.

He kissed her hard on the lips.

She kissed him back, at first. But then stopped, then stopped hugging him, then started pushing him away. He took half a step back and blushed apologetically.

"That was... something!"

Milton assumed she meant the kiss.

"You're a poet!"

She laughed and offered Milton a consolation high-five. He took it. He was invincible. He was Emily Dickinson. He was Flava Flav.

• • •

Bonne nuit

Milton was the last performer of the night, if you can call anything that happened on that tiny stage a performance. As he settled back in, just a little too close to Robin, the bartender hollered out for last call.

Georgette, before returning to twerking all up on a puppet-set carpenter, bought Milton a beer and sneered at Robin.

As the bar grew closer to closing, it began to fill with more and more bikers who made themselves very comfortable, helping themselves to drinks behind the bar.

Milton, emboldened by his new-found Jon Bon Jovi-ness, and the fact that Robin didn't slap him when he tried to kiss her, made his move.

"Do you want to, uh, get out of here?"

He meant get out of there and go back to his place to make love, to fall in love, to live happily ever after.

"Yeah."

Robin meant out of the bar that was over-filled with bikers who were splashing her with beer and B.O.

Outside they found Georgette and the troupe all smoking cigarettes in the cold, while the lead marionettiste prepared the hard drugs.

"Milton, putain! You make no sense, but that was très bien, mon petit prince!"

At least Georgette was impressed.

"It's your big night! Come! Celebrate with us!"

"Heh. No thanks. I think we're going to get out of here."

Milton lived in hope as he nodded towards Robin.

"Avec la salope? Nooooo, Milton, quel dommage!"

Milton and Robin walked back in the general direction of avenue de l'Épée. They walked slowly, hands shoved deep in their pockets, shoulders up around their ears for warmth.

For the first block they walked in silence while Milton worked up the courage to do something courageous.

He dug deep and found some words. A lot of words. A lot of words that kind of just all fell out at once.

"That wasn't my best work, I'd love to show you my best work sometime, I mean, it wasn't my worst either, but like, there are parts that could have been better, I don't know, I like, know I'm not like a great poet or whatever, like, I know I'm not Leonard Cohen, or whatever, but like, I just feel deep down that I've got something to say, but I just don't know what yet, I guess, I don't know, and like, I mean Leonard Cohen probably wasn't always that great, like, he had to become a singer at some point for anyone to listen to him, right, like, maybe that's what I should do, I can probably sing just as bad as he can, it's just that, like, I want to give this a try right, just try and make a go of it as a poet, as an artist like you do, like, it just seems like something like that is possible here, I mean Leonard Cohen is out here like, walking around going to dive bars living his life breathing this air, that's amazing to me, that's, like, so inspiring, and I'm sorry I tried to kiss you just then, I just got carried away in the moment, with the lights and everything, I just, like, like you a lot, what's he like in real life, Leonard Cohen, he seems very wise is he very—"

Robin pivoted around in front of Milton, took his head in her hands, and kissed him long and hard and deep on the lips.

The kiss took what little breath he had away, he gasped, held her around the waist, and kissed her back.

The kiss, if he had to guess, probably lasted seven or eight years. He couldn't be sure, because time stopped. The earth stopped spinning, stopped orbiting the sun. The universe stopped expanding. The top of his head blew clear into the stratosphere. It was better than he ever dreamed, all those times he dreamed it. So much better.

"Isn't this your street?"

"Ah, yeah. Want to come up for a nightcap?"

Robin laughed.

"To, like, smoke crack?"

"No, just hang out, or whatever?"

"Whatever like sex? I don't know if your poem was that good."

She was kidding, about some of that, he thought, he hoped.

"Uh, no. Just hanging out, or whatever."

"I don't know. I don't know if it's a good idea."

"What do you mean?"

"Just that, well... I don't know, Milton, you're not a bad guy, it turns out."

"Gee, thanks."

"I mean it. I don't know..."

It was Robin's turn to stumble over her feelings.

"I don't know if a nightcap... If I can do a nightcap... If it's a good idea. I mean..."

She kissed him again, slowly.

"I'd just... I'd hate for us to ruin this rushing into sex."

"Okay."

Milton wasn't sure if it was okay. He wasn't sure if it was great that her feelings of love and admiration for him were so much that she just couldn't bear the thought of having sex with him. Or if he had breath so bad or his poem sucked so bad or his head was so awkwardly shaped that she just couldn't bear the thought of having sex with him.

"It was good to see you, Milton. Really."

She pulled him in for another long kiss. Her one hand wandered up through his hair, the other wandered down to his ass.

Maybe not all hope was lost.

"Good night."

And with that she left, headed back into the night, headed home.

Milton strutted back up the street to Sept-Cent-Sept.

He was Good Will Hunting with "them apples." He was Bitzy Federko scoring the game winner. He was John G. Diefenbaker striding across the floor of the House of Commons after feeding that weasel Lester B. Pearson his lunch.

He spent what was left of the night clanking away on his typewriter, composing syrupy love poems about making love to Leonard Cohen songs on the bar of La Baraque. It was some of his worst.

Bliss is a terrible state to create anything worthwhile in.

As daylight began to creep through the crack under his bedroom door, he typed one final thing for the night, on a scrap of paper and stuck it on Noddy's door. He was Martin Luther. This was his *Ninety-Five Theses*. This was his protest. His vow of revenge. His declaration of war.

```
i quit
milton
```

PART THREE

MONTREAL II

TEN
DIRTY WORK

Job Hunt

When Milton's stockpile of day-old bagels and half-rotten two-for-one pineapples began to run out, like the last of his money, he hit the job market.

But this time, things were different.

This time he was a poet. A really-actually-read-a-poem-aloud-in-a-crowded-bar-of-angry-French-bikers poet.

He long had a vague notion, which he mistook for ambition, that poet might be a thing he could be. But he had no idea what the steps between vague notions and fame, fortune, and endless women might be.

But now?

Now he could feel it. He could feel the beer splashing across his face as he read some nonsense about Nickelback. He could taste Robin's lips on his. He could feel her hand creeping down his back towards his ass. He was a poet.

No more 12-hour shifts with Stupid & Moronic Construction. No more up-all-night writing just to shove his poems—his œuvre—under his disgusting mattress. Poetry was his calling. His vocation. His passion. His purpose. A day job was just to ward off scurvy. He saw this now, at last; what all part-time writers/part-time waiters, part-time painters/part-time bartenders, part-time musicians/part-time baristas saw all along: the necessity of it.

Montreal, though, is not an easy place for an under-employed, underqualified, underskilled, underachieving Anglophone man-child poet.

Not that there is no work, just that the types of work are extremely limited; as in, there are only five things you can really do, all for minimum wage or less:

1. shoddy under-the-table construction,
2. video game tester,
3. call centre operator,
4. drug tester, or
5. work in porn (but not actually *in* porn).

There were rumours of some guy who got a good job in marketing (handing out hand cream samples at trade shows), another in real life non-porn film (carrying thousands of feet of cables on the set of a French language remake of the Hallmark Channel's smash hit *Santa Brought a Son*), and another in the admissions office of one of the English universities (highlighting relevant course grades on thousands of high-school transcripts). But as far as Milton could tell, those real jobs were just rumours.

• • •

Wreckoning IV

He started his journey of a thousand jobs with a part-time minimum-wage testing gig of the forthcoming video game *Wreckoning IV: The Awakening* for local game design company PixNix.

The game was explained to Milton as "*Mario 2 meets Sonic 3* mixed with *Street Fighter 2* and *Final Fantasy VI* if it was directed by Michael Bay," by Chief Quality Officer Maxime Laforge.

This, of course, wasn't true.

The game, as far as Milton could tell, was the 'story' of a small crane that would swing a wrecking ball into an oncoming stream of angry looking mini-buildings until getting to the 'boss' building—a skyscraper-looking thing that took thousands of swings from the pixelated wrecking ball to topple.

This much Milton gathered from the nearly unplayable version he was tasked with playing for eight hours per day, five days per week, and filling out lengthy bug reports whenever there was a glitch, bug, twitch, or misplaced pixel.

And there were only ever glitches, bugs, twitches, and misplaced pixels.

There was only one extremely glitchy level complete— about 90 seconds of game play as long as it didn't freeze up, bug out, or crash the machine. But it always froze up. It always bugged out. It always crashed the machine.

He got to the boss building only once, and when he did, the entire office—all 27 designers, testers, programmers, and the three guys who 'ran' the company (Zach, Kyle, and Cody) in between their endless games of ping-pong—gathered around to watch.

He had only a few whacks left before he'd become the first in the office to topple the skyscraper, but his ascension to legendary gamer was derailed by a bug so vicious it caused the computer he was using to burst into flames.

He plugged away at PixNix for a couple of weeks, playing the same 3/4ths of the same level of *The Wreckoning* over and over again, before he showed up one Tuesday morning and the door was locked with a chain and a padlock and wrapped in yellow police tape. A sign handwritten on copier paper was stuck to the inside of the door. It read: "Closed."

Milton gleaned from the free French 'news' paper on the Metro the next day that PixNix was shut down by an early morning police raid and the three ping-pong dudes were arrested under suspicion of launching the E-Wreck-Shun

Fig. 34. Closed

Virus, which had been released a few days earlier as a bit of Trojan virus code that was part of a pop-up ad for penile enhancement pills on lovecams.net.

The virus had been active for only a couple of days, but had already resulted in the spontaneous combustion of thousands of computers, including hundreds of machines at the Canadian Revenue Agency Taxation Services Centre in St. Catharines, Ontario.

Most of the fires were small enough to just leave a molten puddle of computer, but at least a dozen houses and one entire mattress warehouse burned down because of the virus.

So much for video game testing.

• • •

CallCo Inc.

Milton didn't have to wait long to find the next shit job on the list.

Ruddy had just gotten a job through a friend of Ava's friend's friend-with-benefits with a telemarketing company called CallCo Inc.

CallCo ran one of the largest call centres in North America way out in Boucherville—three metros and a bus from Milton's apartment.

The company did pretty much anything you could do on a phone: polling, customer service, sales, TTY transcription for the deaf, and, although the internet had all but killed 1-900 numbers, they still had a few contracts for phone-sex services.

CallCo Montreal was referred to as "Planet Montreal" by corporate. It was part of a solar system with other heavenly bodies like Planet Pensacola, Planet Charleston, Planet Toledo, Planet Wichita and at least a dozen other planets strategically placed in cities with collapsed industry, low rent, and plenty of desperate unemployed folks.

Montreal was chosen not so much for how it resembled the crumbling post-industrial rustbelt ghost towns of Middle America, but because the constant threat of Quebec nationalism kept the rent low, and the steady stream of unemployable Anglophone Upper Canadian students and perma-teens kept the unskilled workforce flush.

The CallCo building was a massive former warehouse or airplane hangar or indoor wheat farm in an industrial park way out in the middle of what seemed like nowhere.

From the outside it looked like any of the other non-descript light-industrial buildings in the area, just with fewer trucks backed up to the loading docks.

Inside were acres and acres of fluorescent-lit beigeness, acres and acres of beige ceiling tiles splotched with brown water stains, acres and acres of industrial off-grey carpeting worn beige with traffic, and acres and acres of beige press-board desks lined up in rows like tombstones, divided by chest-high beige cubicle dividers. Each desk had a cheap beige office chair, a telephone, and an old beige desktop computer with a giant CRT monitor.

At any given time, day or night, there were over three thousand people all talking on the phone in the same room at the same time.

If you stuck your head up above your cubicle divider all the voices selling phony herbal remedies, or cancelling lost credit cards, or asking about preferred candidates in an upcoming election, or asking, "Oh yeah, you like that big boy?" disappeared into an unrelenting buzz like TV static.

If your assigned desk were any distance from the door, and they were all some distance from the door, you'd have a headache by the time you walked the quarter mile to your cubicle.

The acres and acres of Planet Montreal, like all the others, were divided into imaginary "continents," then "countries," then "states," then "counties," then "towns," then "neighbourhoods," and each cubicle was called a "house" or a "home" and given a unique address.

Like the real universe, each part came with names, flags, cultures, customs, and petty dictators.

There were the Research, Sales, Service, and Erotica continents. Within these, there were countries like Outbound, with states like Xerox, counties like Parts, towns like Toner, and neighbourhoods like WC5755. In this neighbourhood, a collection of 12 cubicles, 12 people at a time over three eight-hour shifts per day, all day, every day, would cold-call businesses to try and sell them toner they probably didn't need for the WC5755 copier machine they probably didn't own.

Each continent had its own colour, and everyone working in that section was required to wear a standard company-issued, employee-purchased (via direct deduction of $1.32 each pay period) vest, which had printed on it the 'flag' of their 'country,' and name of their 'state' and 'town,' along with a box to write in their neighbourhood with company-provided off-brand Sharpies.

The vests went with each cubicle/'house' and were left slung over the backs of the cheap office chairs after each shift. They were never washed, so they smelled like armpits and cigarettes.

The entire corporation was overseen by the Supreme Commander and his board of directors, aka The Alliance. Each planet was ruled by an Overlord, continent an Emperor, country a President, state a Governor, county a Reeve, town a Mayor, and neighbourhood a Junior Floor Shift Manager, who all had been subject to indoctrination in the CallCo Universal Management Training System™, a.k.a. C.U.M.T.S™.

C.U.M.T.S™ was a proprietary program developed by visionary Supreme Commander Vladimir Ilich Smith. It boiled down parts of *The Art of War*, *The Prince*, Chairman Mao's *Little Red Book*, Mussolini's *The Doctrine of Fascism*, a rare surviving copy of the KGB's original 1954 field manual, and Stephen Covey's *Seven Habits of Highly Effective People* into the most advanced call-centre management system on earth.

C.U.M.T.S™ involved a complex program of employee—or 'subject' as they were called—surveillance and intimidation coupled with an escalating series of reprisals and reprimands for offenses ranging from failing to meet quotas, taking bathroom breaks, bringing fish or curry for lunch, showing up a few minutes late, being irresponsible enough to get pregnant, or, worst of all, taking no for an answer on a call.

At the start of each shift, each outbound worker would be given a daily call list, which contained about 25 percent more calls than was humanly possible to get through in eight hours, and would begin dialing and delivering a meticulously rehearsed (on subjects' own time) script designed to keep the person on the other end of the phone from hanging up until "quotas were met": sales made, upgrades agreed to, subscriptions extended, surveys completed, climaxes achieved.

If call quotas were filled, a subject could get meagre bonuses—usually CallCo Inc. swag, like travel mugs and t-shirts. If they did exceedingly well, they might be promoted to more lucrative neighbourhoods or towns. Subjects who showed the most company loyalty, met their quotas, and proved particularly adept at espionage and ratting on their colleagues could even be enrolled in C.U.M.T.S™ and start to climb the CallCo Inc. intergalactic ranks.

• • •

As Seen on TV Land

House 37720-B (B as in the second of three shifts), Product Neighbourhood, Infomercial Town, As Seen on TV County, Inbound Country, Sales Continent. This is where Milton started out.

Inbound sales was the easiest. People weren't being interrupted during *Jeopardy* and being sold something they didn't want or asked their opinion about the affability of some former prime minister's layabout son they didn't care about. They were calling to book a trip. Or calling because their wife left them and they'd been drunk for three days and were up in the middle of the night watching infomercials and thought that three packs of Super Putty for $29.99 or a super-sized pack of super-absorbent rags or an imaginary hand job was just what they needed to turn it all around.

From 11:00 a.m. to 7:00 p.m. Tuesday through Saturday, in a grass-green vest emblazoned with the Sales flag—a dollar sign on a large block arrow, which was supposed to be money coming in, but looked more like money going out—Milton took orders for Super Putty, the Potty Putter Bathroom Putting Green, Wax Vac Max the Ear Wax Vacuum, Booty Booster Ass Enhancing Panty Pads, the Sitty Kitty Cat Toilet Seat, Spray Mane Spray-on Hair, Micro Egg Microwave Egg Poaching Cups, and a dozen other tangible signs of the decline and looming collapse of civilization.

Even with the exceedingly tight security—CallCo had its own 300-person heavily armed on-site militia and secret police, the CallCo Green Berets, a.k.a. the CallGB—the poor pay, the not being allowed more than a single 24-minute break per day, and the constant harassment from the Junior Floor Shift Manager for failing to upsell vulnerable old women the Sock Knitter attachment to go with their new Purrfect Fur Cat Grooming and Wool Making Machine, Milton didn't mind the work.

It was pretty easy. He would ride the metro-metro-metro-bus to work and back each day with Ruddy and Ava's friend's friend-with-benefits, Jay, and talk about bands and girls and which band was playing at which girl's house party this week. Then sit in his cubicle and pretended to talk on the phone while secretly writing poems to Robin all day.

Despite this, Milton turned out to be a decent call-centre employee. He never hit his upsell targets, but no one did—

they were set impossibly high on purpose—but he'd usually show up, usually close to on time, and usually feign an effort.

Unlike the dying rustbelt cities elsewhere, which were flush with desperate unskilled workers with mortgages and mouths to feed, the subjects of Planet Montreal were over-educated, socially progressive, and generally unencumbered, downtown Anglophone 20/30-something adultescents with limited employment prospects and ambiguous yet staunchly held ideas of social justice and workers' rights—insofar as they would sign an online petition to ban fracking or cause a stink at their call-centre job to try and get unlimited smoke breaks.

With great fervour, various factions from different countries would stage protests, walk-outs, and sit-ins in Emperors' offices.

In response, Presidents and Governors would give Subject Happiness Incentive Training™ to disgruntled employees.

In accordance with the C.U.M.T.S™ manifesto, Subject Happiness Incentive Training™ is a sophisticated system of covert espionage activities meant to gently encourage wayward subjects to fall in line.

Lunchroom clocks would be adjusted to shorten already short breaks, chairs would be tampered with to make them even more uncomfortable, dead rodents would be left in desk drawers, car heating vents would be pissed in, a small bit of Super Putty would be surreptitiously placed under a single keyboard key to make it stiiiiiiiiiiiiick, homes would be broken into and toilets upper-decked.[24]

For the most part, Subject Happiness Incentive Training™ would dissuade any further stand-taking. However, every so

---

[24] While technically a contravention of the Geneva Convention, upper-decking is a popular espionage technique that involves pooping in someone's upper toilet tank, where it festers undiscovered and pollutes the victim's home for weeks.

often a part-time sociology grad student/part-time Outbound Pudding Subscription sales ideologue would stoke enough discontent that Subject Happiness Incentive Training™ wouldn't work. In this case, management would invoke the Direct Enhanced Experience Protocol of Subject Happiness Incentive Training™.

When subjects were in D.E.E.P. Subject Happiness Incentive Training™, they would be detained overnight by the CallGB and re-educated using the Ludovico Technique.[25] That usually did the trick.

Yet, despite all the elaborate attempts at psychological and actual warfare, CallCo Inc. still couldn't motivate the thousands of millennials, paid paltry sums, to show up every day on time. During and over the days immediately following Osheaga, Montreal's Coachella, nearly 40 percent of Montreal CallCo Inc. employees called in sick or just didn't bother showing up. Which meant Milton was one of the better subjects.

After a few weeks of showing up and mailing it in, Milton was rewarded for his half-assed effort with a CallCo Inc. travel mug. Not long after he was given a key ring. Then a golf visor, a four-coloured pen, a foam stress ball shaped like an old rotary phone, and then a tie-dyed t-shirt with the corporate logo splashed across the front.

Within a couple months, both he, Ruddy, and Jay were all promoted from As Seen on TV County to Grocery Store Give-Away Redemption County.

None of them could quite figure out how it was a promotion, but they were assured it was.

The crowd in Prime Time and Day Time Television Commercial towns were noticeably upset to see the three relative newbs skipping right over the upper echelons of As Seen on TV county.

---

[25] The finer points of the Ludovico Advanced Interrogation Technique are outlined in the documentary *A Clockwork Orange*.

Fig. 35. Subject Happiness Incentive Training™ Swag

The scuttlebutt around the Sales continent breakroom was that it was a three-way race between Milton, Ruddy, and Jay for Continental Employee of the Month, which brought with it a plaque on the wall with your name on it and a $15 gift card to an Arby's franchise way across town that was owned by the Emperor's wife.

• • •

Escape from Planet Montreal

The race would never be settled, however.

On a rather ordinary Thursday morning, Milton had to abruptly end a call with a woman from Santa Fe who was arranging a $2 rebate on microwave popcorn, because the fire alarm went off.

Someone on Research Continent, who was particularly miffed with the new parking policy—any car parked for more than two hours on company property, even if the owner was working an eight-hour shift, would be impounded in the corporate lot and a fine of $300 would have to be paid to free it—had figured out a way to bypass the CallCo Inc. impassable firewall and access the internet.

The hacking of the CallCo Inc. firewall was originally just an act of civil disobedience meant to quietly protest the parking policy injustice by wasting company time amidst the soul-sucking, mind-numbing drudgery of the never-ending surveys on customer satisfaction with long-burning composite fire logs.

Maybe, someone on Research Continent thought, as they first logged into Facebook, they'd share the hacking method with others in the centre to spread free internet like some kind of forbidden samizdat. But, as is inevitable on the internet, this Someone on Research Continent decided, before spreading this newfound freedom, to pop over to lovecams.net for a quick under-desk wank.

It was unlikely that Someone on Research Continent was able to finish before the E-Wreck-Shun Virus burst their machine into flames.

Within seconds, thanks to the robust network at CallCo Inc., hundreds of computers were on fire, then the pressboard desks, then the pressboard cubicle dividers.

The law requires commercial buildings to have fire suppressing sprinkler systems. But, in CallCo Inc.'s cost-benefit analysis, paying to arrange for the dancers from Club Super Sexe to attend the annual fire department staff retreat cost much less than installing a new system to meet code. So the fire spread quickly, engulfing Research, then Erotica, then Sales, Service, Accommodation, and then it overtook the corporate offices.

The evacuation was pandemonium. CallCo Inc.'s security measures meant that everyone was locked in the burning building, forcing them to smash through the few windows with whatever chairs and CRT monitors hadn't burned yet.

Milton, channelling John G. Diefenbaker, hurled the massive Inter-Continental Employee-of-the-Year plaque—which was really just a nice-looking three-foot-square wooden shelf for a bronze bust of Overlord Gilles Faucon, winner seven years running—through a window next to the Sales break-room and crawled through the broken glass, cutting himself quite badly.

Jay followed close behind, carrying Ruddy, who had screamed until he passed out, over his shoulder.

By the time the fire trucks arrived, Milton and Jay managed to get Ruddy back awake and calm enough to get on the bus back home.

Miraculously, only two people died. Gilles Faucon insisted, as the "captain of the ship" that he was to go down with it, so he did. And the other casualty was Someone on Research Continent who succumbed to smoke inhalation, according to the official coroner's report.

Fig. 36. E-Wreck-Shun Virus

It was announced a couple of hours later, before the fire was even out, that CallCo Inc. was closing their Planet Montreal effective immediately and their business would be moved to the new Planet Flint.

Milton was once more without a job. But worse this time, so were five thousand other unemployable Anglo-Plateau hangabouts.

• • •

Factotum

With the city now awash in Miltons looking for the same shit work, Milton couldn't find anything.

Even Ruddy had to resort to going to work with Noddy. But Milton refused.

He wasn't going to tear out old bathrooms and ride around in old pick-up trucks with angry old men to help Noddy. He was a poet. He had standards. And screw Noddy.

Besides, how much money did he really need to live and write poems? Not a lot. By his not-so-great math, he figured he could live on about $20 per day. Half of that was rent and bills. The other half was day-old bagels, half-rotten half-price pineapples, the odd ream of paper, and several nights out per week. So he began scouring Craigslist for odd jobs.

Business was slow, but he did manage to pick up a gig modelling for a drawing class. He didn't get paid though, because the instructor kicked him out when he refused to go the Full Monty.

He made $40 helping three different people move different appliances into their houses.

He sold 42 books he'd bought from Guillaume and Gweltaz over the past few months for $20—about 10 per cent of what he'd paid for them.

Georgette clued him into donating plasma, which scored him $35 the first time, but everyone else had the same idea so when he went back a second time, they said they didn't need any more.

He got the same response when he showed up at the sperm donor clinic.

He took to wandering the halls at the med schools in the city and joined every research trial he could.

They paid much better than plasma donating.

He got a $25 iTunes gift card for answering an hour's worth of questions about his sexual history—it took him seven minutes.

He made $200 cash, a massive pay day, for spending the weekend in the laboratory with 30 other guinea pigs who were testing a new drug to treat lupus, which Milton falsely claimed was in his family—he didn't even know what it was. The drug caused all of his body hair to fall out and his skin to turn orange, but he felt fine otherwise. Besides, it was $200. Which should have lasted him 10 days, but rent was due.

The hard times made him cut back what little expenses he had even further.

He began rummaging through the dumpsters behind the Parc Avenue fruiteries and St. Viateur Bagels to get his pineapples and bagels for free. Sure, they were much more rotten than the half-rotten two-for-ones and the stale day-olds, but the price was right.

He'd also go with Ruddy and Ava to every St. Henri free-gan potluck he could. He'd take the same bag of petrified bagels that no one would touch, and help himself to all the garbage soup and zucchini loaf he could eat.

He went to every art gallery opening and book launch and gorged himself on squares of cheese, damp crackers, and stale pita chips full of just-turned spinach dip.

When he ran out of paper to type his poems on, he'd just handwrite over old poems. When his last pen died, he snuck into Noddy's room while he was at work and borrowed a carpenter's pencil.

When all the papers were un-reusable, he started sneaking the communal rolls of paper towel from under the kitchen sink and typed his poems on the long scrolls, just like Jack Kerouac. Sort of.

He had only seen Robin a couple of times since the night of the kiss. Once at a house party where Ruddy and Ava's band, Spigot, was playing. She greeted him with a big hug, but that was it.

Ruddy and Ava were experimenting with Japanese noise performance art, which meant four straight hours of eardrum bursting screeches and wails.

The best Milton could do was scream in Robin's ear about "how great it is to see you", and "you look really good," and "I've been thinking a lot about you," and "we should hang out sometime," and "I've been writing some new poems for you," and "I love you," and "will you marry me and have my babies."

Robin couldn't hear a word he said but smiled and nodded and shouted "hey" and "yeah" back, which Milton took as a sure sign that she was feeling something too.

Near the end of a 37-minute long atonal droning "song", Robin mimed something about a watch and sleep, hugged Milton, gave him a peck on the cheek, and left.

The next time he saw her he was walking back home after helping carry a piano down three flights of stairs in exchange for a tin of cookies.

They almost collided when Milton came around the corner of Parc and Bernard not watching where he was going.

Robin was with someone; some guy Milton had never met before. He said his name was Chad or Max or Derek or something. Milton couldn't remember because he couldn't hear what Chad or Max or Derek said over the sound of his world crashing down around him.

Robin and Chadmaxderek were late for their bus down-town, but she mentioned something about going to Florida soon, for her next film project. She gave Milton a hug. He probably held it too long and squeezed too hard. Things got awkward and quiet so Robin and Chadmaxderek kept on towards the bus.

Robin and Chadmaxderek were jokey and flirty with one another, he could tell. He could tell they were probably talking about him, making fun of his poetry, of that hug, of his still-orange skin and lack of body hair. Probably.

Milton had just met him, but he hated Chadmaxderek with the fire of a thousand suns.

ELEVEN

FIFTEEN MINUTES

Kneejerk

In amongst the requests for dog walking and basement cleaning, which all seemed to only pay in creepy foot massages and tins of cookies, Milton replied to a Craigslist ad during a daily visit to the library: "underground music mag looking 4 writers."

> *underground music mag... looking 4 writers...*
> *send samples*

If Milton was going to become a famous poet, this was how it was going to go. This was to be his *Kansas City Star*. The steady onslaught of Mile End douchebags and noise bands was to be his Western Front. The Green Room and the Diskotek and the Club Musique Bar, with their pukey dance floors and busted bathrooms and two-for-$7 beers were to be his mustard-gassy trenches.

> hey
>
> i found your ad looking for writers on craigslist i have just moved here and i am looking for opportunities to write i am very excited to work with your publication i have a diverse range of musical interests from indie rock pop to

country to jazz and classical bands that please me include
bleed december legitimate businessmens social club future
creature oakleaf cowboys sunset standard time potholz
double yous moms from mars tornadoughnauts and many
others i am interested in doing music reviews and also
writing feature articles i am not sure what else to tell you
so i will stop now hope to hear from you soon

milton ontario

He heard back right away. His first acceptance letter, his
first try. He didn't know what all the fuss was about, this
writing stuff was a breeze. A guy named Wayne Willet replied
with one of those e-telegrams written by a semi-literate:

cool... wanna review some cds... meet me at javajean on
milton... im there most days til 6 working on shit... im the
guy in the hornrims... like every other guy in the plateau...
lol... ww

The Java Jean on Milton was McGill Ghetto Ground Zero.
It was a half hour on foot from Milton's apartment. Back
down Parc, through the park across Des Pins and into the
Ghetto.

When Milton arrived, the place was full to the frot-
hed- milk gills. The my-senator-father-is-paying-for-my-lit-
degree-at-McGill was so thick in there it steamed up the
windows. He had to running-back his way to the counter.

"Tay, see-voo-play?"

"What?"

"Tea. Please."

Wayne was in the middle of the crowd; Milton guessed
it was him because he had about 15 years on everyone in the
place, and he was the only one with a stack of 40 CDs on
his table.

"Wayne?"

"Hey, man."

They shook clammy hands.

Wayne closed his laptop, and Milton sat down with his tea behind Wayne's pile of CDs.

Wayne looked about 45, but he could have been 30 or 60. His horn-rims were the most assertive thing about him. The rest was softness and defeat. His hairline crept up his forehead. His face, body, and personality were all round and soft. Sitting there, through the thick London fog of steamed milk and flat white privilege, he looked a lot like the busted-up mattress Milton had been sleeping on.

Wayne was the editor of *Kneejerk*. Actually, Wayne was *Kneejerk*. He called it an Underground Music Magazine. But anyone else—had anyone else ever seen it—would call it a blog. A blog whose owner had convinced enough small record labels to waste postage sending records for Wayne and his cadre of Craigslisters to review.

"So, you like Future Creature?"

Wayne wasn't much for small talk. He jumped right into business.

"Yeah, they're pretty good."

Wayne mumbled something about Future Creature being derivative of Galaxy Wax from Austin, or Athens, or something and asked if Milton was into Twee.

"You into Twee?"   .

"Yeah, they're pretty good."

Milton had no idea.

"You might dig some of these then."

Wayne shoved a stack of CDs across the table at Milton.

"Take whatever you want."

Milton flipped through the stack. He didn't recognize a single band but he picked four CDs. One because the case was an elaborately folded piece of brown cardboard with a dick drawn on it, two because the band names were funny puns of Canadian bands—Gordzilla Bigfoot, and Steven Page Turner Overdrive—and one because Wayne said, when he picked it up, "You heard that? It's sick."

Fig. 37. Wolf Knuckle, Gordzilla Bigfoot,
Steven Page Turner Overdrive, and anonymous dick band

"Uh, no, but I like their other stuff."

Assuming Wolf Knuckle had other stuff.

Milton slid the four CDs in his pocket and blew on his tea. Wayne looked at his long-empty cup with distant eyes and raised eyebrows like someone looking at their watch as a way to hint it's time to get going. Except he wasn't moving.

"So, uh, when do you want the reviews?"

"Whenever, man."

"How long do you want them to be?"

"Whatever, man."

"Any advice? I've never reviewed CDs before."

"Nah, man. Just go for it."

"Okay."

They sat staring into their mugs for a while.

"Do you pay per review or per word?"

"Aw, nah, man, no pay. It's good exposure though, and you can keep those discs."

"How many people read the magazine."

"Aw, nah, no magazine, man. It's all online."

"Oh. How many people read it online?"

"300 hits last month."

"Cool."

"..."

"Well, I've got a... uh... thing."

Milton patted the square bulge in his pocket.

"Thanks for these. I'll get you the reviews right away."

"Cool, man."

Milton headed home, through the park, and back to the library where he went in and googled "twee."

twee | twiː |

adjective (**tweer** | ˈtwiːə | , **tweest** | ˈtwiːɪst |) *British*

excessively or affectedly quaint, pretty, or sentimental: *although the film's a bit twee, it's watchable.*

• • •

Goosehumps

Milton didn't have a CD player to listen to his new CDs and didn't have a laptop to write up the reviews.

He had to sneak into Noddy's room while he was at work, kick the beer cans and trash out of the way, eject the Rush or Mötley Crüe or Ron Hynes or Figgy Duff from his CD player, and listen to anonymous dick band, or Gordzilla Bigfoot or Steven Page Turner Overdrive, or Wayne's favourite, Wolf Knuckle.

The anonymous dick band was actually called Goosehumps. And they were terrible.

First of all, it took a good three minutes to figure out how to get their CD out of the elaborately folded cardboard package. Once entirely unfolded it was just a picture of a penis, drawn with a Sharpie, and a handwritten *Goosehumps: Duck the Police*.

Milton listened to the CD three times in a row. Sitting on the floor next to Noddy's bed (he was afraid to sit on the actual bed—he, more than anyone other than maybe Joey Flipchuk, knew the dangers of STD-enhanced super bedbugs), hunched over with his head in his hands.

The entire CD was about 18 minutes long. It contained four "songs," one of which was 12 minutes long.

It landed somewhere on the map of musical genres between jazz, rap, folk, and twee Brit-pop, with some hints of techno and Norwegian death metal. It was like a soup of wounded animal, jellybeans, and shards of glass, all in a chocolate-gasoline broth.

The overall effect was a migraine headache and a sneaking feeling of what might be regret, not just for what Goosehumps does to one's ears, but for everything, ever, always.

But Milton had a job to do. Fame to pursue. Dreams to make come true. He was intent on reviewing every CD. Intent on finding something to say about the shit soup that was Goosehumps.

The result was about four rolls of double-roll SuperSorb paper towels' worth of scroll-style typewritten gibberish about, primarily, R.L. Stine's *Goosebumps* series of children's horror novels with wild tangents going off in all directions at all times, all loosely in the style of Roch Carrier's children's book *The Hockey Sweater* reimagined as a bad epic poem acid trip-slash-doomsday cult-leader manifesto.

```
the industrial revolution
and its consequences
made the winters of my childhood
long
long
seasons
they have greatly increased
the fact that
we lived in three places
the school
the hockey rink
and curled up under our blankets with a
flashlight reading stories about zombies
murdering
families
not unlike our own
```

Milton barely slept for three days writing it. Up until the wee hours crashing away on his typewriter, causing several cursing bouts from Georgette.

"Putain, Miltan! Shut up your typing!"

When he was finally finished, he ran down to the library and began transcribing the rolls, riddled with spelling and grammar mistakes, into some form he could email to Wayne.

The transcribing alone took him an entire day.

Wayne responded with a very concise: 'thx,' and within minutes it was live on the *Kneejerk* website, unedited. Milton sent the link to his mother. He'd never been so pleased with himself. He was truly, at last and finally, a published poet.

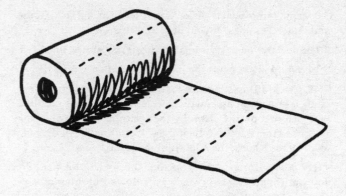

Fig. 38. SuperSorb Double Roll

Within two days, Milton's record review of a bad record in the form of a 35,000-word epic poem about childhood horror-book trauma and a meditation on small-town Saskatchewan life, condiments, international finance, movie theatre vs. microwave popcorn, and 75 other unrelated things had gone viral.

• • •

Viral

9:08 p.m.: Milton sends the review, titled "Duck, Duck, Goose and Other Traumas" to Wayne for editing.

9:11 p.m.: Wayne posts it on the Kneejerk website, unedited.

9:14 p.m.: Milton sends the link to his mother via email.

9:42 p.m.: Milton's mother forwards it to everyone in her church prayer group email chain, and all of their children who are cc'd on the chain by their mothers, who all think they need more Jesus in their lives, including Joey Flipchuk, aka Horace Khack, the adult film megastar.[26]

11:17 p.m.: Horace Khack shares the article on his Live Journal (bigdink6669), which is followed by hundreds of thousands, with the comment: "nerdzzz got werdzzz lol 8=========D"

12:17 a.m.: Within an hour of being shared by Horace, the article hits one million views.

---

[26] Soon after graduation, Joey, with his sudden-onset penile hypertrophy, moved to California and became the world's biggest, in all senses of the word, male adult film star, under the name Horace Khack. The pornography trade magazine, *The Balls Deep Journal*, reported Horace got between $10-12 million for the remaking of Billy Crystal's entire filmography as porn. Including hits like: *This Is Anal Tap, The Penis Bride, When Harry Humped Sally, Titty Dickers, Mr. Saturday Allllll Night, Forget Penis, My That's Giant!, Anal-ize This, The Adventures of Cocky and Ballwrinkle, 69*, Anal-ize That, Gynotopia: Quest for the Really Big One*, and *The Cum-edian*.

Fig. 39. When Harry Humped Sally

1:32 a.m.: Myron Linkletter, a writer for *Late Night with Brett Carmichael*, unable to sleep, checks on Horace's Live Journal and clicks the link to Milton's article thinking it will be some hardcore pornographic content to help him sleep.

2:14 a.m.: Myron Linkletter sends an email to the entire writing staff for *Late Night* with the note: "wow!"

6:47 a.m.: Brett Carmichael checks his email before heading into his office in Manhattan. He clicks the link.

7:13 a.m.: Brett Carmichael sends an email to his writing staff, in response to Myron Linkletter's original note, simply saying: "top10"

9:17 a.m.: During their morning production meeting Brett Carmichael and his senior staff decide to make Milton's article the subject of today's daily top ten list feature.

9:53 a.m.: During the writers' meeting, senior writing staff instruct Myron Linkletter and Alex Dolittle to prepare the evening's Top Ten list inspired by Milton's article.

12:47 p.m.: Milton wakes up.

1:13 p.m.: During the *Late Night* writer's check-in meeting, Myron Linkletter and Alex Dolittle share their first draft of their "Duck, Duck, Goose and other Traumas"-inspired Top Ten list.

2:34 p.m.: Milton returns to the library to check his email: no messages.

3:28 p.m.: Brett Carmichael reviews the third draft of tonight's Top Ten list and signs off, with a few changes.

4:17 p.m.: Brett Carmichael reads the Top Ten list during rehearsal.

5:49 p.m.: Brett Carmichael reads the Top Ten list during the live taping of *Late Night*.

6:03 p.m.: *The New York Times* entertainment reporter Lloyd Palooka, who was attending the *Late Night* taping in an attempt to get some time with celebrity guest Tom Cruise for a retrospective on *Days of Thunder*, ducks out of the studio and phones the editor's desk, urging them to stop the presses. He tells managing editor, Bob Merkin, he's just been tuned onto a major breaking news story that will likely bump the latest on the forthcoming presidential primary from the front page.

"Stop the presses, Bob. I've just been tuned into a major breaking news story that will bump whatever bullshit National has for A1."

He tells Bob Merkin to check the website kneejerk27. angelfire.com.

6:22 p.m.: *The New York Times* managing editor Bob Merkin calls the production desk and tells them to bump the previous front-page story about upstart Senator Obama's burgeoning campaign for president to below the fold to make room for a new story; he can't say what the story is just yet.

"Just make some goddamn room, this is really something."

6:23 p.m.: Bob Merkin calls Lloyd Palooka back.

"All right you sonofabitch, you've got A1. I need the story. And I need it yesterday."

Lloyd suggests, instead of him writing a new story, why don't they just run an excerpt from "Duck, Duck, Goose, and Other Traumas."

"Fuck it, we'll do both. Give me 400 words to put this cock-up in context. Otherwise the world will think we've lost our goddamned minds."

6:24 p.m.: Bob Merkin calls Josiah Gritzwald, The Times' assistant legal counsel.

"I need you to get me the rights to this blog thing from Canada. We're running it on A1 and I need it done last week. Palooka is working on the story."

Fig. 40. Flip phone

6:25 p.m.: Josiah Gritzwald calls Lloyd Palooka and they agree to divide and conquer. Josiah will try and track down the editor of the website where the article appeared, and Lloyd will attempt to track down its author.

6:26 p.m.: Josiah Gritzwald emails the address on the Contact page of kneejerk27.angelfire.com, kneejerkwayne27@free mail.ru, asking someone to call him immediately.

6:26 p.m.: Lloyd Palooka emails the address listed under the author's name on the article, miltonortanio@hawtmale.com, asking for Milton to call him immediately.

6:27 p.m.: Josiah Gritzwald's email bounces back with a note: "The account you are trying to reach is over its quota."

6:27 p.m.: Lloyd Palooka's email bounces back with a note: "The address you are attempting to reach does not exist."

6:28 p.m.: Josiah Gritzwald calls *The Times*' Assistant IT Director Janet Hooschow to ask her to trace the IP address of kneejerk27.angelfire.com. She determines that "Duck, Duck, Goose and Other Traumas" was posted in Montreal.

6:29 p.m.: Josiah Gritzwald texts "blg frm mntrl" to Lloyd Palooka.

6:31 p.m.: Josiah Gritzwald calls Michelle Boulanger, a Montreal freelance journalist who sometimes writes stories for *The Times*, with a request to help find Wayne.

"I need your help finding the guy who runs this website. I need you to find him in the next half-hour. It's urgent."

6:31 p.m.: Lloyd Palooka calls his ex-girlfriend Michelle Boulanger, a Montreal freelance journalist who sometimes writes stories for *The Times*, with a request for help finding Milton. The call goes straight to voicemail.

Lloyd thought their break-up, which happened several years ago, was amicable enough, and enough time had passed, that she wouldn't be blocking his calls, so what the hell?

He leaves a frantic voicemail.

"Hey, Mish, this is Lloyd. Look, I'm sorry if you are still harbouring some anger or whatever towards me and don't want to talk to me right now, I get it. Part of me wishes it never ended. It was intense and carnal and, well, pretty great in a lot of ways. But I've moved on with my life and thought you had too. Look, I really need your help right now. It's important. I need you to…"

His message was cut off by the voicemail lady saying "END OF MESSAGE" and disconnecting.

6:32 p.m.: Lloyd calls Michelle back. It goes straight to voicemail again. "THIS MAILBOX IS FULL. PLEASE TRY AGAIN."

He throws his cell phone against the wall of the *Late Night* studio lobby, leaving a large dent. The security guard comes over and asks him to leave and escorts him out of the building.

• • •

Parapluie de nouilles

6:35 p.m.: Lloyd, with his flip phone broken in two, finds a payphone in Times Square. He picks up the receiver, plugs in a half-dozen quarters, and holds the receiver to his ear with his shoulder while dialing Michelle's number, which he knows by heart.

He gags at the distinct smell of feces coming from the phone receiver and drops the phone and starts coughing.

A homeless man sitting against the wall nearby says to him, "That there's the ass-wiping phone, my dude. That one on the other end there, that's the talking phone."

"What about the middle one?"

"You don't wanna know."

Lloyd spits out the shit smell stuck in his mouth and digs in his pocket for more quarters. He's all out. He trades the homeless man a $10 bill for a dozen quarters he's collected in a paper coffee cup. The pay phone "on the other end" still smells awful, but not quite shit awful. Lloyd plugs in some quarters and dials Michelle's number.

6:36 p.m.: Michelle picks up.

"Michelle, it's Lloyd, please don't hang up."

"I'm sorry. Lloyd who?"

"Lloyd Palooka."

"Excuse me? Palooka?"

"Lloyd... Palooka... From *The Times*... *The New York Times*... From New York. From the NAAJ Conference in 2001... Remember? The Bed-In at the Queen Elizabeth?"

The 2001 edition of the annual National Association of Arts Journalists conference was held the week of September 10, 2001, in Montreal at the Queen Elizabeth Hotel. The attacks of 9/11 occurred on the second day of the conference, and, unable to travel, the NAAJers, as they called themselves, were sequestered in the hotel.

The emotional rawness of that moment, the expense accounts, and the well-stocked hotel bar all added up to a number of impromptu trysts, including two days that Lloyd and Michelle spent, like John and Yoko did 32 years before in the same hotel, confined to their room.

Lloyd kept calling it a "Bed-in for peace" and going on about how if they didn't love one another with their full hearts at that exact moment the terrorists would win.

Michelle found him incredibly annoying and regretted everything. Immediately.

"OH! Lloyd. My god! Your last name is Palooka? You work for *The Times*?"

"Yeah. I'm an editor."

Technically he was the Junior Entertainment Editor—a made-up position for a junior beat reporter who happened to walk in on his boss and his boss's boss's wife necking in the executive bathroom during a Christmas party.

"I need your help, it's urgent."

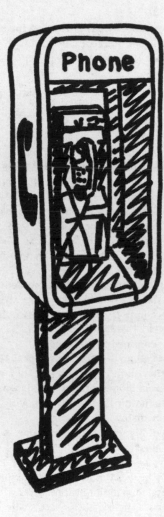

Fig. 41. Pay phone

6:39 p.m.: Michelle phones her friend Julie, a night dispatcher with the Montreal police, asking for a favour.

6:42 p.m.: Josiah faxes a 19-page contract to the Kinkos at the corner of St. Dennis and Sherbrooke for Michelle to pick up to get Wayne to sign.

6:49 p.m.: Michelle picks up the contract.

6:59 p.m.: Wayne, who'd fallen asleep in Java Jean is roused from his sleep by a teacup smashing on the tile floor, dropped by a trainee barista. He wipes the sleep from his eyes, the drool from his chin, closes his dead laptop, packs his bag, and sets off for home.

7:12 p.m.: Wayne stops at Parapluie de Nouilles for some take-out chow mein.

7:16 p.m.: Bob Merkin calls Lloyd Palooka, the call goes to voicemail.

"What the fuck is going on over there, Palooka?"

7:17 p.m.: Bob Merkin calls Josiah Gritzwald and asks.

"What the fuck is going on over there, Joe?"

7:18 p.m.: Josiah Gritzwald calls Lloyd Palooka, the call goes to voicemail.

"What the fuck is going on over there, Lloyd?"

7:24 p.m.: *Times* publisher Larry Gleckman calls Bob Merkin and asks, "What the fuck is going on over there, Bob? I heard you've pulled A1."

"We've got something big, Larry, just hold on to your ass."

7:29 p.m.: Wayne arrives at his apartment, a tiny studio off of Square St. Louis, to find the door slightly ajar. He pushes it open slowly and finds Michelle Boulanger sitting in his kitchen, on the foot of his bed. She snaps his picture with a small point-and-shoot digital camera. He drops his Parapluie de Nouilles in fright and chow mein spills across the floor.

"Aw man! My mein!"

"Wayne Willet, I'm Michelle Boulanger, from *The New York Times*. Are you the owner of the blog kneejerk27. angelfire.com?"

"It's a magazine."

"Sorry, magazine."

"Yeah, it's mine."

"I need you to sign this, and give me the number for Milton Ontario, right away."

Wayne wasn't the swiftest, and it took him a moment to get over the spilled chow mein and grasp the situation.

"How much do you pay?"

"It depends upon the licencing agreement the author has with the website."

There was no such agreement, only a clammy handshake and four CDs.

"Oh, the site owns the rights."

"Then you'd get $10,000."

"I'll need payment in cash before I can sign anything."

7:31 p.m.: Michelle calls Josiah Gritzwald from Wayne's living room/bedroom/kitchen with the news.

"This Kneecap twerp is a real pain in the ass, he won't sign until he's paid."

"In cash."

"In cash."

7:37 p.m.: Michelle and Wayne pick up a $10,000 money transfer from the Kinkos at the corner of St. Denis and Sherbrooke.

7:41 p.m.: Wayne cashes the $10,000 money transfer at May Day Loans on St. Denis. Less their cashing fee, Wayne gets $6,000 cash in $100 bills. He signs the contract in May Day Loans.

"Ok, where's Ontario?"

"A couple blocks up that way, why?"

"No, you idiot, where is Milton Ontario, the author of the article?"

"Oh, I have no idea. He just emailed me through Craigslist."

If Michelle had a gun, she'd have shot Wayne in May Day Loans.

"Thanks for nothing, asshole."

Michelle walks out. Wayne heads out back towards Parapluie de Nouilles.

• • •

No Name Brand™ Pasta Spread

7:42 p.m.: Michelle calls Julie, asking for help locating Milton Ontario. After a few seconds of clarifying that it was a person's name and not a Toronto suburb or either of two Montreal streets, Julie checks her system.

"No one by that name in here. I can check credit card and phone records, but I'm supposed to have a warrant."

"I don't have time for that, Jules."

Michelle and Julie had been friends since high school; Michelle laid it on thick.

"Pleeeeeease! I need this for a story. It's a big deal. I just need to talk to the guy. He's just a source. It's nothing sinister."

"I'll get in so much trouble, Mish."

"Who told your mom that bag of weed in your room was theirs in high school, Jules? You owe me."

"Ok, fine."

7:45 p.m.: Julie has checked all databases she can access without special clearance. No one named "Milton Ontario" has a cellphone in the entire country. But there is a Milton Ontario with a Saskatchewan driver's license, with an address from some place named, "Get a load of this: Bellybutton, Saskatchewan. There's also a Milton Ontario with a long maxed-out Visa with payments far overdue. The most recent purchases were all for under $4 from Fruiterie Parc near the corner of Parc and Bernard. $4 almost every day last month. Also, someone with that name has 27 books checked out of the Mile End Library, and they've listed 707 avenue de l'Épée as their address. He owes $80 in late fees."

"Why didn't you open with that, Jules, jeez?!"

"It's a guy named Milton Ontario from a place called Bellybutton, Saskatchewan, who buys $4 of stuff almost every day from the same fruit stand and has 27 books checked out, including *How to Draw Breasts, Behinds, and Other Erotic Forms* and *Who Needs College?: A Drop-Out's Guide to Dinner Party Conversation*, and like 30 R.L. Stine novels. His address is the least interesting thing about him. I should probably report him to counter-terrorism."

7:56 p.m.: Milton is in his room—still refusing to be in the same room as Noddy—tucking into a bowl full of overcooked spaghetti with a splash of 99 cent No Name Brand™ Pasta Spread, courtesy of Georgette's pity over his ongoing hunger strike. Through the wall he can hear Ava and Ruddy smoking cigarettes and rehashing their misunderstandings of the Habermas–Gadamer debate as misunderstood breakfast metaphors.

"Bacon and eggs can't be separated from their cultural and historical contexts, you tool! That's why all-day breakfast is an abomination!"

And Noddy chewing giant mouthfuls of fried horsemeat with his mouth open and talking loudly about the history of the Newfoundland Fishermen's Union towards Larry, who was over to visit Georgette and stayed to hang out even though she left for a date with Chris hours ago. All this over a blaring QHL game, when Michelle Boulanger bangs on their door.

Larry answers the door. Michelle snaps his picture.

"Hi, Mr. Ontario. I'm Michelle Boulanger from *The New York Times*. Did you write an article for a blog called knee-jerk27.angelfire.com titled 'Duck, Duck, Goose and other Traumas'?"

Noddy, Ava and Ruddy all stop talking mid-sentence and

crane their heads towards the door.

"Uh, Ontario? Just a minute. Ruddy! Door for you."

Michelle snaps Ruddy's picture.

"Hi, Mr. Ontario. I'm Michelle Boulanger from *The New York Times*. Did you write an article for a blog called kneejerk27.angelfire.com titled 'Duck, Duck, Goose and other Traumas'?"

"Aw, I'm not Mr. Ontario. I'm from Ontario though. What's up?"

"Are you the author of the blog article 'Duck, Duck, Goose and other Traumas'?"

"Nah, that might be Milton. MILTON!"

Milton ducked into the hall. Michelle snapped his picture.

"Thank you, Mr. Ontario. We don't have much time. I'm Michelle Boulanger from *The New York Times*. Did you write an article for a blog called kneejerk27.angelfire.com titled 'Duck, Duck, Goose and other Traumas'?"

"Uh... Yeah, that's me."

"Can I ask you a few questions?"

"Uh... what about?"

"You, your article, it's for a story I'm writing for tomorrow's paper."

"For tomorrow's paper? Like *The New York Times New York Times*? From New York? New York City, New York?"

"Yeah, that's me. Look, there's not much time, my deadline is in just a few minutes."

8:24 p.m.: The phone rings at the desk of managing editor Bob Merkin, who had gone home two hours ago when the headline was settled as "Upstart Senator to Presidential Hopeful," and wasn't thrilled to be back at the office, missing his only daughter's flute recital:

"This better be Palooka and you better have 400 words that don't need a lick of red."

"Hi Bob. It's Michelle Boulanger."

"Mish! Hi. How are you? It's been a long time. How have you been?"

"I have your story."

"My what?"

"About the weirdo in Montreal."

"I thought that was Palooka's story?"

"Not any more."

8:38 p.m.: 38 minutes after the deadline, which was a fairly normal occurrence, Production Designer Brenda Settleson hit send on an email of the final digital proof of the front page for tomorrow's paper to the *The Times*' production facility in College Point, Queens.

10:52 p.m.: After a game that saw 14 fights, the final buzzer goes with the Saint-Jean-sur-Richelieu Reno Depôt Hammers beating the Sherbrooke Monsieur Chicken Fightin' Martyrs 7-5.

Noddy's recounting of the history of the Newfoundland Fisherman's Protection Union, which he claims was started by his maternal grandfather, continues as the game ends and switches to *La Nuit du Sport*.

11:28 p.m.: "And that's how it became the Fish, Food and Allied Workers Union."

11:30 p.m.: *La Nuit du Sport* ends and Noddy changes the channel.

11:34 p.m.: *News at Night* ends with "one last check on the weather," and *Late Night with Brett Carmichael* begins. Tonight's guests are actor Tom Cruise, comedian Carrot Top, and pop band Arcade Fire.

11:47 p.m.: *Late Night with Brett Carmichael* returns from a commercial break.

Fig. 42. Late Night with Brett Carmichael, Top Ten

DIRTY BIRDS

Late Night With Brett Carmichael

MUSIC PLAYS

> BRETT CARMICHAEL
> Welcome back, uh, welcome back ladies
> and gentlemen. Tonight's Top 10, Paul,
> Tonight's Top 10 is a real doozy.

> PAUL LORY
> Is that so?

> BRETT CARMICHAEL
> It is, Paul.

> PAUL LORY
> Well, I look forward to it then.

> BRETT CARMICHAEL
> *(Laughs.)*
> That's good, Paul, I'm glad you're
> looking forward to it.

> PAUL LORY
> Very good.

> BRETT CARMICHAEL
> So, what happened Paul, what happened was one
> of our writers, My-ron Link-letter.

> PAUL LORY
> Oh yeah, I know Myron.

> BRETT CARMICHAEL
> *(Laughs.)*
> Oh yeah, Paul, you've seen him around?

> PAUL LORY
> Yeah, I've seen him around a couple times.
> He's a good guy.

BRETT CARMICHAEL
So, this Linkletter guy. He's big into
the internet, apparently.

PAUL LORY
I've heard of it.

BRETT CARMICHAEL
(Laughs.)
So, last night, after we're all in bed,
Myron is up on the internet and
he discovers this article.

PAUL LORY
Is that all he was doing?

LAUGHTER

BRETT CARMICHAEL
Now Paul, Paul, we don't want
to know that!

LAUGHTER

PAUL LORY
Well it is the internet!

LAUGHTER

BRETT CARMICHAEL
(Laughs.)
It is. It is the internet. So, Myron's out
there on the internet in the wee hours, Paul,
and he discovers this article and reads it,
I guess, and thinks it's quite something, Paul.

PAUL LORY
Sounds like it.

BRETT CARMICHAEL
So, he goes into the email there, and emails
it to everyone. All of us.

DIRTY BIRDS

>   PAUL LORY
>   I didn't get it.

LAUGHTER

>   BRETT CARMICHAEL
>   *(Laughs.)*
>   Eeeeehh… Well, almost everyone.
> But I wake up this morning, and there's this
> article in my email from Myron. And I get into
>   the office and it's all anyone is talking
>   about. All day. This article.

>   PAUL LORY
>   I've never heard of it.

LAUGHTER

>   BRETT CARMICHAEL
>   The article, Paul, you should really
> check your email, the article is called
> "Duck, Duck, Goose and Other Traumas" on
>   this blog from Canada, Paul.

>   PAUL LORY
>   My people!

LAUGHTER

>   BRETT CARMICHAEL
> And it's written by this guy, Paul,
>   get this, named Milton Ontario.

>   PAUL LORY
>   I have an aunt who lives there.
>   It's a nice place.

LAUGHTER

>   BRETT CARMICHAEL
> No Paul, not the place, the person.
> This guy's name is Milton Ontario.

> PAUL LORY
> I see. Yeah, I've never been there.

LAUGHTER

11:48 p.m.: Ava and Ruddy in stereo: "MILTOOOONNN!!!"

> BRETT CARMICHAEL
> *(Laughs.)*
> Well maybe you'll have to visit.

> PAUL LORY
> Maybe I will.

> BRETT CARMICHAEL
> Anyway, Paul, this article by this
> Ontario fellow is quite something.

> PAUL LORY
> Is it?

> BRETT CARMICHAEL
> So I'm told. We've got writers to do the
> reading around here. They just roll me out and
> plug me in at 11:30.

LAUGHTER

> PAUL LORY
> That's how you've managed to keep
> your hair all these years.

LAUGHTER

> BRETT CARMICHAEL
> *(Laughs.)*
> Exactly. This Ontario fellow's article, it's
> gone, as the kids say, viral, Paul. Viral.

> PAUL LORY
> That doesn't sound good.

DIRTY BIRDS

BRETT CARMICHAEL
Not good at all, Paul. But I'm told
it's not contagious.

PAUL LORY
Well, that's a big relief.

LAUGHTER

BRETT CARMICHAEL
You're telling me!

PAUL LORY
Yeah, I just told you. It's a big relief.

BRETT CARMICHAEL
Yes. Anyway, Paul, tonight's Top Ten list,
that shtick we do every night at this time.

PAUL LORY
Yes. I'm familiar with it.

BRETT CARMICHAEL
Tonight's Top Ten, Paul, is about this article,
"Duck, Duck, Goose and Other Traumas."

PAUL LORY
From Ontario!

BRETT CARMICHAEL
Just like our very own Paul Lory,
ladies and gentlemen.

APPLAUSE

11:49 p.m.: "MILLLLLLTOOOOOOOOONNNNN!!!!"

BRETT CARMICHAEL
Here it is, folks. From the home office in
Milton, Ontario, tonight's Top Ten Reasons That
Guy Reviewing Your Debut Album on that One Blog
from Canada Might Actually be the Unabomber.

MUSIC PLAYS

11:50 p.m.: Milton emerges from his room. "What?"

> BRETT CARMICHAEL
> Number ten: He's got strong opinions he
> expresses at length that he really wants
> everyone to read.

Number nine: It's on the internet and it still
smells like gun powder and maple syrup.

Number eight: There's a Tragically Hip song
about him.

> Number seven: He knows who the
> Tragically Hip are.

Now hold on. Hold on, Paul. That's not fair.
Now. Now, the Tragically Hip are a great
Canadian band, Paul.

> PAUL LORY
> From Kingston, Ontario.

> BRETT CARMICHAEL
> Exactly, Paul.
> *(Laughs.)*
> We should get them on the show sometime.

> PAUL LORY
> I'm shocked they haven't been.

> BRETT CARMICHAEL
> Me too, Paul, me too.
> *(Laughs.)*

Number six: Canada's Parliament is a cabin
in the woods in Montana.

Number five: It's pronounced poo-teen,
not Putin.

Number four: He's still hosting his blog
on Angelfire.com.

Number three: He says he listened to your
entire album.

Number two: He keeps sending you bombs
by email.

And the number one reason that That Guy
Reviewing Your Debut Album on that One Blog
from Canada Might Actually be the Unabomber.
Are you ready for this, Paul?

PAUL LORY
Am I ever!

BRETT CARMICHAEL
It's a bad review, but he says he's saw-ry.

LAUGHTER.

MUSIC PLAYS

· · ·

The Big Times

Milton didn't know what to make of the whole thing. He'd typewritten the rambling review, if you can call it that, on a roll of paper towel in a three-day fever dream fueled by hunger hallucinations.

After sending "Duck, Duck, Goose and Other Traumas" to Wayne, Milton slept for hours, got up, showered with Noddy's Axe body soap, borrowed some of Georgette's toothpaste to grind the fur off his teeth, and moped around the house until Georgette offered him a bowl of pasta.

He spent the rest of the night, until Michelle Boulanger knocked on the door, hiding from Noddy in his room, listening to the dueling conversations through the thin wall: Noddy ranting and roaring about fishermen's unions to Larry, Ava and Ruddy bickering over Gadamer and Habermas and the hermeneutical imperative of experience vs. tradition and breakfast food.

"Like, it's in the fucking name, Rudd. Break-fast. Like breaking the fast. Like you were just, like, sleeping and so you weren't, like, eating or anything, and now you're up and 'breaking that fast' with the first, like, meal of the day. So, like, when you eat like bacon and eggs for supper it's not breakfast, that's just bacon and eggs for supper. Tradition doesn't get to trump language just because a bunch of slave-owning colonial assholes liked to eat burnt pig guts when they woke up each day."

After Brett Carmichael's top ten, the entire room sat in stunned silence, staring at Milton. All except for Noddy, who belched loudly, crushed an empty beer can in his hand.

Ruddy broke the silence.

"Milty, are you, like, famous now?"

"Oh my god! That's so crazy. Like, did you really write all that?"

Milton shrugged.

"Congratulations, son. That's a nice feather in your cap."

Larry stuck out his hand to shake Milton's.

"What are you going to do now, Milty?"

"I don't know."

He thought about Robin. He wanted to call her. He wondered if she was watching. She wasn't. She was in Florida, getting ready to shoot her next film, making out with Chadmaxderek. He didn't have her number. He didn't have a phone.

"Go to bed, I guess."

"Fuck that, b'y, let's get shittered. You hit the big time!"

"Maybe."

Milton couldn't imagine getting shittered now. He couldn't imagine anything. He just got up off the couch, walked down to his room, closed the door, turned off the light, and laid down on his bed and stared into darkness until morning.

night, partly cloudy in the evening, turning cloudy lat, low 38. **Tomorrow,** sunshine and clouds, high 53. Weather map appears on Page D8.

OVERNIGHT SENSATION

Unhinged viral blog post read by millions warns of zombie apocalypse and economic collapse

MONTREAL, QC–Overnight on Thursday, the incoherent ravings of an unhinged Montreal poet became the most widely viewed item in internet history.

The 35,000-word blog post entitled, "Duck, Duck, Goose and Other Traumas," was posted to the website knee-jerk27.angelfire.com by Milton Ontario, 22.

At press time the web-page had over three million views in less than 48 hours ,according to the site's owner Wayne Willet, 44.

Mr. Ontario says the post, which he refers to as a "poem," began as a review of the album "Duck the Police" by Juneau, Alaska, band Goosehumps.

"It just grew from there," says Mr. Ontario.

The piece was originally written on an antique manual typewriter, typed onto rolls of paper towels over three sleepless days and nights in Mr.

Ontario's windowless room in the apartment he shares with several artists and construction workers in the trendy Mile End neighbourhood of Montreal.

The piece went viral after it was shared on the Livejournal.com page of adult film star Horace Khack.

Mr. Khack hails from the same small Saskatchewan village—Bellybutton—as Mr. Ontario.

"From there it just sort of happened, I guess," says Mr. Ontario.

Mr. Ontario refused to comment on his relationship with Mr. Khack.

The piece is written without proper punctuation or any formal structure and covers a range of disconnected topics from nostalgia for youth horror novels, to hypothetical zombie invasions, unrequited love, and failed revenge plots.

The most bizarre and off-the-wall section is a lengthy screed against the unseen flaws of the global financial system and something Mr. Ontario calls in the "poem" "the disease/disease/disease/of sub/prime loans," referring to the popular means by which banks provide affordable mortgages to middle-class Americans.

"This man is clearly an idiot," says Walter Gordan, vice-chairman of the investment bank Bear Stearns.

"These financial instruments are the backbone of our strong economy," says Mr. Gordon.

Mr. Ontario, who has an Artistic Sciences diploma from the Polytechnic University of Saskatchewan and is currently unemployed and single, says he doesn't have any training or knowledge about finance.

"I don't know anything about money, I'm broke," he claims.

He stated that he learned about the existence of subprime mortgages at a party.

The more than three million page views of "Duck, Duck, Goose and Other Traumas" in under 48 hours surpasses previous record holder, "Yarnkatz"—a video of kittens playing with a ball of yarn—according to internet tracking firm Hitz.com.

In the morning, after Noddy's work boots plodded down the hall and out the door, Milton got up.

He got dressed and snuck into Noddy's room to borrow five bucks in change out of the clamshell ashtray full of change and cigarette butts on his bedside table. He ran down Parc to the newsstand past the library. It wasn't open yet, so he sat on the curb and watched the sun come up.

The old man who ran the newsstand showed up shortly before 7:00 and unlocked the door, Milton followed him in. The old man was surprised, and/or thought he was being robbed, and hollered at Milton.

"MONSIEUR! EXCUSEZ MOI!"

"Day-sole-ay, New York Times, see-voo-play."

The old man prattled off a long, angry soliloquy in French while he walked into the back and hauled in a bundle of papers, cut the straps, and handed one to Milton.

"Duh, see-voo-play."

He handed Milton a second.

"Quatre dollars soixante."

Milton handed the old man a handful of Noddy's change and unfolded the top paper. There was a photo of Milton looking rather like a serial mail bomber holding up a wad of paper towel.

"Say mwah!"

• • •

Supernovice

Almost overnight Milton had become a pop culture phenomenon.

The Associated Press wrote about his post, so he appeared in every paper that didn't write their own stories, which was most of them.

The hashtag #duckduckgoose trended on Twitter for three straight days.

The *Kneejerk* article became the most shared link on

Facebook of all time.

He was on the front page of *Yahoo!, Boing Boing, Buzzfeed, Huffington Post*, featured on *Slate, The Onion*, and *McSweeney's Internet Tendency*, and was the subject of a Google Doodle.

Vanity Fair was about to bump their annual Hollywood issue back a month to put him on the cover, but changed their mind after seeing a higher resolution photo of Milton.

The Canadian edition of *Time* magazine did put on its cover Michelle Boulenger's poorly lit, black and white shot of a haggard and sleep-deprived Milton brandishing a paper towel manifesto with the headline, "The Face of Millennial Terror."

He was a Final Jeopardy clue that all three contestants got wrong, leaving the winner, Roy Hobbles, a retired teacher from Denver, Colorado, with just $1.

He was featured on thousands of local and national newscasts in Canada and the U.S.—in roughly equal frequency as both a hard news story about the danger of millennials and a soft human-interest story about the stupidity of millennials.

He was interviewed remotely by Fox News, MSNBC, Larry King, Barbra Walters, Charlie Rose, *60 Minutes, Good Morning America*, and *Regis & Kelly*, and live in-person by CBC, CTV, Global, TVO, Radio Canada, a dozen local radio shows, CSIS and the FBI.

The traffic to kneejerk27.angelfire.com crashed the Angelfire servers for the first time since a bootlegged copy of Elton John's special Princess Diana version of "Candle in the Wind" was posted on di4ever.angelfire.com the day of her funeral in 1997.

The automated Angelfire pop-up ads on *Kneejerk*, which Wayne refused to pay $2.99 per month to replace with his own, made the company nearly a million dollars in the first week alone.

Fig. 43. Time Magazine

Unfortunately for RocketSox.com, a company that printed pictures of people's pets on novelty socks and Angelfire's lone advertiser, they were on the hook for the entire million dollars, and went bankrupt.

An online t-shirt seller from Chinese Taipei sold 47,000 t-shirts with a stylised likeness of Milton's *Time* magazine cover surpassing their previous bestseller shirts featuring a stylized likeness of long-dead Argentine revolutionary Che Guevara.

German, Japanese, French, Portuguese, Spanish, Polish, and Russian publishers bought the translation rights to "Duck, Duck, Goose and Other Traumas" from Wayne for about $5,000 each, without royalties or residuals. The Polish hardcover edition made it to number four on the *Gazeta Wyborcza's Best Seller List*.

Goosehumps, which made only 200 copies of *Duck the Police* originally, selling seven and mailing 12 to music blogs and magazines and blogs masquerading as magazines, were signed by EMI to re-release it. It made it to number two on the Billboard Top 40 Albums chart, but was unable to surpass Avril Lavigne.

Between that deal and digital downloads, the members of the band, which had long broken up, each made over a million dollars.

The drummer, Gary Thompson, made an extra $250,000 by selling the 181 original copies of *Duck the Police* in their original elaborately folded cardboard package with the hand-drawn picture of a penis that were in a box in his garage. That was until the rest of the band found out and threatened to sue. Gary relented and they settled out of court for an undisclosed amount.

"Duck, Duck, Goose and Other Traumas" also triggered an avalanche of angry hate emails to both Wayne and Milton. So much so, that they crashed the email servers of freemail.ru, the obsolete Russian email-hosting service Wayne used.

Milton's Hotmail.com account survived, but he was so overwhelmed with emails—most of them from angry investment bankers and hedge fund managers who were personally offended by Milton's "gross and irresponsible mischaracterization of subprime mortgages and derivatives, you pathetic waste of life"—he abandoned his account.

Early in the ordeal, Milton and Wayne met at the Java Jean to congratulate one another for becoming internet famous. Wayne confessed that *The Times* had paid him for the rights to the post, and that Milton's share was $100. It was the last time Milton saw Wayne.

Between *The Times* deal, translation deals, and appearance and licensing fees he collected "on Milton's behalf," Wayne had more than $500,000 cash, which was more than enough for 30 acres of Belize farmland.

In all, Milton's meteoric rise to Trivial Pursuit answer earned him $100 and seven TV network mugs.

And as fast as it began, it ended. The world spun around, Beyoncé and Jay-Z got married, a new iPhone came out, the presidential primaries were picking up steam—"Yes We Can!" and what not—and that was that. Milton's 15 minutes were up.

TWELVE

NINE TO FIVE

Entry-Level Data-Entry Clerk

In several months of bouncing between terrible jobs and destitution, Milton had done some pretty desperate things for Craigslist strangers.

Everything from rubbing the bunions of a 72-year-old widow in Little Italy for $15 to handing out explicit strip club pamphlets to tourists on rue Sainte-Catherine promoting the "Spectacle des œufs" while in full leather BDSM regalia, complete with whips and gimp mask, for, he found out after, free admission to the show.

He figured he'd stolen $50 in change from Noddy's ashtray, probably that much again in Georgette's teabags and groceries.

He'd eaten dumpstered pineapples that were in no shape to be eaten. He'd held his nose while he selectively nibbled at the least mouldy parts of very mouldy bagels.

He'd pawned everything of value, save for his typewriter.

With the $100 from Wayne running out and rent coming up soon, he had run out of options.

Milton resigned himself to having to beg Noddy for his old job back.

To help him build up the courage, to overcome his pride,

or eat himself to death before Noddy got home, he ordered a large pizza with the last few dollars from his "Duck, Duck, Goose and Other Traumas" windfall and ate until his stomach ached. About 9 slices into an extra-large 28-inch from Pizza Maurice, Georgette knocked on his door.

"Milton, someone call my phone for you."

For the last several months, Milton, when not helping move a couch that a hermit had died on and rotted into for $10 or delivering Parapluie de Nouilles for tips, sent hundreds of resumes to hundreds of seemingly legitimate companies for hundreds of seemingly legitimate jobs. Hundreds. Everything from shelf stocker—of which he had vast experience—to Junior Vice President.

He didn't have a phone, so he put down Georgette's number.

There hadn't been a single call for months.

Apparently, he forgot to tell her.

"I'm not your secretary, Milton! Putain!"

The woman on the other end of the phone spoke quickly and Milton missed her name, the company name, and what the job was, just that they wanted to interview him tomorrow at 9:00 a.m. He couldn't find a pen or pencil, so he wrote the address in the film of dust on his bedroom wall.

The address Milton etched in the dust was somewhere on rue Sherbrooke in Westmount between two Metro stations. He figured it would be no problem to catch a metro then a bus and make it there in plenty of time. Which meant, of course, that he mistimed his trip and landed between buses, which ran less frequently in the wealthy Anglophone Westmount. His options were to wait for the next bus and be really late or walk and be pretty late.

He walked for the first two blocks before he saw a clock in the window of a dep and then started running. He ran about 20 blocks at a full sprint to the offices of Medi-Drug

Inc., arriving at 9:07. He was soaked with sweat and steam poured off him as he panted his way into the reception area, completely out of breath.

"I'm... I'm... I'm here for a job interview."

"Is everything alright, sir?"

"Yes... Just... My... My... Car broke down..."

"Oh dear! Please have a seat. I'll let Cathy know you are here. Would you like a glass of water?"

"Yes... Yes... Please."

"Hi, uh, Milfron, is it?"

Cathy Dixon was the beaming HR Manager. Fresh out of business school, she was all chemically whitened teeth and sensitivity training.

"Milton, yes."

"Oh, sorry, Milden. Yes. Right this way."

Cathy led Milden to a large boardroom filled with a giant table. He sat on one side, and Cathy took a seat directly across from him next to a short nerdy-looking guy hiding behind thick glasses and one giant eyebrow.

"This is Tom Turacos, the Deputy Assistant Manager of Data here at Medi-Drug. He's our 'numbers guy'."

'Numbers guy' was in air quotes, which confused Milden more than usual.

"Tom, this is... uh... Milden Ontrayo."

Milden held out his hand to shake Tom's, but Tom just stretched a pained smile across his face and shrugged.

"Germs."

The job was for an entry-level data-entry clerk. Days and days, weeks and weeks, months and months, of typing numbers into spreadsheets. Everything was coded, Cathy explained, so it would just be a seemingly random bunch of numbers. Months and months of never-ending random numbers.

"Do you have a high tolerance for monotony, Milden?"

"Yes, I'm from Saskatchewan."

Cathy and Tom took turns asking Milden various questions he didn't really understand. He knew vaguely what a database was but didn't have the faintest what a SQL Table was or how it was ingested.

He was determined not to go back to S&M, he'd do whatever he could to get the job, so he lied through his teeth.

"I'm a little rusty with SOQ tables, it's been a few years since I studied them in school, but I believe I got an A in that class. I'm really a secret data head under this rugged exterior, like you, Tom."

Milden was the only one who laughed.

As the questions got increasingly particular and difficult, Milden's bullshittery got increasingly forced to the point that his dad became a physician who studied pediatric diabetes and was about to co-author a ground-breaking article on insulin receptors in children under five in *Kids Diabetes Quarterly*.

"So medical research is in my blood, you could say... Like insulin..."

"I'm not familiar with that periodical," was all he got.

The final question was a softball.

"Milden, this final question is a softball. What are your hobbies and interests?"

Finally, one he could half answer truthfully.

"Oh, I'm a writer when I'm not pursuing my passion in medical research."

"Oh, interesting. What kind of writing?"

"I'm a poet."

"Poetry is a dead medium that has long been surpassed by newer forms like television—"

"Oh Tom, stop it! Poetry! That is so interesting! Lorraine, one of our VPs, is a poet! Wait here, she'd love to meet you."

Lorraine Donnatella was the Vice-President of Regulatory Affairs. Her thick Italian lilt carried through walls and down long halls and often from her fourth-floor office to the reception desk on the first floor. She was all exclamations, hair spray, and hot red lipstick.

"Hello dear! So, you're the poet! That's so wonderful! I've never met another poet before! What kind of po-ems do you write?!"

"Uh, well, uh… free verse, I suppose. Experimental modern sorts of po-ems."

"Get outta here! Modern po-ems are beyond me! My god! That's so impressive!"

"Lorraine is a poet too, Milden."

"Aw hush, Cathy, you're being kind! I took a limerick class at the United Irish Societies Centre with a fella I was seeing a few years ago! That's a whole other story! Haha! Let's just say my love of poetry lasted longer than my love for that no-good cheating scumbag! If you know what I mean! But limericks sort of became my thing! In birthday cards and such! Y'know! There once was a girl from HR, whose MBA would take her far, she worked all she could, and the money was good, so now she can afford a new car! Nothing fancy!"

"That's good."

"You're too kind!"

"So, are your po-ems like published or anything?!"

"Yeah, a few. I was in *The New York Times* a few weeks ago, actually. And I've done public readings and things like that."

"Get outta here! No way! Look at you! *The New York Times*! A real poet, Cathy! How exciting! I can't wait to read it! Are you single?!"

"Uh… yeah."

"Get outta here! A handsome fella like you! I want you to meet my daughter! You'd love her! She's a stunner like her mother! Haha! What are you interviewing for!?"

"Uh…"

"He's interviewing for the data-entry clerk."

"My gawd! That will bore you half to death! It's no work for a poet!"

"I don't mind, honestly."

"I won't hear it! No! Cathy, what's D.E.C. one pay?"

"13.75."

"No, no, no! Milden the poet—my gosh, that's even a poet's name!—how would you like to be my executive assistant for, say, $15 an hour?! Us poets have gotta stick together, hon!"

Milton was terrified of Lorraine, but the alternative was S&M until it put him in an early grave.

"Uhm… sure. That'd be great."

"Then it's settled! How wonderful! A real poet! My god!"

Lorraine clapped her hands together, grabbed the sides of Milden's head and planted a big, wet, lipsticky kiss on his sweaty forehead, turned on one of her super high heels, clicked down the hall and sprinted up the stairs.

"Oh, that Lorraine! Congratulations, Milden! Welcome to Medi-Drug!"

Cathy stuck out her hand to shake Milden's. Tom muttered "unbelievable" under his breath as he and his eyebrow pushed their way past Milden and out the door.

• • •

Medi-Drug Inc.

Medi-Drug Inc. was the pharmaceutical arm of a large multinational corporation. One of them great big companies that make drugs for keeping old dicks hard on one coast, casserole dishes on the other, and nuclear-tipped intercontinental ballistic missiles somewhere in the middle.

Medi-Drug was a pretty small corner of this global mega-conglomerate super empire. And while this particular corner did jack up prices of life-saving medicines to the highest the

Fig. 44. Weapons of mass production

market would bear, it was, on balance, probably better for the fate of humanity than the nuclear-tipped intercontinental ballistic missiles part, slightly.

Not that Milton was in any position to be particularly choosy or moralistic about what he was doing. His choices were between helping to shake down the poor and the sick, ducking out of the way of hammer-tossed power tools and plumbing fixtures, or dying of starvation in his windowless room.

Plus, it was more money than Milton had ever made in his life, came with full benefits—not that he would dare set foot in a doctor's, dentist's, or optometrist's office for having to try and explain anything to them in his très mal français—and a company cellphone.

The job itself was something that Lorraine made up on the spot in the interview, so Milton's actual job description was fairly non-existent.

She was the VP of Regulatory Affairs, which meant she was responsible for ensuring Medi-Drug met the 37 bajillion government regulations dealing with drug research and the mountains of paper it produced.

Regulatory Affairs was the most powerful department in the company.

Black pens were forbidden. All original paperwork had to be filled out in distinguishable blue. Every scrap of paper had to be scanned and copied three times and stored in three different secure physical locations for a minimum of forty years. Every digital file had to be printed and backed up hourly and likewise stored on three separate encrypted media in three different secure physical locations.

Any documents with potentially identifying data had to be stored in triple-secure safes, of which there could only be two keys (as opposed to four keys for the regular filing cabinets), as well as double biometric security (retinal and fingerprint scans). And those were just the documents.

The drugs themselves were stored in tamper-proof containers in a climate-controlled vault in the basement with three layers of security as well. They were delivered by armoured transport, no matter if they were diet pills, the cure for cancer, or the latest highly addictive designer opioid.

Employees needed special clearances and background checks in order to access data or medications. There were dozens of licences and permits required for different things, and scores of reports and inspections and site visits and spot checks to be completed throughout the year.

All of this, and anything else anyone did or even thought of doing, had to be written down in formal standard operating procedures, against which employees were closely monitored and audited quarterly. Those who kept to procedure got bonuses, those who wavered got fired.

It was a massive amount of work, but Milton did none of it.

There was a Department of Document Management whose job it was to photocopy and scan and file and schlep boxes to the basement or into courier vans to be sent to off-site warehouses. There was a Department of Compliance, whose job it was to write reports and prepare for inspections and site visits and spot checks and keep the various licences and permits in order. And there was a Department of Standards, whose job it was to write, train, and monitor employee compliance with 179 standard operating procedures—a number that was growing by the week.

Across these three departments there were at least 30 employees, plus 11 other people whose jobs Milton could never quite figure out. The entire Regulatory Affairs Division, or Reg. Div., took up most of the fourth floor of the four-storey building that housed Medi-Drug on the corner of rue Sherbrooke and avenue Metcalfe.

Milton's job was pretty much to sit at a small desk outside of Lorraine's office, get her a coffee "with a droppa! Justa little droppa!" when she needed it, answer and dial the phone for her, greet the steady stream of Data Entry Clerks, Research Directors, Trial Administrators, and Medical Consultants summoned to her office, and then listen through the never-thick-enough walls to her scream obscenities at them for deleting an email or writing a note in black ink or losing a patient record or dropping a bottle of experimental drugs and having them skitter across the lunchroom floor and under the fridge.

"*Madonna*! What in the name of our blessed virgin were you doing with them in the lunchroom anyhow?! *Coglione!*"

In all it was between 30 to 45 minutes of actual work per day. The rest of the time Milton had nothing to do but discretely write poems and letters to Robin in spreadsheets and by hand on toner test sheets and printer-jam misprints and fax machine spam (in blue ink, of course).

C	D	E	F
me	Y-Prime	Variance	ΔE∂
646345	0.23423455	they are an incorrigible lot	0.002992
673452	0.11254634	the lot of them	0.050302
347742	0.12453632	incorrigible	0.059583
423342	0.09194814	inporridgable	0.003040
323425	0.12948590	idefatigable dregs and druids on battery acid fluid	0.005039
868692	0.22383940	with lucid dreams of i love lucy love scenes	0.028859
739502	0.17982759	and desi and his why i oughtas	0.004586
235234	0.09837281	ala chicken breast sandwiches	0.003757
625562	0.10245029	and away we go	0.030395
592392	0.18972648		0.003938

· · ·

The Hyperreal

The Medi-Drug miracle saved Milton from having to stoop to ask for Noddy's help.

Noddy was, after all, the one who'd slept with the love of Milton's life. That very same love of his life who'd gone to Florida and could be gone for years, if she came back at all. That very same love of his life who he spent most of his days writing letters to. Letters he would never send because they were too personal, too embarrassing, too mundane. Mostly, though, letters he would never send because he didn't have her email address or mailing address or any way to reach her. He'd google her often for clues of her where-abouts, but nothing would ever turn up. So, eff Noddy, was Milton's general sentiment. Eff Noddy.

Noddy, though, didn't feel the same way.

He continued to knock on Milton's door and declare apologies into its 40 layers of lead paint every so often.

"Dude? What did I do? I knows I fucked your bird the once there, but that's it, b'y. I messed up. But I haven't seen her since."

Milton just pretended Noddy wasn't there. The odd time they bumped into each other in the hall or going opposite directions in the stairwell, Noddy would give a hearty "whaddayat, b'y?" and Milton would just stretch his lips in not-quite-a-smile and duck past.

Noddy grew sadder and sadder and Milton could hear him through the thin walls asking Georgette, or Larry, or Chris, or Ava, or Ruddy.

"What's his deal? He okay? You talked to him lately?"

He was worried. Milton was his protégé, his "little buddy," and now he wasn't.

For weeks after the Robin 'incident,' Milton had laid in his misery and dreamed of elaborate revenge plots. Mostly to do with reporting Noddy to the city building inspector, or poisoning his horse meat, or switching his Coors Lights with Heinekens. But he didn't have the heart for any of it. And after what happened with Joey Flipchuk and the super bedbugs, he didn't know if there was much of a point anyway.

It turned out, the best revenge Milton had ever venged was just going on with his life and being a bit of a dick about it.

To avoid running into Noddy, and with more money than he knew what to do with, Milton spent almost every night out.

Either on his own or with Ruddy and Ava going to rock shows or art shows or house shows, or with Georgette and Chris to heckle a rival troupe's puppet rock opera, or one night with the few people from work to a Meat Loaf concert.

Yet for all the going out and being around people who were having a good time and looking to meet people and hook up and fall drunkenly head over heels in love and get pregnant in the accessible bathroom, Milton met no one, made no new friends, didn't fall in love, never hooked up, got no one pregnant. He stood alone, even when with a group, his arms crossed in front of him, watching.

Watching music.

Never dancing. Never really listening or feeling or ingesting the music in ways that people do that makes them tap their toes or fall in love. That makes them see clearer or further or differently. That makes them stand taller and walk lighter and laugh deeper. That makes a single tear climb down their cheek as they sway in unison with a few hundred other sweaty bodies, holding their flip-phones up over their heads while the encore drags into its fifteenth minute. That makes them bundle up the memory and place it in a box marked "Precious" and put it away in the backs of their minds where it will stay safely until their father is found blue on the kitchen floor, or while they're sitting in the chemo lounge with an IV in their arm, or when they're dropping their youngest off at their first day of university,

or any other moment when the only thing that helps someone keep putting one foot in front of the other is climbing
up into that mind attic and pulling out that old dusty box
marked "Precious" and unwrapping the fifteenth minute
of "Paradise By the Dashboard Light." The warmth of that
moment. The glow it gives off. The glow of all those cell
phones. The glow you carry around with you at just the
thought of it.

There was none of that for Milton.

He just watched.

His mind was somewhere else. His heart was somewhere
else. Somewhere in Florida making a movie about vultures.

Yet he kept going, despite never seeming to have a good
time, because it's where he thought he should be. Because
it's where people he thought he'd theoretically like or be like
were. But it wasn't and he didn't. Not really.

They were all Ruddys and Avas. All dancing very seriously, feeling very seriously, dressing very seriously, looking
out through their horn-rims from under their asymmetrical
androgynous bowl cuts very seriously.

All grabbing a beer and going for a smoke outside and
debating the incomplete bits of Baudrillard they'd half
read for class that week and whether or not if they went and
got all-day breakfast after midnight it would be real real or
hyperreal.

"I mean, of course the eggs are really real, like real real,
but the entire experience, the faux-1950s diner, the gang
of chums, the witty banter and in-jokes, all of it is just
Tarantino, which is just Hughes, which is just Hawks, which
is all just this re-creation of a re-creation of a re-creation,
so of course we're living in the simulacra, and eating eggs
in the simulacra, but they're still eggs—and let's go to Palais
instead of Dinette, because their coffee is better."

All everything very seriously all the time. But not at the
same time.

No one really gave a shit about any of it. Not really. Even for the most serious of them. Even for the ones in the actual bands making the actual music everyone was actually dancing to. It was all just fantasy football and half-hearted attempts to get laid.

Everything and everyone had honed this highly refined sense of irony to the point that irony became the core principle of their very being. It became their existential state.

The kind of empty and agonizing limbo that living in irony creates became manifest as all these grown-assed teenagers walking around the Plateau in their norm-core Garfield sweatshirts, in all their hardcore-noise-mope bands, in all their dick-missile art projects, and garbage-soup potlucks. Nothing was really real, just hyperreal.

Everyone was playacting like this was real life. Like they were adults. Like any of this mattered. Like anyone could possibly give a shit about their shitty art, or even their feelings, or even if they existed at all.

They were all children on an island in a sea of working-class Francophones who were clinging to some shred of meaning, dignity, and identity their grand-père du grand-père du grand-père brought with them from the old county and drove the Indigenous out to impose and fired muskets into a sea of Red Coats to defend and kept their heads down and their mouths shut to keep safe and spoke up and tore down and took hostages and dumped bodies in car trunks in municipal airports to send the message to back the fuck down.

Stuff that in a cosmic sense didn't really matter either. But in the stuff of everyday life, the love and the hate and the drudgery and the misery and the chapped lips and the sore backs and the cracked heels and the root canals and the cataracts and the growing stench of death sense—it matters most of all.

And in that sense, all that matters is getting through,

is surviving, is passing your vendettas and indignities and prejudices on to your children so they might cling to that same tenuous, fraying thread and that one lump of blood-soaked stolen mud that ties them and their rheumatism and their pigeon toes to you and you to their grand-père and their grand-père to the Franks and the Gauls and the Romans and to Jesus Christ himself.

And that is salvation.

That is eternal.

And salvation and eternity might be myths, but they're the myths that get you out of bed in the morning.

Play-acting adulthood at Anglophone summer camp wasn't any of that. Not salvation. Not eternity. Likely not even into next year or beyond graduation, when everyone would move back to Toronto for a while and then back to the suburb they came from and settle for a bad job and a mediocre spouse and the 1.8 average kids.

But that year or two or seven in Montreal, that one summer, will play on a loop in the back of their minds, in the shower, through the dog-day afternoons in accounting, in the evening as they close their eyes.

That time they pretended to be something becomes the thing they depend upon to get them through their eternity of being nothing.

But the make-believe is the very thing that dislocated them from everything that came before in the first place. From everything permanent and eternal. It isn't survival and salvation that gets them out of bed in the morning. It's nostalgia. It's the opposite of eternal salvation. It's terminal damnation. Tying your very soul to fading recollections of time wasted. Of time spent being ironic and thinking it clever. Of being clever and thinking it smart. Of being a poet and thinking it mattered.

And where does that leave us? It leaves us slip-sliding from something into nothing. Into atheism, into cynicism, into nihilism, into suicide or the suburbs.

And what do we leave behind?

At the very most, 1.8 asshole children.

You might get the sense, if you were an anthropologist sent from a fancy British university to study this tribe of transient, rootless, listless lit majors and poet secretaries and barista musicians play-acting at living, that no one was having a good time. That they were just taking the piss, pulling your leg, all in on some elaborate practical joke—just not a very good one. And you'd get the definite sense that the one straight-faced kid off to the side with his arms folded in front of him staring straight ahead while an orgy of prog-rock foolishness spilled off the stage and pooled around his feet, that that one kid wasn't in on the joke.

Yet Milton kept going. Milton kept thinking, kept hoping, kept praying—as he walked home alone in the cold and the dark replaying every mumbled drink order, every brush against every sweaty elbow, every accidental eye contact— that maybe one of these times he'd get it.

If only Robin would come back from Florida and take him by the hand and whisper that Noddy was all a horrible mistake and teach him how to dance in a way that looked aloof but not silly.

If only.

• • •

Corporate Ladder

While all the going out and getting not nearly enough sleep and showing up to work most days at least a little hung-over and at least 20 minutes late wasn't so great for making friends or advancing his poetry career or getting him laid, it was great for Milton's Medi-Drug career.

Lorraine was fascinated by him.

Medi-Drug was a company made up almost exclusively

of moms and dads. Every conversation revolved around daycare pickups and school trips and soccer practice. Every day in the lunchroom there'd be a cake for so-and-so's birthday or because so-and-so is having another baby.

Everyone who worked there, in their tan slacks and floral blouses living really real and really boring lives, looked the same and sounded the same and lived the exact same. The parking lot was filled with Hyundai Santa Fes with two car seats in the back and handfuls of Cheerios ground into the upholstery.

It was a living Dilbert theme park.

It was a special kind of hell.

To have someone living any kind of life other than that was so refreshing to Lorraine—the queen of the t-crossers and i-dotters, the enforcer of regimented sameness.

Each morning she'd coax out of Milton details of his night before. Where'd he go? Who with? Who'd he see? Who was there? Did he meet anyone? Does he have his eyes on anyone?

"Here's my daughter's number! You should take her out! You'd get along great! Just wear a condom! I'm not ready for grandkids just yet! Could you imagine?! Me a grandmother?! I'd die!"

Milton quickly began stretching the truth to tell better stories. He began inventing recurring characters and plot arcs and nightly subplots with lovers and villains and intrigue and polyamorous relationships and good-old-fashioned cheating and betrayal. It was Lorraine's favourite soap opera. She couldn't get enough.

And after Milton agreed to go to a Meat Loaf concert with Lorraine and her daughter—who turned out to be 17 and not the least bit interested in even looking at Milton— he was promoted to Assistant Director of Regulatory Affairs. Much to the cockeyed dismay and angry hushed chagrin of all the moms and dads.

Fig. 45. Ass. Dir. Regulatory Affairs

"Between you me and this rubber tree, hon! There's barely a brain cell in this entire department! And don't get me started on those fools downstairs! My god! They're like the boys my daughter brings home! Dumb enough to shame even an Italian mother! *Madonna*!"

The promotion didn't bring with it much more work. Milton still spent the majority of the day scratching poems and mundane love letters on scrap paper, but Lorraine gave him more and more responsibility.

Milton, of course, had not one clue what the hell he was doing or how anything worked. He was some kind of office boy-toy, not any kind of real actual employee. Yet the moms and dads, with their actual need for their actual jobs, and their healthy fear of Lorraine, did all the actual work Milton might actually be expected to actually do, had he been an actual employee at all.

THIRTEEN
THE GHOST & THE KING

Line One

Somehow Noddy got Milton's work cellphone number and called him one day around 9:30 a.m. Milton didn't recognize the number, so he didn't answer. Then it called back. Then again. Then again. Then finally he answered.

"Milton, b'y! You gotta get down here!"

"I'm at work."

"I'm serious, b'y. It's serious."

"Yeah, so am I. I'm at work!"

"Yeah, but no, b'y, I'm not fuckin' with ya, I got some-body for you to meet."

"I don't have time for this, I've got a lot of work to do."

"Yeah, take the morning off and git your arse down here, b'y. You gotta meet this fella."

"I can't."

And he hung up.

Noddy called back, Milton never answered. So, he called again and again and again and kept calling. Milton put his phone in the drawer, but the constant vibrating shook his entire desk. He shut the phone off and disconnected the battery—just to be safe.

It took Noddy about half an hour to track down Milton's

office number. Caught off guard, Milton picked up.

"Regulatory Affairs, Milton Ontario speaking."

"Dude! Don't hang up! Don't hang up!"

Milton hung up.

He unplugged the phone, put it in his desk drawer—just to be safe—and went back to writing a letter to Robin, that he'd never send, about what he did every day at work.

very important split-second decisions.

A	B	C	D	Varia
Record	Date	X-Prime	Y-Prime	
1838495839	060707	1002am another important phone call from another	0.543646345	0.23
2335355467	081507	important client as a director i get dozens of very	0.453673452	0.11
6767646534	120507	important calls each day and have to make all kinds of	0.345347742	0.12
8742453693	220107	very important split second decisions	0.352423342	0.09

A knock on the door interrupted his letter writing.

"Um, Mr. Ontario, there's a call on line one for you. They say they're a very important client who's had a hard time getting you on your private line. They sound agitated."

"Thanks, my phone is having some troubles, I'll take it in the boardroom."

Milton walked to the boardroom at the opposite end of the hall, shut the door behind him, sat on one of the light blue swivelling office chairs discoloured from use, picked up the handset, and pushed the flashing "Line 1" button.

"Don't hang up. I'm an arsehole, I know. But this is big, for you. Serious."

Click.

Milton walked back to his office and shut the door behind him.

1269467428	081206	0.08503958		0.546323425	0.12
9673568852	300407	0.09885998		0.349868692	0.22
3466428492	140307	0.10458689		0.682739502	0.17
3566837995	030707	0.07375784		0.423235234	0.09
3462173808	270407	1007am yet another important call this day is		0.345625562	0.10
8767980920	200207	turning out to be a real doozy		0.534592392	0.18

Part way through the 11:00 a.m. management team meeting, as Milton doodled "Robin Ontario" into his notebook while Tom Turacos and his eyebrow rounded the 30th minute of a 53-minute presentation on data validation protocols, there was another knock on the door.

"I'm sorry to interrupt. Mr. Ontario, there is a... um... a man in reception. He says he's your brother."

"My brother."

"Yes, sir. He says your mother is sick."

Downstairs Noddy was sitting in the small waiting area next to front reception. He was reading the medical journal *Sexual and Reproductive Epidemiology*.

"B'ys, the porn mags you'se got in here suck, no tits and just going on and on about the clap and shit."

"Noddy! Wha... What are you doing here?"

Noddy scooped Milton up and slung him over his shoulder fireman-carry style.

"C'mon, b'y."

• • •

I'm Your Man

Noddy carried Milton over his shoulder for six blocks to the metro station, down five flights of stairs, and on to the downtown platform. When he finally stopped, Milton managed to wriggle free.

"What the hell?!"

"It's fine, b'y. You'll thank me, you'll see."

"I'm going to kill you, you'll see."

Milton was incensed, but he was out of the Data Validation TED talk, so he decided to not murder Noddy. Not yet.

They rode the green line to the orange line and then the orange line to Mile End. Milton followed Noddy off the train, out of the metro station, and several blocks snaking through familiar Mile End streets to a fairly ordinary brick row house.

There was a pile of S&M's handiwork on the front sidewalk.

"Wait here, don't leave. Lemme make sure he is still there."

"If I came all this way to see a freaking raccoon..."

Noddy disappeared into the house before Milton could finish protesting. So he just shivered on the sidewalk in his dirty, wrinkly, ill-fitting dress shirt and church basement bazaar nickel tie.

On the brink of dying from exposure, Sam appeared in the door and waved him in.

"How are ya, mate?"

"Ready to kill that jerk."

"Get in line! They're in through there."

Milton walked between two piles of rubble and around a corner in what might have once been a living room and into what might have once been a den. He was greeted by Noddy, pants around his ankles, his dick and balls tucked back between his legs, doing the Cyril Sneer.

"I hate you!"

Milton tried to kick Noddy but missed.

"Bahahahahaaha! Fuckin' classic!"

"I'm leaving. I'm moving out. I've had enough of this."

"Go on, b'y. Don't be a sook."

Noddy walked through more piles of rubble, down a long hall towards a closed door.

"LENNY!? You decent?! Hahaha!"

He pushed through the door.

There, in what might have once been a kitchen, tied to a kitchen chair, looking old and tired, sat Jesus Christ Himself: Leonard Cohen.

"Is that...? Is he...? Did you...? What the...? You can't...! It's not..."

"Calm yer tits, b'y. It's fine. Lenny here didn't feel like paying for work, so I referred his account to collections... hahahaha."

"Collections…? Lenny…?"

"They'll be here in a bit, but in the meantime, I thought you'd wanna meet him. He's a big poet and shit, ain't he?"

"You don't know who Leonard Cohen is?"

"Nah, my son, I know the singer one, but not this poetry skeet."

"Dude, it's the same guy! And you've got him tied to a chair!"

"No shit, buddy! That's the same guy? He's so old! And why would a fella be a poet when you get so much more puss singing? Ain't that right, Lenny?"

Leonard Cohen shrugged a nod in agreement.

"How long have you had him here?"

"Sam and I found him poking around here last night, nabbed him. Just like jigging cod, b'y."

"You can't kidnap Leonard Cohen!"

Leonard Cohen shrugged a nod in agreement again.

"I didn't kidnap nobody, b'y, unbunch your nuts. It's forcible confinement at the most. Even then, this is his fucking house."

"Have you been feeding him? Letting him use the bathroom? Anything?"

"Nah, b'y. He pissed hisself a bit, but he's a grown man, he's fine holdin' it in."

"You can't… How…?"

Milton began untying Leonard Cohen.

"I wouldn't do that."

"You can't tie up Leonard Cohen! What the… Who ties anybody up?! What is this?"

"Serious, b'y. If the fellas come by and he ain't tied like they like, we'll be right next to him."

"What fellas? What is going on?"

"The fellas. Tony and the b'ys."

"Tony? Who the hell is Tony?"

"Y'know, Tony. Buddy with the porn place we worked on."

"Love Cams Tony? That guy?"

"Yeah, turned out he's a big mob guy."

"Mob guy? What are you talking about mob guy?"

"Like the mob, y'know. The b'ys like Tony Soprano, 'say hello to my little friend,' and shit."

"That's just made up, there's no mob guys. What the...?!"

"Nah, b'y. Serious. Tony's a bad motherfucker. He bought into S&M way back when. Takes a cut, gets us work, pays us a lot of cash for flipping these shitbird houses."

"No way. No way. No way! I'm calling the cops. I'm leaving here and calling the cops. I'm taking Leonard Cohen with me. I'm calling the cops and they can sort this out and you can all go to jail for a long time and leave me and Leonard Cohen alone."

"Easy now, my son. I don't like it none either. Especially since it's the singer guy too. You're deadly, b'y."

Leonard Cohen nodded in appreciation.

"But nobody's calling no cops. They probably got me on forcible confinement, money laundering, fraud, construction without licences or permits, racketeering, who knows what other bullshit they'll pile on, put that with my probation and record and I'm looking at 20-plus years. They got you for accessorizing all that shit, and I doubt Lenny here won't finger ya to the judge, so that'll be more yet, but since you're probably still a virgin they'd only give you 5 to 10 worth of prison romance. And Sam, poor fuck, would be sent back to Bumfucktopia or whatever shithole country he's from..."

"I'm from New Zealand, mate! I'm whiter than you are, ya silly bugger."

"No way! Nuh-uh! No! No! No! No! No! I'm not... I never... I didn't... I have witnesses at work, you kidnapped me, against my will!"

"But none of that matters, because if we cross Tony and the b'ys, he'll just kill us all. Pop. Pop. Pop. Like nothin'.

Then we'd all be dead and I'd never get to fuck your mother. Bahahaha."

Milton began pacing and pulling at fistfuls of his hair.

"Pull your shit together, b'y. We're fine. You're fine. I'm fine. Lenny here is fine, besides pissing hisself. It's all fine. I know how to handle Tony. Just chill, b'y. It's fine."

"Fine?! FINE?! It's not fine! How is it fine?! You're a mob lackey. You've gotten me tangled up in this. You've gotten Sam tangled up in this..."

"Hey, mate. I'm nobody's lackey. Organized crime is the only real legitimate form of government left, not like the fascists in so-called 'real' government. This is all good for me."

"Okay, but me... And Leonard Cohen! You've kidnapped Leonard Cohen! He's a national treasure! He's a brilliant genius! You... You piece of... crap!"

Leonard Cohen nodded once more in agreement.

Milton, in a rage, picked up a scrap of what was once countertop and swung it at Noddy. He overshot and missed, allowing Noddy to grab him by the church basement bazaar nickel tie, slap him hard across the face again, hoist him up a couple inches off the floor, and pin him against the wall.

"Jeez, b'y. You've got your dick in such a twist. Get your shit together. I brung ya here as a favour, to meet Lenny here before the b'ys fuck up his shit. But I'll have to send you back to your herpes factory if ya don't cool it."

"Fine. Fine. Fine. I'm fine. I'll be cool. I'll be fine. Just let go of me and let me talk to him."

"Promise?"

"Yeah. Yeah. Just let me go."

"Pinky promise."

"Jesus Christ, let me go."

"Not until you pinky promise you'll stop being a little bitch, b'y."

"Argh! Fine. I pinky promise."

"No, really, we have to do the thing, the pinky thing."

Noddy stuck out his pinky finger towards Milton. Milton locked his pinky around Noddy's and they shook.

"Pinky swear, and if you break it the mob kills you and I get to fuck your mom at your funeral."

"Screw you, Noddy!"

"Bahahahaha!"

• • •

Cautioned to Surrender

"Leonard Cohen, I'm really sorry for this. My friend here is an idiot, and I will try to get you out of this. I promise."

"Son, all our friends are idiots and all our lovers will betray us, yet we go on loving anyway."

"Uh, yeah. Have they fed you anything? Can I get you something? Is there anything here?"

"I believe there are some tea and oranges that come all the way from China over yonder in the larder, there."

"Larder?" Milton looked at Noddy, "What's a larder?"

Noddy shrugged.

"The cupboard, my boy, the cupboard."

Milton found a couple of old oranges and a few tea bags in the larder over yonder. There was an old dented kettle with a splash of water of unknown origin or age on the dusty stove. Milton turned the knob on the stove to make tea and started peeling one of the oranges as he made his way back to Leonard Cohen.

"Well, my child, it shan't be long before our four horsemen return to take my legs. Your comrade, and the mastermind there, Captain Newfoundland, tells me you are a poet of some note."

"Oh God, I'm not much of anything. I write poems, but I'm nothing yet. There was one that got kind of big on the internet a while ago, in *The New York Times* and on TV and a bunch of stuff. But not much besides that."

"What do they call you?"

"Who?"

"The world? Your mother? The agents of the state?"

"Like, my name?"

"Yes, as a start."

"Oh, um... Milton Ontario."

"Milton. Ontario. You're not *the* Milton Ontario, are you?"

"Heh... Uh... Maybe?"

"That poem... That thing... 'Ducks and Geese'... That thing in *The Times*. That was your handiwork?"

"Oh, yes. Uh... Leonard Cohen, sir, that was me."

Milton had never been so proud. So full. So invincible than in that exact moment when Leonard Cohen, Leonard Freaking Cohen, recognized him. Him! Milton Ontario.

"That was horrid, son."

"I b-b-beg your pardon."

"I don't think I mumbled or stuttered, I think I made myself clear; it was a horrid piece of writing. I couldn't for the life of me understand why someone would go through the trouble of writing such a wretched thing, but people do stupid things all the time. Humanity must add to its collective list of embarrassments the publication and inconceivable sensation that abomination became for the time it did, before, mercifully, it vanished from all but the smallest sliver of our consciousness."

"So... You read it?"

"Read it?! Reading implies writing, implies the thing before the eyes has meaning, is the product of craft, communicates something. That pox on the English language was just a large pile of empty syllables."

"But you read it?"

"Let me ask you a very important question, and let this be the only bit of wisdom I give you for free."

"Yes, please."

"Did it get you laid or paid?"

"I beg your pardon?"

"That atrocity. Did you receive sexual intercourse or vast sums of money for its creation and unfathomable, but thankfully brief, success?"

"Uhm… I made like a hundred bucks, I guess."

"Of course not. Of course the father of that bastard pile of phonemes couldn't manage to parlay even a week of fame beyond measure into anything worthwhile. Not even enough to buy a back-alley hand job from a busted old junkie. I implore you to put down your pen, burn your word processor, and only use paper to wipe your own ass from now on, son, if you can manage even that."

"Damn, b'y."

"I beg your pardon?"

Milton, Noddy, and Sam all traded confused and amazed looks with one another and leaned in closer to hear Leonard Cohen's final verdict.

"Listen, my son, and listen carefully. This is important. Poetry isn't words on a page. It's not a song or a lyric or the tune a bird sings. It's nothing you clearly think it might be. It doesn't articulate any great, unknowable, unreachable, incomprehensible pain buried in the pit of our souls. Poetry, my son, is merely the act of turning words and lyrics and tunes and melodies into lovers and money. When I first started, I wasn't much good at it either—no one is—but I had at least the sense to know what it was, and know what I needed to do, so I taught myself to play the guitar and got richer than God and bedded more lovers than Jesus. Poems don't need to make any sense or have any profound meaning, they just needed to be the proper arrangement of tones and notes to catch the ears and pocketbooks of virile men and women. And if you get really good at it, you can just write poems and songs about making love to those virile men and women, even to other men's women and other women's men. Endless streams of lovers will throw themselves at you.

Even to this very day, this wretched old man can have his choice of lovers or be sent piles of money for just humming a few bars of 'Hallelujah'. And no one, not its creator nor its creator's Creator knows what the hell that song is about. So, for you to write such hideous poetry, such poorly crafted dreck, is on its own on affront to all sense. But that you call it poetry, that you think that it getting you on the Twitter and in the newspaper where the whole world can point and laugh at you is enough, that you didn't get laid or paid because of it, that's unforgivable."

Milton's feelings were starting to be a little bit hurt.

"Please, now, might I have the last of the oranges and the tea and perhaps a cigarette before we get on with this cops-and-robbers charade, mes amis?"

Milton gave the last orange and drop of tea to Leonard Cohen, and Sam gave him one last cigarette.

"He's vicious, b'y. I'd a smacked the lips right off him if he said that shit to me."

"He's not wrong, mate. I can't believe you didn't get a little laid after all that."

Leonard Cohen nodded in agreement.

"Who says I don't have some irons in the fire?"

"I do. I live in your house, b'y, you've never had a girl over ever."

"Screw you. Screw all you guys, I've got some irons in the fire. Shut up."

• • •

Lonesome Heroes

Milton, Noddy and Sam took seats on buckets and boxes and piles of rubble around Leonard Cohen to drink tea out of dirty mugs and wait for "Tony and the b'ys" to show up and do whatever it was they were going to do.

At first, they all sat in silence except for Noddy humming "Hallelujah" to himself, with Sam joining in on the chorus.

Noddy abhors a silence, so before long he launched into one of his History of the Republic of Newfoundland seminars; this time it was actually about Labrador.

He prattled on about how "the Newfs hung on to 'er just to put 'er to the French, then to put 'er to the Canadians, then to put 'er to the Quebeckers." About how "shit runs downhill, b'ys, so nowadays Newfs fuck Labrador just as hard as Canada fucks the Newfs. We're raking the nickel and the iron and the hydro out of 'er as fast as she'll cough 'er up, and the Inuit there don't get shit else but a hard go."

Leonard Cohen nodded along in agreement.

Milton could only take so much.

"Will you just shut up. This is nuts! We're just sitting here like it's another coffee break. It's not. Leonard Cohen is tied to a chair and the mob is on their way to kill him and probably us. What the hell are we doing?"

Noddy eyed Milton like he was about to smack him again.

"You're fixing for another smack in the lips, are ya, b'y?"

"No, I just want to know how we're getting out of this mess?"

"No mess to get out of, b'y. She's fine, sure. Luh, I told ya. Our first few jobs were flipping repo'd houses and offices for Ton'."

"Repo'd?"

"Repossessed... Read much? Jesus, some daft, you are. Places Tony and the b'ys would collect for unpaid debts and shit. He'd hire us to gut 'em, flip 'em, sell 'em. He'd make bank and the renos would let him launder a bunch of cash. First, we didn't know it was a mob thing, but Tony's a decent guy so when he saw he could trust us he cut us in on it. I got four crews going now for him. None of the b'ys working knows it's for the mob, just me and Sammy here. But I also had legit clients and kept getting more work because we's the cheapest in the city. So, Tony helps us with that for a small piece of it, and one of the things he does is collections. If fuckers don't pay, like ol' numb nuts Will Shatner here, we refers them to collections and they collects how they collects, and if they can't collect the full amount plus interest, they collects the house and a few kneecaps and that's it."

"What do you mean that's it?"

"Well I don't think they kill all of them. But I figure Lenny here is good as gone since he's heard way too much. Besides, he was a bit of a dick about your poetry, which I always thought was pretty good. So, he can fuckin' swim with the bitches."

"The fishes, mate. He's going to swim with the fishes."

"If you say so, buddy."

"No! We can't let them kill Leonard Cohen! Even if he was a bit of a dick to me. I'm sorry, Leonard Cohen, that was a bit mean what you said to me."

Leonard Cohen nodded in agreement.

"That's not up to us."

"Well you got to stop them. You have to say something. You have to save his life."

"I don't got to do shit. Tony's my boss, and he's a mean motherfucker, so he does what he wants."

"Please, Noddy?! I thought we were best friends. Brothers."

"Okay, b'y. Fine. I'll try and get Tony to go easy on him. But no promises."

The torn-to-shit house returned to silence save for Noddy's humming, this time "Suzanne," with Sam's accompaniment in the chorus.

Noddy made it through Leonard Cohen's back catalogue at least three times, which was remarkable not just in how well he knew it, but the fact that he didn't fill the silence with a lecture on triangular trade, or something.

Milton's heart rate gradually returned to normal. He sat

on a bucket, leaning against the wall with his eyes closed, shivering in the cold, quietly waiting for the hit squad to arrive and murder Leonard Cohen.

They arrived with a great bustle and stomping of snow off of boots in the foyer at the other end of the house. It was pitch black by this point; most of the lights had been torn out, but Noddy had opened the fridge to shine a bit of light on Leonard Cohen.

A huge Italian voice boomed: "EH, NEWF?!"

"Yeah, in here, b'ys."

Clomp, clomp, clomp and four men—three giant, one tiny—took up all the space that was left in the kitchen. Milton stood as far back in the dark corner as he could.

"Fellas. The boys here tell me ya got a live one."

"Just a cheap fucker not paying his bills, might listen to reason though, he's not a bad guy."

"Not a bad guy? Nobody's a bad guy when you've got them by the balls. Tell me, sir, are you not a bad guy?"

"Hello, Anthony, my son. Good to see you."

"Ah! *Vaffanculo*! Godfather, is that you?"

"It appears so, Anthony. I've been a guest of these three gentlemen since last evening; they seem to think I owe them money. They're not bad guys, but they make it difficult not to soil oneself, being tied to a chair night and day."

"Muthafuckah! Three? Where's the third?"

"Well, he's a poet too, so he's hiding in the shadows, naturally."

The giants all turned and looked at what they could see of Milton. The nearest one grabbed him by the church basement bazaar nickel tie and dragged him out into the middle of the kitchen and threw him down at the feet of Leonard Cohen.

"Who da fuck are you?"

"I'm... I'm... Milton Ontario."

"I didn't ask where you're from. What's your fuckin'

name cutie pie?"

"It's... it's... Milton Ontario. That's my name."

"Milton Ontario? What kind of fuckin' name is that?"

"I don't know. I'm... I'm from Saskatchewan."

"Milton Ontario from Saskatchewan?! What the fuck is Milton Ontario from Saskatchewan doing in the Godfather's fuckin' kitchen?"

"Godfather? I'm... I'm Noddy's roommate. He thought I might want to meet... I'm a poet too."

"This true, Newf? This little shitstain your roommate?"

"Uh, yeah Ton'. He's all right, b'y. He just loves poetry shit, so I brought him to meet Lenny before... y'know. Milt and I, we's like brothers but I fucked his girl and he's been crooked as sin at me ever since, so I thought meeting Lenny would..."

Tony, who was a lot smaller than Noddy, slapped him hard across the mouth.

"That's Godfather to you, you fuckin' halfwit."

"Yessir. Sorry."

"Lemme get this straight. You and the Aussie, you couple of geniuses, figure the Godfather owes you money so you tie him to a fuckin' chair, let him shit and piss himself all night and all day, bring your little girly friends over to play pattycake with him, and expect me to do what now?"

"Well he owes us money. Like, fifteen hundred bucks."

"He's the fuckin' Godfather. He don't owe you shit. Least of all fifteen hundred bucks. *Madonna!*"

"Well I didn't know he was the singer, I just thought he was the poet."

"Did your father fuck a fuckin' moose to fuckin' make you? Untie the Godfather right fuckin' now."

Noddy stumbled over to Leonard Cohen and began fumbling with the rat's nest of extension cords that bound Leonard Cohen to the kitchen chair.

"Any of you b'ys have a knife or anything, these knots

are bad in the dark like this."

One of the giants grabbed Noddy by both shoulders and tossed him out of the way like he weighed nothing. He tore the extension cords off the chair in one swipe. Leonard Cohen rubbed his wrists and stood up.

"If you gentlemen will excuse me for a moment, I've got to go see a man about a horse, as the poet says."

He winked at Milton as he walked by and made his way out the back door. The three boys, three giants, and the mob boss stood in silence and listened to the septuagenarian icon haltingly piss against his neighbour's back porch.

• • •

Worm on a Hook

Leonard Cohen returned to his kitchen and took a seat back in his kitchen chair.

"Godfather, it's a terrible travesty what these shitheels have done to you. Two of these fucks work for me, so I am ultimately responsible. I will have the boys dispose of these three little turds immediately. And for me, I t'row myself at your mercy, Godfather. I'm still a young man, and I am your humble servant for as long as I live, but if this shittin' and pissin' yourself at the hands of a few of my guys is too much, I understand and will take my medicine. I just ask that you make it quick. Just one to the back a tha head."

Tony made gun fingers and pulled an imaginary trigger.

"Well, Anthony, you do make a very good point: having to sit in one's own waste for quite some time is rather unpleasant, and certainly doesn't lend one to overwhelming feelings of clemency. In fact... Give me a piece."

All three giants and Tony held guns out to Leonard Cohen. He stood and took Tony's.

"In fact, gentlemen, it makes you rather eager to get on with the meting out of justice, to get on with it straight away and by your own hand so you can get home and change your drawers. You three—the poet, Captain Newfoundland, and the Kiwi, get over by that wall and on your knees."

"Wait!? What? No! We didn't... I didn't... I tried to save you, Leonard... Godfather."

Tony punched Milton in the gut.

"When Godfather says get on your fuckin' knees, you get on your fuckin' knees."

Milton doubled over in pain and crawled over to the wall to get on his knees next to Noddy and Sam. Tears were streaming down his face.

"The trouble, mate, is organized crime has the strictest justice code, which works wonderfully for everyone until you accidentally kidnap the boss."

"It wasn't kidnapping, b'y, just forcible confinement. Shut up."

"Shut the fuck up you fuckin' fucknards!"

Tony cracked Sam on the back of the head with the same scrap of countertop Milton had swung at Noddy earlier. Tony didn't overshoot though, and knocked Sam out cold. He slumped on the floor in a limp heap.

"Please, Leonard... Godfather... Please? I love you and your work. And thank you for telling me about poetry. I see it now."

"Son, one final piece of advice, reminding the man holding the gun inches from the back of your skull of the objectively worst bit of tripe he's ever read in his long life and how you are its author is not the most effective way to save your own hide."

"I'm sorry. I'm so sorry."

Milton sobbed.

"Neither is crying, I'm afraid."

Leonard Cohen cocked the gun. Milton felt the cold steel barrel dig into the back of his head. He sobbed again.

"Do... do... you like drugs?"

"I'm sorry?"

"Drugs. I work for a drug company, I'm pretty high up. I could get you drugs, lots of drugs, to sell or whatever."

"Now you play your ace. Sadly, the time for negotiation passed long ago."

There was a moment, only a split second, where everything—all time, all space, all history, every moment of Milton's sad little life, from his sloppy-drunk accidental conception on the banks of Lake Diefenbaker in his father's 1972 Chevy pickup truck to this very moment, an instant before a bullet was about to crash through the back of his skull, tear through his jello brain, and smash through the bridge of his nose before lodging itself in the wall.

All of it stopped.

The memories. The moments. The things that happened and the things he'd forgotten piled into one another like a chain-reaction multi-car wreck on the icy Trans-Canada Highway.

Then there was nothing. Then there was quiet. Then there was that spot. All of the infinite universes and infinite possibilities for what he might have been, for how this might have gone, everything reduced to that one spot.

He focused on that spot, where the bullet would lodge in the wall. He crossed his eyes and focused on the spot until it doubled, and each double began moving in opposite directions. And as it did, the last activity his brain would ever have, the last image it would ever conjure, was the feeling, the electric shock, of that one brief accidentally-on-purpose kiss with Robin at La Baraque after he read his Nickelback poem. The euphoria of reading poetry to a crowd for the first time, the warmth and safety of her embrace, her eyes in that moment and how they sparkled with booze and light, and that spark, that jolt, that kiss. He'd die a virgin, but he'd always have...

BANG!

. . .

Fig. 46. Gun

Hallelujah

The sound of the shot was deafening.

It made Milton's ears throb and ring. Every dog in the neighbourhood started barking. Tony, the pint-sized mob capo, collapsed in a dead heap next to Milton, his body slumped across the backs of Milton's leg.

Milton looked down, Tony's dead face looked up at him. He looked surprised. He looked dead. His face had what looked like a giant leaking zit on its right cheek; warm blood oozed out the zit, down his cheek, and onto Milton's leg. All Milton could think was how, between the blood and the fact he'd pissed himself, his pants were likely ruined.

Leonard Cohen sat back down in his chair.

"Tell me about these drugs, Poet."

"Uh, the place I work, it's a drug company. Lots of drugs. I can get you some. As much as you want."

"What kinds of drugs, my son?"

"Pills, lots of pills, all kinds of pills. Pain killers, stiffy drugs, diet pills, experimental drugs, all kinds of drugs. I can get them for you. I can get you a lot of them."

"I'm sure you could, but unfortunately most places with 'all kinds of drugs' take certain measures to ensure employees don't take any poetic licence with the merchandise."

"They do. Lots of security. But I'm kind of in charge of all that, of the security and the inventory management and storage and everything. I can get it for you and not get caught. They'll never know."

"And why would I trust that you, the author of the worst tire-fire of a poem I've ever seen? I should shoot you for that affront to civilization alone. Why should I trust you with a task like this, trust you to follow through and not take advantage of an old man?"

"Because I am a poet too. Just like you. Sure, I suck at it. But I write it to get laid, I swear. In college I wrote a collection of poetry for a girl, Ashley, from my high school, and I got it bound in leather made of pressed reindeer hearts from Iceland. I thought for sure it would win her over."

"But?"

"But she married some doctor who can't even drive a John Deere S800 at an idle in a parade."

"That sounds like something a woman would do."

"See?! You know! We're the same. Sort of. Not really. Not at all. But I'm trying really hard to be a poet. And I've become an Assistant Director at this company in three months because my boss loves the fact that I'm a poet. It might not be getting me laid or paid yet, but it could. It could get you paid. It will."

"To measure a man, I've always said, put a gun to his head and see what kind of song he sings. I'm impressed with you, Poet. I'm still not, and will never be, impressed with your awful writing, but I'm going to give you a chance."

"Oh thank god. Thank you, Godfather. I won't let you down. I swear."

"Here is what I am going to do. Anthony, may he rest in peace, was right, the penalty for tying the Godfather to a chair and forcing him to soil himself is death. But I'm offering the three of you a suspended sentence. You are going to take as many pills as you can manage without raising suspicion— don't let your ambition get the better of you, do it in a way that remains undetectable—and you're going to give them to Captain Newfoundland and his Kiwi sidekick, here. S&M will continue to operate as it currently does, with a new supervisor—obviously, poor Anthony is no longer up for the job—but on top of the subpar renovations, you will now also be the intermediaries, ferrying the goods the young poet procures to your new supervisors—a pair of old friends of mine who run a bookshop in Mile End—who will see that they make their way through the proper channels to market. None of you will ever see me again unless there is a problem. In which case, I will be the last person you see. In exchange for this new work, and the added risks that go with it, in addition to keeping your beating hearts, you will also be paid appropriately for the goods and services you provide. For, as our unconscious Kiwi friend points out, in not so many words, organized crime is the most perfect form of social organization and it adheres more stringently to the sublime tenets of economics and justice than any other. So, you will earn a fair wage commensurate with your services rendered to the greater good. Should anything go wrong, anything at all, I reserve the right to execute the sentences on each of you at any time. Is all of this understood?"

"Yes... Yes, Godfather, thank you."

"Yes, Lenny, b'y, works for me."

Everyone conscious and alive in the room looked at Noddy with WTF faces.

"What, b'ys? 'Godfather' is just foolish."

"He's not wrong. You two take our Kiwi friend home, give him my apologies on behalf of Anthony when he awakes. I know Anthony would feel very badly, could he feel anything. You three take Anthony home; he needs no apology, though. And I too am going to go home, to get out of my soiled drawers. Gentlemen."

And with that, Leonard Cohen disappeared out the back door and into the darkness. The three giants folded Tony into a contractor-sized garbage bag. Milton and Noddy carried Sam out the front door and on to become the top suppliers of illicit pharmaceuticals in all of North America.

FOURTEEN

KINGPIN

Three Per Cent Assumed Net Loss

It didn't take much for Milton to become a drug kingpin.

He couldn't just walk in and start filling his pockets, there were cameras, and double-locked vaults with retinal scanners, and people might notice. Instead, he found an even easier way.

As Assistant Director of Regulatory Affairs, he was responsible for overseeing the receipt of each shipment of drugs. The numbers on the shipping receipts rarely matched the numbers of actual containers of drugs, they were always off just slightly one way or another. There was an assumed net loss of three per cent in the system, so he just had to keep it below that to not raise suspicion.

On intermittent orders, he'd short-count the shipment and the "lost" cases would be reported to the supplier and replaced, covered by insurance. When the replacement drugs would arrive Milton would lock them in a safe in his office and take a case in his backpack whenever he left the building. If and when they were audited, everything would always check out.

He was good at it.

It was the only thing he was ever actually good at.

Careful execution of his plan allowed him to steal an awful lot of drugs. So many that he'd have to make a couple trips per day to drop them off with Noddy. Two backpacks full, one at lunch, one after work, every day. And as fast as Milton could move them out, Noddy moved cash back in. Thousands and thousands of dollars of cash. More cash than either of them had ever seen.

Noddy schooled Milton on managing his ill-gotten gains. About not spending too much at once, about not paying cash for a new Cadillac, about building credit and spreading debts between loans and credit cards to give himself cover, about money laundering, and how if he knew a friend in a cash business, like construction, say, that friend might help him clean some of his money.

Noddy began laundering Milton's money. It was a pittance compared to the amount he was doing for the mob. Milton would give Noddy a pile of cash, he would give him pay stubs and paycheques for 80 per cent of it and keep the rest.

Milton was now moonlighting as a design consultant for S&M Construction at $120 per hour—more than a Dog-Fucking Instrumentation Man would ever make on an overtime shift in the Alberta Oil Patch.

Medi-Drug ran trials on every kind of drug imaginable. So the drugs Milton was stealing were a real hodgepodge and were sold in a variety of ways. Some pills were worth more than others, but they were all worth something.

Some days Milton would score—that's what it's called in the biz—a few cases of some experimental treatment for erectile dysfunction, or maybe some new opiod pain killers—those kinds of drugs fetched the highest street value.

Other times it would be more specialized or obscure or mundane medicines, like hormone supplements or multivitamins or phony baloney herbal remedies, which would all usually be ground up into "cocaine" or "heroin" or

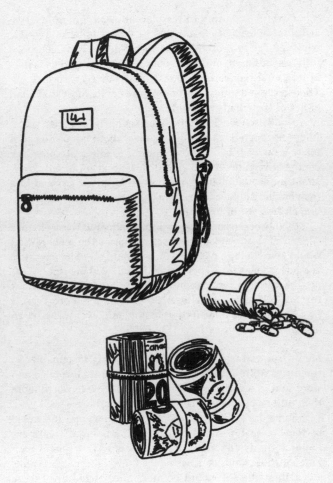

Fig. 47. Amateur pill pusher's survival kit

"meth" and sold to pro athletes, stockbrokers, bankers, and puppeteers.

If there were a lot, they could be sold in bulk to the governments of poorer countries, or if they were top secret, they could be sold at huge markups to competing pharmaceutical companies.

The backpacks were going out fuller and fuller and coming back stuffed to the brim with more and more cash.

It was a great time to get into dealing drugs.

• • •

The High Life

Milton was so far removed from the smugglers and the mules and the dealers and the enforcers breaking kneecaps that he didn't think of himself as part of some elaborate criminal enterprise. He told himself, beyond a desperate ploy to keep Leonard Cohen from murdering him, it was just like taking a few pens from work and giving them to his roommate.

"It's just pens... It's just pens..."

This is what he told himself. This is what he repeated under his breath for the first few weeks of walking out the front door each day with tens of thousands of dollars in stolen pills on his back.

"It's just pens."

Whatever his roommate did with them, and whatever lives those pens lived afterwards, that was none of his business.

"It's just pens... It's just pens..."

It's what he started believing as the stealing got easier and easier, as his confidence in the scheme grew and grew. To the point that, while he genuinely believed he was doing nothing, or barely anything, wrong, he grew more and more cocky in general.

He gave less and less of a shit about trying to be anything other than himself—or himself high on the delusion that he was at once both a criminal mastermind and an innocent.

He became better at his job. His poetry got marginally better. He began to formulate his own opinions and express them to Noddy and Georgette and Ruddy and Ava and Chris or Larry on nights they were all gathered around the living room yelling at one another over the too-loud, unwatched QHL game.

"No, forget that, Ruddy. You don't get it. You never get it. Ava is right. Beauty isn't spread evenly through existence like peanut butter. Peanut butter isn't even spread evenly through existence like peanut butter. Beauty is a statement of value. It's an aesthetic construct used to differentiate things that are pleasing from things that are not. It's not inherent in all existence. You tool. It's not even inherent in this room. No offence, Av. It's more like crunchy peanut butter."

He began ordering expensive scotch, on the rocks, even though he hated the taste of it. He started smoking cigarillos, even though he couldn't take a drag without having a coughing fit. He started wearing black turtlenecks and fedoras. He started going out more, drinking more, even drinking enough to dance once in a while.

Him and Noddy would bathe themselves in cologne every night and go to La Baraque and buy girls drinks.

Noddy would take a new girl home every night, while it took Milton a while to warm up to the idea. But a thickly-cologned mysterious man in a black turtleneck buying endless drinks with a big wad of bills has a certain appeal for a certain type of person who hangs around a certain type of place.

He got a hand job, the most action he had ever gotten from anyone, on a Tuesday night in the alley behind La Baraque thanks to a puppet theatre lighting tech named Ginette.

Milton was hanging around in the alley while they smoked their crack—which was actually ground-up Medi-Drug diet pills—as the puppet troupe would do, and one thing led to another led to a fumbling back-alley hand job.

From then on it was open season.

Fig. 48. Amateur poet's survival kit

He was still Milton, so it was still always 30-seconds of fumbling and rubbing and slobbering and awkward, sticky goodbyes and good nights. It was still always in the alley, or in a dark corner, or once on the hallway toilet in La Baraque with a biker named Flo who was a good six-inches taller than him. It was still always a bit of a letdown.

He'd always assumed there was more to it. He'd assumed it was part of something else that added up to something bigger. But it never did.

It always felt vaguely disappointing and kind of wrong. He never really felt great about any of it. And he never worked up the nerve to take any of his paramours home for the real thing. He was still Milton, after all.

But it beat the alternative, so he kept at it.

At first, he'd fall in love each time, if even for a night, with whoever was on the other end of the fumbling and slobbering and rubbing.

He carried around the lackluster memory of Ginette for weeks, thinking that maybe, possibly, potentially, she could be the one. But she wasn't.

Of course she wasn't.

She was high on diet pill dust at the time, in that alley, at 3:00 a.m. She called him Martin and patted his head after.

Gradually he stopped falling in love. Gradually he stopped trying to remember their names. Gradually it stopped meaning anything at all.

• • •

Moan for Man

The bikers at La Baraque hated Milton and Noddy hanging around even more than they hated the puppet troupe.

But word got around that the "les deux tête carrées" were the Godfather's top suppliers, and the Death Riders depended, like everyone, on the Godfather's generosity, so they tolerated them.

Tolerated to the point that Milton, feeling pretty good in his black turtleneck, with a wad of money in his pocket and a half-dozen scotches in his belly, put his name on the monthly stand-up comedy open mic list and not a single biker threw a single beer at him the entire time he read one of his latest poems, which included several parts where he closed his eyes and shook his entire body.

```
go
mean
for
man
go mean for man
man oh man
go mean for me

go mean for the unwashed and unshaved
go mean for the unkempt and the unclean
tugging at the frayed ends of the earth
go mean for man
man oh man
go mean for me

go mean for mountain goats and homeless cats
go mean for the dirty birds and the cowboy
boot crossdressers with something to prove
go mean for man
man oh man
go mean for me

man oh man
oh man
go mean for me
go mean for me e e e
```

"I see you've been practicing the whole poet thing."

Milton just got off the stage, nary a beer thrown at him, even after he knelt in silence with his eyes closed and his arms outstretched for what seemed like an hour after finishing his "poem." It was a familiar voice behind him.

"Oh my God! Robin! Hi! How are you?!"

They hugged long and hard. She touched his cheek.

"It's good to see you. I like this new look. And that poem was... something."

"Heh, thanks. It's a bit different, I suppose. What are you doing here? I thought you were in Florida?"

"Yeah. Long story. Want a drink?"

"I do."

Milton and Robin sat and talked for a long time at the bar. He caught her up on everything—well, almost everything—that had happened to him since she left: the fame, the misfortune, the unemployment, the real job, the meeting Leonard Cohen, the turtlenecks, the expensive scotch, the cigarillos.

He left out the parts about nearly being executed by Leonard Cohen, about becoming a drug dealer, about the sloppy back-alley hand jobs.

She was impressed.

"Wow, I'm impressed!"

She caught him up on the fact that her new film was off to a shaky start.

"It's called *Turkey Vultures*."

"Great name!"

"Yeah, thanks. It's about the vultures in Florida who feed on roadkill gators. There are thousands of them. All over the place. Especially in all these suburbs that have become like ghost towns with the economy like it is. They're really beautiful-ugly birds. I've got a good start on things, but this one is different than *Dirty Birds*—more cameras, and the sound, Jesus, the sound. *Birds* was basically silent, but for the couple parts that I just overdubbed. But this time it's all live sound—vultures make these really guttural trilling sounds, they're really quite remarkable—but it's a nightmare with the ambient noise. So, I have this big crew, which is like a whole thing. And then one of the stupid sound guys brought his stupid dog to work one day, and the dog got loose and was running around on the road, and caused this big traffic clusterfuck, and we couldn't get the dog back, then an alligator jumped out of the ditch and got the dog, then a car runs over the gator. It was all so traumatizing.

But then all these vultures show up, so I tell them to keep shooting. Well, guy with the dog flips out. Calls the cops on me! We have to shut down shooting while they do this big investigation thing. We're like hemorrhaging cash while this is going on. And of course, most of my crew is from here, and none of us have work permits, so we all get deported. So, here I am. I found a good lawyer who can get us back down there with the right permits, but it's going to cost a lot. Right now, I'm just trying to get some money together so we can go back down and finish the thing."

As they talked, Robin kept circling back to this: how she needed money to finish her movie.

They talked about the economy: "Worst since the '30s they're saying."

"I'd believe that, you should see how bleak things are down in Florida."

About the U.S. election: "You really think this Obama guy can win?"

"Not if that hockey mom has anything to say about it."

"Then he doesn't stand a chance."

About Noddy, who was down to his underwear and wrestling a biker twice his size in a kiddie pool of scrambled eggs that was meant for the evening's post-open-mic entertainment.

"I can't believe I hooked up with him!"

"Me neither."

Even about Milton's poetry: "I'm not writing nearly as much as I used to."

"Why not?"

"I don't know, just too busy with work and things. It's just become this kind of secondary thing, I guess."

No matter what they'd talk about, the conversation

would always wind its way back to Robin's current predicament.

"Yeah, it's hard when external things keep you from making art, like work or money, or lack thereof. I'm so bummed. Being so broke. I don't know if we'll ever get to finish *Vultures*."

They talked until the bartender shooed them out of the bar.

This was the longest they had ever talked. Milton didn't want the night to end as they got up and made their way to the alley for a final cigarillo and to see what the puppeteers were getting up to.

He wanted to kiss her.

He wanted to take her back to his place.

He wanted to run away with her and live happily ever after.

He wanted to do all of this all at once and didn't want it to start in an alley while puppeteers smoked prenatal vitamins and humping behind the dumpster.

"I might be able to help you get your movie made."

"What? How?"

"I've got some money saved up, I can give you some, if you want. Why don't we go to my place and talk it over?"

"Okay. That'd be amazing. Thank you so much!"

She said yes!

Well, she said okay, but that was enough to make Milton float home ten feet off the ground.

They talked and laughed all the way back to his apartment. She held onto his arm. They laughed. It was sweet.

He led her up the stairs, fought his sticky front door open, brought her inside, and kissed her.

She kissed back.

They kissed. He kissed her harder, she kissed back harder. They began wrestling one another out of their clothes down the hall to Milton's room.

"This is your room?"

"Yeah."

"It's pretty small, and, well, gross, isn't it? And what's that smell?"

"It's not great. I'm going to move soon, probably."

Milton turned the lights back off, so it was completely dark. They went back to kissing and undressing and feeling their way around one another in the dark. Robin's body, next to his, felt like perfection.

"Ew! Are there no sheets on your bed?"

"Uh, yeah, they're... uh... in the wash. Just lay on top of the blanket."

Milton laid Robin down on top of the cheap blanket he'd bought at the lingerie/baby clothes/housewares store on Parc to replace his winter coat and always damp towel he'd been using for months and months.

He kissed her neck, and down her collarbone, across her perfect breasts, down her stomach, and along the waistband of her panties. She moaned softly and pressed her hips towards Milton as he kissed down the inside of her thighs.

"Thank you so much for offering to help with *Vultures*. It means a lot."

Milton stopped kissing and sat up on the bed.

"Are you just... Are we just... Is this just because of that?"

Robin sat up and half wrapped herself in the blanket.

"Because of what?"

"Are we just doing this because I offered to help you out?"

"What? No! God no! I'm drunk and horny and you're here too."

"That's it? Just because you're drunk and I'm here?"

"No, I mean, probably a bit. Like, it's probably a bad idea. I had that thing with your roommate, and you seem to have feelings, and... I don't know. Just shut up, this is nice. It was nice. I'm sorry."

She reached for Milton in the dark and grabbed his knee. "Probably a bad idea?"

He tried getting off the bed to turn the light back on, but planted the full weight of his knee on top of Robin's ankle, she yelped as he, in an attempt to avoid breaking anything, tried to quickly adjust his weight and instead became ensnarled in the blanket and toppled off the bed and onto the floor, crashing into the unstable table and sending a pile of books and dirty dishes and 44 pounds of 98-year-old Underwood No. 3 typewriter cascading to the floor.

The typewriter landed with a curious cracking thump, later to be discovered because of the 6-inch hole it drove clear through the floorboards.

Milton, stunned and drunk on the floor in his tiny white briefs and his black turtleneck, in the pitch dark, attempted to regain his bearings and his feet by reaching out in the dark for something to hang on to.

He found the blanket and pulled on it to pick himself up, but instead he pulled Robin, half-wrapped in it, onto the floor too.

They both lay in a tangled pile of blankets and books and typewriters and dirty dishes on the floor and laughed until they were out of breath. Then they just lay there, on the floor, in a pile.

Robin was laying perpendicular to Milton, on top of him, across his legs. She stroked his shin and sighed quietly. Milton played with her still-socked foot while his legs fell asleep and went numb.

He stared up into the darkness as he grew more and more sober and more and more tired. She closed her eyes and hummed "Bird on a Wire" softly. He wanted to say something to save the night. To rally. To keep it going. To turn it into a 'thing'. To rid himself of the suspicion he was being gamed and make it real and meaningful. To make her have 'feelings' too. To make her fall in love with him. But he couldn't think of anything more convincing than lying in the pitch blackness with his boner and his turtleneck, running his hand lightly over the top of her foot.

This made him hate himself even more than usual in that moment.

He had all this money and power, all this courage he never had before. He was getting (almost) laid and getting paid often and a lot. He had everything. Except sheets on his bed. And a window in his bedroom. But mostly everything. Everything was going his way. But in this moment, the most important moment of his entire life, all he could do was tickle her foot.

• • •

Morning After the Night Before

They woke up a few hours later in the same position—on the floor, Robin still lying on top of Milton—to a banging on the bedroom door.

His head pounded, his shin—which took the brunt of the table in the fall out of bed—throbbed, and his long-asleep legs burned with pins and needles.

"What time is it?"

"Hey. Good morning."

"Hi. What time is it?"

"I have no idea."

The banging on the door continued.

"Putain! Milton, get the fuck up!"

"What do you want, George?"

"Nohdee phones for you. He's in jail, says you 'ave to bail 'im."

"What?"

"Nohdee is in jail, connard!"

Robin moved her legs off Milton and attempted to get to her feet in the darkness.

"I think I should go."

"No, yeah. Don't worry. Of course. It's fine."

Milton's attempts at helping to extract them from the pile of trash on the floor only made things worse. They clashed heads really hard and both squealed and rubbed their foreheads.

Georgette kept knocking.

"Milton! Putain!"

"Yeah, give me a second!"

Milton was feeling his way across the floor on his hands and knees to find the light switch when Georgette threw the door open and flipped on the light. The one bare bulb hanging from a loose wire on the ceiling behind Georgette's tribal scarf décor/fly trap flooded the room with a blinding red light. Milton and Robin both covered their eyes.

"Jesus! Turn it off!"

"Ah, désolé, Milton. I did not know you 'ad a girl with you."

Milton peeked through his fingers and could see Robin, the love of his life, sitting on the floor in a pile of trash, in just her socks and underwear. She was exhausted and a mess. She was beautiful. He felt like he was going to throw up.

"Why are you on the floor? C'est quoi ce bordel?"

"Just turn the light off, George. Jeez!"

Robin got up onto the bed and turned her back to Milton and Georgette. She looked around for her clothes in amongst the mess. Not finding anything she picked the first shirt she could find off the pile and pulled on a wrinkled, dirty, tie-dyed CallCo Inc. t-shirt.

"Nohdee is in jail, Milton. After you leave the bar last night, 'e gets arrested. 'e calls me and says you have to come bail 'im. Said you can get cash."

"Gah! Yeah. What an idiot. Okay, just give us a minute."

"Tout de suite!"

Milton pushed the door closed on Georgette.

"Whee, toot sweet."

He turned and smiled awkwardly at Robin. They squinted at one another through the burning light and their respective hangovers and embarrassment. Milton searched for something important to say.

"Sorry," was all he could muster.

"I have to pee."

While Robin peed, Milton kicked aside the pile of rubble they had bucked off the table and bed so that he could get to a far larger pile in the far corner.

Robin came back in while Milton was filling a backpack full of rolls of money from a large cardboard box full of rolls of money, that lived at the bottom of the pile.

"Holy god! What is that?!"

"Ah... don't worry about it.

"That's like... So much money!"

"Yeah, I don't really know how much."

"Where'd it come from?"

"It's just my savings. It's all legit. I just... uh... Don't trust banks. Heh."

When the backpack was full, he started filling a plastic grocery bag that was balled up in his pile of garbage.

"I guess I've got to bail this dummy out. I'm sorry for the mess... and... everything."

"It's okay."

Milton finished filling the plastic grocery bag and handed it to Robin.

"Take this."

"To bail him out with?"

"No, to finish your movie."

"I can't take this much. This is nuts! I thought you wanted to lend me a few bucks. But this... This is too much! I'll never be able to repay you. I don't even know how much it is."

"It's probably a hundred grand. I don't know. But don't

worry about it. It's not a loan. It's a gift."

"A gift? I can't... You can't... We can't... I'm not for sale."

"An investment then. Just give me a producer credit, or whatever. Nothing else. No strings."

"That's it? No strings? You don't want sex or a blow job or anything."

"Not like this, not for this. I'm... You're... It's not like that."

"What is it like? This is a lot of money."

"I don't know, Robin. I... I believe in you. I guess."

"I can't take it. It's too much! Seriously. Who gives someone a shopping bag full of money? What are you, a drug dealer?"

"Haha... No... Never mind where I got it. It's yours now. I insist."

Robin tried to hand the bag back to Milton.

"I can't take this. It'd change things too much. And why do you have it? Last time I saw you, you were basically homeless. Now you're handing out bags of money to women, in your underwear and turtleneck! This whole thing is too much."

"God! Fine. Okay. It's a long story, but Noddy dragged me into a bit of a mess so I'm selling leftover pills from work to a... to a company. It's all legit. I get paid in cash. It's been going on for a while, so now I've got this big box of money. I can't spend it all. I don't want to spend it all. I want you to have it for your movie. It's an investment, not a bribe. I swear."

"Wait. You're selling pills?"

"Just the leftover ones."

"Like you're stealing pills and selling them for cash."

"It's not stealing, it's like dumpstering, basically."

"Basically?! Are you a drug dealer? Like, an actual drug dealer?"

"God no! Are you kidding? Could you imagine me doing

anything like that? I give them to Noddy who sells them to another guy who sells them to somebody else. Who knows where they actually end up?"

"So, they don't go to a company?"

"Well, a kind of company. I don't know. It's complicated. But it's fine. I swear."

"It all sounds shady, dangerous, and illegal."

Georgette banged on the door again.

"Milton! Merde! Nohdee is on the phone for you!"

"It's all fine, I swear. But I want you to take this and make your movie. Really. And I need to go down and bail out Noddy. He's a horrible person, but he's like my business partner... or something... I guess."

Georgette swung the door open. She covered her eyes with one hand and held out her phone to Milton with the other.

"I won't look at your naked girlfriend, just talk to this asshole, putain!"

Milton took the phone.

"Hello."

"Jumpin' Jesus, b'y. Will ya get your arse down here already. Do you know how many guards I had to blow to get a second phone call?"

"Yeah, I'm coming. What's going on?"

"A big pile of bullshit. Just come bail me out. I don't know what it'll cost, bring, like, 20 Gs."

"Yeah, fine."

He hung up, handed the phone back to Georgette.

"Putain, vous êtes deux imbéciles, des putains de pathétiques."

Milton pushed the door closed on Georgette again and held the grocery bag back out to Robin.

"Will you please take this? Please? I'm begging you."

"If I do could I get in trouble? Honestly?"

"Gah! No! Look. I take pills from work, I give them to

Noddy, he gives me a bunch of money, and gives the pills to someone else. I have no idea what happens to them from there. Neither does he. If we get caught, we'll be in shit, but we're just small fish who don't know anything, and you have nothing to do with any of it. For all you know, I just cash my paycheque each week and keep it in a box in my room. Weird, sure, but I'm from Saskatchewan. After my grandpa died, we found $50,000 in small mouldy bills in a potato sack in the root cellar. So, you'll be fine. I promise. And you can make your movie. Here..."

Milton dug another grocery bag from the pile and dumped several more handfuls of money in it.

"Take more. It's fine. I swear. Take it all if you want. This is mostly just extra I can't clean so I can't really spend it."

"What do you mean, 'clean'?"

"Like money laundering, like in the movies. It's messed up, I know. But you're fine. I promise."

"Oh, Milton. How'd you get tangled up in this mess? This isn't you."

"Well, when there's a gun to your head you do what you have to keep... uh... the bad guys from pulling the trigger."

"What? What bad guys? Are you in danger?"

"I have a box of 'extra' money in my room and am on my way to bail out my dumb-ass partner in a criminal plot I'm in the middle of... I'm always in danger."

"Oh my God, Milton. I had no idea you were like this."

"Yeah. I know."

"But it's also kind of badass."

"Badass?"

"I don't know. It's like, horribly stupid, but you're different than before. It's kind of... I don't know... hot."

"Hot?"

"Yeah, a little. I don't know. You should go."

"Uh... I guess..."

"Thank you for all this. Maybe I can see you again before

I go back down there?"

"Yeah, that'd be nice. Tonight?"

"Sure, meet me at La Baraque at eight?"

"It's a date."

Robin stepped around the piles of junk on the floor, took the bags of money out of Milton's hands, planted a deep, long, hard kiss on him, and grabbed his ass.

"See you at eight."

FIFTEEN

THE NIGHT
PAT MURPHY
DIED

Intent to Distribute

It was after 10:00 a.m. by the time Milton got out the door. With a backpack full of about $40,000 in drug money, he took a cab downtown to the police station. By noon, Noddy and Milton were back in a cab going home.

Milton's bag of drug money didn't get searched, he didn't even end up needing any of it.

Bail in American movies works differently than bail in Canadian real life. The police decided, mostly to get rid of Noddy who had all the drunkards and assorted detainees singing "The Night Pat Murphy Died" all night, to let Noddy go without a bail hearing. He was released on his own recognizance and only had to pay a $43.95 processing fee.

> *Oh, the night that Paddy Murphy died, is a night I'll never forget*
> *Some of the boys got loaded drunk, and they ain't got sober yet.*

On the cab ride, Noddy explained to Milton what had led to his arrest.

"What the heck, dude?"

"You're after taking that bird home, yeah? You bang her?

Not bad, eh? The tits on her! My son!"

"No. Tell me what happened with you?"

"Get a blowy at least?"

"Shut up! What'd you do?"

"Nothing! Me and the b'ys are hanging out behind The Barack with them puppet queers. Well one of them takes to running their stupid mouth about some shit and gets a smack from one of them bikers. Then another fella gets a smack and before ya knows it all holy hell's busted loose. When the cops shows up, I got buddy down on the ground just feeding him lefts. Right? Buddy swallowed his teeth, sure. Look at me mitts, barked up real good. So, the pigs hauls me off him and puts me in cuffs. Well they searches me and finds a couple bottles of shit, and now they're charging me with disturbing the peace, possession with intent, and resisting 'cause I shoved a cop after he started grabbing at me arse when he was frisking me. So that's just fuckin' wonderful."

"Wait! What? Possession with intent? What does that mean?"

"Intent to distribute."

"Distribute what?"

"Just a few pills, b'y. Ain't nothing."

"My pills? The pills? The ones I give you? The pills that saved our lives? Those pills with intent?"

"Relax, b'y, it was just a few. I just got to find a doc to write me a 'script and it'll all go away."

"Oh, it'll all go away? Just need to find a doctor to prescribe pills that aren't even approved by the government yet? That say "TRIAL DRUG" right on the bottles? It'll all go away?! We're screwed! We're either going to prison or Leonard Cohen is going to throw us off a bridge."

The cab driver, who supposedly spoke no English, watched in the rear-view mirror with a smile as Milton tied into Noddy.

"You idiot! You're going to get us both killed. Why?!

Why the hell did you keep any? You just have to take a bag from me and hand it to another guy. That's it! Free money! I'm taking all the risk you... you... friggin' nincompoop!"

"Jeez, b'y. Calm yer tits. Do you know how much one of them bottles is worth retail? Buddy buys them from us for pennies a pill and sells them for like 50 per. We're getting fucked, b'y."

"No! We aren't! We're being allowed to live! And we're making more than enough! I've got a box of extra money in my closet I can't even lift. Of *extra* money! Money I can't spend, because I have too much of it."

The cab turned off onto an unknown side street and headed towards the highway to take the extra-long way home.

"Hey, buddy, where the fuck you taking us?!"

"Just sit tight, my friends."

"This fucking guy is taking us on a ride now that you're blabbing about all the money you can't spend. Nice going, b'y."

"If we survive this, I'm going to murder you, I swear to god!"

• • •

Cancer

The cab, now somewhere in the guts of the far-flung neighbourhood Côte-des-Neiges, stopped at a light. While stopped, an old man got into the front passenger seat.

"Ho, buddy, whaddayat? Cab's taken. Ya blind?"

It was Leonard Cohen.

The light changed and the cab drove on. Leonard Cohen didn't say a word, just sat staring straight ahead as the cab exited back onto the highway. Milton and Noddy sat in the back and watched him silently. The silence seemed to go on for hours.

And hours.

And hours as the cab sped down the highway to nowhere in particular.

"Gentlemen, I'm just an old man, my memory isn't as sharp as it once was, so please correct me if I am wrong, but I believe when we last met we came to an arrangement in which you would provide me with a steady stream of goods in exchange for your lives and great deals of money, and we were to never meet again unless there was a problem. And, well, here I am. Leads me to believe there has been some kind of problem."

"Nah, b'y. No problem. Cops just got cocked up. Das it."

"Possession with intent to distribute and resisting arrest are serious charges. If the offender happens to also have a record as long as his growing nose, the prison sentence could just have enough weight to cause him to talk out of turn, especially if his only skill in life is talking out of turn."

"Nah, b'y. I ain't no fuckin' rat. And these bullshit charges won't stick worth shit."

"What do you think, Poet? Is this a surmountable challenge? Was I a fool to drop everything I was doing and go out of my way to join you two for a scenic drive through Côte-des-Neiges?"

"No, sir, Godfather, sir. I mean, yes. I mean... It's okay. I think it's okay. Noddy did a stupid thing, but he's sorry, and he won't do it again, and... Uh... Everything else is going really well. I'll make sure it keeps going fine. No one suspects anything."

"So, our dim but verbose friend here is the issue?"

"Eh, buddy, I don't care who you are, you don't go calling me dumb to my face, b'y."

The cab driver reached under his seat, pulled out a Taser, reached back without taking his eyes off the road, stuck it in Noddy's leg, and gave him a jolt. Noddy jerked stiff where he sat.

"Jesus fuckin' thundering Key-rist!"

"So, Poet, are you saying if we eliminate the weak link in this operation we can return to our previously fruitful arrangement?"

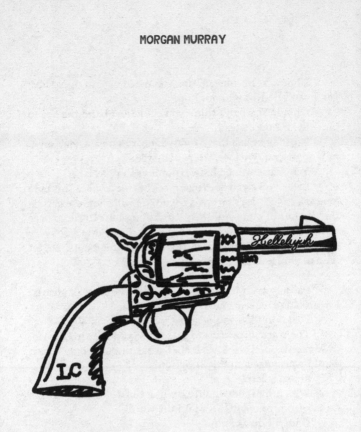

Fig. 49. Leonard Cohen's revolver

"Uhm... Yes... I mean, no. You mean get rid of Noddy? No. I can't do this without him."

"Oh no? You don't think you could just hand the bag to our Kiwi friend instead?"

"No, it's not just that. Noddy is my roommate. He's my... he's my friend. We look after each other."

"You really want a blowy, don't ya, b'y?"

"Let me give you one final piece of free advice. This man here is a cancer. He's no one's friend. He will continue to suck the life out of you until there is nothing left. Until you are dead. Which could be very, very soon if you don't act very carefully and deliberately in the next few moments. So, let me ask you, how do you get rid of cancer?"

"Uhm... I don't know."

"Pardon me, Mr. Ontario, you'll have to speak clearly, I'm an old man, remember."

"I... I don't know. I'm sorry."

"There are three ways to get rid of a cancer, Mr. Ontario: irradiate it, bombard it with chemicals, or cut it out. Which would you suggest in this situation?"

"S-s-suggest?"

"Which method would you like to use to remove this cancer from your life before it kills you?"

"Uhm... I don't know."

"I beg your pardon?"

"I... I don't know."

Leonard Cohen pulled a small silver six-shooter revolver with an ivory handle and 'Hallelujah' engraved along the barrel from inside his jacket, cocked it, and handed it to Milton.

"I find it works best if you irradiate it right between the eyes from close range."

Milton took the gun in his hands and held it like it was some kind of sacred offering. He stared at it like it was the strangest thing he had ever seen. It weighed a lot more than he thought it would. He was shaking and numb, frozen.

"Poet... I said that I prefer to irradiate the cancer right between the eyes. It's very easy, just point and squeeze. From this range, you should be able to hit him with one of the six bullets. Here, hold it like this."

Leonard Cohen adjusted in his seat and helped Milton grip the gun better, he helped him hold it up to Noddy's forehead.

"That's it. Just point and squeeze."

Tears ran down Milton's face. His vision blurred. The world spun around him as the cab hurtled down the highway.

"Just point and squeeze."

"I ca-ca-can't."

Milton sobbed. Noddy stared at Milton, wide-eyed, terrified, a single tear ran down his cheek.

"Fuck dat! Don't do it, b'y! Shoot him!"

"Just point and squeeze. It's easier than poetry. Just point. And squeeze."

"I CAN'T!"

"Don't do it, b'y! I'll be some rotted if ya shoot me."

"Yes you can, my son. You're a poet. He's a cancer. Just point and squeeze."

"I'm sorry!"

"Don't do it, b'y!"

"I'm sorry!"

"Just point and squeeze!"

"I'm sorry!"

Milton closed his eyes, jerked the gun away from Noddy's forehead, and squeezed.

BANG!

...

The bullet ricocheted off the C-frame of the car next to the rear window behind Noddy's head, off the metal passenger headrest upright inches from Leonard Cohen's head, and lodged itself into the right shoulder of the cab driver.

The car, travelling about 140 kilometres per hour, jerked violently into the neighbouring lane, glanced off a cement truck, shot back across three lanes, launched itself off a concrete barrier, and took flight for what seemed like a weightless eternity, before landing nose first and toppling end-over-end several times and coming to rest on its roof.

Traffic in both directions stopped.

Flames licked up out of the engine compartment.

An eerie silence came over the midday highway.

Milton, the only one wearing a seatbelt, was the first to come to. He hung suspended upside down. He coughed through the thickening smoke and looked up to see Noddy below him—twisted in a heap and covered in a sparkle of broken glass. He reached out. His shoulder screamed in pain and shot lightning down his arm.

"Psst... Noddy. Hey. Nod. You okay?"

Noddy didn't move.

Leonard Cohen, in a mangled pile in the front of the car, didn't move.

The cab driver, crumpled around the steering wheel, groaned but didn't move.

He poked Noddy harder.

"Hey... Noddy. Wake up... Please."

Nothing.

"Please!"

With his good arm, Milton reached up and unlatched the seatbelt. He crashed down hard on top of Noddy and his bad shoulder. He screamed in pain.

"Jesus, b'y! will ya go on and scream in some other fella's ear?"

"Oh, thank God! I thought you were dead! Are you dead?

Are you hurt? We need to get out of here!"

"Well, I ain't feeling good enough for ya to be humping me. Go on and get off me, b'y."

Milton one-arm crawled through what was left of the window in the back of the car and helped Noddy drag himself out behind.

Traffic was stopped and people were starting to get out of their cars to come help.

"We have to get out of here, Noddy. Before anyone sees us."

Milton ducked back inside the smouldering car, grabbed the backpack full of money and stuffed Leonard Cohen's gun inside.

"Well let's get after 'er."

Noddy's leg was twisted and bloody, he could barely walk. Milton threw the bag over his good shoulder and put his good arm around Noddy and helped him limp towards the side of the road.

Just as they reached an off-ramp embankment, Milton looked back to see two black SUVs pull up to the burning car and a handful of giants with big guns poured out.

As they disappeared down the embankment, they heard the gas tank on the cab explode and felt a wave of warmth roll down the hill after them.

• • •

The Runs

Milton and Noddy slid down the embankment, crawled under a rusted chain-link fence, and into a large, full mall parking lot. They limped into the middle of the parking lot and laid on the ground between two cars, out of sight of the highway, to catch their breath.

"Buddy! The fuck? You tried to shoot me, b'y! Not fit!"

"I missed on purpose, you idiot."

"Why didn't you just shoot the old fart instead of the cabbie, Jesus! Nearly got us all killed."

"I didn't want to shoot anyone! But maybe I should have shot you!"

"I wish you did, for how bad my head hurts. Next time don't shoot the buddy driving the car. Shoot the buddy trying to kill us."

"Shut up. I'm glad your head hurts."

"Well, ya broke my Jesus leg too."

"Good."

They both laid on their back and stared up at the grey, sky. Milton's shoulder was badly dislocated, his arm hung limp by his side. Noddy's leg was badly messed up, likely broken, at least sprained, and he'd smacked his head pretty good off the roof of the cab, splitting it open at his hairline, sending thick sheet of bloods down his face. He looked more like a ghoul than usual.

"Meeting you is the worst thing that's ever happened to me."

"Jeez, b'y. You're a bit of a sook, ain't ya?"

"A year ago, I'd never even held a gun in my whole life, and the strongest drug I ever even took was a Tylenol. Next thing, I meet you and I'm dealing drugs and just shot a guy and got into a crazy car crash and got away just before it exploded, and now I'm on the run from the cops and Leonard Freaking Cohen and his army of meatheads with a pile of drug money and a gun."

"What's this now?"

"I wish I never met you!"

"No, no. You still got the cash and the gun? Oh buddy! We ain't dead yet."

"I wish I was!"

"But we ain't, b'y. We can get out of this mess you made."

"Yeah right. How?"

"There's a metro just up the road. We get on it and disappear. That's it. Run."

"Where are we going to go? What are we going to do? We both look like crap and if we go anywhere in public someone will call the cops. I'm sure Leonard Cohen owns all the cops in this town, and everyone in every jail, and before the end of the day we'll be dead in a cell somewhere. And that's if Leonard's guys don't find us first. They know where we live, who we hang out with, everything. We can't just go home and pack a bag and hop in a cab to the bus station."

"Well, you look like shit. Ya needs to scrub that sour look off your face. I just needs to mop the blood off me and get a new pair of pants. The arse is outta these ones."

Noddy slowly turned to show Milton his bare arse.

"Luh, just there. It's a Walmart. You'll fit in just fine there. Go buy me a few duds."

Milton and Noddy bickered until Milton relented and got himself to his feet and started towards the Walmart.

"Check out the maternity section, b'y, single moms are dyin' for a nice boy like you."

Milton, looking like he had just been on the losing end of a car wreck, staggered into Walmart.

He found a change of normal-looking clothes for himself and a pair of *Simpsons* sweatpants, an "I'm with stupid" t-shirt with the arrow pointing up, and a "Nice Bum, Where Ya From?" ball cap for Noddy.

His arm was killing him and he was covered in broken glass, so he also got a first-aid kit, some rubbing alcohol, and a jumbo pack of super-long Twizzlers.

Back in the parking lot, Milton dumped half a bottle of rubbing alcohol on Noddy's busted up face. He screamed so loud Milton was sure the cavalry would be coming any second. Milton made Noddy wrap bandages around his own head, and splinted his leg with a pair of windshield wipers he tore off a parked car.

Noddy managed to dress himself and looked suitably like a complete idiot. Milton changed his clothes, bandaged his arm, and put it in a sling from the first-aid kit.

Looking only slightly better than they did before, they limped their way to the metro very slowly. When they finally made it, they stopped at the top of the two escalators, one heading down to the uptown platform, the other heading up to the downtown platform.

"Where are we going?"

"Give me half the cash, b'y, I'm going uptown, you take the other half and go downtown."

"What, why?"

"I'm fucked, b'y. I gots nowhere I can go. I can't go home, I can't go out west, too many bad fuckers knows me. And I'm skipping bail. The only chance I gots is if I can get into witness protection. The cops here are all in the Old Fart's pocket, so I'm taking a train to Toronto to see if they're interested in taking down the Montreal mob. You need to get on the next bus to Sin Jawns."

"What are you talking about? St. John's?!"

"I'm gonna call my uncle Greg, he's a prof at MUN, b'y. He'll look after ya. He owes me."

"What the heck am I going to do there?"

"B'y, you gotta trust me. There's probably already a hit out on the both of us. Every two-bit goon will be looking to pop us for a few grand. So, don't be thick in the head. No one knows ya in Sin Jawns. Just change your name, grow a beard, get some glasses, and you'll be fine. Greggy's clean, no one knows I knows him or he knows me. He'll look after ya."

"Then what."

"Settle down, find a woman, join the circus, fuck if I know. If things go well in Toronto in a few months all this shit should have blown over then you can do what the fuck you want."

"I just want to go home."

"Give it a bit, then you goes home."

Noddy looked at Milton with a face that was almost apologetic. A trickle of blood ran down his temple. He playfully punched Milton, really hard, in the bad shoulder, Milton yelped in pain, but the punch put his shoulder back together and he instantly felt better. Slightly. Noddy unzipped the bag on Milton's back and fished out a bunch of money.

"Well, keep your dick wrapped, b'y. I'se be getting' on."

"Okay. See you. I guess."

Milton took the up escalator to go downtown, Noddy took the down to go uptown. They stood directly across from one another, avoiding eye contact for several minutes until their trains came, both at the same moment. Noddy grinned and flipped Milton the bird. Milton pretended not to see him.

PART FOUR
NEWFOUNDLAND

SIXTEEN

ST. JOHN'S

Ferry

St. John's was much further from Montreal than Milton ever imagined.

The bus trip went fairly quickly through Quebec, hugging the shore of the St. Lawrence as it grew wider and wider. Hundreds of farms, sliver-thin, stretching from the water, up the valley to God knows where. The opposite in every possible way from the massive flat squares of Saskatchewan.

New Brunswick isn't big, but the road winds through hills and bush and it seems like the dead of night even in the middle of the day, and it just goes on forever. The sun doesn't start shining again until Nova Scotia. Then rolling hills to Cape Breton—the distillation of quaint maritime charm—then the world ends.

North Sydney is the end of the line. But it's still 16 hours from St. John's.

It's further from Montreal to St. John's than it is from Regina to Montreal, which is across most of a continent.

Newfoundland is so far from everywhere it has its own time zone.

Newfoundland is its own planet.

Milton dug into his bag of drug money and bought a

walk-on ticket for a massive ferry, which is about 100 times bigger and costs about 100 times more than the cable ferry across Lake Diefenbaker.

The MV Caribou sails for six hours through the night across the Gulf of St. Lawrence to a tiny fishing village called Port aux Basques, where Milton will endeavor to find another bus to take him to St. John's.

Milton tried to sleep on the floor of the ferry. But the gentle rise and fall of the ship through the night was just about more than his Prairie guts could stand. He turned a pale shade of corpse and fought nausea the entire crossing.

The second the ship docked, he was fine.

He walked off the ferry into a cloud of thick, cold fog.

It was Fall when he left Cape Breton, but the six-hour crossing was actually eight months into the past, into winter.

The thick, cold fog was like cement that pushed through his skin and meat and into his bones. When he looked down, he could barely see his own feet. At least, he thought they were his feet.

He made his way through a vast parking lot full of fog-hidden cars about to board for a return to Fall. Milton walked with his hands in front of him to avoid bumping too hard into anything that would sneak up on him in the fog. He made his way over to the ferry terminal and went inside to get a bus ticket.

The short, square woman at the counter—from what Milton could make out through her thick accent which sounded like Finnish without spaces between the words—explained, that:

"m'duckyissasin'boutdabussinb'ynotenoughtraffic for'ertokeeprunnin'folkslikeflyin'thesedaysI'sposebutif yasneedtogettoTownm'loverGerrythere'llgiveyaalift."

She pointed to a guy in a neon Ski-Doo jacket smoking a cigarette and drinking coffee out of a Styrofoam cup sitting directly below a no-smoking sign. Milton assumed that meant he was the bus driver.

Gerry wasn't the bus driver. There was no bus. Gerry was an entrepreneur.

When it wasn't fishing season he'd supplement his pogey[27] hauling lost tourists from Port aux Basques to "Town" in his 1997 Ford F-150 Extended Cab for $100 cash, and bring back 50-pound bags of potatoes and five-gallon pails of pickles and 48 double rolls of toilet paper and 5x7 high-impact plastic baby barn garden sheds and anything else his neighbours would order from the only Costco on the entire giant, empty island.

"Sorrym'sonshesfullerthanamummersgutontibbseveb'y ift'weren'tsomauzyI'dtakeyainthepanbutyerapttofreezesome dayonclothesouttheresureby."

"How much for a ride?"

"Nawm'songotsafullloadgottacallGerryb'yhe'llgetyat' CornerBrook."

Gerry pointed to a rotary phone on the wall under a handwritten sign that read "Gerry's Taxi – Dial 1."

"Are you... Is that... Gerry... Taxi...?"

"Yesb'ydasrightgivesGerryacallan'he'llgetyatoawarm bedferdanight."

"Gerry... Right..."

Milton, without taking his eyes off Gerry, walked backwards towards the phone and dialed 1 for Gerry.

The phone rang at the information counter, 15 feet away. Brenda picked up the phone.

"Gerry'scab."

Milton had no idea what was happening or who he was talking to.

"Uh... Hi... I need a bus to St. John's. Please."

"Nawm'duckydisisGerry'scabyawan'Gerry'sbuswhich isn'tabusjustGerryjustluhissasinthere'snobusnomoresin butdassittheworldischangin'."

---

[27] Employment Insurance.

"Is this... Am I talking... to you?"

Milton pointed at Brenda across the corridor.

"Y'sdearwhatcanIdoforye?"

"St. John's! Please!"

"Gerrysay'e'adnomoreroomin'istruckm'ducksinthatis tooI'll'avemeGerrycome'roundan'pickyagetyatoawarmbed forthenightsure'e'llbe'eredaoncesittight."

"Uhm..."

Gerry finished his coffee, dropped his cigarette butt in the cup, got up, threw the cup out, threw some words at Brenda, and made his way out to his waiting truck. Milton followed him out and watched him climb into his truck.

There were five other men in the truck already, all of them twice Milton's size, with moustaches, ballcaps, and a mix of snowmobile-branded winter coats. They all turned and looked at Milton, half-nodded, and, in unison, took sips from giant travel coffee mugs. Gerry got in the cab and started the engine. Nodded to Milton and drove away.

• • •

Gerry

Milton sat down on the curb, under the weight of the cold and fog. Just sat. Sat and stared into the thick grey abyss for a long, long time.

Sat and stared into the thick grey abyss for a long, long time and slowly lost all feeling.

He was on the run from a very bad man and the very bad men that worked for him. There was a price on his head.

A hit.

He didn't even think hits were real. He thought they were some made-up movie stuff. But apparently not. Apparently, whatever is left of Leonard Cohen, or whoever took his place after he bounced down the highway, can post on Facebook, or something, that he will pay to have someone who done him wrong murdered, and just like that they are murdered.

And that someone who done someone wrong? That someone who crossed the most powerful and ruthless criminal
and finest poet and songwriter in all of Canada? This time,
that was Milton. Milton Ontario. Mike and Sherry's son from
Bellybutton, Saskatchewan. Milton Ontario, who on the advice
of one of the worst people in all of existence to take advice from,
has fled to Newfoundland— NEWFOUNDLAND!—to try and
save his own life.

Hypothermia was beginning to set in, the kind you can
only get from Newfoundland fog, as Milton got drowsier and
drowsier sitting on the curb, trying to calculate how long it
would take Leonard Cohen's thugs to find him and throw him
into the frozen sea.

He began to nod off, when a rust- and maroon-coloured
1992 Reliant K car squealed its worn-out brakes right next to
him, almost running him over.

From the few syllables that Milton could make out, this
was either the most Newfoundland hitman ever, come to take
his life, or Gerry's Taxi come to take him to St. John's.

Either was fine at that moment, so he crawled in beside
a middle-aged man with a face worn by weather and hard
living, a thin grey moustache, a Polaris ball cap and an
Arctic Cat jacket, with a travel mug of coffee in one hand and
a cigarette in the other.

"ThenamesGerryb'yaftermefadderan"isfadderbeforedat
nowmesonyalookslikeadrownratfrozenintherainbarrel
whereyaofftoIcantakeyaasfarastownyacan'aveyourselfastay
inaproperplacem'sonliketheGreenwoodInnan'yecanget
yerselfafinescoffatSorrentosderoneofdemrightfancyItalian
placestookmeoldladythereBrendathemissusworkingthe
counterthereforourannivers'rythirtysixyearsthisMarch
pastwe'vebeenatitgoodlongwhileexceptforashortspell
intherewhenIwasworkin'outwestan'heardshewasdiddlin'
GerryfromUpperFerryderyaproblydon'knows'ibut'e's
thafellawit'thequeereduparmtheregot'ercaughtintha

Fig. 50. Gerry's Cab

winchon'eesbrudder'scrabboattwisted'erright'round
likelicoricesoI'mupinFortMacan''hearol'UpperFerryGerry's
diddlin'Bren'an'Igetswildgoesoffm''eadforaweekstuck'er
inevery'ookerIcouldfindan'whateverwasleftwentright
upmenosenowm'sonInearlygotrunoffforthatIwasright
wreckedan'Bren'callsmet'askwherethechequeisshes
gotstabuytheboysnewbootsan'IjustsnapsrightIsaysto'
'erIsays'LuhBren'Iknowsy'beendiddlingSkipperwith
thetwistedflippersoy'ain'tgettin'onecentfromme'well
m'sonshewasrightrottedwit'meturnsoutitwasIsleo'morts
BrendawhoworksatthecountertherewitmyBren'datwas
bonkin'TwirlyArmGerrynowmesonBren'smarriedtoo
toTooTallGerryfromthaFerrybutdatain'tnoconcerno'
minenowisitb'ybesidesmykhack's'boutrottedofffromall
theFortMaccrackI'ad'erinferaweekstraightsowhoamI
tojudgeIt'oughtthatwas'erb'yy'sm'sonIt'oughmean'
Bren'wast'roughbutb'yshe'sagoodwomanbetterdenI'd
everbewouldn'tyaknowshetakesmebackwhenI'mbackon
nex'longchangeevent'houghIgotthaclapbutdasitb'ywhat
cany'dobeentenyearssinceneverbeenbacktoFortMacsince
nom'sonthatplaceisnotfitnotfitatallnowwherewasitya
wannagom'son?''

It took several more pleading-not-understanding-a-word
minutes, and three more never-ending Gerry stories—about
his dog Coot who's "gotsagirlfrienduptheroadan'keepstakin'
offafter'ercan'tevenlet'imouttopiss'imselfor'e'llbegonefer
t'reedays"; his son Little Gerry Jr, who's "smartasawhipbut
uglierthanthearseendofasculpinwhichain'tgreatbutbetter
thanthereverseI'spose"; and his mother Bertie, who's "olderden
daGrandeBanksan'crookedasallsinan'willknockyaonyer
arseifyacross'erbless'er'eart"—about 45 minutes, for Milton to
reverse negotiate with Gerry to drive him all the way to St. John's
for $150.

Milton had offered $500, but Gerry insisted that was
much too much, that he couldn't possibly do it for more than

$100. Milton countered with $300, Gerry with $50. Milton, confounded by Gerry's negotiation style, which he would discover was an island-wide phenomenon, offered the original $500. Gerry said, "ifyaneedstapaysomet'ingdasfinebutIwon't takemorethanone-fiftyanddasit." So that was it. But Milton planned on tipping generously for the 900 kilometer cab ride.

Amongst his never-ending stories, Gerry attempted a conversation with Milton. Or at least he'd stop every so often for a draw off his cigarette, which would give Milton a chance to say something.

With some prompting, Milton carefully told Gerry some of his story: about how he was from Saskatchewan—to which Gerry interjected with a story about working out west and his cousin who's "stillgoin'at'eroutder'e'sinGrandeCache drivin'truck'elikesitalrightbetterdenworkin'foralivin'"— about how he was a famous poet and how he knows Leonard Cohen, "the singer one,"—to which Gerry interjected with a story about his wife Brenda, "Lennyder'e'sdafellawhosoun's likeBren'whenshegetsondaLambsb'yy'sm'sonlikeder garglin'rockstheboth'of'em"—about how he'd gotten tired of the big city hustle and bustle in Montreal—"y'sm'son udderdenEdmontonIain'tneverbeeninaplacesobigasdatan' Ican'tstandsittoocrowdedeveryoneupyerarsealldatime"—and how, at the suggestion of his roommate from Newfoundland, he was coming out here for a while.

Those were the magic words, "roommate from Newfoundland." It launched the pair into a protracted game of six-degrees of Noddy.

"Who's'ean'who's'esfadder?"

"You wouldn't know him, he's from St. John's."

"IknowsplentyafolksfromTownm'sonbesidesnoonefrom TowntheyallfromtheBayan'movestotown."

"Well, his name is Noddy."

"Nom'son!Y'don'tmeanNoddyButtsfromdaSea'orse?"

"Butts?"

"Y'sb'yalittlemout'yskeetalwaysgoin'on'boutConfederation and'owwe'swasrobbedan'somerealtinfoil'atshit'boutyaybig."

Gerry held his hand up a few feet above the seat of the car.

"Yeah, that's him. Wow! Small world, eh?"

"O'm'sonnotsmall'noughwhyoneart'wouldyoudo anyt'ingdatdullsticksaysmesondatfellaisnotfitnotfitatall don'beatanyofdatwhatever'e'sgotyaintogetonoutdaonce b'y'eain'tfitain'tfit."

"Now you tell me!" joked Milton.

Gerry wasn't joking.

A few hours on through the thick, thick fog they pulled off at a gas station on the edge of a town called Badger. Gerry fueled up the car after fighting with Milton to not take any money.

"Ye'ungry?"

"I guess. I can just grab something here."

"Nom'sondisain'tfoodwe'llstopinonm'cousinlivesjust updaway."

Gerry pulled the car onto a small, narrow side street with a few small houses.

Badger made Milton homesick for the first time in a long time. It was the same patchwork of little houses that weren't old enough to be historic but not new enough to be nice, like Bellybutton. Just with much thicker fog.

Gerry turned into the driveway of a small white house with red shutters and as he drove up to the house a man in plaid chopping firewood emerged from the fog. He looked just like Gerry. His name was Jerry.

Gerry and Jerry spoke even quicker. It was just a blur of mashed together vowels and apostrophes. Milton would catch every tenth word or so. Something about this fella from the mainland who knows Noddy Butts from the Sea Horse, followed by great laughter and head shakes.

Jerry waved Gerry and Milton inside. The small house was warm and humid and smelled like fresh-baked bread.

Inside was Jerry's wife, also Brenda, who immediately began fussing over her guests.

"Comem'lovetakeaseatletmefixyaaplate."

Gerry and Jerry and Milton sat around the round kitchen table with a plastic sheet over a white lace tablecloth.

Gerry and Jerry hummed and buzzed back and forth at one another. From the bits Milton could decipher, there was a lot of talk about the weather, the woods, their sons out west, nan, and more laughter and disbelief that "disfella'ere" knew "datdimButtsfella".

In no time, Brenda put down a plate piled high with canned ham and white bread sandwiches, and mugs of milky tea.

"G'wonnowfillyerbootsm'duckies."

The sandwiches vanished and tea disappeared, and Gerry and Jerry seemed to have covered every possible topic there was upon which two cousins could possibly discuss, all in less than half an hour, and Milton and Gerry got back in the K-Car and pulled back on the highway.

Gerry returned to his life story. They were rounding the 1992 cod moratorium "daarsefelloutta'erb'y," and heading towards the difficult years that landed him out west in a work camp, far from Brenda and the boys, with nothing and no one "'ceptferdabottlem'sonan'datdon'loveyabacknone."

Going the speed limit, and only stopping for gas and a feed of fee and chee[28] in Gander, about halfway, it takes a mortal human about ten hours to make the trip from Port aux Basques to St. John's.

Gerry though, including a stop for lunch in Badger, and for smokes in a town called Goobies, which appeared to Milton to just be two gas stations on either side of the highway, plowed his antique K-Car through the thick fog with the accelerator pinned to the floor. He pulled up to the bright orange front door of a bright green row house on

[28] Fish and chips.

Upper Battery Road—perched on the cliff face next to the harbour in the most picturesque neighbourhood in the entire city, if ever the fog cleared long enough to see it—in less than seven hours.

"Thereyebem'son."

Milton thanked Gerry effusively and held out $300 in greasy drug money.

"N'awm'sonIcan'ttakedatfromyayerknottedupwit'dat Buttsfellayou'llbeneedin'allda'elpyacangetg'wonnowtake caresayerselfb'y."

No amount of insisting could change Gerry's mind, so Milton, thinking he was clever, left the money in the door handle of the car after he shook Gerry's hand and got out. A week later an envelope with $300 in greasy drug money and a note came in the mail:

> ye forgot this in me car.
> —Gerry

• • •

Fog City

Milton stepped out of Gerry's K-Car into the thick, cold, dark fog of St. John's. Noddy had given Milton an address and not much else, just "my uncle Greggy will look after ya."

This was the place.

The Battery neighbourhood was a cluster of houses and shacks stuck to the rock face that descended from Signal Hill—a high hill that guarded the entrance to St. John's Harbour and overlooked the entire city—down to "The Bubble," the city's sewage outlet pipe that fed raw sewage directly into the harbour.[29]

---

[29] "The Bubble" was world-renowned among birdwatchers because of the rich variety of rare sea birds that would flock to the delicious sewery bounty. Sadly, the bubble was burst for ornithological enthusiasts in 2009 when a modern sewage treatment facility was built across the harbour.

Most of the houses in the Battery were built quickly by amateur carpenters after most of the city burned to the ground in 1892. With winter coming, they were slapped quickly up on the jagged cliffs.

Every 40 years or so an avalanche or rockslide down the hill would dump a few of the houses into the harbour, or hurricane winds would rattle the houses overnight and dozens would wake up to find their roofs floating in the water below.

A hundred years ago, this was prime real estate for fishing families to get easy access to the water. Now it was full of professors and artists and students.

The neighbourhood was interwoven with a series of impossibly narrow streets that began as footpaths. In most places there was just enough space for a small car to pass between the front door of one house and the back door of another. When it snowed the usual several feet each winter, many of the streets became unpassable and cars just piled up on the one road in and people hiked the rest of the way.

Milton got none of this.

The entire place, Newfoundland from Port aux Basques to this bright green house he stood in front of on the eastern edge of the world, was socked in with fog. He could just make out the width of the house in front of him. He knocked on the bright orange door.

Milton nearly fainted when a man who looked exactly like Noddy, just slightly older, answered the door.

"Hi. I'm Noddy's friend, uh... Morgan Murray."

Man-Noddy smiled a wide prodigal-son-returns-home smile and hugged Milton.

"Come in, come in. Welcome to Newfoundland, Morgan. Noddy told us his dearest friend would be coming. It's great to meet you."

Standing behind the man was a woman with long grey hair, warm brown eyes, and a rough grey sweater. She hugged Milton too.

"Welcome, Morgan. It's so nice to meet you."

They took Milton into the kitchen, gave him tea, opened a package of Jam-Jams and sat around the kitchen island getting to know one another.

Greg Butts was Noddy's uncle. He studied seabirds and taught marine biology at Memorial University. His wife, Susan, who moved here 25 years ago from Milton, Ontario, "for a one-year post-doc," researched middle-class alienation and taught in the Women's Studies department.

All Noddy had told them was that his roommate was interested in seabirds—specifically seagulls—and wanted to do his master's with Greg.

Greg explained how the deadline for admissions had passed and the semester was nearly over, but since he was the associate dean, he might be able to call in a few favours so Milton/Morgan could start right away.

They asked Milton about where he was from, how long he'd lived in Montreal, about his job—which he said he lost due to the economy, to great sympathy from Greg and Susan—and about his interest in seabirds.

Milton didn't mention the poetry or that he was on the lam from Leonard Cohen, the most dangerous man in the world, nor the several-teen-thousand in drug money or loaded gun in his backpack, his only piece of luggage.

Neither of them had seen Noddy for a long time. They were glad to hear he was still alive; they had been worried about him. Not worried enough to try and track him down and see, but that "since his mom and dad died, he sort of went off the deep end and got in with the wrong people. It sounds like you are a good influence on him."

Milton mirrored their concerned, solemn faces back to them and agreed.

"I try."

When the tea was all gone Greg took Milton into the damp basement and showed him to a small spare room with only a bed in it.

"It's not much, I apologize, these old houses don't have a lot of room. But you are welcome to stay here as long as you'd like, or find a place on your own. If you do stay, we'll work out some rental arrangement to cover food and expenses, but we're more than happy to have you stay with us. Sue and I never had kids so it's nice to have the company."

They made plans to go to the registrar's office on Monday. Milton thanked Greg, closed the door behind him, crawled into bed, and slept for 24 hours.

• • •

University Entrance Exam

The registrar was a sweet, mousy woman, who flipped through Milton's handwritten application to the School of Graduate Studies for a master's degree in Marine Biology while Greg and Milton sat across the desk from her and watched.

"This all looks fine, Mr. Murray, except for this here."

She turned the paper towards Milton and pointed with a pencil to the section listing his previous education.

"I'm sure it's just a mistake. Where you put diploma in Artistic Sciences at the, uh, Polytechnic University of Saskatchewan, did you mean a double degree in Arts and Sciences from the University of Saskatchewan?"

Milton agreed.

"Very well. And he meets the admission requirements for the program, Dr. Butts?"

Greg agreed.

All three signed an admissions form, the registrar handed Milton a temporary student ID card, and Milton/ Morgan Murray, was officially a grad student.

Milton knew nothing about seabirds, nor marine biology. It took him five years to finally complete a two-year diploma in a made-up discipline at a soon-to-be-bankrupt Saskatchewan trade school. But he wasn't about to protest against this act of bureaucratic kindness, even if it was a horrible mistake.

He followed Greg through a labyrinth of underground locker-lined utility tunnels that connected all the buildings on campus, up several flights of stairs to the top floor of the Science Building, and down a hall with a trash can every fifty feet catching drips from the ceiling, and through a door marked "Marine Biology."

Greg introduced Milton to Brenda, the department secretary, "who runs things." He started rhyming off a bunch of different forms and Brenda began handing them to Milton with rapid-fire instructions.

"Now, my love. Fill all of these out to get your library account and email set up, this one is for your supervisor, is that you, Greg? Get this filled out and signed by Greg, and this one is your thesis proposal, it doesn't need to be done right away, but by the end of the term it will need to be approved, this is a year-long program, not two, so you just have to complete a major research paper, not a full research thesis, it's a new thing the university is trying, and this one is to choose your classes, you need to take at least six over the year, three are required and three are electives from this list, classes start again soon, so if you have any questions about choosing, Greg here can help you with that, I don't know your situation, but if you need financial assistance fill out this form for student loans, the deadline is next week, so we need to hustle on this one, and this one is for department scholarships, the deadline was last Friday, but we can sneak yours into the pile when no one is looking, just get it back to me by the end of the day, this one is for a TA position, you'll help with marking and maybe some teaching depending on what Greg is teaching next term. Any questions?"

"Can I borrow a pen?"

· · ·

Grad Student Lounge

Greg led Milton back down the hall to the Grad Student Lounge: a plain cinder block room with one small window, one small table, and several small chairs.

A student, a tall guy in cargo shorts and dad sandals with socks—in spite of the weather—was in the room fiddling with cables attaching the one ancient computer to the one ancient printer.

"Ross, this is Morgan, Morgan this is Ross Saunders."

They "hey'd" at one another as Greg left and Milton sat at the table and began shuffling through the forms.

Ross grew increasingly frustrated with his cable-fiddling and picked the printer up off its little cart, and tossed it against the brick wall, bits of plastic busting off and skittering everywhere.

"Fucking thing! At Queens they didn't have shit like this!"

He sat down across the table from Milton and pulled a joint out of his bag.

"You mind?"

Milton was surprised how quickly grad school started to resemble working in a call centre.

"No, go ahead."

"Want some?"

"No thanks. I've got too many forms to fill out."

"Yeah, fucking place is all still paper and pen like it's the fucking stone ages. And why do they need all that information? The corporatization of the university is a travesty, they can't even get a printer that works, yet we have to pay all this money, it's fucking madness."

As Ross smoked the printer rage away, they swapped origin stories.

Ross was from Oakville, but did his undergrad at Queens in Kingston. His thesis, a second draft of which he was trying unsuccessfully to print, was titled: "Changing Migratory and Distribution Patterns of *Egretta Thula* in Northwestern

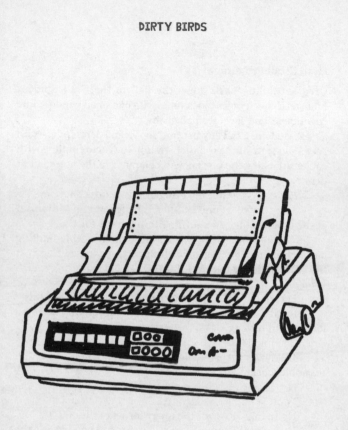

Fig. 51. Printer

Atlantic Maritime Climatological Zones Characterized by Warming Sea Temperatures and Increased Salination, 1983-2003."

He responded to Milton's blank stare by explaining, "It's about how global warming is fucking with Egrets."

Milton kept staring blankly.

When it was Milton's turn, he stuck to the fiction of graduating from the University of Saskatchewan and explained how he'd taken a gap year to live in Montreal, but was looking forward to "hitting the books" to pursue his passion: seagulls.

"Seagulls? Are you serious? You know marine ornithologists call them sea*rats*, right? I mean, they are totally over-represented in terms of biomass share because of how they proliferate on land. There was a petition circulating around ornithol conferences last year to get them declassified as seabirds and reclassified as terrestrial birds. One conference I was at, one ornithol suggested they be renamed Dirty Birds, someone else Dump Pigeons. It was hilarious."

"No... I didn't know that."

"Yeah, it's a big controversy right now. I'm surprised you're not up on things like this, coming in to study them and all."

"I've been swamped with other stuff lately. I guess I'll have to catch up."

"Well, the Seabirds Student's Association is hosting a screening and a debate tomorrow. Some hippie made a movie called *Dirty Birds* about dump seagulls in India. It's sort of become the *objet d'art* for the declass-side of the debate. It should be fun. Though I wouldn't want to be you. It's pretty lonely on the non-declass side."

"Wait, what? *Dirty Birds*?"

"Yeah, you seen it?"

"Um... no... But I've heard of it."

"Well you should come, tomorrow night at seven at the Great Auk Pub."

DIRTY BIRDS

Ross took one final drag, flicked ashes behind the radiator next to him, got up, took his things, pushed the smashed printer back into the corner with his foot, and left.

SEVENTEEN

GRAD
SCHOOL

The Great Auk Pub

The Great Auk Pub is in what would be an alley in any other city, but in St. John's the entrance was just off a set of stairs that went from Water Street below to Duckworth Street up above.

Milton couldn't find it for the longest time and walked in long circles in the thick fog down Duckworth and up Water for over an hour before he found a group of young-ish people in cargo shorts, socks and dad sandals, who led him down the two flights of stairs and into the pub.

The pub was dark and smelled like stale beer, deep-fried fish, and piss. It was deceptively large for a stairwell alley joint. The entrance is near the pool table at the back of the bar, which was decorated for the occasion with two ratty-looking stuffed seagulls.

Ross was sitting on the pool table.

He responded to Milton's friendly smile with a straight-forward, "It's five bucks."

Milton paid and headed to the bar to get a drink, weaving his way through a mess of small tables full of people yelling over the blaring Great Big Sea.

Greg was at the bar getting drinks for him and Susan.

He bought Milton a local beer and invited him to sit with them at a large corner booth right next to the stage with a few other students and professors.

They all raised their glasses to Morgan when Greg introduced him as they sat down and gave him a gentle ribbing when told Morgan was interested in studying seagulls.

"So, you must have seen this film, then? No? Never? My God, it's seminal!"

Milton nodded like he could hear over the "It's the end of the world as I know it and I feel fiiiiiiine" and smiled politely.

At about 8:30 p.m., with the bar filled to the brim, Ross walked on stage and began tapping a feedbacky mic.

"Welcome to the Seabird Student's Association monthly mixer. Tonight we are thrilled to have gotten the rights to screen *Dirty Birds*, an award-winning film by Toronto filmmaker, Uh... Robin Davis. As you probably know already, there is a controversy brewing in ornithological circles about the classification of certain species of gulls. One of the key people in this debate is Dr. Greg Butts, and I'd like to invite him up to say a few words about the controversy and introduce the film. Thanks."

"Thanks, Ross. Thanks everyone for coming. It's nice to see this many people out to chat about seabirds. Ross is right, there is a bit of a controversy brewing. I'll give you the Cole's Notes version. Basically, a number of scientists, including myself, are recommending that several common species of gulls in the *Larus* genus, particularly *Larus heermanni*, *Larus canus*, and *Larus delawarensis* be reclassified into the *Cathartes* genus, as the behaviour of these particular gull species has changed so dramatically over the past century due to human interaction that they now more closely resemble the behaviour of vultures and buzzards and other scavenger birds than their seabird ancestors."

Someone in the back loudly boo'd.

Fig. 52. Dirty Birds

"Hah. Thank you. So, that's all well and good. Right. If you are an ornithologist it's a kind of turf war over the fates of these gulls, but I know not everyone here is a bird scientist, so in laymen's terms, why this matters is that we're basically saying these bird species have had their evolutionary trajectory altered by their behaviour and by human interactions. Which matters a lot, and to more than just seabird nerds, because we're saying that behaviour can have evolutionary consequences, which would be the biggest amendment to Darwin's theories of evolution since he first posed them almost 150 years ago; and also, we're saying that human behaviour can directly alter the evolutionary trajectory of animals. That's big. These are both really big deals. I won't say much more now, but afterwards a few of us are going to have a discussion about this and what it all means for the discipline as well as life on earth more broadly. But before this, we've got this film: *Dirty Birds* by... Uhm... Robin Davis. This is a beautiful film that won the *Palme d'Or du court métrage*—best short film—at the Cannes Film Festival last year, and it is a great honour for us to get to show it here tonight. Take it away, Ross."

Ross powered up the projector and a loud fan whirred to life. The screen at the front of the bar was filled with blue and blinked: "Source Not Detected."

Ross began fiddling with cables and mashing buttons. The projector began counting down on the screen to power off. Ross mashed a few more buttons and the screen went blank. His face turned bright red as he mashed more feverishly and began violently yanking on cables.

Another student sitting at Milton's table, Lori, the Seabird Student Association Vice-President, who was tucked back in the corner, began climbing over people's laps to get out and race to Ross's aid. She kneeled all of her weight on Milton's crotch as she passed by, and he let out a sharp grunt that fluttered across the bar. Everyone felt it except for Lori who joined Ross in furiously mashing and pulling on things trying to get the projector to work.

The longer they mashed and tugged the more hands joined in. There were seven or eight of them frantically trying to get the thing to work. Finally, someone flipped open the lens cover, which had gotten closed in all the fondling, and the cluttered desktop of Ross's laptop was visible, including a conspicuous file labeled "Anal-ize This."

Ross inserted a DVD and his laptop whirred. A small window opened with the silhouettes of two seagulls circling. Ross couldn't find where to click to make it Fullscreen, so he just enlarged the window; "Anal-ize This" was still visible in the background.

"Is that okay, can everyone see it?"

Someone in the back yelled, "Press Control and F5!"

"What?"

"Control and F5!"

"Why?"

"Make it Fullscreen!"

Ross began mashing every laptop button but Control and F5. The video stopped playing. Then the program playing it closed. Then several awkward moments of button mashing while everyone in the room read the contents of Ross's desktop, which included among the mess of files and folders "Titty Dickers" and "Cocky and Ballwrinkle."

The blue blinking "Source Not Detected" returned. Lori and others re-converged for yet more clicking, mashing, pulling, plugging and fondling. Eventually they got the projector turned back on and the movie playing in full screen.

"I can't hear it!"

Ross began fiddling again. He asked if anyone had speakers. No one did. With Lori's help he managed to turn the volume up to Max on the laptop and point the feedbackey mic towards it. Any sounds coming from the mostly silent film could only be heard clearly from within about five feet of the laptop. Everyone in the bar leaned forward and strained to hear the faint squawking of the gulls.

• • •

Dirty Birds

Dirty Birds opens with a bright white ball of sun in a faintly grey, cloudless sky.

One seagull circles into view—someone at the back of the bar boos loudly. Another seagull appears. The two seem to be part of some choreographed routine. They turn in identical circles going in opposite directions. When one circle grows bigger, the other does the same simultaneously.

Leaning his head towards the laptop, Milton could make out the faint cry of one of the gulls over the whirring of the DVD and projector fan.

Another gull joins the pair, then another, and another, until the sky is filled with them. The one faint cry becomes two, then ten, then a cacophony of hundreds. The camera pans down across the sky until the sun washes out the entire picture.

DIRTY BIRDS
A FILM BY ROBIN DAVIS

The camera continues panning down to reveal the horizon—the slums of Calcutta—then further, to reveal that we're in a landfill. Truck after truck dumps large piles of garbage onto one giant mountain of garbage. Bulldozers push the truck-sized garbage piles deep into the face of garbage mountain. The roar of the engines can be heard beneath the roar of the gulls.

Thousands of gulls fill the sky above all the garbage. They dive into the pile and emerge with bits of trash. The camera slowly zooms in on the chaos. The slums blur and disappear into the background. The trucks and bulldozers blur and disappear into the background. The garbage mountain blurs and disappears into the background. The thousands of birds become hundreds, become tens, become one full bird, becomes just its head, as it stands on a pile of trash and begins digging at a plastic bag. It pulls something out. A large scrap of rotting bread. The gull throws its head back, unlatches its jaw, and swallows the large piece of bread whole. It re-engages its jaw, hops twice, and begins to fly.

The camera stays trained on the gull's face as it begins to zoom back out. Slowly the single bird becomes ten, becomes hundreds, becomes thousands. Slowly the garbage re-emerges, then the trucks and dozers, then the slums of Calcutta.

The camera follows the bird as it flies up. The garbage and trucks and dozer and houses fall out of frame. It's just birds and sky. Thousands then hundreds then tens then two. Circling around one another in some kind of dance. Then one, the gull with the belly full of rotten bread, circling as the camera continues panning upward towards the sun until the picture is washed out by white light.

THE END

Credits roll over "Anthem" by Leonard Cohen:

DIRECTOR – ROBIN DAVIS
WRITER – ROBIN DAVIS
PRODUCER – ROBIN DAVIS
PRODUCTION DESIGNER – ROBIN DAVIS
CINEMATOGRAPHER – ROBIN DAVIS
EDITOR – ROBIN DAVIS
FIRST ASSISTANT DIRECTOR – ANDREW SIMMONS
SECOND ASSISTANT DIRECTOR – LANCE POCHARD
TITLE ARTIST – ALTON SALAAM
SOUND DESIGNER – GASTON CHARLES
SOUND ENGINEER – RUDDY TURNSTON
ASSISTANT SOUND ENGINEER – AVA WEBBER

"ANTHEM" WRITTEN AND RECORDED BY LEONARD COHEN
COURTESY OF COLUMBIA RECORDS.
SPECIAL THANKS TO THE CITY OF CALCUTTA SANITATION
DEPARTMENT.
MADE WITH THE GENEROUS SUPPORT OF TELEFILM CANADA,
CANADA COUNCIL FOR THE ARTS, ONTARIO FILM FUND, ONTARIO
ARTS COUNCIL, MISSISSAUGA FILMIC ARTS INVESTMENT FUND,
AND THE HAMILTON PUBLIC LIBRARY.

• • •

Mutually Assured Collegiality

Milton was mesmerized.

His mouth fell open with the first frame of the film and stayed open the entire seven minutes. A string of drool fell out of the left corner of his mouth and made its way past his chin and towards his lap.

He'd never seen anything so beautiful in all his life.

As it played, he didn't see dump seagulls fighting over scraps of rotten trash, he saw the first smile Robin ever smiled at him. He didn't hear dump trucks and trash dozers and screaming birds faintly over the hum of a DVD player and a projector. Milton just heard Robin's intoxicating laugh.

He didn't feel pity for the birds, or embarrassment at the trash and waste of man, or any pangs of guilt or any morality at all, he just felt her arms around him, her lips on his, the softness of her stomach as he kissed his way down, down, down.

As a smattering of applause for the film turned into awkward waiting for what came next, underscored by low bar chatter, he could smell her. He could taste her. She was there with him. And it was only him and her there. Together, at last. Alone, at last.

Alone until Lori crawled back over Milton, kneeling hard on his growing erection, on her way to help Ross turn off the video, which had begun playing again from the start.

The sharp grunt from before was replaced by a sensual moan, just loud enough to be heard throughout the bar, just loud enough to turn a few curious heads in time to catch Milton trying to recoil his string of drool and erection and hide his reddening face.

No one knew who he was, so they just looked silently at one another with very concerned looks. That split-second of judgy agony was mercifully interrupted by Ross pounding on the top of the projector, trying to stop the movie from playing a second time through.

As the attention turned from Milton back to the academic death match that was shaping up on stage—a handful of bookish folks sitting around a pub table, holding microphones all wrong, blowing into them at the wrong times, making them hiss and squeal unnecessarily, asking "is this on," and looking at the microphone like it had just told them it was their real dad when they heard their voice projected through the bar—Milton returned to his fantasy.

As Greg took up a passionate, table-thumping speech on behalf of the Behavioural Evolutionists, the "Evolutionaries" he called them, and how strongly he believed his facts were more factual and more irrefutable than the other side's, and how at least seven gull species needed to be reclassified as terrestrial birds—"Comprehensive surveys and migratory tracking data from 18 sites around the world have found that more than 80 per cent of the populations of each of these species migrate between human waste sites as opposed to their more traditional marine-adjacent nesting and feeding sites. Likewise, most gull species have always been monogamous breeders; however, we're seeing an increase in poly-amory related to these landfill birds. This is fascinating in its own right, but we're also seeing increased breeding variability that is accelerating differentiation within the species, as traits better suited to survival in a landfill, traits like aggressiveness and mouth size, are becoming preferred and more prolific than marine traits, like diving and swimming. This means, without a doubt, that the changes in behaviour have begun to reshape both the psychology and physiology of these species. If these trends continue, the Common Gull will look more like a Turkey Vulture than a Tern within a century"—Milton relived his first meeting with Robin at the anarchist potluck in the abandoned furrier in St. Henri, over and over again in his head.

As bird psychologist Dr. Tom Robarts took up the case of the other side, the supremacy of his facts over Greg's, and the urgent threat that radical reclassification of species posed to the integrity of the ornithological sciences, and even the fate of the University, one of the most ocean-focused schools in the country—"It is beyond reckless to begin taxonomical reclassification of species based on preliminary studies that, despite showing notable special differentiation, which I will admit is significant, would move their study between distinct and major subfields of ornithology—from marine genera to terrestrial genera, for instance. This stops being a scientific question, at this point, and becomes a vastly different question of the internal politics of these fields of study and the principles and practices and traditions which sustain them, of the institutions which support them, of a certain hierarchy and distribution of expertise and equipment and methodology, and, ultimately, funding. It opens a veritable hornet's nest of complications for both theoretical and practical concerns of the study of these species, and this doesn't even begin to broach the deeper implications of these purported 'findings', which are philosophical, social, and moral"—Milton relived the night they first kissed, after he read his poetry for the first time at La Baraque, over and over again, imagining they didn't stop with just that kiss.

As Dr. Reginald Abergavenny III, the chair of the philosophy department, began blowing into the microphone and thumping it loudly, nearly deafening everyone in the room, as he launched into a lengthy "unpacking" of the "implications" of "problematizing the phenomenon of history as the deciding factor in speciation and differentiation"—"I am from a place where my people are the indigenous inhabitants, or as indigenous as 37 generations of Celtic Briton from Derbyshire can be, so I've got a bit of a different perspective, I suppose, than my colleagues here who are descendants from New World settlers. It's truly a shame there couldn't be a North American Aboriginal on this panel, because I'm sure we would share a similar perspective. That being: heritage is a foundational principle of the continuity of a species. And while I do appreciate the contention that behaviour is a determinant of destiny—if I may translate it from ornithological-ese to the Queen's English—I survived the Blitz as a boy, and continue to carry the words and spirit of Sir Winston Churchill very near to my heart, so Lord knows I understand the consequence of behaviour on shaping not just the individual being but entire societies, or populations, or flocks, as it were. I'm afraid my dear friend, Dr. Butts, is perhaps a tad overzealous in his extrapolation of certain of the gulls preferring to lunch on rubbish as opposed to having to earn their dinner at sea. It's a more useful allegory for the history of Newfoundland itself and the consequence of post-confederate non-industrialization, than a fundamental re-think of the principles of progeny and progeniture"—Milton relived the night that Robin ended up back at his apartment, in his bed, in nothing but her socks and underwear, in his arms, and how it might have gone different. How it might have ended in making love and happily ever after, instead of passing out, pent-up and broken-hearted in a pile of trash.

As the panel opened the floor to questions and the loud-mouth in the back, who identified himself as a Thayer Hartlaub, Ph.D. student in the biology department who hailed from New England, and stood up and shouted a long, rambling non-question question about how the defense of taxonomical progeniture was, fundamentally, a "case for National Socialism and racial purity at worst, or of white supremacist American nationalist exceptionalism at best"— Milton imagined he and Robin both completely naked and lying next to one another on his bed in an alternative version of that one wonderful night.

As Dr. Abergavenny cut off Thayer Hartlaub's anti-Nazi rant to plead his own defence: "I survived the fucking Blitz you little American shit, so don't you dare lecture me about the dangers of National Socialism"—Milton imagined the feeling of Robin's nakedness against the tips of his fingers.

As Thayer Hartlaub began to yell louder and point angrily towards the stage and go on about "you're just jealous the Germans reached the end point of colonialism before you Brits did, you dinosaur"—Milton felt the tips of Robin's fingers on his naked skin.

As 78-year-old Dr. Abergavenny stood up and flipped the pub table off of the stage, sending several glasses of beer spiralling into the crowd, and took off towards Thayer Hartlaub, Milton felt the warmth of Robin's mouth on his.

As Thayer Hartlaub, in an effort to get through the crowd that was trying to intervene between him and the septuagenarian head of the philosophy department, climbed onto a high-top table and launched himself, top-ropes style, onto Dr. Abergavenny and a throng of academics, Milton imagined his weight on top of Robin, her legs wrapping around his hips, her hands pulling him into her.

As Dr. Abergavenny shattered a beer bottle on the corner of a table and pressed it into Thayer Hartlaub's cheek in an attempt to remove his eye, Milton imagined Robin reaching down between his legs to gather up his hard, throbbing...

Milton's concentration was broken by Thayer Hartlaub's

blood curdling scream as Dr. Abergavenny's beer-bottle shiv broke skin.

Milton tried to shake it off and return to his dream, but a beer bottle exploded against the wall next to his head and he snapped-to in the middle of chaos.

Beer glasses and bottles were flying. A chair was shattered over someone's back.

Dr. Dolores Fienberg, the head of the Women's Studies department, hit Dr. Robarts between the shoulder blades with a pool cue. A second swing splintered the cue across his back and sent him to the ground, where Dr. Fienberg began stomping him.

Greg wrestled the beer-bottle shiv away from Dr. Abergavenny before he could get Thayer Hartlaub's eye. But Dr. Abergavenny remained in the middle of the mass of swinging fists and flying bottles with a bluing Thayer Hartlaub in a rear naked chokehold, shrieking at the top of his lungs.

"We shall go on to the end. We shall fight in France, we shall fight on the seas and oceans, we shall fight with growing confidence and growing strength in the air, we shall defend our island, whatever the cost may be. We shall fight on the beaches, we shall fight on the landing grounds, we shall fight in the fields and in the streets, we shall fight in the hills; we shall never surrender!"

• • •

Thayer Hartlaub

Milton didn't have a dog in the fight, just an erection, so he watched a bunch of middle-aged professors and late-twenty-something grad students, all with no upper body strength, trying to murder one another for a while.

When the manager of the bar pulled the fire alarm and the sprinklers came on, Milton snuck the *Dirty Birds* DVD out of Ross's laptop and got out the door just before the paddy wagons showed up.

In the department offices and halls of the Science Building the next day, everyone laughed the fracas off, except for Thayer Hartlaub, who, sour over his three stitches, bad case of pink eye, and being a litigious American, filed assault with a deadly weapon and attempted-murder charges against Dr. Abergavenny.

Pressing charges as a result of an academic dispute, however, even when a 78-year old phenomenological ontologicalist with increasingly alarming Nazi leanings nearly takes your eye, is highly frowned upon in academic circles. As soon as charges were filed the academy started putting the screws to Thayer Hartlaub.

First, his preferred parking pass for Ph.D. candidates in Lot 17 was revoked without explanation and he was reissued a pass for Lot 47—an unlit dirt lot behind the hospital, about a 30-minute walk, on a nice day, to the Science Building.

Then his mailbox in the department office, where he collected intra-campus mail, special-order library books and journal articles, student assignments, and his power and telephone bills for the basement apartment he was renting in the once fashionable suburb of Cowan Heights, was given to the new master's student, Morgan Murray. Thayer's mailbox was moved to the basement of the Physical Education building, another 10 minutes out of the way on the trek from his car to his office.

His office was flagged for emergency asbestos abatement and he was forced to relocate to an empty residence room in the antique Hurley Hall undergraduate male-only residence, which throbbed with rap-metal 24/7 and reeked of weed and B.O.—and was another 10 minutes further away from where he had to park.

He wasn't assigned any teaching for the coming term, and lost out on the $1,175 for the 42 hours of class time and 300 hours of marking that came with each course.

His automatic renewal of the 74 books he currently had

checked out from the Queen Elizabeth II campus library was mysteriously disabled. This wasn't discovered until a letter sent two weeks later was received an extra two weeks later, because of Thayer Hartlaub's infrequent checking of his intra-campus mail. By then, the dollar-per-day-per-book late fees were over $1,500. He had to ask for an advance on his student loan to pay the fine.

The next time he checked his mailbox, which he made a point of doing more frequently after the library fines and his power having been temporarily shut off because of a missed bill, he had three letters of resignation from the three internal members of his Ph.D. committee.

Dr. Rhoreston Tittlewatts, a marine biologist, claimed his 97-year-old grandmother was in poor health and he would be completely too preoccupied with her assured imminent death to possibly review and adequately invigilate a dissertation about something as frivolous as adorable seabirds.

Dr. Maria Armiston, an animal behavioural psychologist, claimed her 97-year-old father was in poor health and she would likely be required to drop everything at a moment's notice to fly back to Wisconsin to tend to him and, thus, could not possibly be relied upon to serve on any type of committee in the interim.

And Dr. Larissa Munk, a marine paleobotanist, claimed her 97-year-old aunt, on her mother's side, who had raised her after both her parents were killed in a paragliding accident in the South of France in 1961, had recently contracted a rare case of dementia and required around-the-clock care, so she would be taking administrative leave to provide it.

Without a committee, Thayer Hartlaub wouldn't be able to defend his nearly complete dissertation: "Gendered Responses to Inter-Colony Aggression and Violence in North Atlantic Puffin Populations."

After a tour of the department and 17 variations on the word "no," he had no choice but to transfer to the Geology

Technologist program in the Polytechnic University of Saskatchewan in Moose Jaw and take up moderation of the Facebook group "MUNStinks!"

When both Thayer Hartlaub and his lawyer, Jerry Fitzgerald, who had quit private practice to enter provincial politics, failed to appear at Dr. Abergavenny's pre-trial hearing, all charges were dropped.

Equilibrium returned to the university in time for the next edition of "The Bolshevik Society," a quarterly quasi-fight club/Russian literature seminar in the rec room of Russian Department Chair—or Tsar, as he insisted on being called—Dr. Sergei Krinklinski's suburban home, where Dr. Abergavenny was the three-time defending champion for his take on Vladimir Solovyov's defence of Aristotle's noumenonical essentialism, and his willingness to fight dirty.

EIGHTEEN

THE LAM

Tern, Tern, Tern

Milton, all the while, grew into his life as a pretend grad student/real-life schmuck on the lam. He took Noddy's advice and avoided reaching out to anyone from his past life or making friends with anyone who could be working for Leonard Cohen. Which could be anyone.

He did call his mom at her work at the Bellybutton Regional School library every few weeks. He figured the chances of Cohen's men bugging a small rural school library were slim.

Of course, he didn't tell his mom about being tangled up in the criminal underworld and that his life was in danger. But she was thrilled he was in medical school, albeit all the way out in Newfoundland, and thrilled that he had a girl-friend, a filmmaker who was out of the country for a few months working on a film, but when she was back, he'd bring her home for a visit.

Mrs. Ontario was happy as could be for her son, who seemed to finally be applying himself.

Milton didn't know if Leonard Cohen survived the crash. He kept an eye out, thinking that if a national icon like him died in a car crash it'd be in the news. But there was nothing.

So he stayed on high alert. He kept the bag of what was left of the money and the loaded Hallelujah gun with him at all times and slept with it under his pillow.

He couldn't, however, keep from reaching out to Robin.

Certain that Leonard Cohen would be listening to her phone calls and reading her mail and emails and whatever else, Milton cleverly started making fake Facebook accounts of old men and young Russian mail-order brides and sending Robin friend requests and vaguely creepy messages hoping that one would stick and he could get her to agree to chat in an encrypted chatroom for Chinese cos-players.

Until that worked out and he could run off and be with Robin happily ever after, Milton returned to the monastic life of his PUS days, spending all day sleeping in, in Greg and Susan's dank, dark basement, sending Robin creepy Facebook friend requests, and concocting free-verse academic papers on seagull DNA.

At night he would eat a frozen TV dinner and watch endless Russian dashcam videos and pirated episodes of *The Amazing Race*, before slopping out of the always wet, always foggy, and always slushy Battery to a grocery store in a converted old hockey stadium, where he stocked shelves until 1:00 am.

Then he'd return home, jerk off to his stolen copy of *Dirty Birds*, and fall asleep dreaming of the day he'd get to see Robin again.

Academically he was doing okay too. Much better than he expected and much better than a fake marine biologist should have.

He didn't know the first thing about birds, or research, or academic writing, and the things he was supposed to read were dreadfully boring and totally incomprehensible. But his training as a poet, such as it was, served him well.

The technique he had more-or-less mastered of regurgitating a large quantity of words pretty much at random, turned out to be the perfect technique for crafting top-notch academic papers.

In fact, things started going a little too okay.

His essay, "Tern, Tern, Tern, to Everything there is a Season," a term paper for BIOL6780: Climate Change and Marine Life, won the School of Graduate Studies Paper of the Year award.

It opened:

> Terns, terns, terns. To everything there is a season, and a time to every purpose within the atmosphere choked with greenhouse gases: a time to be born, and a time to die; a time to plant, a time to reap that which is planted; a time for increasing sea levels and ocean salinity and temperatures; a time to break down, and a time to project increasingly frequent extreme weather events; a time to weep at the inability to mobilize political will behind mitigation efforts, and a time to laugh at climate change deniers as waters rise and wildfires rage; a time to mourn the passing of our earth, and a time to dance on our mass graves; a time to cast away stones, and a time to gather precious stones together as they will be the final currency; a time to embrace the end, and a time to refrain from embracing and install hi-efficiency light bulbs; a time to get active, and a time to lose hope; a time to keep consuming, and a time to be a cast away when the ocean overtakes us; a time to rend the old world, and a time to sew anew; a time to keep silent and watch the world burn, and a time to speak truth to power; a time to stop worrying and love the bomb, and a time to hate the player not the game; a time of warming ocean temperatures, and a time of piecemeal responses to global cataclysm. Terns, terns, terns, these majestic seabirds are the canary in our flooding coal mine.

Winning Paper of the Year meant he appeared on the front page of the campus newspaper and throughout social media. He appeared on the local evening news during a weekly segment called "Some Smart"—a promotional series the University marketing department paid to have run on the small local TV station, disguised as news. And he was fêted at an end-of-term event at the campus graduate student pub, Bitters—it was commonplace at Memorial (perhaps more so than at other universities, which all function at a certain level of rampant tacit alcoholism) to hold academic events in pubs, bars, and nightclubs.

All of the hoopla over "Tern, Tern, Tern," and the plastering of his face all over town and the internet guaranteed that, despite changing his name and his best efforts to grow a beard to disguise himself, if Cohen's thugs were looking for him, they'd find him.

So, when it came time for choosing summer research internships, Milton signed up for the most remote field work assignment possible: a seabird census in the Gannet Islands Ecological Reserve—a cluster of small, remote islands some 40 kilometres off the coast of Labrador in the sub-arctic Labrador Sea.

• • •

Seabird Sanctuary

The Gannet Islands are seven tiny islands in all, which are just low barren bumps of rock sticking out of the frigid Labrador Sea. They range in size from a few square kilometres to a few square meters.

There were no gannets—the large, beautiful, majestic seabirds—on the Gannet Islands. Just three warring bird colonies. Razorbills—the large, awkward cousins of the extinct Great Auk; puffins—the small, awkward, drunken cousins of Toucan Sam—and common murres—a miniature version of the razorbill that behaved like the puffin.

Fig. 53. Gannet Islands Ecological Reserve

It was like a refuge for rejected penguin prototypes.

As part of the Gannet Island Seabird Census Research Project, graduate students were hired to spend the summer counting birds and observing their behaviour and interactions.

The largest of the islands, Gannet Island proper, was the basecamp. It was large enough for three Ph.D. students who shared a yurt with a generator, satellite TV, and a port-a-potty.

On the next three smaller islands were three master's students, one per island, in pup tents, including Milton.

Fires were forbidden, so the students on the smaller islands kept warm—as even in the 'summer' the temperature struggled to stay above freezing—with small propane stoves.

The smaller islands had no port-a-potties, let alone generators or TVs. To maintain "ecological integrity" all waste, including human, had to be captured in a bucket and taken off the island when supplies were brought over from the big island every two weeks—as sea states allowed.

Being that Milton was the newest arrival and in a program that was the laughingstock of the department—"a one-year master's program? What a joke!"—he was put on the smallest of the islands, colloquially called Lāna'i, after the puniest Hawaiian island. Two colleagues from his program were shitting in buckets over on Maui and Oahu, while three Ph.D. students were on Hawai'i, sending out regular taunting updates on the walkie-talkies of who got the rose that week on *The Bachelor*.

A seabird colony, if you've never seen one, is really just an island of bird shit that hundreds of thousands of screaming, fighting, fucking birds all work diligently to keep shitting on.

For a student research assistant taking part in a census count of a colony, it's really just three months of never-ending bird shit.

For the first two weeks Milton lay awake all night each night while shit fell on his tent like pouring rain and the swarm of birds screamed in an ornithological orgy of mating and murder.

There was a red blinking lantern and a low-frequency noise-machine attached to the outside of his tent to deter the murres, who were the nastiest of the locals, from dive-bombing his tent in the middle of the night.

A decade or so ago, a student, being attacked by a bazaar of rabid murres, ended up killing a dozen of these protected birds with a frying pan.

This year's group of students were told in no uncertain terms that if they killed any birds by any means, they'd be kicked out of the university and charged under the Protected Seabirds Act.

With the first two-week re-supply, the Ph.Ds sent over earplugs with a note.

"You might want some of these, rookie."

Able to sort of sleep, Milton settled in and spent the rest of the summer under a steady barrage of bird shit and deafening screams, eating cans of cold beans and cans of cold condensed soup in his tiny tent, shitting in a bucket, and sitting on a rock in a winter rain suit "counting" birds.

• • •

Gannet Island Seabird Census Research Project

To count birds, a seabird census taker identifies a portion of nesting area, or rookery, and counts the number of birds that land there over a set period of four or five hours through a pair of binoculars. They also snap a digital photograph of the area before, during, and after taking their count, to be verified in the lab when all of the data is compiled.

The counter must use landmarks, which is particularly difficult on these featureless shit-soaked islands, to carefully demarcate and identify different areas. Each day they count another area, until the entire island has been counted, and then they repeat.

Over a three-month period, an average census taker on the smaller Gannet Islands should be able to get six counts of dozens of areas about the size of a curling rink. These counts are compared to one another, and the photographs, to give a rough estimate of the populations of each of the bird colonies on the island.

This census is done every decade, as changes in colony size can indicate various things about the birds themselves, as well as the changing environmental and climate conditions.

It's excruciatingly tedious and difficult work—the birds don't exactly sit still to let you count them—so Milton gave up after a couple of hours of trying to make sense of a vibrating mass of flapping, fighting, fucking, shitting birds, and instead began filling the expensive waterproof field notebooks he was given with an epic love poem dedicated to Robin, written as an elaborate seabird allegory.

Each day he would sleep as long as he could, wake up, drink a cup of cold, bitter coffee, eat half a can of beans or condensed soup, and carefully attempt to climb from his tent and into his rain suit without taking too many direct shit-hits—impossible—and then go sit on a rock.

He would snap a picture of a different chunk of rock covered in birds and their shit and sit and write and write and write as the bitter Arctic wind howled around his plugged ears.

> it swoops and circles and drags and rages
> screaming for attention
> drowned out by all the other screams
> louder screams
> more insistent beckoning screams
> sirens inviting you
> enticing you
> insisting you

Fig. 54. Rejected penguin prototypes

crash upon the rocks
like so much endless shit

. . .

Cartwright, Labrador

Partway through their three-month stint, the students were picked up from their shit perches by a hired-out lobster boat and taken to Cartwright, the nearest town, a down in the mouth former fishing village of about 900, on the shore of Labrador.

Milton's research team, a half-dozen students who hadn't showered for six weeks, staggered off the lobster boat into in the village's only motel, got cleaned up, and then spent the next three days getting black-out drunk and, for everyone other than Milton, hooking up.

Even in Cartwright, one of the most remote villages in the entire country, Milton spent his nights in the motel bar on edge.

He would sit in a dark corner, nursing a single beer, and watch the faces of every swarthy fishermen or miner on long change or scattered tourist. Anyone could have been a Cohen thug. After a few hours he would sneak to his room by making towards the bathroom before ducking out an emergency exit, walking around the back of the motel in pitch darkness, and sneaking in through another emergency exit he had propped open with an ice bucket.

Once in his room he'd triple-lock the door, push the mattress and the box spring from the extra bed and the big dresser that held the big old tube TV up against the door, and lie awake listening for footsteps in the hall or voices from the parking lot or cars pulling in or out. But mostly, all he could hear was his research teammates flapping, fighting, and fucking down the hall.

By the third day of being on ultra-high alert, Milton looked forward to getting back to his desert island. By the end of the summer, he actually preferred the solitude and didn't mind the torrential shit and horrible racket. It became sort of comforting and familiar, like living next to a river.

On a desert island in the middle of an icy sea, completely and utterly alone, socked in with fog, wind smashing him in the back, sitting on a rock, being screamed at and shat upon relentlessly by surly, recalcitrant seabirds, composing love poems to his not-quite lover was the most comfortable and most himself Milton had ever been.

He was almost sad to climb into the lobster boat for the last time in early September, not long after the last icebergs were drifting away south, and the first bits of sea ice were drifting in from the north.

• • •

Gander International

After one final rager weekend in Cartwright, the Gannet Islands Seabird Census Research Project Team got on a small plane to go back to St. John's the day after Labour Day.

Or at least they tried to.

The fog was so thick, as it was every single day, that they circled around the St. John's Airport—which, for some reason, had been built in the foggiest possible spot on the island—for an hour before backtracking to Gander.[30]

---

[30] Gander was built as an airplane gas station in the 1930s for its half-way-ness between New York and London. And it quickly became a bustling international hub. In the 1950s, the Newfoundland government built a world-class terminal worthy of the Sinatras and the Monroes who would often pass through. This was to be Newfoundland's ascension to world-class. The clocks on the wall in the terminal read Gander, London, New York, Montreal, and Moscow. But this was still Newfoundland—the place French explorer Jacques Cartier called "the land God gave Cain"—so, in accordance with the immutable laws of nature, the story of Gander International turned into an absurdist tragicomedy. A couple of years after the glorious new terminal opened, the jet engine became a thing and planes no longer needed to refuel in Gander. Gander and all its promise had become more-or-less moot. Except for a pile of diverted 9/11 flights, which inspired the Tony-winning tourist advert, *Come From Away*.

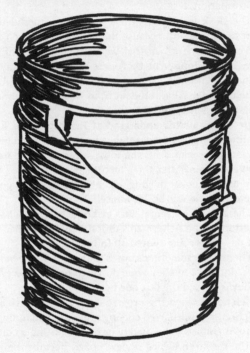

Fig. 55. Amateur ornithologist field work survival kit

The research team got off the plane and walked into the once majestic terminal building at Gander International.

They wove their way through this dusty mid-century modern monument to dashed hopes and broken dreams, to the information desk.

The desk agent told them the next scheduled flight was in two days, and because the annual fishermen's union conference was in town that week, there were unlikely to be any hotel rooms, but they were welcome to stay in the terminal.

Belcher, a master's student from New Jersey, almost had an aneurysm when told this.

He had done his undergrad at Princeton and his high schooling at a private boarding school in Switzerland. This entire summer had been the most offended and disgusted he had ever been. After three months of shitting in a bucket, the lip of the bucket digging into his unblemished porcelain Princeton ass, he was beside himself.

There were no rental cars either. The entire Labrador delegation to the fishermen's union conference had gotten in the day before and rented all four cars.

There were sometimes buses that went between Gander and St. John's, but they were down to once per week now, and they'd missed the last one by a day.

Belcher phoned the project supervisor, Dr. Heermann Von Schrenck, and started cursing him out, demanding a ride back to St. John's immediately or he'd be filing a complaint with the research ethics review board because he may or may not have collected all of his own shit on the island and there may be a rogue turd sitting on a rock in the middle of the Atlantic at just this very minute about to choke the life out of a razorbill.

Not wanting to risk the humiliation and potential loss of his research chair that would come with one of his research assistants killing another protected seabird, Dr. Von Schrenck agreed to pay for taxis to ferry the six of them the rest of the way to St. John's.

Trouble was, there were only two taxis in all of Gander. They were operated by two brothers, Gerry and Jerry Sheppard. The G/Jerrys wouldn't both go to St. John's.

"WesnotsendingbothcabstoTownwhadifamissushas ababyanneedsalif'tada'ospitalBrendaattheBigStopshe's'bout tapopanydaynowcan'triskit."

So all six weary bird counters crammed themselves into Gerry's 1997 Pontiac Trans Am, four in the back and two in the front with Gerry, for the three-hour ride back into Town.

Milton, the rookie who lived in the Battery, was the last to get dropped off. Worried that Cohen's goombahs might be waiting for him to walk in the front door, he had the cab drop him off in the pitch blackness and thick fog on top of Signal Hill—high above the Battery—so he could sneak down the back way.

Dr. Von Schrenck had promised to pay for the cab but didn't say exactly how he was going to do that, so Milton dug into the bottom of his backpack and handed Gerry $300 in slimy drug money. Gerry didn't have any kind of receipts, so he ripped the top off of his cigarette pack and wrote:

Gerry got ya drove, $300-

Fig. 56. Gerry's Cab

NINETEEN

LITTLE
SPOON

Stranger

It was late, past 10:00 p.m., by the time Milton crept, slipped, tripped, staggered, stumbled, fell, barrel-rolled, and crawled down the jagged rocky cliff face in the dark and fog to his house. He could see the lights in the kitchen were on and he could hear laughter. He snuck up behind the house and slithered around the backside to get a peek in the kitchen window.

Greg and Susan were sitting on one side of the kitchen table, the side facing Milton. Susan was staring into a cup of tea with a tired, forlorn look on her face. Greg was laughing uproariously at whatever a third person, some guy with his back to Milton, was saying.

This stranger could just be a visitor, a friend—a friend of Greg's apparently. It could be nothing. But, if it was nothing, why wouldn't Susan just get up and go to bed? Why sit there staring angrily into a teacup? Maybe she wasn't just sitting there. Maybe she was being held there against her will.

Maybe this was a Cohen tough sent to kill Milton and anyone he associated with.

Maybe Greg was trying to defuse the situation. Laugh it off. Get the killer to drop his guard long enough to make a move. Maybe this was it.

Milton slowly slid his hand in his backpack and felt around for the cold steel of the gun with five bullets left and took it out.

He poked his head back up into the light of the window to take another look at his Angel of the Death. The man didn't have a gun in his hand; in fact, he was flapping his arms wildly, clearly telling a very elaborate story. Greg seemed genuinely entertained. Susan was genuinely annoyed. The flapping man started mime-humping the table.

"What. The. Hell. Is. He. Doing. Here?"

Milton slid the gun in the waistband of his jeans, and walked in the front door.

Noddy jumped up from the kitchen table and wrapped him up in a big hug.

"You motherfucker! How the hell are ya, b'y? Am I glad to see you!"

Milton couldn't muster any words. He didn't know what to make of this. Noddy was being hunted by the same evil, violent, ruthless, cold-blooded killers as he was. Noddy was the one who told him to disappear. Noddy was the one who schooled him about going on the lam, about not trusting anyone, about going to Newfoundland and keeping a low profile. Yet this clumsy dumb-ass was sitting in the kitchen of Milton's house flapping his arms and humping the table.

Surely, he'd been followed. Surely, an army of giant square men with Uzis would be smashing through the door at any second to end it once and for all. Unless...

Unless Noddy flipped.

Unless, in his carelessness and stupidity, Noddy got caught by Cohen's men, probably at the metro station in Montreal the day Milton left, and to save his own skin had promised Milton's in exchange. And now, he was here to collect.

Noddy hugged Milton tighter.

"I missed ya, b'y. Whaddayat? Yer looking like a Jigg's Dinner been drug through a cat's arsehole, b'y."

"Why. Are. You. Here?"

"Greg and the missus looking after ya?"

Milton shook free from Noddy's bear hug and took a step back into the corner, he reached behind him with his right hand and took hold of the gun. He clicked off the safety.

"What are you doing here, Noddy? I thought... I thought you were going to be gone for a while."

"Nah, b'y. I was just telling da b'ys here I finished that there job a bit early, so I thought why not pay ya's a visit? I haven't been to Town for a good while, ain't that right, Greg b'y?"

"No. It's been... it's been some time."

"But I've bored poor Sue, here, right to tears, and Greg's probably had enough of me yapping at him, let's you and me go up the road and get a beer, b'y, catch up."

"I don't know, Noddy, I've had a long few days travelling, I'd rather just go to bed."

"Nah, b'y. I came all this way to see ya, don't go playing hard to get. C'mon now, just a beer."

Milton cocked the gun slowly.

"I'm... I'm pretty wiped. How about tomorrow?"

Milton had to get rid of Noddy and get out of town immediately. He needed to get back home, back to Bellybutton. Move into his grandma's cabin on the edge of Lake Diefenbaker. Not even Noddy could find him there. He was an idiot for coming to Newfoundland in the first place. For trusting Noddy at all, ever. An idiot.

"Oh, go on with ya now, one beer never killed no one, b'y. I'm buying. Let's go. I've got some news for ya about our buddy out in Montreal."

Noddy wouldn't take no for an answer. Milton couldn't just shoot him in front of Greg and Susan. So, he agreed to "one beer" and resolved to find a way to either shake him or shoot him on the way.

• • •

Narrows Lounge

The nearest bar was the Narrows Lounge in the lobby of the Battery Hotel—a once-stately hotel perched atop Signal Hill looking out into what might have been the best view in the city, were it not for the fog.

There weren't a lot of places that Noddy could go in the city, thanks to his proclivity for burning every bridge possible and fleeing nearly a decade ago. But the Battery Hotel was a pretty safe bet.

Since the '60s it had fallen into some kind of mix between the Bates Motel and the Overlook Hotel. The rat-infested barn of a hotel had a hard time convincing tourists the views were worth it, and no locals would trek up the hill when there were 3,000 other bars with cheaper beer and perfectly good views of the fog down below.

Not that it mattered.

Milton didn't plan on making it up the hill and into the hotel with Noddy.

They walked along one of the ox cart paths/streets out of the Battery and doubled back to head up Signal Hill towards the hotel. Noddy yammered on excitedly like he used to when they were walking through Outremont to catch the 80 in the pre-dawn darkness on their way to ruin perfectly good mansions in Westmount.

"Buddy, am I glad to see you! I've been going nuts on my own all this time. You holding up all right?"

The double-back point was a fork in the road between street lights—one way went up the hill, the other went down into Town—in the fog it was completely dark. This was the place.

"B'y, I haven't been totally alone, though. Met this chick on the bus to Toronto, fuck b'y, the tits on her. Gave it to her right there in the bus, in the shitter. It's all sloshing around and smells like the inside of your mother's arsehole in there, but I'm just fuckin' having a go at her."

Milton reached back and took hold of the gun.

He really didn't want to have to shoot Noddy. He figured he could just get Noddy to lay down in the gutter or something and then make a run for it.

Noddy had his eyes closed while he mimed "fuckin' having a go at her" as they walked into the darkness at the fork in the road.

Milton began to pull the gun from the waist of his pants just as Noddy slapped him on the back in playful fraternal delight with his bus-fucking story.

BANG!

The shot woke up every dog in the city, as well as the rooster and a couple of goats that lived in the yard of the house at the fork in the road.

Lights started flicking on in the windows of houses nearby.

Noddy let out a "Jesus Christ!" as he burst into laughter and took off running up the hill.

Milton, not sure what had just happened, followed.

They arrived at the doors of the Battery Hotel panting out of breath.

"What in the Christ was that?"

Milton pulled out the Hallelujah gun and showed Noddy.

"Don't know what happened, must have misfired, or something."

"Sweet Christ, and you kept Lenny's gun. You're a bad muthafucker, Milton. You don't look it, you look like a sculpin fucked a moose and shat you out, but you're all right."

He slapped Milton on the back again. Milton flinched.

"Put 'er back in your holster, Tex, let's grab a beer."

Milton clicked the safety on the gun and tucked it back into his pants. He followed Noddy into the hotel bar.

• • •

Dancing Horses

Over beers Noddy explained what he'd been up to since they last saw one another.

He had taken the bus from Montreal to Toronto.

"Fucked that chick in the shitter, tits on her like Coast Guard buoys, b'y, out to here!"

He planned to go to the police and rat on Cohen and get into witness protection, but wasn't sure how far Cohen reached, and if he could trust the cops in Toronto. So, he got back on the bus and headed further west.

"Fucked another chick in a Tim's bathroom in Thunder Bay. She was the coffee girl, had an arse on her like nan's baked bread."

Each time he told Milton about his cross-country sexcapades, he'd perform various sex acts on his stool.

His plan, such as it was, was to find some Asian gangsters in Vancouver who'd probably like to take down the big East Coast boss. But he only made it as far as Regina.

"Was giving it to this chick in the mop closet of a 7-11."

He began 69-ing his stool.

"She had a mouth on her like your mother. The things she said would make a nun blush. You'd a liked her. But by the time I gets done the screwin', the friggin' bus left without me."

Marooned in Regina, Noddy wandered around until he stumbled upon the RCMP Academy, where every Mountie in Canada is trained.

"I figures, if there's any straight cops, they got to be in the Academy, right? So, I goes in and asks to talk to the boss. They punt me around like a football for a while before I ends up with some stupid fuck of a detective. By this point, I didn't really give a shit. So, I told the b'ys the whole story. Well, I left you out of it, I feel some bad that I dragged you into this whole mess. They takes me into protective custody at the barracks there, got me cleaning the stalls of them stupid friggin' dancing horses. Shit was up to my knees every fuckin' day. Don't know what they feed them pigs. Must be cop doughnuts or some shit. They got some big top-secret task force trying to figure out who runs what they calls the 'Maple Syrup Gang,' but being stupid fuckin' cops, they didn't have a whiff before I tells 'em. So, they got me shovelling shit, getting me ready to go into deep hiding—probably chop my balls off and send me down to Argentina to hide out with a bunch of Nazis or some shit—and I catches wind that they're going to take Lenny out. And it dawns on me, if I can bust out, find you, find Lenny without us getting whacked first, and warn that old fart the cops are coming, he would call off his dogs, and we could stop running, and looking over our shoulders, and you could move back to Sask-scratch-my-ass and marry your prize sheep like you always dreamed."

"Wait! What? You escaped protective custody in the most concentrated collection of police in the country?"

"Y's b'y, nothing to it, just stole one of them dancing horses."

"And now you want to track down the most dangerous man on the planet who wants nothing more than to kill us and somehow convince him that you know some top-secret police plan?"

"Yes, b'y. That's what I said. Geez, clean out your ears."

"And how are you going to prove this to Leonard Cohen?"

"I has it on paper."

"What paper?"

"Some top-secret plan thing that was sitting on a desk there. I just nicked it."

"Nicked it? What's it say?"

"All sorts of shit. It's our get-out-of-jail-free card, b'y."

"Let me see it."

"Can't."

"Why not?"

"She's up me hole."

"What?"

"I got 'er stuck up me arse."

"What? Ugh! Why? Gross!"

"Safest spot for 'er, b'y. Been up there a week now. She's looking a bit ragged."

"Oh god."

"Well it ain't the most comfortable I'se ever been, but I had worse up there. This one time, when I was working at the Seahorse..."

"I swear to God, I will take out this gun and shoot you if you finish this story."

"Jeez, b'y. It was just a bunch of coke a few of the girls wanted me to hide. Get your mind out of the shitter. But, this other time, I was pretty fucked up on 'shrooms, and..."

"I will murder you! I'm not joking!"

"Okay, okay. So ya in?"

"In what?"

"To find Lenny and give him the contents of me arse. Get us out of this here shit we in, b'y. C'mon, keep up."

"No. I'm not. I don't want anything to do with any of this. I want to finish my degree and move to the Galapagos Islands and live on the beach counting budgie birds and never be seen again."

"Yeah, well, I figured out what island in the middle of the Labrador you'se been on, and what day you'se got back by just doing a bit of Googling in a public library for about 10 minutes. Now, I'm smarter than the average shitbird crook that works for Lenny, but how long do ya figures before they track you down and pop ya? These fucks don't fuck around, and they don't like loose ends, and you and me, b'y, are as loose as there is. I give ya two more weeks of fucking around in never-never land here before yer bobbin' face down by the shit bubble in the harbour with the shit gulls picking at yer guts."

DIRTY BIRDS

"Pretty sure that's what's going to happen if I go with you anyway."

"Nah, b'y, it'll be best kind. Deadly. You even got a gun and hopefully some money—because I ain't got neither."

"Screw you, Noddy."

"Hey now! Go on, b'y. Don't be sour. I just saved your life and am about to take you on a great adventure, maybe even get ya laid."

"No. It won't be an adventure. It will get us killed."

"That mean you're in?"

"I... I don't know. I need to sleep on it."

• • •

Royal Canadian Mounted Police Gendarmerie royal du Canada

TOP SECRET
OPERATION SUGAR SHACK

BACKGROUND

For decades all organized crime in Canada, and perhaps beyond, has been directed out of Montreal through a secretive organization that law enforcement agencies refer to as THE MAPLE SYRUP GANG (MSG). For the last 27 years, law enforcement agencies, including the RCMP, the SPM, OPP, CSIS, CF and the FBI have attempted to infiltrate this criminal organization to determine the organization's structure, leadership, and the range of its criminal activities. Despite these agencies' best efforts, no agents or officers have been able to infiltrate the organization as undercover operatives, nor has any meaningful information been collected from confidential informants (CI), nor any significant plea-bargain testimony from apprehended witnesses, regardless of the incentives promised. All potential leads and evidence have concluded in dead ends thanks to an apparent complex network of cover criminal organizations such as bike gangs and

ethnicity-based gangs and mafias. Whenever arrests have
been made or contraband seized in these cases, the criminal
activities targeted by these measures continue unabated.
The identity of those involved in this shadow organization
that leads criminal activity in this country and abroad
remains a mystery.

An individual turned themselves in to officers at the RCMP
College in Regina, Saskatchewan. This CI has provided in-
depth information about the structure, leadership, and a
number of the criminal activities undertaken by the MSG.
Previous evidence and witness testimony, which until now
had been indecipherable, clearly corroborates this CI's
accounts.

CI REPORT

1. According to CI accounts, the leader of MSG is none
   other than popular musician, Leonard Cohen. During the
   CI's last contact with Mr. Cohen, the CI and an associate
   were being threatened by Mr. Cohen in the back of a
   speeding car. The CI and their associate were able to
   subdue the driver of the car, causing a single-vehicle
   collision, and escape from the scene. The CI has not
   seen Mr. Cohen since, but the CI's accounting of these
   events align with the dates of Mr. Cohen's last known
   public appearances, and account for his subsequent can-
   cellation of a series of concerts throughout North
   America and Europe.

2. The CI identified Guillaume Vautour and Gweltaz Mouette
   as close associates of Mr. Cohen. Mr. Vautour and Mr.
   Mouette run a used bookstore as a front for a money-
   laundering business, in the Plateau area of Montreal.
   Upon investigation, it has been discovered that the
   building in which the bookstore is housed is owned by
   Mr. Vautour, and taxes have not been paid on the building in 45 years.

3. The CI indicated that local law enforcement, politicians,
   and officers of the courts have been corrupted by the
   MSG.

4. The CI indicated that they partook in various criminal
   activities under threat of imminent death, on behalf of
   the MSG. These activities included illegal construction
   and renovations, money laundering, and drug trafficking.

5. The CI stated Mr. Cohen frequents the bar La Baraque
   in the Mile End area of Montreal.

6. The CI provided a last-known address for Mr. Cohen, which is a home in the Mile End area of Montreal owned by LC Holdings.

7. The CI stated they overheard associates of Mr. Cohen's bragging about fixing the 1993 Stanley Cup finals in which the Montreal Canadiens miraculously pulled off an upset victory over Wayne Gretzky and the Los Angeles Kings.

8. The CI insisted his report include testimony against the legality of the confederation of Newfoundland on account of "those crooked fucks on the join side," led by long-time premier Joseph Smallwood.

SITREP

Acting on this new information, undercover operatives have been able to ascertain the whereabouts of Mr. Cohen and have identified Mr. Vautour, Mr. Mouette, and a number of other suspected associates and members of the MSG continuing to operate this criminal enterprise in Montreal. Mr. Cohen operates in heavily guarded and secretive locations and commands a large and heavily armed quasi-militia of thugs and petty criminals. Direct confrontation would require a large show of force which would undoubtedly tip off Mr. Cohen and send him underground. In order to apprehend Mr. Cohen, alternative methods of amassing the requisite force must be employed.

OPERATION SUGAR SHACK

Last year, in conclusion to the Festival Tout de Nuit, a complimentary breakfast was provided to the public at the main branch of Banque Nouvelle France (BNF) on Sainte-Catherine Street. As has been well documented, the event escalated into a violent riot, looting, and destruction of millions of dollars of property in downtown Montreal. While those responsible for inciting the incident were never apprehended, hundreds of others were arrested and charged with offences ranging from misdemeanour loitering to felony vandalism and theft. The Festival organizers are hesitant to hold another public breakfast event as part of this year's festival, but the Commissioner of the RCMP has used top secret back channels to communicate with the festival chairperson, who has been identified as a trustworthy associate, and convinced them to hold another breakfast event. At this event, which will certainly be heavily manned with SPM tactical officers after last year's incident, undercover operatives will incite another riot. Due to Montreal's natural volatility, this riot will spiral out of control quickly, as it did last year. This event will be organized in such a way as to confine and preoccupy the potentially corrupt SPM forces, and force the Mayor of Montreal to declare an immediate state of emergency and request RCMP and Canadian Forces intervention. RCMP and CF forces will then move on MSG targets and apprehend Mr. Cohen and his associates.

• • •

Sleep On It

Milton got up from the bar and headed out of the hotel.

Noddy slammed the rest of his beer and the rest of Milton's and followed him back down the hill to Greg and Susan's, pestering him all the way.

Susan had gone to bed, but Greg was still up. Noddy burst in the front door.

"Greg, b'y, we need a borrow of your car."

After an hour of begging and pleading and a long list of terribly unconvincing lies, Greg relented, mostly out of fatigue.

"Okay, fine, so long as Morgan drives..."

"Who in the Christ is Morgan?"

Greg laughed.

"And you promise to have it back here in two weeks at the very, very latest!"

Noddy kissed Greg on the lips.

"Yes b'y, hand to God, Scout's honour, all that. We'll look after 'er. Even put a bit of gas in 'er when we're done."

Then he turned to Milton.

"Long drive tomorrow, b'y, we better hit the sack."

He said "sack" just as he tapped Milton in the balls hard enough to cause him to double over and gasp for breath.

"I didn't say I was going with you yet."

"I'll bunk in with you. Be real romantic, b'y, hahaha."

Noddy followed Milton down the narrow stairwell into the cellar.

"You sleep in this shithole? Frig, b'y. It's right motley down here."

"It's fine, just shut up."

Milton grabbed his toothbrush and headed back up the stairs.

"Where ya off to, b'y?"

"I'm just brushing my teeth; you should try it some time."

When Milton returned to the cellar, Noddy was doubled over, doing the Cyril Sneer, the knotted top of a plastic sandwich bag sticking out of his butt.

"Argh! I hate you so much. You know that?!"

"Hahahahahaha! If you weren't looking at my arse, b'y, you wouldn't be looking at any arse at all. You dies for it."

Noddy, wearing only a pair of holey wool socks and his thick coat of disgusting, snarled, body hair, grabbed the only pillow and climbed under the covers.

"Wait, hold on, you're not sleeping naked!"

"Nah, b'y, got me socks on, don't be a prude."

Noddy rolled over, with his back to Milton, and stuck his bare ass out at him, and farted. The top-secret RCMP document he was hiding in his ass in a plastic sandwich bag made a kazoo sound as it flapped in the breeze.

"I hate you."

"Hahahahahaha!"

Milton sat on the hard wooden chair at the small table he used as a desk, and opened the laptop he had bought second-, third-, or more-hand from a pawn shop for $100.

He checked his email and Facebook for the first time in three months. He was hoping for some, any, response to any of the dozens of fake accounts he'd been secretly sending Robin messages from. There was nothing. But buried in his notifications was a Facebook event invite:

World Premiere: Turkey Vultures, a new film by Robin Davis, Bar La Baraque, Montreal, 8:00 pm, September 6, 2008.

That was in three days.

Milton closed his computer, shut off the light and climbed over a loudly snoring Noddy and into bed—on top of the covers, fully clothed. He laid on his back, staring into the darkness. He elbowed Noddy hard in the stomach.

"Hey, jerk, I'll come with you."

"Yes, b'y. Deadly!"

Noddy put his arm around Milton and pulled him into little spoon and fell back to sleep immediately. His boner poked into the deep scratch the bullet from earlier had left in Milton's right ass cheek.

PART FIVE
MONTREAL III

TWENTY

RETURN

Road Trip

Noddy and Milton drove, and Noddy talked, straight through from St. John's to Montreal in Greg's 1997 Subaru Forester.

They set off before 8:00 a.m. and Noddy drove the first leg to Gander at about 150 kilometres per hour, turning the ordinarily three-hour-long trip into just over two.

They stopped for a "piss an' a pop" at the Gander Truck Stop and Milton took over.

Noddy sat in the passenger seat drinking Coors Light, smoking cigarettes, and talking at Milton about the history of the pulp industry in Newfoundland.

"Just another bunch of arseholes from the mainland fuckin' the arseholes from the island, this time for pulp instead a fish."

After the bat-out-of-hell sprint to Gander, Milton's speed limit obedience made it feel like they were going backwards.

"C'mon, b'y, pull da ballast outta your arse."

As they crept through Grand Falls-Windsor at a sane speed, Noddy grabbed the steering wheel and jerked it towards the ditch. Milton slammed on the brakes and they skidded sideways to a stop in the middle of the busy Trans-Canada Highway.

"Get out. Go on. Get."

Noddy wouldn't let Milton drive for the rest of the trip. He sped, drank, smoked, and talked and talked and talked the rest of the way.

"The conditions in them lumber camps, by. Make your pop's sweaty arsehole seem like the Ritz."

Of course, neither of them bothered to check the ferry schedule from Port Aux Basques to North Sydney, so they arrived at the ferry terminal just in time to watch the ferry pulling out and had to wait 12 hours for the next crossing.

Noddy made Milton pay for their ferry tickets from his dwindling stockpile of drug money, and they pulled into the front of the line to wait for the next ferry.

Noddy sat on the hood of the Subaru drinking his warm Coors and smoking cigarettes, staring out into the thick fog. Milton tried to recline the passenger seat and get some sleep, but the spectre of assured death and/or true love hanging over their race back to Montreal kept him from sleeping much at all.

Eventually he gave up and joined Noddy in leaving two bum-shaped dents in the hood of Greg's car. Noddy handed him a warm Coors, and launched into a long, passionate soliloquy about Joey Smallwood walking the Newfoundland railway bed to unionize the island's railway men.

"They brung his shoes into my school there the once. Holes worn right through."

Milton didn't listen, like he never listened. He just lay back on the windshield and stared into the fog.

"Noddy, what's going to happen? When we get back to Montreal, what's the plan?"

"Plan? For what? I'm gonna get some good poutine, and maybe find some broads, that's what."

"No, you idiot. With Leonard Cohen and all that? How are we going to get out of this? I can't do this anymore. I need to be able to live my life and my life isn't in Newfoundland."

"Ah, go on, b'y. Things are just fine in Newfoundland."

"I'm sure it is for some people who don't know any better. But I had a life in Montreal. I had a job, almost had a girl, was making a name for myself with my poetry. Things were starting to happen and then all this happened."

"B'y, what girl did you almost have? Your job sucked balls, and ya was a joke, b'y. Carmichael didn't say your poetry was good, he made fun of ya. Even Lenny told ya you suck."

"Robin."

"Robin? The bird chick? You still hung up on her? I thought she left."

"She's coming back; why do you think I agreed to come on this death march with you?"

"I thought you grew a set, or something, but apparently you need to come so you can collect them from this chick."

"She's not a chick! She's an artist—a filmmaker, a genius, you have no idea."

"Nah b'y, I have a pretty good idea, remember?"

"Shut up! That was just sex."

"That wasn't sex, b'y. That was fuckin'."

"Gah! Never mind."

"Don't go getting all in a sook now. Look, here's what's what: how old are ya?"

"Just leave me alone."

"Nah, b'y. I'm serious. How old are ya?"

"24."

"Jesus, b'y. You're a fuckin' baby."

"Shut up, Noddy. Just leave me alone. Okay."

Milton moved to get off the car, Noddy grabbed his arm.

"I'm serious, b'y. You're 24 and what have you ever done?"

"Let go!"

"Nah, b'y. You've done fuck all. Ya just get off your mother's tit and come to Montreal to live some fantasy dream life like the rest of them spoiled rich pricks in the Plateau."

"Same as you!"

"I mean it, b'y. What have you ever done before this?"

"Lots!"

"Lots? Like what? Giving handies to dirt farmers in the back of the farm store don't count. Doing a bullshit diploma at a bullshit school don't count. You're a baby, b'y."

"Shut up."

"You are. I'm not being an arsehole. It's the truth. You done nothing at all your whole life, and that's fine, parents raise pussies nowadays, your mother and father fucked you like that. Ya lived a charmed life. That's fine, b'y. Nothing wrong with that. But ya come to Montreal with your head so far up your own arse your eyes are going brown..."

"They are brown."

"...and just like your whole life you're expecting the entire universe to kiss your arse, and tuck ya in at night. But it ain't like that, b'y."

"How would you know about any of it?"

"How would I know?"

• • •

Heart's Content

"B'y. I grew up poorer than dirt around the Bay in Heart's Content. We couldn't afford toys, so my mother just cut holes in our pockets. But it was all we knew. We was poor. My nan and pop were poor before that, their people before that and all the way back to 15-dickity-6. In '91 I was 14. My father was a fisherman, b'y, but he couldn't pay his crew no more so my mother pulled me and my brother out of school and made us go to work with me father. There was no fish left on the Grand Banks, where my people had been fishing for centuries, so he gets the old guy next door to sign over his license for the Labrador where there was supposed to be a bit of cod left. It was a three-day steam on me father's shitty little rig to the Labrador, and we gets there and there ain't a goddamned fish left in 'er. We caught more fishing gear than fish. So, my father's fucked good. The bank's gonna take the boat and the house and the Pontiac, and he loved that Pontiac, b'y. So, he goes below and drinks an entire 40 of rum in one go, like water, and gets belligerent and starts bawling. He digs out some old rabbit hunting rifle he kept on board for security, or whatever, and he starts just going off—'fuck this boat,' POW, 'fuck this radio,' POW, 'fuck this rigging,' POW— shoots up the whole goddamned boat. My brother and me, we's just stunned. He runs outta bullets and we tries to talk him down, but he cold-cocks me brother with the end of the rifle and takes a swing at me too. Then he digs into his pocket and finds one more bullet and loads it into the rifle and swallows half the goddamned thing and POW. Blows the back of his head to sea and falls over the side after it."

"Oh my god! I had no idea."

"Course you didn't, you think poet is a job, and the worst thing that ever happened to you was you stubbed your toe or some shit. So, my brother and me, we's in the Labrador, in December, ice is coming in, boat shot full of holes by the old man, radio shot up, whole thing's right proper fucked. It's a three-day steam back home and me brother says me father never actually got a license for up the Labrador, so we're poaching too, and if we gets caught we're double fucked. So, we head 'er for home and run into some weather around Fogo way and shit gets good and tangly and we head 'er for shore but don't make 'er and wreck just off Fogo. My brother can't swim worth a shit, so he's fuckin' drowning and bawling like a baby on me, so I grabs him and swim us both to shore, but the arsehole freezes to death on the way anyway, so I'm dragging me dead brother a half mile to shore, and by the time I makes 'er he's stiff like a fuckin' board, b'y, but he's me brother, so I drags him up on the beach and hauls him up on me back and starts walking for a couple miles to the nearest house. And I'm right frozen too, b'y. Can't feel my arms and my legs, and getting right sleepy, which means I'm about to kick 'er too, and my clothes are frozen stiffer then a Bayman's prick on check day, but I gets to this old nan's house and she thaws me out and I gets a ride back home with me brother piled in the pan of some feller's truck. Then I get blind drunk and been that way pretty much since. A few months later, Ottawa shuts the whole fuckin' thing down, the Moratorium, and we were all fucked. No money in fishing to begin with, but at least it got ya something to eat. After that we only had our boots to chew on. Four hundred-some-odd years being poor, broke, and stupid, but being able to keep enough food in our bellies to keep from dropping dead, and in one day we were all, an entire island of us, fucked."

"Yeah, you've told me about how tough the moratorium was."

"Ya don't know the half of it, b'y. Ya can't fathom misery at that scale. Forty-some-odd-thousand families lost 'er overnight, and everyone else who relied on them for their own bread followed right behind. And it wasn't Gerry Butts in Hearts Content who took the fish outta the goddamned sea, it was the trawlers. The Japanese and the Russians and the Portuguese and the Spaniards dragging bottom and sucking every last bit of life outta the richest fishing ground man had ever seen. And the fuckin' feds did fuck all about it but put a bullet in us all. We was gutted. We was cooked. We was done. That's it. Ya can't fathom, b'y. I was there and it still boggles the mind."

"I'm sorry, Noddy, I really am."

"What are ya sorry for, b'y? You a Russian trawler? Your pops the Minister of Fisheries and Oceans? What the fuck good is sorry? Everyone's always sorry, no one ever does a goddamned thing about it. Just let the stupid Newfs starve. So, you goes to town and starts stealing every fuckin' thing that ain't bolted down just so you can eat. I lived under the overpass on Water Street for four years, b'y. Everyone else left. Everyone else sold their gear to the government or went on pogey to get enough for a bus ticket out west to find work. I couldn't afford either, my gear was on da bottom off Fogo. But I gets a woman, Barb, she moved in under the overpass with me. We'd steal gas and thin it out with rainwater and get fucked up on it. I should be dead from that. Killed Barb. She got some diesel out of an old Volvo on Waterford Bridge Road, and that shit will kill ya dead. And it did. And what do ya do with a body when you don't know her people and live under an overpass? I just left her there. And I loved her too. We talked about getting cleaned up and getting jobs and a real house and getting married and having a batch of kids and growing old together. But I couldn't live under that overpass no more, so I moved into the 'rippers. It was the bar open the latest downtown, and where it was easiest to steal liquor. And each night I'd get da shit knocked outta me by the bouncers, and eventually they got tired of it, or their hands got sore, or they found Jesus, and they stopped beating on me and gave me a job as the DJ."

"Wait, I thought you grew up in Town and worked on the docks when you were a kid."

"Who told you that?"

"You did, when we were working together."

"Nah, b'y. I grew up in Hearts Delight."

"I thought you said Hearts Content."

"Same shit."

"I'm pretty sure they are different towns. And that all those little towns hate each other."

"Well, Hearts Desire can fuck right off, but Hearts Delight is fine."

"And Sam told me your dad was a politician, and I looked it up and someone named Gerry Butts was Minister of Fisheries for three months in the '80s."

"Sam's full of shit."

"And Wikipedia?"

"It's full of shit too."

"You are full of shit, Noddy. Jesus."

"That's no way to talk to a fella who seen his dad kill himself. Hahahahaha!"

"Go to hell."

"Hahahahaha."

In lieu of tearing the windshield wiper off Greg's car and stabbing Noddy to death with it, Milton climbed down off the hood and got back in the passenger seat. Noddy hollered at him through the windshield.

"Aw, c'mon, b'y. Don't be a sook. I'm just saying life ain't fair. That's it. Nobody's going to give ya nothing. You need to grow a set of balls already and take what you wants from it. Man up, b'y."

"Shut up!"

Milton shut his eyes and pretended to sleep until he eventually fell asleep.

. . .

Deb

Milton woke up the next morning to Noddy starting the engine to pull onto the ferry. They parked at the front of the ferry on the lowest level and got out of the car and went above deck.

"I'm going to find some pussy at the bar, you coming?"

"No, thanks. I'm good."

"Suit yourself. Can I borrow a hundy?"

Rather than fighting with Noddy about the futility of trying to pick up women on a ferry, or the absurdity of spending $100 at the ferry bar at 7:00 a.m., Milton dug into his backpack and pulled out a wad of slimy small bills and handed them to Noddy.

He then turned and walked in the opposite direction and found the quietest corner on the boat he could, took a dog-eared, bird-shitty notebook and cheap pen out of his backpack, found a blank page, and began writing. He wrote for six hours straight as his guts bobbed up and down with the sea.

> hell
> hath no fury
> like this mess im in
> and im in it gladly to find you
> with satan himself guiding me
> back to you
> hell
> hath no fury
> like a heart that yearns
> like flesh that burns
> like a stomach that turns
> for you

When the voice came over the intercom telling everyone to return to their cars, Milton packed up his notebook and found his way back down to the car.

As he approached, he noticed something bobbing up and down in the back seat through steamed-up windows. Something light coloured and about the size of Noddy's ass. Milton got to the car and opened the back door. Noddy was humping someone he'd picked up at the bar.

"Get! Not yet! Go away!"

Milton closed the door and leaned against the hood until the grunting and howling stopped and the car quit rocking. The back door opened, and Noddy tumbled out onto the deck with his pants around his ankles.

He stood up and pulled up his pants.

"Whaddayat, b'y?"

"Are you done?"

"Yeah, fucked right out. This is... uh..."

A woman, readjusting her clothes, clambered out of the car.

"Nice to meet you. I'm Deb."

Deb stuck out her hand to shake Milton's, but she had her underwear bunched up in one hand, and her purse in the other. She laughed awkwardly instead, gave Noddy a peck on the cheek, said, "Call me," and went back towards her car.

"Not bad, eh, b'y? A boat 10."

. . .

Fries, Dressing, and Gravy

They rolled off the ferry in Cape Breton and Noddy drove the remaining 1,500 kilometres in one shot. It took them less than 12 hours, including three Tim Horton's drive-thrus, and three roadside "piss stops."

Noddy didn't stop talking the entire time.

He went on and on about all the ways the Maritimes and Quebec paled in comparison to Newfoundland. On and on about all the ways that Halifax wished it was St. John's. On and on about how the accordion is an actual instrument and the fiddle is just "fingernails on the Christly chalkboard." On and on about how garlic fingers were "just pizza with nothing on it."

But mostly, he went on and on, at least 10 of those last 12 hours, about the superiority of Newfoundland's most cherished rotgut midnight snack—fries, dressing, and gravy—compared to the "worst case of actual shit being passed off as food," the maritime delicacy, the donair.

"FDG is working man's food: spuds, bit of bread, bit of gravy. Something your nan can make to cure your hangover. It's deadly, b'y. But donairs? Sweet merciful Christ! Shameful. Some rich capitalist fucks somehow convinced half this goddamned place that turned meat rolled on the floor and covered in a bit of turned Miracle Whip is not just worth eating, but something worth bragging about as if it doesn't taste and look the spitting image of dog shit. Not fit, b'y. Not fit at all."

Which led down a long and winding tangent about exploitation of the working class by the "rich capitalist fucks," and how donairs were the very embodiment of the

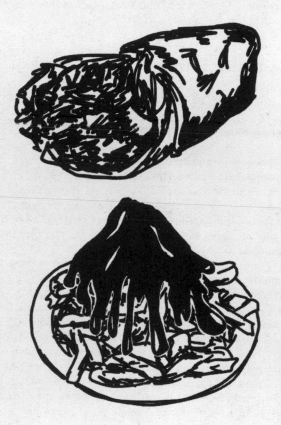

Fig. 57. Atlantic Canadian delicacies

"true trickle-down economics, a bunch of working folks happily eating leftover dog shit."

Milton ignored Noddy as best he could and pretended to sleep the entire way.

Having his eyes closed helped, especially when Noddy would pass a string of seven cars going uphill on a solid yellow line with a gas truck coming straight at them.

He did awaken for the brief moment when Noddy passed a couple of dozen cars on the shoulder while they were stopped at a construction site.

He almost took out the flag person, and then proceeded to play a game of chicken with the lane of on-coming traffic. Turns out, there is enough room in a single lane to fit two cars, as long as one of those cars is piloted by a crazy asshole who hits every one of the hundred pylons set out along the centre line.

Milton screamed. Noddy laughed.

"Sorry, Greg. You might be getting a call from the piggies over that one."

As they approached Montreal, Noddy pulled off at a strip club in a Verdun strip mall.

"Might as well have a last meal, b'y, while we're still on this side of the dirt."

Milton rolled his eyes, and followed Noddy through the blacked-out glass door with a tinfoil silhouette of a woman.

Noddy picked a table right near the stage in a half-empty bar with only a smattering of lunchtime patrons—used car salesmen, professional online poker players, stay-at-home dads, and surly mobsters who'd surely recognize both of them and shoot them both in the back on the way out.

Milton shrunk down in his chair and tried not to make eye contact with anyone. They ordered beers and steak-frites, and Noddy passed the time flicking loonies at a dancer half-heartedly wiggling to The Eagles.

"This fuckin' guy can't play music worth shit."

The dance ended when the song ended and a commercial came on for the Aquazilla waterpark, and the new Pontiac Vibe, followed by a traffic report—she was dancing to the radio.

Noddy inhaled his steak and then started stealing pieces off Milton's plate. When the food was gone, and Noddy had flicked all of their change, Noddy got up from the table and belched loudly.

"Well, b'y. Pay the bill and saddle up. Here goes nothing."

• • •

Homecoming

They drove back into the city as the sun began to set over the western half of the island and headed straight for de l'Épée.

Even though they had both left town without a word of notice, hadn't called since, and Georgette was probably pissed they stiffed her on the rent, they weren't sure where else to go.

They parked up the street and watched the sparse traffic on the tree-lined street until the sun had set completely. They were being careful, as careful as an ignorant fool and a naïve fool can be while trying to outrun the police and the mob.

When the coast seemed clear they snuck into the alley, through the shadows between brick row houses, up the rusty, rickety fire escape, and through the kitchen window of Sept-cent-sept, where Georgette was cooking some rich-smelling French dish in her sweatpants.

"Georgie, you minx, get a look at ya, like an angel from heaven!"

"PUTAIN! NOHDEE ET MILTON!! FUCK YOU COCK-SUCKERS!!! TA GUEULE!!! PUTAIN!!!"

For a split second, before hugging them, Noddy and Milton weren't sure if she was going to try to stab them with the kitchen knife she was holding.

"Where did you go? Putain! You leave wit'out saying anyt'ing. I t'ought you died. I called police. Dey didn't know. Putain!"

"Yah, sorry Georgie, we got into a bit of shit and had to leave town."

"Well fuck you, connards!"

"Any bad looking guys been poking around for us?"

"Ah, oui, putain! Dis guy with no neck come 'ere asking for you a while ago."

"What'd you say?"

"Oh... Tu sais. Pas beaucoup."

A smile grew across Georgette's face.

"Georgie, did you fuck that meathead?"

"Nohdee! Tu es dégueulasse!"

"Georgie?"

"Peut-être. Un petit peu."

All three shared a laugh. It was the best they'd probably ever all gotten along.

Georgette explained, in insufficient detail for Noddy's taste, that the same "meat'ead" had come around a few times a few months ago looking for Noddy, saying he was owed money. Eventually Georgette and the "meat'ead" started dating, but he took offence to Larry and Chris.

"No man will tell me what to do. So, I tell 'im to, 'ow you say, 'get bent'. 'e cry like baby and go away."

He go away, but not before he helped Georgette clean out Milton's and Noddy's rooms. They found thousands of dollars in either room, Georgette kept a bunch of it for missed rent and "pain and suffering," and the "meat'ead" kept the rest, said it was "what he was owed," and it would make Noddy "square." He hadn't said anything about Milton.

When the police came by a couple months later, Georgette thought it was just a really slow response to the missing persons reports she'd filed, but they had a warrant for Noddy for his skipping bail.

With that, she was convinced the two of them had gotten into some kind of shit and weren't coming back, so she put an ad up on Craigslist and got two new roommates that afternoon—Lara, a Comp-lit major at Concordia from Brampton, and Koel, an English major at McGill from Ajax.

Lara was a bit "chiqué," but she kept to herself, and Koel was fine except when him and Ruddy would get drunk and pester Ava about semiotics.

"Dey won't shut up about signs et signifiers et... putain!"

All caught up on the news, Noddy helped himself to a large mouthful of whatever Georgette was cooking. It scalded the inside of his mouth, causing him to spit it back into the pot, which drew a slap from Georgette.

They made their way down the hall, where Ruddy and Koel were locked in an intense argument with Ava.

"No, you idiot! You, like, don't understand! Pierce is absolutely right that every sign is relational and dependent upon an interpretant, and if you take it even further, you start to verge into hermeneutics and the pending weight of history and culture. De Saussure's notion of the arbitrariness of signs only makes sense in a vacuum. It might be fundamentally important, but it misses that relational aspect that makes it social."

"No, no, Av, you're missing the point. It's like this. Say you've got a toaster, everyone knows what a toaster is, you see it sitting there on the counter, it's obviously a toaster. But there is no natural law that decrees 'metal box with two slots in it' is a toaster, per se."

"Yeah, Av, it's a convention, but it's totally arbitrary. Why not call it an umbrella?"

"Because, you idiots, there's, like, no such thing as a toaster without bread and butter and jam. It's a product of a society, of a culture, that, like, refines grains to produce flour and make bread, and then slices that bread, and stuffs them into the slots of a hot metal box to change the chemical structure of the bread to make it taste different, and some-how, like, more acceptable to eat in the morning. And all of that is the outcome of a long history of baking and the War and industrialization. Your toaster isn't anything without any of that, it might as well be an umbrella."

"Exactly, that's what I said!"

"No, it's..."

"All you fuckers are wrong, it was Ruddy's mom and her sweet, sweet, ass that did it."

"NODDY! MILTON! OHMYGAWD! George said you were dead."

The rest of the night was like nothing had changed, except there were two strangers sparring with Ruddy and Ava while being yelled at by Noddy about some slightly derogatory aspect of Canadian history they didn't know the "real" story about.

Milton sat in the middle of it, like always, and didn't say a word. He just stared at the QHL game (Saint-Jean-sur-Richelieu Home Depot Hammers were getting licked by the Rapide Lube Monstres de Huile de Jonquière) playing at full volume and tried not to breathe in too much second-hand smoke.

Except tonight, his and Noddy's impending certain death at the hands of Leonard Cohen—singer, songwriter, poet, national treasure, mob boss—hung in the air with all the smoke.

* * *

Kia Ora

The next morning Noddy woke Milton up early and told him to get the gun and the money and come with him.

Milton had slept fitfully on the couch and when he first woke up, thanks to Noddy giving him a Wet Willy, he had forgotten the past year.

Crossing the most dangerous man in the country, stealing pills to sell to the most dangerous man in the country, being on the lam in Newfoundland grad school from the most dangerous man in the country—all of it, hadn't happened. It didn't exist. It wasn't even a bad dream. It was nothing. He was just arriving in Montreal for the first time. About to fulfill his destiny as a world famous poet.

But as Noddy pressed his bare ass into Milton's drowsy forehead, top secret RCMP plans crinkling, and farted loudly, it all came flooding back.

Milton relived, in split-second high-definition, every mounting misfortune and bad decision. His heart, which through the night had returned to its normal spot in his chest, dropped back down to where it had been clogging his lower intestine for the past year of constipation and terror.

"C'mon, b'y, let's go."

Noddy explained, after much begging, pleading, and cajoling from Milton, and between revisionist retellings of the 1959 Badger Riot[31] on the walk to the bus to the metro, that his plan, their plan, was to find Sam.

If Leonard Cohen hadn't killed him after they'd disappeared, Sam would probably be gutting a house in Westmount somewhere. And if he was gutting a house in Westmount somewhere, he'd probably know what had happened to Leonard Cohen, and maybe even know how they could find Leonard Cohen.

Failing that, they'd go into La Baraque and pick a fight with the biggest guy in there, and, assuming they survived, word would get back to Leonard Cohen.

"Can't we just call Sam?"

---

[31] On March 10, 1959 police and company strike-breakers clashed with striking loggers in the small town of Badger, Newfoundland and Labrador. A police officer from the Royal Newfoundland Constabulary was killed in the mêlée.

"Nah, b'y. That Aussie Pinko don't believe in phones, and I don't know about you, but I'd rather not get the shit smacked outta me."

For an entire day they wandered up and down the streets of Westmount, ducking into any house that looked the least bit under construction, and playing Franglais charades with unimpressed contractors and angry homeowners. But no Sam.

Shortly after 5:00pm, after being threatened with police, mace, and a shotgun—which Noddy swore wasn't loaded, "You can hear when he cocked it, he was full of shit"—they gave up and walked down into the Atwater Metro station to go back to Sept-cent-sept and drink more of Koel's beer and work up the courage to go get the shit beat out of them at La Baraque.

Noddy was taking a piss on the wall towards the front end of the crowded rush-hour metro platform and Milton was trying really hard to look as disgusted as the other commuters when he saw Sam standing on the opposite platform, laughing.

"*Kia Ora*, fuckwits!"

Noddy finished peeing and jumped down on the rails and scampered across to where Sam was standing. Milton, in favour of not getting hit by a train, took the escalator up, walked across the station, and took the escalator back down to find them standing on the platform.

Noddy was grinning ear to ear.

"B'y, you look like shit!"

"Thanks, mate. You two look good. Not like you just crawled out of a tomtit's asshole at all."

Noddy kept hugging him and grabbing his face. At one point he gave Sam a kiss on the lips.

They went back upstairs, found a case of Molson Ex in the dep and sat in the mall food court drinking and catching up.

Sam hadn't seen or heard anything about Leonard Cohen, other than what a thug sent to rough him up told him: that Noddy had fucked over the Godfather and Sam was suspected for being in on it. Sam swore he wasn't, took his beating honourably, and convinced the thug that he was still loyal to the Godfather.

He was allowed to continue sloppily renovating vast Westmount mansions as a front for laundering millions of dollars in drug money. That was going so well that Sam had several crews working around the city. And he was smart enough to mind his own business and not fuck up the steady flow of work and cash coming his way.

"Talking to you pair of assholes could mean the end of me, but fuck them, mate. The mafia is just another form of government. They just want to run your life and steal your shit."

"But we need to find that ol' fart Lenny, b'y."

"Wish I could help, mate, I'm just his hired monkey. There are about 500 mouth-breathing troglodytes between him and me in the food chain. If ya really need to see him, just go to La Baraque and ask one of them. If they don't kill ya, word will get back."

"That was our plan B, thanks for nothing, b'y."

"No problem, mate, just let me know when ya go, I want to watch."

TWENTY-ONE
INTO THIS FURNACE

World Premiere

Despite the last several days, like the last several months, feeling like a bad hallucination. Despite having spent the entire day wandering aimlessly around Westmount. Despite having tied his fate to Noddy. Milton was very much aware of what day it was.

It was the day. The day he came back for. Not the day to sort things out with Leonard Cohen. Not the day to finally rid himself of the walking, talking, belching, farting, swearing, screwing human yoke that was Noddy. Not the day to free himself. But the day of Robin's premiere

He'd hoped that all this inconvenient mob-wanting-him-dead business could have been solved before the big day, but it wasn't. "What odds," as Noddy would say, they were going to La Baraque anyway.

Milton made up an excuse to go back to Sept-cent-sept before they went to the bar. He hadn't had a good night's sleep or a shower in weeks, he looked very much like he had just "crawled out of a tomtit's asshole."

He showered and shaved. Koel wasn't home, so he helped himself to some clean clothes, while Noddy helped himself to the contents of the fridge.

"You ready, Cinderella?"

"I guess."

They walked the familiar blocks to La Baraque in the balmy, late-summer evening.

Milton had lived in Montreal for not much longer than he'd lived in Newfoundland, but this neighbourhood, these tree-lined streets, these brick rowhouses with their rust-and-peeling-paint metal staircases, the fixy bikes chained eight deep to every lamp-post and light pole, the gangs of mommy bloggers with their designer baby buggies. This felt like home.

The homieness of it, the normalness of it, made it feel like everything was fine. Like those few moments upon waking. But things weren't fine. Things were bad. Very bad.

The inevitability of his virgin death became plain as day the second they rounded the corner onto Hutchison Street and La Baraque came into view.

Robin's premiere was a much bigger deal than Milton had anticipated.

Along with the usual jumble of choppers and hogs and other stupidly named motorcycles, there were two giant spotlights on either side of a red carpet that stretched from the street to the front door of the dive bar.

There were a dozen photographers and reporters buzzing around. Scores of ordinary, non-biker/non-mobsters were being kept behind barricades guarded by a handful of surly biker-bouncers in tuxedo t-shirts.

Franco-ska-metal blasted over speakers out into the street.

Along Hutchison, people were on their balconies watching, wondering what the hell was going on.

As Milton and Noddy got closer, a grey van pulled up to the red carpet and two men in matching grey and red overalls got out. They opened the back door and removed two large pedestals and set them next to the giant spotlights. They returned to the van and pulled out two massive crates covered in sheets. Carried the crates over to the pedestals, and when they removed the sheets, they revealed a pair of caged turkey vultures.

Wearing thick leather gloves and clear welding face masks, the two men took the turkey vultures out of their cages and set them on the pedestals, attaching a cord fastened to the turkey vultures' legs so they couldn't get too far, and slapped an entire raw chicken on the small platform.

Throughout the rest of the night the giant ugly birds would flap their wings to try and escape. When they'd hit the end of their short leashes they'd let out an angry, guttural, deathly gargle until one of the men would throw them another chicken.

"What in the Christ is going on?"

"It's Robin's new movie premiere."

"Robin?"

"You know, Robin, the love of my life, you slept with her, I hate you because of it and everything else."

"Oh, right. Her. She was a dead lay, b'y."

"Yeah, you mentioned."

"Did you know about this?"

"No... not at all."

When they got up to the barricade, Milton asked one of the bystanders, a burnt-out hippy puppeteer in a *Dear Heather* t-shirt that Milton vaguely recognized, why all the hubbub for a small independent short film about birds.

"Hey, why all the hubbub for a small independent short film about birds?"

"It's not often that Leonard Cohen executive produces a film!"

You could almost hear a record scratching.

"Pardon me?"

"Yeah, man, Leonard Cohen is the executive producer of this. No one has seen or heard from him in months, but apparently this is directed by his wife or his girlfriend or his daughter or something. There's a good chance he'll be here."

"Wait, what?"

"Yeah, there were rumours going around discussion boards that he might be dead, or he might have gotten married, or might have gone back to the Buddhist monastery, or a whole bunch of things, after he cancelled his tour last Fall. He hasn't made any public appearances in over a year. And then word got around that he executive produced this woman's film, some Roberta woman."

"Her name is ROBIN!"

• • •

Red Carpet

Before long Sam showed up, then Georgette and a bunch of her puppet friends arrived for their usual drink-to-the-point-of-smoking-meth-in-the-alley, then came Ruddy and Ava and Owly and Pochard and Booby and Wren and a bunch of the gang from the anarchist potluck. Koel and Lara were there too, but neither seemed particularly wowed by the whole thing. Koel did shoot Milton strange looks, like he recognized the clothes he was wearing from somewhere.

Most of the potluck gang were on the guest list, so they talked to the tuxedoed bouncers and went in the bar. It convinced Milton that he was on the list too, so he approached the smaller of the two bouncers who was still several times the size of Milton.

Milton tried really hard to play it cool.

"Hey, yo, the name's Milton Ontario, I'm friends with the director."

"Milton? The-fuck-kind-of-name is that?"

"Uhm... my name."

"Well you ain't on no list, Milfred Ontario."

The bouncer never even looked.

"Are you sure, the director and I are quite close. I'm also friends with Leonard Cohen. Please check again."

"What did you say?"

"Please check again?"

"No, before that you little peckerhead."

"I said... I said... I'm friends with the filmmakers."

"Yeah, which ones?"

"Robin Davis, and... um... Leonard Cohen."

The bouncer grabbed Milton by the collar with one hand and lifted him off the ground.

"Don't you ever say that fuckin' name again, now get out of here before I get upset."

"Gargle," was all Milton could cough out.

Back on the ground he rejoined Noddy.

"We need to get in there, Noddy!"

"No shit, Einstein."

"It's Sherlock."

"What is?"

"The saying is 'no shit, Sherlock.' Everyone knows that."

"Whatever, let's go around the back, b'y, see if we can get in there."

Milton and Noddy coolly circled around the back of the building. The back door was guarded by another giant bouncer. Noddy tried to sweet talk him.

"Eh, b'y, buddy here has fifty-bucks for ya if you'll let us in."

"Take a hike you little worms."

"He'll also throw in a handy."

"Get lost, turds."

"Fine, a blowy?"

The bouncer sized Milton up, like he was actually considering it.

"Piss off."

A giant roar rose from the crowd at the front of the bar. Milton ran as fast as he could back around to the front. By the time he got there, the commotion had died down but the crowd was still buzzing.

"What happened?"

"LEONARD FREAKING COHEN! THAT'S WHAT HAP-
PENED!"

"Was he alone?"

"No, he was with some brunette."

They had to get into the bar.

• • •

Mission Impossible

Milton circled back and found Noddy down the alley sitting
on a garbage can smoking a cigarette and drinking a beer.

"Where'd you get that?"

"What, this horsepiss? I had 'er in my pocket. Did you
get in?"

"Does it look like a got in?"

"Nah b'y, it looks like you're sniveling like a fuckin'
baby."

"Leonard Cohen apparently just went in. We have to get
in there."

"No shit, Smallwood."

"Yeah. But how?"

"Like Tom motherfuckin' Cruise, b'y, through the roof."

"No, I'm serious."

"So am I!"

Noddy pointed his cigarette up at the four- or five-foot
gap between the La Baraque fire escape and the building
across the alley.

"That way."

Noddy dumped out the garbage can he was sitting on
and set it under the just-out-of-reach retractable ladder on
the building across the alley from La Baraque—the La
Baraque fire-escape ladder was missing altogether.

He climbed on top of the garbage can and reached up as
high as he could but was still a couple of feet short.

Fig. 58. Fire escape

He lunged for it but didn't come close and crashed onto the asphalt. He got to his feet rubbing his shoulder and limping in a wincing circle.

"Sonofabitch! Set it back up, I'll give ya a boost."

"Great idea."

Noddy climbed back on top of the can and helped Milton up next to him. There wasn't much room for the two of them, and the can had a wicked wobble.

"Climb up, b'y."

"Climb up what?"

"Me, ya dense arsehole. You're stunned as my arse, Jesus. What did ya think I meant? The wall like Christly Spiderman?"

Milton put his arms around Noddy and started trying to climb him like he was the rope in high-school gym class.

"B'y, you're as useless as a leaky pogey boot."

Noddy grabbed Milton's crotch and boosted him up.

"I was never this handsy with Brenda under the over-pass even."

"I thought her name was Barb."

"Just grab the Jesus thing, would ya?"

Milton climbed until he could just grasp the bottom rung of the rusty fire-escape ladder.

"Got it!"

Noddy dropped him and the ladder and Milton clattered down to the ground. When he hit the ground, he lost his grip on the ladder and it clattered back up again.

Noddy was laughing too hard to catch it on the rebound, so they had to re-enact the back-alley sex act of getting the ladder. The second try was a winner and they climbed the fire escape to the very top.

At the top, the four or five feet between that fire escape and the La Baraque fire escape seemed more like forty or fifty feet.

Milton refused to go first, so Noddy hopped up on the rickety, rusty handrail and sprung across to the other side like nothing.

Milton began to follow, but looked down, which was forty or fifty feet, and felt himself splatting on the ground. He staggered back and closed his eyes to try and stop the city from spinning around him so fast.

"C'mon, b'y, take the fuckin' red pill, ya pussy."

"Yeah. Shut up. I'm coming."

Milton haltingly climbed the handrail and half-squatted on the top rail.

"Let's go, b'y. Jesus. We's all going to be dead of old age before you jump."

Milton closed his eyes and jumped.

Well, he sort of jumped, sort of fell.

He was scared to let go of the rail he was on, which wasn't a great way to get away from the rail he was on, so he just sort of flopped across the gap but managed to grab hold of the bottom rail because the gap was actually closer to four feet than five or fifty.

Noddy laughed while he struggled to climb back up and over the railing and onto the platform.

From there the pair climbed down the fire escape to the second-storey window of what looked like a storage room. Milton tried to open it, but it was locked, so Noddy leapt up, grabbed the fire escape overhead, and swung his two work boots into the locked window.

SMASH.

His boots didn't shatter the glass so much as just kick two boot-sized holes in the glass and cut his legs to ribbons. He managed, rather ungracefully, to swing himself back out of the shards of glass and cursed up and down as he bled through his shredded, filthy jeans.

"Lord, motherfuckin' Christ in a Chrysler! That smarts!"

Milton took off Koel's shoe and gingerly hammered the rest of the glass out of the frame and carefully climbed into the dark storage room.

• • •

Break & Enter

The second floor of La Baraque was a large storage room full of empty beer kegs and broken furniture bordered by a long hallway with an office at one end and a staff bathroom, with an actual door, and the stairs down to the "kitchen" area behind the bar at the other.

A group of voices walked past the storage room door towards the office.

Milton opened the door a crack to take a look. He could tell from their backs that the voices belonged to a couple bikers who ran the bar, a couple of old men, a couple of thugs, a limping Leonard Cohen, and Robin.

He nearly had a stroke.

The sight of Cohen made him nearly shit himself in fear. The sight of Robin made him nearly shit himself for completely opposite reasons.

They all filed into the office. Robin sat on the end of a couch facing the doorway and down the hall. Other than a biker with his back turned, she was the only person Milton could see.

He closed the door, leaned up against it, and slid down to the ground. His head in his hands.

"What's on the go, b'y?"

"I saw Leonard Cohen. And I saw her. With him."

"Who?"

"Robin, you idiot!"

"Robin?"

"Yes, the girl, you know, the one you..."

"Oh yeah, the one I fucked, that you love, that I fucked. Yeah, great rack."

Fig. 59. Broken window

"Argh!"

"Get out the way, I need to go talk to Lenny, b'y, clear all this shit up."

"Not while she's with him. You'll get her killed too. Let me get her to leave the room first."

"Well git with it, b'y. I'm bleeding out here."

Milton opened the door again and looked down the hall. Robin was still sitting on the couch. She was talking casually with the group of murderers she was with. She was beautiful. She wore a stunning green dress. It showed off her bird tattoos.

Milton stared for a long time.

"Ya trying to ESPN her over here or what? Get on the go with it already?"

Milton began to wave from the darkness of the storage room to try and get her attention, but it wasn't working. He stuck his arm out a bit further and a bit further until Noddy said "fuck it" and shoved him out into the hallway.

Milton stumbled into the wall but managed to keep quiet enough to avoid drawing the attention of the well-armed killers 15 feet down the hall. It did get Robin's attention, though.

She was shocked.

Milton stood up straight and straightened his shirt and his hair and sheepishly waved.

She smiled back.

SHE SMILED BACK!

He beamed. He blushed. Noddy stepped out beside him, bloodied, filthy, crazed. This was even more of a surprise for her. Someone in the room with her spoke and she laughed and looked away.

"Jesus, b'y. I'd totally hit that again if you don't want to."

When she looked back Noddy waved her out, and Noddy and Milton ducked back into the storage room.

An eternity passed before there were footsteps in the hall and a soft tap on the door. It opened and there she was, lit like an angel by the one bare bulb in the piss-smelling hallway. Milton's heart stopped entirely.

"What are you guys doing up here?"

"Hey babe, whaddayat? No hard feelings from before. When we smashed bits. And I didn't call. Remember?"

"Yeah, thanks."

"Turns out Romeo here is all in love with you and shit, and I didn't know before we fucked."

Noddy patted Milton on the shoulder.

"All yours, Cupid. Just be sure you wrap your wiener, don't know who she's been with."

Milton died of embarrassment.

Noddy spun Milton around and dug into his backpack for the gun. He cocked it, stuck it in the back waistband of his pants, nodded to Milton and Robin.

"Nice knowing ya, b'ys."

He left the storage room and headed down the hall to the office.

Within seconds there was shouting and crashing and banging and three gunshots. Pop-pop. Pop. Bullets pierced the storage room walls and made small beams of light that cut through the darkness.

Downstairs, the gunfire was drowned out by the chaos of the bar and Franco-ska-metal.

In the storage room it was drowned out by the growing drone of blood rushing to Milton's head as his face flushed with embarrassment.

"Hey, Milton."

• • •

Heart to Heart

"Hey, Robin."

They hugged long and hard.

Milton melted.

"How are you? My god, you look like you've aged a thousand years since I last saw you. What happened? I never heard from you again after... After we... After you gave me all that money."

"I know, I'm sorry. Noddy... Well... Things got bad... Things are bad... It's all bad... He's probably dead already."

Something Noddy-sized slammed into the wall beside them, and they both jumped. Another bullet—pop—poked another beam of light through the wall above them.

"Definitely now."

"What are you talking about?"

"Leonard Cohen is a bad guy. I left you to bail out Noddy, and Leonard Cohen tried to kill us both, but we got away and I went to Newfoundland and hid out in grad school, and Noddy was supposed to go into witness protection, but he ended up stealing secrets from the cops that he was going to try and give to Leonard Cohen in exchange for our freedom, and he's had them up his... uh... butt... for like a month, and now he's probably dead, and I'll probably be any minute now. It's a whole thing."

"Wait. What? Hold on. Go back. Leonard Cohen? *The* Leonard Cohen? Are you kidding?"

"No. I'm not. That gun Noddy has... had... that is Leonard Cohen's gun. I took it from him when we escaped. All this money..."

Milton dumped the last couple hundred dollars in grimy drug money out of his backpack and onto the floor.

"This is Leonard Cohen's money. Just like the money I gave you. He's like the Godfather of the Canadian mafia."

Robin laughed and laughed and laughed.

"Leonard Cohen? A mob boss? Are you nuts? He's like

the sweetest, most sensitive man."

"How do you know him?"

"Uh... Well, after I didn't hear from you for a while I came back to town to try and find you. I ended up at La Baraque and he was there sitting at the bar, so we got to talking and turns out he's a fan of *Dirty Birds* and offered to help fund the completion of *Turkey Vultures*. He had such great insight into my work, it was such an honour just to hear him talk about it... That voice! My god."

"You were looking for me?"

"Well yeah, I was mad you didn't call or anything so I went back to Florida. But I got kind of lonely, I guess, or something. I missed you. Apart from the crew, who were all weirdos, and all these hundreds of creeps on the internet trying to pick me up, I was kind of lonely, and I don't know... I have a nice time with you."

"And then Leonard Cohen..."

"Yeah, just downstairs, it was wild."

"You and him?"

"Yeah, we really hit it off."

"And you...?"

"And I...?"

"Did you...?"

"Did I...?"

"Are you...?"

"Am I what, Milton?"

"Are you and him a... I dunno... a couple now or something?"

"Hahaha. What? Leonard Cohen? He's old enough to be my grandfather. That's disgusting. And a bit insulting. He likes my work, Milton. That's it."

"So... you're not...?"

"Not what?"

"Dating Leonard Cohen?"

"Ha! No. I'm not dating Leonard Cohen."

"Not even a little bit?"

"Not even a little bit."

"Oh thank God!"

"I guess so."

"So... Now what?"

"Now what what?"

"What happens now?"

"Well, whenever whatever is happening next door is done, I'll go downstairs and play my movie. You're staying to see it right? You've got an executive producer credit. Thanks again, by the way."

"I wouldn't miss it for the world. That's why I'm here. That's why I've walked into the bowels of hell and am looking death in the eye. To see you and your movie."

"I know you're a poet, but you are weird as hell sometimes when you talk."

"Well, I'm not looking death in the eye right *now*. Noddy probably is. And I can't really leave this room. If they find me, they'll kill me too. I just needed to see you. I just needed to..."

"I really think you're wrong about this Leonard Cohen stuff. Seriously, he is the most generous and kind and brilliant man I've ever met. He's a genius."

"He's also very dangerous. Trust me."

"Well then what are you going to do?"

"I just... I came here to see you. I just had to see you. I just had to..."

"Had to what?"

"Had to tell you how I feel."

"How you feel?"

"Yeah."

"Well how do you feel?"

"I... Robin... I... Think I'm..."

"What?"

"Iloveyou. There. I said it. I... Iloveyou."

• • •

Love is a Lie

Robin just stared at him. A smiled threatened to form at the corner of her lips but her furrowed brow wouldn't allow it. They both looked at the dark floor.

"Geez, Milton, I'm really flattered. Really, I am. You are a great guy. But, like, we hardly know each other."

"I think I know enough. I think I knew enough from the moment we met."

"The moment we met? I don't even remember that."

"At that potluck in the fur place, with the garbage can soup."

"There are a lot of those."

"Anyway. That's fine. I should go."

"No, don't go. Wait."

"Well you don't love me back. That's fine. I'm an idiot."

"You're not an idiot. And it's not that I don't love you back. I don't even feel like I know you."

"But we kissed, and made out, and almost... You know. And the chemistry. I felt it."

"That's what kissing and making out usually feels like, Milton."

"So, it wasn't love?"

"It wasn't not love. What the hell is love anyway? You're talking like you want to get married and have a bunch of kids and grow old together. That's a kind of love, I guess. But not even. My parents and all my aunts and uncles are divorced and remarried a bunch of times, and I've been in long-term things that didn't work, and it's not love that makes or breaks those things. It's understanding one another, knowing one another, and being committed to work on staying together, to taking it seriously. It's more of a contract than, like, a soulmate thing. And that might be really unromantic, but people, life is really unromantic. It's not, like, poetry. People are beautiful but also disgusting. When we were sleeping on your floor that night, you were asleep and you farted really loud on my leg, like right on my leg, I felt it. It was so warm and gross. It was disgusting. It smelled so bad. But the rest of the night was really beautiful, in its way."

"Oh god. I'm so sorry."

This was not going how Milton had dreamed it up.

"It's fine. Those things happen. It was real."

"But I don't want to get married or anything like that. I'm just, like, in love with you. And you're not in love with me back. Which is fine. Seriously. And I'm really sorry for farting."

"It's okay. I farted on you as payback."

"Good."

Milton headed back towards the window.

"Milton, wait."

"I said what I wanted to say, now I should go. I'm sorry."

"Stay. Talk to me."

"What's the point?"

"The point is, that *other* love you think you want. You think you're in. It's a lie too. It's all a lie, really. You've had some hormonal reaction to some pretty girl you met at a party, and you're mistaking that boner you've got for her with a meaningful connection. But seriously, we hardly know each other. We're friends, and we almost hooked up that one time, but I feel like I don't know anything about you."

"Yes you do. You know me better than anyone. I've shown you my poetry, I've told you things, you've seen me naked... almost... I'm closer to you than I am to anyone. I just spent three months on a rock in the middle of the Labrador Sea, three months, counting birds and writing poems..."

"What?"

"I'm getting my Master's in Marine Biology specializing in seabirds, because of you. They played *Dirty Birds* the first day of school. It was the most haunting and breathtaking and beautiful thing I've ever seen."

"Wow. Thanks... I guess."

"And I sat on a rock in the middle of the sea counting

birds for three months, getting shit on for three months, just writing letters and poems to you. And all those creeps on the internet hitting on you. Those were all me trying to find a way to contact you in secret. Ever since that very first day we met. You've been the only thing I can think of. You're the first thing on my mind when I wake up, I think of you all day long, you're the last thought I have before I fall asleep, and when I dream, I only dream of you."

"Again, I'm truly flattered... I think. And I really think you have the whole Leonard Cohen-is-a-killer thing wrong. But, pining for someone on a rock in the middle of the sea, or whatever, that's not love either. That's, like, obsession."

"I'm sorry."

"No, it's okay. I'm not disgusted or anything. It's truly flattering. It's truly romantic. Truly. I mean that. But it's not enough for you to just come in and dump this on me and expect me to leap into your arms as we ride off into the sunset. That shit only happens in bad movies and terrible books."

"And poems."

"And poems. And it's not real. And if it is really happening it's probably wrong. Way wrong. Trust me. I've done it before. I've made terrible mistakes because a kiss felt nice and I mistook it for happily ever after. When really it was just a restraining order waiting to happen. Don't fool yourself. Don't try to fool me. Sure, you've shown me some poems, and we made out a bit, and all that. But you're like an invisible man, almost. I've spent all this time with you, and I barely know you. I know about all these things that have happened to you. But I don't know what those things have done to you. I don't know what you see when you look at the world through your eyes. All I really know is how hard you work, how many knots you tie yourself up into to seem one way, or to seem normal, or to fit in, to be like everyone else. Even your poetry is all bluster and subterfuge, it's just to seem poetic without having to actually be poetic. When you talk to someone like Leonard

Cohen, the poet, not the murderer, haha, when you talk to him, you see "Hallelujah." You hear his words and just the sounds and meanings of those words change how the world looks and it suddenly appears different because he's given you a glimpse of what he sees when he looks at the world. The joy and the pain and the struggle and misery and sex and triumph. It's all there. It's a perfect piece of art. That's what it does. It lets you walk around in his skin for a while and feel the world brush up against you so you understand everything a little bit different, a little bit better. If you let it. If you let yourself open up, and be vulnerable, and, like, free. But right now, you're in a prison of appearances and bullshit. It's all pretense, Milton. And that's fine for a lot of people. It's fine for a lot of average people. They find things they like and then drape themselves in the airs of those things and wear them around and go to parties and get laid and collect a bunch of stories to tell their grandkids and then settle down in the suburbs and become automatons until they drop dead of a heart attack at 82. They never really make anything or mean anything. They just come and go and fade away like they were never here. This city is full of twenty-something teenagers playing at poetry or whatever, that's where they're all headed. But there is something about you, Milton. Something that makes me think that maybe, just maybe, you aren't the fade-away type. That maybe you can be something. Mean something."

"Like what?"

"I don't know. I can't decide that for you. But you're much more committed to the idea that there might be something more to all this, some deeper meaning to be found. You just haven't found it yet."

"Well where is it then?"

"I don't know. That's up to you to figure out. That's up to you to make something of yourself. To make the world bigger by your being in it. Not to make it shrink or stay the same. I'm trying to do that by making these films. Such as they are.

It's not a lot, but it's what I see, and what I want to show people, and share with people, and put something out in the world that's constructive and meaningful, that connects and builds. That sows love, really meaningful love, the kind that is based on connection and understanding and knowing and responsibility and hard work and sharing what we see in each other with each other, so we are all a little bigger for it, all a little better for it, so we all live forever in each other and for each other and so we don't fade away to nothing, so we don't disappear. So we don't die."

"I don't want to die. I don't. I want that. What you said."

"But it's not a thing you pick up at the grocery store. It's not a thing at all. It's the collection of every second of your being and what you do with it. What direction you walk in, what you manage to carry with you and do along the way. This is what you're missing. Poetry isn't a party trick you play to get laid or impress your so-called friends, or whatever. Poetry, or whatever you do, is the way you plant yourself in the world, the way you pour yourself out into the world to quench another's thirst, the way you exist and the way you persist. The way you add to it and build it up and make things better."

"You... Amazing..."

Milton was about to pour his flattery all over Robin and tell her how wonderful she was, how great she looked in that dress, how incredibly smart she was, how incredibly horny her words made him, how badly he wanted to kiss her right then, take her right then, make love to her right then, but there was a loud banging on the door.

"Oh shit."

Milton turned to climb out the window

"I was never here."

"Milty! You bust your nut yet, buddy? Put your dick away, I'm coming in."

Noddy wasn't dead.

Not yet.

• • •

All Sordid

Noddy burst through the door.

"All sorted, b'ys. You two fuck?"

"I should probably, uh... get back to things."

"Yeah. Okay. It's... You're... I... I missed you."

"Yeah, I'm glad you're back. Come down and watch the film when you guys are done whatever this is."

Robin left Milton and Noddy alone in the dark, dank storage room.

"So, did ye guys bone?"

"What do you mean sorted?"

"I mean, did you feed her your meat?"

"No, what do you mean it's all sorted? What's sorted?"

"Yeah, in a minute, b'y. I want to hear about you did-dling that bird bird's bird."

"Noddy, shut up and tell me!"

"Calm your tits, b'y. It's all good. Lenny liked what I had up me arse, we had a few laughs, caught up. Got my old job back."

"What about me?"

"Yeah, did you bang her or what?"

"No... C'mon, Noddy."

"What? She do that thing with her elbow while you were going at it?"

"Her elbow? What...? No... Shut up. What did Cohen say about me?"

"Oh, I forgot to ask."

"What? Why? What? You're such a... Such a... Gah!"

"It never came up. Give it a rest."

"Well I'd like to know if I'm going to get killed or not."

"Hard to say, but probably not. Let's go watch this chick's flick and you can buy me a beer and tell me all about flicking this chick's tits. She do that thing with her nose?"

"Nose...?

"Wait now, was that her or the broad on the boat with the nose thing?"

"I wish I still had the gun."

Milton glumly followed Noddy out into the hall and down the stairs into the bar.

His soon-to-be-most-likely-probably murderers were still whooping it up in the office with his never-to-be-unlikely-probably not lover.

TWENTY-TWO
TURKEY
VULTURES

Bird on a Wire

The air left the room when Leonard Cohen entered the small grungy bar. It was all gasps and whispers. A microphone was set up next to the large projection screen and he limped over to it.

"My friends, good evening. Welcome. There is a rather famous story about an encounter I had with a rather famous woman at the Chelsea Hotel in New York City. This, of course, was the indomitable and incomparable, Ms. Janis Joplin. The woman who made the film you are about to see reminds me very much of Ms. Joplin. Ladies and Gentlemen, to share with you for the very first time her new and breathtaking film, please welcome the truly one of a kind, Ms. Robin Davis."

Robin, in her stunning green dress, joined Leonard Cohen on stage. Their embrace struck Milton as a little too familiar and lingered perhaps a bit too long. Robin sheepishly waved to the audience, tucked her hair behind her ear, thanked everyone, and awkwardly said, "Play the movie, I guess."

The lights went down, and the screen was black.

Slowly the bright white ball of a Florida sun, in a faintly grey, cloudless sky, filled the screen and flooded the room with its glow.

One turkey vulture circles into view—someone at the back of the bar whoops loudly—then another vulture. The two seem to be part of some choreographed routine. They turn in identical circles going in opposite directions. When one circle grows, the other does the same. The only sound is the faint whooshing of wings cutting through the wind.

Then another vulture joins, and another, and another, until the sky is filled with them. Silently gliding in identical circles. The camera pans down across the sky until the sun washes out the entire picture.

TURKEY VULTURES
A FILM BY ROBIN DAVIS

A couple audience members whoop and holler.

The title fades as the camera continues panning down to reveal the horizon—the swamplands of Florida—then further to reveal that we're next to a highway. Pickup truck after pickup truck whizzes by. The camera comes to focus on a point a few miles down the road, where dozens of vultures are swooping and landing and walking their lumbering walks.

Slowly it zooms in on the crowd. The swampland blurs and disappears into the background. The highway blurs and disappears into the background. The pickup trucks blur and disappear into the background. The dozens of birds become several, become a few, become one full bird, becomes just its head, as it stands on an alligator that's been run over by a pickup truck.

The star hisses at the other vultures, and tears some flesh from the gator. Hissing and tearing, tearing and hissing. The sound makes it visceral. The film is black and white but you can see the blood, you can feel the hot sun, you can smell the rotting gator. Hissing and tearing.

Another vulture attacks the star. They jostle and the star hops twice, and lifts into flight. As it begins to zoom back out, the camera stays trained on the vulture's face.

Slowly the single bird becomes a few, becomes several, becomes dozens. Slowly the highway re-emerges, then the pickup trucks, then the swamplands. The camera follows the bird as it flies up. The highway and trucks and swamps fall out of frame. It's just birds and sky. Dozens then several then a few then two. Circling around one another in some kind of dance. Then one, the vulture with the belly full of gator, circling as the camera continues panning upward towards the sun until the picture is washed out by white light.

THE END

The credits roll over "Bird on the Wire" by Leonard Cohen:

DIRECTOR — ROBIN DAVIS
WRITER — ROBIN DAVIS
PRODUCER — ROBIN DAVIS
EXECUTIVE PRODUCER — LEONARD COHEN
EXECUTIVE PRODUCER — MILTON ONTARIO
EXECUTIVE PRODUCER — JOSEPH FLIPCHUK
PRODUCTION DESIGNER — ROBIN DAVIS
CINEMATOGRAPHER — ROBIN DAVIS
EDITOR — ROBIN DAVIS
FIRST ASSISTANT DIRECTOR — ANDREW SIMMONS
SECOND ASSISTANT DIRECTOR — LANCE POCHARD
TITLE ARTIST — ALTON SALAAM
SOUND DESIGNER — GASTON CHARLES
SOUND ENGINEER — RUDDY TURNSTON
ASSISTANT SOUND ENGINEER — AVA WEBBER
"BIRD ON THE WIRE" WRITTEN AND RECORDED BY LEONARD
COHEN COURTESY OF COLUMBIA RECORDS

SPECIAL THANKS TO THE FAKAHATCHEE STRAND STATE
PRESERVE, COLLIER COUNTY SOLID AND HAZARDOUS WASTE
DIVISION, FLORIDA STATE DEPARTMENT OF HIGHWAYS AND
GATOR REMOVAL.
MADE WITH THE GENEROUS SUPPORT OF TELEFILM CANADA,
CANADA COUNCIL FOR THE ARTS, ONTARIO FILM FUND, ONTARIO
ARTS COUNCIL, MISSISSAUGA FILMIC ARTS INVESTMENT FUND,
AND THE HAMILTON PUBLIC LIBRARY.

. . .

The Story of Isaac

The bar remained silent through the credits; dozens of people closed their eyes and listened to "Bird on the Wire."

When the screen went black, and the bar went dark, the place erupted into deafening applause and whistles and cheers.

The music, though, continued. Just the same few chords being repeated. A spotlight lit the stage and there was Leonard Cohen with his guitar. He stepped to the mic and sang a live version of "Bird on the Wire."

Like a bird on the wire
Like a drunk in the midnight choir
I have tried in my way to be free

The cheering and screaming and hyperventilating was louder than the music. The entire bar throbbed. People's ears would be ringing for days just from the frenzy of seeing Leonard Cohen on stage with his guitar.

When the song ended, Leonard Cohen continued to strum, and he spoke.

"I'm an old man now, past my prime, it's been 40 years since the Chelsea Hotel, it's been at least that long since I was in Greece and saw some birds sitting on a wire and wrote this song. So, as I slowly crumble, way must be made for the new generation of poets —such as Ms. Davis. What a

Fig. 60. Bird on a Wire

beautiful film, my dearest Robin, thank you for that. We have also been graced, rather unexpectedly, by an up-and-coming young poet, one whose work has been featured in no less than *The New York Times*. I first saw him read his poetry on this very stage, many months ago. It was... it was something to behold. I would like to call him to the stage to share some of his work with us. Please welcome Mr. Milton Ontario."

Milton's name emerged from Leonard Cohen's lips in slow-motion. Milton could see the words, see his own name, tumble like heavy bricks out of Leonard Cohen's mouth and crash holes through the stage at his feet.

Milton. Crash. Ontario. Crash.

Then time slowed again even slower as slowly, slowly, slowly Leonard Cohen pointed and every face in the packed bar turned towards Milton.

Robin's jaw hit the floor.

He was in hell.

His face burned red hot. This was the payback. This was his punishment for almost killing the most powerful and dangerous man in all the land. This was the revenge for crossing Leonard Cohen.

The crowd started chanting.

"Milton! Milton! Milton!"

Noddy cackled in his ear.

"Fuck 'em up, b'y!"

Georgette pushed him towards the stage.

He stumbled towards the spotlight and a dozen more hands hoisted him up beside Leonard Cohen, who smiled and nodded as if to say: "I'm your man. And you are, and will always be, my bitch."

"Go on, son, sing a song for the people."

The only poetry Milton had on him were chicken-scratched ramblings in an expensive waterproof Gannet Islands Seabird Census Research Project notebook that was covered in dried bird shit.

In the light of civilization, everything he wrote on the island read very much like the ravings of a crazed, lovesick castaway.

He stepped to the mic.

"Um... thank you. I... uh... I..."

His executioner grinned like an idiot as he strummed the same dumb chord on his dumb guitar over and over again.

"Like a... ahem... a bird..."

The crowd howled in laughter or disdain or approval, Milton couldn't tell.

He balled his loose hand into a fist at his side, glared at Leonard Cohen, and leaned into the poem's first line:

> like a bird on a wire
> i sit on this rock
> in this endless shitstorm
> of 75 326 birds

Someone in the crowd booed, someone else hurled a beer bottle and it shattered on a large speaker hanging not far from where Milton stood. He read on:

> like a bird on a wire
> my heart is filled with smoke
> and feathers
> and the shit
> of 75 326 birds

Milton grew an inch or two as the crowd whooped and another beer bottle smashed on a lighting rig over his head and rained beer and broken glass down on him.

He grew an inch or two taller as Leonard Cohen, *the* Leonard Cohen, kept strumming that one dumb chord in accompaniment.

He grew an inch or two taller as he wrapped his arms around his death sentence.

This wasn't a mistake. This wasn't putting on airs. This wasn't pretense. This was war. And he, in that moment, thought he was winning.

He was Edward Hilroy. He was Benjamin Frankin. He was em-effing John George Diefenbaker tearing Lester B. Pearson a new one.

So, he went off script. So, he spoke directly to Robin in that moment.

My heart
My heart may be young
But it beats just like yours
My eyes might be brown
But they see just like yours
And I don't love you because of who you are now
But because of what you will be
But because of what I will be with you

He sang the last few lines in a shaky, halting baritone, Leonard Cohen-like, to the tune of Leonard Cohen's one shaky chord.

He fell to his knees.

He raised his one balled fist towards the sputtering and shorting out light swinging above him.

Leonard Cohen laughed drily and wiped a fake tear from his eye.

"I apologize, my friends, but that was particularly bad."

The crowd roared with laughter. Leonard Cohen kept strumming.

A very large, very mean-looking man grabbed Milton and hauled him off stage.

"The Godfather wants to have a word with you upstairs."

He was dragged up into the piss-smelling office and thrown on the couch Robin had been sitting on earlier, to await the execution of his final sentence.

• • •

Moses

Milton could hear Leonard Cohen downstairs launching into another song, a new one he didn't recognize, with the organs and the backup singers and perhaps a saxophone.

> *Like the Lord leading Moses*
> *You're a pillar of light*
> *I brandish my rod*
> *And you give me new life*

The song lasted 14 minutes, including a three-minute saxophone solo, and wrapped up with a less than subtle verse about Leonard Cohen wanting to get with Robin:

> *Your breast is like fire*
> *Your eggs like water*
> *I haven't been so tempted*
> *Since Eve crossed our Father.*

Milton didn't much care for it.

Not the song. Not the organs. Not the backup singers. Not the perhaps-a-phone. Especially not the fact that Leonard Cohen was hitting on his, Milton's, not-quite girlfriend.

Once the applause and ovation and deafening roar died down and things returned to the usual La Baraque simmer, a herd of elephants clomped up the stairs to where Milton was being guarded by Stoneface McBikertattoos.

Robin and Noddy came and joined Milton on the couch, followed by Leonard Cohen and two old men, who Milton recognized immediately—Guillaume and Gweltaz from the used bookstore on Parc, between the Y and the Library.

Apparently, when they weren't running the worst second-hand bookstore ever as a really poor money-laundering front, they moonlighted as two of the deadliest octogenarian hitmen in the world.

The small office became extremely crowded and the smell of whiskey and old man mixed with the stench of piss wafting up from the bar.

"Ah, the poet. So good of you to join us. I'm so pleased you were able to share your talents with the room just now. Our degenerate friend here forgot to mention he had brought you along."

"Hello, uh... Godfa–"

"Buddy, what are ya at up there? I don't know much about poetry, but that thing you read didn't rhyme or nothin', b'y."

"Enough of these niceties, my friends. We have much to celebrate!"

"Fuckin' eh, b'ys, let's get shittered!"

"Might I propose a toast?"

McBikertattoos popped a cork and began handing around red plastic beer cups with a splash of cheap champagne.

"To our esteemed guest of honour, the most glorious Ms. Davis."

Robin blushed. Milton gritted his teeth.

"You have touched this old man's frail body with your mind, and reminded me once more the power of love."

Milton made an audible gagging sound. Robin laughed.

"Oh Leonard, you know I have a boyfriend."

Milton sat up a bit taller. A never-ending grin began stretching across his face.

"Yes, and he's quite a specimen, isn't he?"

"Robin! Really? You mean it?"

He put his hand on her knee. This was it. At last.

"Yeah, I met someone. Didn't I tell you? He's really sweet. A small-town guy with big dreams. Leonard introduced us. He wanted to be here, but his flight was delayed out of Miami."

"Miami?"

'Miami' came out as nothing more than a puff of air. Like a dying man's last breath.

"He's great. You'd really like him."

"Ouch, b'y, if that don't make your dink shrink!"

Not only did Milton's "dink shrink" to nothing, but what was left of his heart turned to dust and blew away.

"Actually, my dear, I've pulled a few strings, and well..."

Leonard Cohen nodded to the thug by the door who nodded down the hall.

"Yo, Robi, you up here?"

"Oh my god! You didn't!"

Robin squealed with delight and tears of joy welled in her eyes. She skipped to the door, threw her arms around him, and planted a deep, long, sloppy kiss on Joey Flipchuk.

. . .

Joseph

Joey Flipchuk.

a.k.a. Horace Khack, a.k.a. Milton's nemesis, a.k.a. world-renowned adult film star, a.k.a. owner of the world's largest penis thanks to Milton's spoiled super-bedbug revenge plot.

Joey flipping Flipchuk.

"Joey?"

The name Milton hadn't uttered in years came out involuntarily.

"Milt, is that you! No way! You sonofabitch! It's been forever. How are ya man? How are your folks?"

Joey, and his three legs, strode powerfully across the room, hand extended to Milton. Milton stayed sitting and limply offered his hand back. Joey wouldn't have it. He pulled Milton up and wrapped him in a bear hug. Milton could feel Joey's massive dong crushing against his leg.

"Robi, you didn't tell me you knew Milty Onterrible."

The bear hug had turned into a headlock and noogies. Milton was brought face-to-face with the enormous bulge in Joey's pants.

"We grew up together. We were best friends when we were small. I used to shoot him in the ass with my BB gun. This is wild."

Joey's knuckles grinding into the top of his throbbing head was the last thing Milton felt, as all feeling and will to live

Fig. 61. Berta Federko's overgrown zucchini

left his body. He slumped back onto the couch as Joey made his way around the room shaking hands and patting shoulders with murderers and mob bosses with the kind of confidence that can only come with having a circus Johnson.

"Have we met before, b'y? Where have I seen ya to?"

"I'm an actor, you may have seen one of my movies?"

"No, I don't think so. I don't watch much TV. You just got one of them faces, b'y, like I knows ya."

The last in the circle was Leonard Cohen.

"LC, very nice to see you again. Thanks for letting me use your plane. And, as always, for introducing me to this beautiful woman."

As Joey and Robin kissed again, Milton melted into a puddle of humiliation and regret, leaving a Milton-sized grease stain on the already very greasy, stained office couch.

"It was my honour, Mr. Khack."

"Aw fuck, no way, b'y. You're Horace Khack! Holy shit. You've got a huge dick, buddy! I jerks it to *When Harry Humped Sally* all the time. Dies for it."

As Noddy and Joey high-fived, Milton, a puddle of heart dust and regret grease, flopped his head back and stared at the very greasy and stained office ceiling.

"Thanks, bro."

"I mean, his bird is massive, b'ys, like a party sub."

"Only a six-footer though, man."

As everyone laughed and laughed, Milton closed his eyes, and his brain, his stupid waste of an otherwise perfectly good brain, began playing reruns from his life, his miserable life, like some cliched movie life-flashing-before-your-eyes scene that reveals what you have to live for. But at that moment, the timing of everything, it was more like his brain was just piling on more misery.

As Noddy held his arms out fish-story style to McBiker-tattoos—"You seen his gear, b'y? Like this, no kidding."—Milton was back at the first day of kindergarten with Ashley

D. walking through the door, the most beautiful thing he had ever seen.

"I always thought I'd be good in porn. I likes to fuck. Ask your missus there."

"Sick, dude. I might be able to hook ya up."

"I ain't packing near as big a tackle as you, b'y, but she's a hairy bird, I calls her the jungle."

Noddy began to undo his pants but was halted, mercifully, by the loud protests of everyone except for Milton and the mute Gweltaz.

"What, b'ys, you've all seen 'er before."

As Noddy tucked his hairy ass back into his jeans, Milton was overcome with the smell of Ashley D.'s lip gloss at Ashley B.'s 14th birthday party. With the wisps of her hair in the prairie wind at recess. With the softness of her grimace as the same prairie wind froze her eyelids shut.

"Dude, people are into all kinds of weird shit these days. Hairy porn is all the rage. We're shooting *Titty Dickers 2: The Legend of Curly's Pubes* next month in Miami, we're still looking for someone to play Curly."

"Yes, b'y! I'm your man."

As Noddy and Joey high-fived again to seal their newly formed acting partnership, Milton fast-forwarded through the heartbreak and torment of losing Ashley D., the first time to Joey and the next time to Dr. McClutchsmoke, through finding hope and then solace in poetry, in Leonard Cohen records, in the possibility of escaping Bellybutton, of escaping Moose Jaw, of escaping his infinite flatness to find something, to become someone somewhere like Montreal— the most romantic city in North America.

"Well, it's been nice meeting everyone. But I just got off a plane. I'm starving. I could eat a horse. What'd ya say, Robi, wanna go grab a bite?"

"Yeah, sure."

Fig. 62: Titty Dickers II: The Legend of Curly's Pubes

"Mind if I comes with you'se? I'm buying. I wants to hear about how ya gets on with that giant rod."

"Sure dude. If you're buying."

"Milt, can I borrow a few bucks? I'm flat out."

As Noddy grabbed Milton's backpack and fished out the last of the drug money, Milton replayed that first flash of Robin's smile in that vermin slaughter-house potluck party, the terror and ecstasy of that first poetry reading, that first hug, that first accidental kiss.

"Thank you for gracing us with your unusually large presence, Mr. Khack."

"An honour as always, LC."

As Robin gave Leonard Cohen a hug and a kiss on the cheek, Milton could smell her hair, could feel her warmth next to him, could feel what her laugh used to do to his heart before it had been reduced to a puddle of dust.

"Thank you for everything, dear Leonard."

"My dear, it was my pleasure."

As Leonard Cohen took Robin's hand and kissed it, Milton felt the months of searching and pages of poems piling up, burying him, the hopelessness, defeat, despair, all erased by one fleeting glimpse of those deep brown eyes.

As Robin sat back down on the couch next to the Milton stain, Milton relived the fame and misfortune, the shitty jobs, and meeting his hero, the great Leonard Cohen. He relived the gun to his head that first meeting, the gun to Noddy's head the second. He relived finding an image of Robin's smile in every moment of terror to give him the strength to go on.

"You want to come with us, Milton?"

As Milton didn't answer, because he had no more words, he was a puddle, a stain, his unhelpful brain screamed through the drug dealing, the endless rolls of money, the turtlenecks and fedoras and scotches on the rocks, the diet-pill smoking puppeteer back-alley hand jobs, and all the confidence that comes with having a circus-sized box of extra money in your tiny closet of a bedroom.

"No? Ok."

As Robin put her arm around Milton and pulled him in for a kiss on the cheek, he felt her arms around him that night, pulling him in for a deep, wet kiss, hands wandering down his back, to his ass. He felt her weight, the substance of her very being, pressed against his. Undressing in his dark room. The feeling of her warm, soft skin. The excitement. The anticipation. The dreams coming true. The destiny being fulfilled.

As Robin planted a kiss on his cheek, Milton, miles away in a fantastical retelling of a story that never quite happened, was about to feel Robin's lips on his that one last time. Feel the soft, moist warmth of her tongue on his, in his dark bedroom that one night, ages ago. Back on the couch, in the real world, the puddle Milton turned his head just as Robin tried to kiss his cheek and met her mouth with his, open, tongue groping for hers, for forever, or something, but only finding half an upper lip and a nostril.

"Ew! What the hell, Milton?"

For a split second, thanks to a half-playful, fully disgusted slap from Robin, he returned to earth, to that couch, to drink in one last bit of embarrassment.

"Sorry," the dying man gasped.

"Yeah, well, call us later if you want to meet up or something."

As Robin took Joey's hand and followed him out the door. Noddy not far behind, asking if Joey required special pants to fit his "massive dank," Milton tried to pull himself together. He tried to fight his way back to reality, un-puddle himself, and follow behind.

There was some small figment of his imagination that still had a beating heart. That was still capable of dreaming of a way to just get up and walk out on Leonard Cohen, go for a beer with Robin and Joey and Noddy and turn the tables on them. On this whole horrible thing. That he could expose Joey for being a phony. For being a bumpkin hiding behind a mutant dick. For not being Robin's type. For not being anyone's type. For being a stupid idiot with a dumb stupid idiot face and an ugly tree-trunk dick who, when Todd Strubey first played "Famous Blue Raincoat" to their grade 9 English class, laughed and called it gay.

That fading last flicker of light in his head clung to the notion that Joey was no good for Robin, that Robin needed to be saved, and Milton was the one to do it.

He struggled out of the puddle and to his feet to follow after them.

"I..."

McBikertattoo pushed Milton back down into the puddle. He wasn't going anywhere. He wasn't saving anyone.

"I... I don't have your number."

As they disappeared down the stairs.

· · ·

Job

With one look from Leonard Cohen, the biker thug and geriatric hitmen left the room and clomped back downstairs.

Leonard Cohen and Milton sat in the room alone. Milton in his puddle of despair and utter ruination, Leonard Cohen whistling the first few bars of "So Long Marianne."

They sat like that for what seemed like hours.

If someone had told 23-year-old Milton that he'd be sitting in a room, alone, with Leonard Cohen, he never would have believed it. Yet, here he was, 24-year-old Milton, sitting alone in a room with Leonard Cohen, and it didn't matter. Nothing mattered. Leonard Cohen was a bad guy. The worst guy. Well, the second worst guy, Joey Asshead Floppy Dick Flipchuk was the worst guy.

They just sat.

Leonard Cohen whistled.

They sat for a long time.

"I saw this... this child, get up on that very stage downstairs many months ago and start sputtering this utter nonsense, and I thought to myself, I thought, well now, this may be a useful idiot, this man-child with his mix of ambition and ignorance. Who speaks in tongues. Who revered me so. I can play him like a harp. And so I did, Mr. Ontario. And my, did you sing. For the past year, my entire enterprise has operated without fear of discovery thanks to coded messages we made up using that rambling nonsense you published in *The Times*. You hand delivered me millions in merchandise in just a few months. But I underestimated you. I underestimated how foolish and weak you truly are. How beholden you are, not to your ambitions, but to your impossible dreams of all this being something, meaning something. How you honour those impossible dreams over all else. Over respect for your elders and especially over your very own life. I had thought that vile nincompoop partner of yours was the cancer, the trouble, the problem. But I was mistaken. He is the useful idiot in the end. And you, my boy, you are but a parasite. An albatross."

Milton didn't have anything to say in his defence. He was a puddle.

"Don't you have anything to say in your defence?"

He half-heartedly shrugged.

Leonard Cohen became enraged. He stood and boomed over the Milton puddle.

"Job answered Jehovah, and said, 'Behold, I am of small account; what shall I answer thee? I lay my hand upon my mouth. Once have I spoken, and I will not answer; Yea, twice, but I will proceed no further.'"

All Milton could do was shrug. Leonard Cohen kept yelling.

"Jehovah answered Job out of the whirlwind, and said, 'Gird up thy loins now like a man: I will demand of thee, and declare thou unto me. Wilt thou even annul my judgment? Wilt thou condemn me, that thou mayest be justified? Or hast thou an arm like God? And canst thou thunder with a voice like him?'"

"I don't... I don't even know."

• • •

Abraham

"Now the Lord said to Abraham, 'Go from your country and your kindred and your father's house to the land that I will show you. And I will make of you a great nation, and I will bless you and make your name great. I will bless those who bless you, and him who dishonors you I will curse.'"

Leonard Cohen took his Hallelujah gun out of his jacket and begun slowly turning the cylinder. Click-click-click.

"And they came to the place which God had told him of; and Abraham built an altar there and laid the wood in order."

He spun the cylinder one last time, quickly. Click-clk-clk-clk-clk.

"And bound Isaac his son and laid him on the altar upon the wood."

Leonard Cohen held up his gun, the same gun Milton had kept under his pillow for the past year, and pressed it hard against Milton's forehead.

"And Abraham stretched forth his hand and took the knife to slay his son."

"I just want to go home."

"And the angel of the Lord called unto him out of heaven, and said, Abraham, Abraham: and he said, 'Here I am'."

Milton wept.

"And the angel said..."

Click.

POSTFACE

Milton had no poetry left. What was left of it was in a puddle in a dive bar in Montreal. He spent the bus ride home filling the last few pages of his expensive waterproof Gannet Islands Seabird Census Research Project notebooks with a running tally of roadkill.

Raccoons	64
Birds	42
Skunks	34
Porcupines	37
Deer	32
Cats	21
Rabbits	16
Moose	11
Beavers	11
Dogs/Coyotes/Wolves	7
Foxes	5
Bears	2
Cows	1
Horses	1
Unknown	36

His parents picked him up at the Regina bus station and drove him home through the infinite flatness of Southwestern Saskatchewan. Through Moose Jaw and Tuxford. Through Keeler and Brownlee. Through Eyebrow and Central Butte. To the shores of Lake Diefenbaker.

"Bumped into Ashley's mom at the post office the other day, hon."

"What are you going to do now?"

"She said Ashley's pregnant."

"Don't think Randy will be giving ya your old job back. Had a bunch of money in the stock market down south, lost 'er all with the crash. Went tits up."

"Twins."

"You should've got a trade."

ACKNOWLEDGMENTS

Someone, not sure who, but someone, surely, thinks that novels are the work of solitary geniuses. Neither of those are even remotely true. Novels are the work of neurotic introverts with vast and endlessly patient support systems. Or at least that has been my experience with this, my first one of these. So, I shall attempt to thank all that need thanking, and thank them in roughly chronological order.

Thank you dad for building that bookshelf that was always full of books in our old house. Thank you mom for reading them to us. Thank you Ms. Peterson for showing me that stories are something I could make. Thank you Mr. Brick for showing me that stories are important. Thank you Aunt Sue for showing me that stories are a worthwhile thing to do with your time. Thank you Will Ferguson for writing in a voice I recognized. Thank you Franz Kafka for writing in a voice I didn't. Thank you Dr. Margo for showing me where the twain shall meet. Thank you Vaclav Havel for showing me how the twain do. Thank you Leonard Cohen for showing me a version of Montreal that might not exist, but was enticing enough nevertheless. Thank you Logy for a masterclass in having the courage to follow your heart and the conviction to live your best shithead years. Thank you Drs. Hynes and Dyer for showing me too much respect and patience. Thank you St. John's for the (figurative, very much only ever figurative) warmth. Thank you Memorial University Collective Agreement which entitles employees to one free class per term. Thank you Lisa Moore for writing the most beautiful book and for leading the most challenging workshop and for guiding, advising, and inspiring all of us wannabe writers. Thank you Sharon and Melissa and Jamie and Carrie and Susan and the few others who stuck around after class and keep on to this day. Thank you Robert Chafe for showing me how powerful stories get made. Thank you Broken Social Scene for picking that story about that guy who gets hit by the bus for that contest. Thank you Breakwater for *Racket*. Thank you James Langer for asking at that book launch party what else I was working on and believing me when I told you and holding me to it and keeping me honest and believing in this book and working so hard on it with me. Thank you Rebecca Rose for trusting James and championing me and everyone else. Thank you Tam for rescuing me from my misery and sitting with me on that rock at the foot of that lighthouse in that sorta-French place egging the birth of Milton and his misadventure on. Thank you Elling for inspiring me and for hiring me and for not firing me and coaching me through the rough patches and cheering me through the smoother ones. Thank you Will Ferguson for being kind 17 years ago and being even kinder six months ago and taking the time and saying such nice things. Thank you Rhonda Molloy for making this thing beautiful. Thank you Samantha Fitzpatrick for selling a million copies. Thank you thank you thank you Katie Bean for a life and a heart and a home and a cover and a small human bean who eats dirt sometimes, but is the most perfect thing, thank you.

And thank you, lastly but not leastly, to you. Yes, you, for reading this, all of this. It's been an honour.

MORGAN MURRAY was born and raised on a farm near the same backwoods west-central Alberta village (Caroline) as figure-skating legend Kurt Browning. He now dads, works, plays, writes, and builds all sorts of crooked furniture on a farm in the backwoods of Cape Breton, where he lives with his wife, cartoonist Kate Beaton, their daughter, Mary, Agnes the dog, and Reggie the cat. In between, he has been a farmer, a rancher, a roustabout, a secretary, a reporter, a designer, a Tweeter, a schemer, a variety show host, and a student in Caroline, Calgary, Paris, Prague, Montreal, Chicoutimi, and St. John's. He has pieces of paper attesting to his competence from the University of Calgary; the University of Economics, Prague; Memorial University of Newfoundland; and a participation ribbon for beef calf showmanship (incomplete) from the Little Britches 4-H Club, Caroline, Alberta. *Dirty Birds* is his first novel.